W9-CRU-736

THE TROJANS

WIRT WILLIAMS

THE TROJANS

Little, Brown and Company · Boston · Toronto

Published simultaneously in Canada
by Little, Brown & Company (Canada) Limited

PRINTED IN THE UNITED STATES OF AMERICA

To Marc Jaffe and Grace Bechtold

Acknowledgment

So many people have given me assistance in the exploration of the motion picture industry that accompanied the writing of this novel that it would be impossible to acknowledge them all. But a very special debt is owed to Jack Raphael Guss.

THE TROJANS

THOUGH the stars hold, the moon is gone. The black of sky already thins. Across the iron-dark sea the horizon is sharpening its edge. Southward from Greece the north wind blows, across the Aegean to these hills outside the walls of Troy. On the hills an army sleeps, the white points of its tents rising in row on furrow-even row from the shadowed slopes.

A horn blows. Yellow lanterns swing in the gray dark. In the tent-paths the first-rising soldiers move. Then from the white tents step the other heroes: sleepy-eyed, black-bearded, heavy-limbed. Iron ladles dip into wooden kegs. Water splashes sleep-numbed faces and spatters in the dust.

The Achaean soldiers put on their brass breastplates; they put on their leggings and their plumed helmets. In the horse camp the chariot-pullers whicker. Iron-banded wheels clatter on dirt and stone. Cooking fires leap and weave orange in the paling gray light.

On the edge of the host stands a hugeness taller than the walls of Troy. As the sky grows light, its shape can be seen. It is a horse and has been made by men: it is a giant horse of wood. The soldiers eye it as they prepare for battle.

Now from the gray sky into the pale cold air a great voice speaks. It comes from everywhere and nowhere: surely it is the voice of some god. It speaks and is silent, and then it speaks again:

"Testing, one, two three four, one two three four. How do you hear me Joe? You read me okay Joe?"

Another voice answers: "Five by five, control, read you five by five."

"Roger. Joe, get Menelaus and his crowd over here, get 'em over right now. We almost set up."

A man dressed nothing like a soldier walks in front of the wooden horse. He carries a sign which he leans against the left front leg of the horse for a moment as he lights a cigarette. The sign says:

HELEN OF TROY
SCENE 42
TAKE 1

The Greek soldiers sat at long wooden tables lined beneath the walls of Troy, and ate a breakfast served from field kitchens: scrambled eggs, roast lamb, Turkish coffee. They ate noisily and with pleasure: tin clacked on china, laughter made bursts, words were unmistakably soldier words.

A man in a dark brown, American, tropical suit stood alone under the papier-mâché walls and watched and listened. He was of average height and the suit clearly had been cut with expensive care: he looked not fat but substantial. His hair was dull gray, and seen more closely, his face was heavy but not heavily lined. Now it was marked with fatigue though the hour was only eight; it was also permanently stamped with discipline and decision. Yet it was not an unkind face: it hinted, even, at a capacity for compassion.

A smile touched the face as its brown eyes moved over the soldiers. They were real soldiers in the real Greek army, and their presence was part of a deal that Globe-International Pictures, Inc. had made with that army. The dark-suited man was smiling because he was thinking of a denunciation delivered upon that arrangement in the Greek parliament a few days before. The man's name was Sidney Tate and he was president of Globe-International Pictures. His smile, never pronounced, faded as he thought of something else. He thought that there was a calculable chance that, before the picture was done, there might be no more Globe-International Pictures.

A tall man in khaki sun-tans and a baseball cap was suddenly at his side. "Good morning, Sidney."

"Morning, Howard."

"We move the monster inside today, rail's almost finished."

Sidney Tate nodded. "I saw it, good." He paused and looked directly at the other. "How about Dayton? Is she here yet?"

"You're droll, Sidney. After all, it's only eight-thirty, she was only due half an hour ago. Wait a bit, wait till nine or ten or twelve or two. Then we'll hear from Miss Dayton. We will if we're lucky."

"She is irresponsible," Tate damned her irretrievably.

"Yes. Yes you could say that."

"I gave you the picture because you were supposed to be able to handle her, Howard."

"I *have* handled her, Sidney. She's been horrible, unbelievable, on this picture, I wouldn't fool you. And yet she's only actually missed two days of shooting. Check that against her track record."

Tate did not answer.

"Check it against her last one, Sidney."

"Do you have any idea what her, tardiness, has cost us?" Sidney said.

"As producer of the picture, Sidney, I have more than an idea. We are now five million dollars over a nine-million-dollar budget. In round figures I figure Dayton has cost us two nine of that. Before it's all over she'll cost us more. And she'll make us five times as much as she costs us when the picture is finished and released."

"When the picture is finished and released."

"It will be finished, and it will be released, and all concerned will wax very very fat."

"I wish I had your ebullience, Howard, and your confidence."

"Think good thoughts, Sidney. In six months we'll be congratulating ourselves for enduring Dayton. Just keep thinking good thoughts."

"Howard."

"Yes, Sidney?"

"I am absolutely serious. Is she going to make it?"

Howard Sills did not answer for a moment. Then he said, "Want me to level with you?"

"Yes."

"I don't know. I go from one day to the next not knowing. I think she will. I hope she will. But I won't be sure until this thing is in. I never saw anybody like her nor even heard of anybody. She's unbelievable."

Sidney Tate nodded, almost in abstraction. He appeared to be staring at the wooden horse, three hundred yards away.

"Sidney, there's more and it's worse."

"Oh?"

"I don't know where Dayton is this morning. She didn't answer her phone at the hotel, and they checked, I have an arrangement with them, they checked and her bed hasn't been slept in."

"Well." Tate offered the word delicately.

"Maybe. Maybe. I hope so."

"Maybe she's already left."

"Nobody's seen her. I've got men out looking for her, Sidney. I'm scared."

"So am I." Tate smiled; his face softened. "It doesn't help though, does it? She'll show or she won't, they'll find her or they won't, we'll survive or we won't. Come on, I'll buy you a cup of coffee."

"Deal," said Howard Sills, gratefully.

The sun curved up and into the southern half of the blue and beat the brown hills with hard light. Tourist police officers in tight collar, tie, and olive jacket stood between the village children and the shooting area, and when a child came too close, an officer gestured him back. The shooting area today was bounded by the open sea to the south, the walls of Troy to the east, and cameras and equipment to the north and west. The tents were outside the cameras on the west, and the road that did not quite circle Mykonos lay above them to the north. Inside the shooting area, on a plain of bare rock and sand, the armies milled, weakly. Inside the walls, hammers thudded wood. Outside, men made black figures against the white horse as they moved on scaffolding on its side.

Abruptly, the day passed from warm to hot: the high Mykonos wind was not blowing. Soldiers held helmets in their hands or dropped them to the ground: fingers brushed sweat from faces. Voices shouted and replied in two languages, and in a third compounded of both. Children shouted at the tourist police, possibly obscenely. The police smiled.

The men came down from the wooden horse.

"She on the set yet?" someone asked someone else.

"Don't be a hick," said someone else. "It's not but ten."

"It's past eleven now," said the chief electrician. "How about Queen Dayton?"

"Not here," said his assistant.

"Ain't that running a little late even for her?"

"You know better."

At noon loudspeakers called over the hill: "All personnel will be on standby until further notice. All personnel will be on standby until further notice."

"Let's go eat," said the assistant cameraman.

"You hear what time we shoot?"

"I hear we may not shoot at all. They can't find her."

"Don't you imagine she's just shacked with somebody?"

"Nobody on this picture. They been looking since nine this morning."

At the tables near the field kitchens:

". . . not on the island . . ."

". . . can't find her anywhere on the island . . ."

". . . no word, no nothing . . ."

". . . Tate's looking himself . . ."

". . . say Sylvia Korbin is gone too . . ."

". . . where in hell could she . . ."

". . . all over the island . . ."

"Well it ain't no skin off mine, I'm on Guild scale and I get paid right by the clock Dayton or no Dayton."

At two-thirty the speakers said: "Shooting is completed for the day. There will be no more shooting today. There will be no more shooting today."

At three-fifty-five, the press (seven men, four women) departed together in two cars for the Hotel Metropole, to file bulletins and then to write full stories. The disappearance of Margaret Dayton was official and certified.

In the center of a room that was one half of a long trailer, sat a man with armor covering his chest. His arms thrust out of it naked: they were long and brown and the muscles in the back of them made long jumping ridges as he moved them; a boxer's arms. His face too was a fighter's face: the broken twisted nose should have left it ugly but made it instead uniquely handsome if aging. He had not been a fighter for thirty years, but had been a motion picture actor for that time. For part of it he had been a great star.

Mace Garrett unlaced the breastplate of Hector and dropped it on the cane seat of the closest chair. He bent over an army footlocker, took out a bottle of Old Grand-Dad, half full, and raised it to his lips. He took one deep swallow, sat heavily on the bed, put the bottle on the canvas floor, swung his legs up and lay staring at the brown canvas overhead. His hand came between the pectoral muscles that had thrilled two generations of movie-watching women, and massaged the flesh.

That's better, he thought, now it don't hurt hardly at all. He framed the words self-consciously: they gave the, thing, shape and substance and so reduced it. Just last the picture, you treacherous son of a bitch, just last the picture, that ain't much to ask.

It was more important that he finish the picture than anything else had been in his life. It had seemed almost certain that he would make it, that he would finish the picture, that his untrustworthy body would discharge those responsibilities his bad judgment had created. Now, Margaret had thrown the odds the other way.

Please get her back, he thought in the same word-by-word stiffness. Please get her back fast.

The street was a space four feet wide. On either side were smooth white houses joined to make a single structure. In one, through an open double doorway, came American jukebox music. Visible through the doorway, a thin man in a white sport shirt faced a plump brown-haired woman across a table and glasses.

The man's face flicked from expression to expression, he regarded the woman attentively, and yet she said to him in French: "You are engaged with something."

"A little," he said. "Forgive me."

"But of course."

She smiled, Nelson Glassgow smiled back, but his vitality was not in it.

He liked and had plans for this charming Greek lady who spoke no English but French. Yet he could not escape the topic he was using her to forget. What the hell was his client up to?

His thought was, *How dare Margaret do this to me,* and when he understood this was his thought, he abandoned it. This was the stereotyped posture of the talent agent, and it was his vanity never to be photographed in a stereotyped posture. So much, he thought, for vanity.

"All the world now comes to Mykonos," said the lady in her

French. "Three years ago there was not such a number. It is unfortunate."

"Yes," said Glassgow.

He saw four American girls, laughing loudly, moving handsomely and sexily, come through the doorway and take a table. It occurred to him that if Margaret Dayton was with them, she might seem less desirable than any. Until, he thought, until the cameras started turning, the world's eyes inside, and she decided to switch on the current and *be* Margaret Dayton.

He was angry with himself as well as Margaret: he wished to feel only the need to chastise but he felt as well a concern deeper than anxiety. He knew her fears and capitulations, her flights and recoveries. Yet she had never vanished before.

If anything had really happened to her, it was his fault. He did not believe that but he could not help feeling it. The greatest pain he had ever known was to be responsible for another's misery. To be responsible for another's total disaster must be that horror beyond imagining. If the other were Margaret, it would be worse.

The lady said something discreetly provocative to him. He replied as best he could.

The hotel room had classic spareness. On an upper level, a single bed: on the lower, the mirror and a dressing table the length of the wall. A well-shaped woman stood before the table, a martini glass in her right hand, and looked toward the open door to her balcony over the Aegean Sea.

Octavia Dayton finished the second martini, and poured what was left in the shaker into her glass. It came to less than half a drink. She sipped it slowly, glanced across the rim of the glass to the wall mirror, then lowered the glass and confronted herself directly.

She appraised, in habit and without vanity. Her rouge was patchy but her hair was a rich red-brown and deeply waved (courtesy of Globe makeup). She was years under fifty, and she looked forty or just under, even in that long trough of anxiety.

She looked at herself, not smiling, and knew that her darkness of the spirit did not come entirely from Margaret's absence; it was not pure fear. Heavy on the edges of her fear was her guilt.

For one instant she had not thought but reacted: if Margaret is gone I am free.

Now there was a penance to do. But what penance?

She had come to make peace with her daughter, firmly and finally, and she had not succeeded.

Abruptly she picked up the telephone. "Mr. Glassgow, please."

She listened to the rings. The difficulties, went back to Glassgow. No, they went back further than that, but he had brought them into light.

He did not answer the rings. She hung up the phone, and drank the martini-flavored ice water in her glass.

The man with white hair sat in the light from a single overhead bulb, the curving walls of the Quonset overhanging like those of a cave. He was Howard Sills. He examined sheets of figures and ledgers of figures, and exhaled: a sound of quiet desperation. He checked his watch; it was still the business day in Beverly Hills. He pulled the phone to him.

He spoke not to the operator but the interpreter hired by Globe-International. "I want to talk to Dr. Carl Bernberger, Beverly Hills, California," and gave the number. He put the phone in its cradle, and waited. Bernberger was Margaret Dayton's psychiatrist.

Sills stared ahead of him and wondered what it would be like if he could see it and how it would look slipping away. Success had come the first time as though it were a debt owed him: the second, each step was a hazard and a hunt. He did not want to lose success but he set less store by it now. There was something else much more important that he simply could not afford to lose. He could not lose it and stay alive in the ways that he wished to stay alive.

Dr. Bernberger was not in the office, said his interpreter. He looked at his list of the other calls to make. He picked up the telephone again and looked at the list: assistant director at Athens and Piraeus (tourist police Paros, Delos, Tinos, and Rhodos), a private investigator in Athens, Rhodos was a fair piece away. Istanbul was not much farther. He wondered if she could have gone there. Get an investigator there through the consulate. He picked up the telephone. It would be a long night.

The horn-rimmed glasses sat on their rims on top of a closed script in a blue leather cover. On the cover, gold letters said: *Helen of Troy Director's Copy*. Max Korbin rubbed his eyes and stood.

He had been trying to make directional notes for Margaret Dayton's next scenes, they were scheduled for the next day, and he had given it up. He picked up the telephone and called security on the set. No, said the duty officer, no sir, there was no word of Miss Dayton or Mrs. Korbin either, nobody had seen either one of them.

Korbin hung up and gazed across the telephone to the wall. Then he stood and went into the bedroom.

He turned the light switch and stood just inside the doorway, looking about. The beds were made, everything was in place. He stepped to his wife's dressing table and opened one drawer after another. He saw only her toilet articles. His eyes found the waste-basket beside the table, and he bent and looked into it. There was one piece of Kleenex blotted with lipstick, and a crumpled piece of paper. He opened it. It had words penciled in her writing: *Vern McGaughey. Suite 1129 Rockefeller Center, New York. McGaugheyprises, New York.*

There was no more; only the address. McGaughey was a large stockholder in Globe-International and an old, old enemy of Sidney Tate.

Korbin stared at the paper, his face tensing with lines of puzzlement.

The man sat completely still in the armchair, staring toward the bulkhead and a porthole in its center. In the circle of space, the horizon swung up and down with implacable slowness, an arcing line between the different grays of sea and sky. Light from an electric lamp touched and bounced from the smooth baldness of his head. His face was smooth, tranquil, and predatory: at its ease and yet permanently watchful. Through the port came the sound of the rhythmic assault of sea on ship, and from a radio speaker above the bed:

". . . Mr. Tate said he had no reliable information as to where Miss Dayton might have gone."

With no change of expression, the man leaned forward and touched one of a panel of buttons on his desk.

A knock sounded, deferentially, on his door.

"Come in," he called.

He looked toward the door and a young man in blue blazer and white flannels entering.

"Yes Mr. Haratunian?" said the young man.

"Call Sardelienne. Please inform him that if the situation we discussed is not adjusted immediately I shall withdraw my support from his government entirely. Emphasize that I mean entirely. I think he will understand that. I do not wish to speak to him myself."

The young man bowed sharply.

"Tell the Athens office the four-hundred-million figure is satisfactory. Accept terms of the merger if they will close in seventy-two hours. A wireless will be sufficient."

The head dipped again.

"And please get me Mr. Sidney Tate on the telephone. Before you call Sardelienne."

"Yes, Mr. Haratunian," said the young man.

Sidney Tate listened attentively to his son, sitting across the table, over dinner dishes, in the suite they shared.

". . . the Mycenaean crypts, of course, tell us a good bit more." Tate nodded in genuine deference; Lawrence was a graduate student in history at Tufts.

The telephone rang.

"I'll get it." Lawrence walked to the telephone, picked it up, spoke, and then extended it to Tate. "For you, radiophone they say." A small chord of excitement was in his voice.

Tate took the phone and said, pleasantly, "Sidney Tate." He paused. "Why *hello,* Richard! So good to hear from you." He heard in his voice the excessive urge to please; disgusted, he curbed it.

"Yes, it is true after a fashion." He chuckled as authoritatively and as unworriedly as he could. "She's had a touch of nerves, occupational hazard. Why of course she'll be back."

He listened and laughed deeply and easily. "She will absolutely be at your party when you come in. It's so generous of you to think of it. It'll do her worlds of good." He laughed again the laugh of a man in absolute control of his own situation. "Sure I'm sure. Thanks for calling. We'll be expecting you."

He put the phone in its cradle and saw his hand was shaking.

He was in a new element: impotence. He would have to learn to stay afloat in it but he did not have to like it. No he did not.

The thing he valued most in his life was at the disposal of the voice he had just heard, and, consequently, of the caprice of a young woman whose brains (he thought) were in her belly.

Aircraft engines made removed but overriding noises over the ragged hum of the terminal. At a counter a compact and dark-haired young woman wrote on a message pad, and studied what she had written: *Next stop Syracuse Sylvia.* She tore it off and handed it to the brown-haired Greek girl waiting, opened her purse, and paid in drachmas. Then she walked through the terminal a considerable distance and sat beside a woman whose hair was covered with a scarf, who wore ordinary glasses, and no makeup. The woman, who looked somewhat plain, looked up from her magazine and smiled.

Between neck-high stone walls, dull yellow under the moon, the gravel road ran straight up the hill in front of him. The slope was not difficult but not easy: Grover Brand felt his heart and lungs working as he walked.

He had not been able to sleep, he had left the hotel, his walk was already taking him toward Troy. At hilltop he stopped, breathing hard, and turned right, toward the Aegean Sea.

Yellow moonlight washed the blue night and made black rocks sharp against flat silver. Below to the right were the bunched lights of craft in the harbor, above them the dispersed points of light of the town, and above these, the steep rising blackness of the mountain.

He had thought he had achieved decision and its bleak liberation: now he knew himself a prisoner still. Of pity? Affection? Love even? Of all those perhaps, certainly not of passion.

To step into the night and close it behind him.

But it was Margaret who was gone. Yet he had no fears for his wife: it was one of the primary articles of his life that Margaret had a special and absolute protection.

From everything except himself, he thought.

He walked on. In time, he could not have said how much, he was on a hill looking down at the plain where this Trojan War was being fought; trailers, and Quonsets, and trucks, and autos, and tents, and above the sea the papier-mâché walls, and facing the walls, with the mysterious menace its model might have had three thousand years before, if there had indeed been a model three thousand years before, the horse.

As it had done at the start of day, the horse still pointed toward the walls of Troy. But now, far advanced on its hidden rail, it was less than a hundred yards away. Huge and immovable, paler than the pale moonlight that fell on it from behind, the horse loomed above the walls. It threw a long, faint shadow that crept darkly up the papier-mâché surface as the moon crawled toward the west.

Brand looked for a moment, turned, and walked back to the hotel.

He was tired, now he wanted to sleep, he would sleep in spite of everything. But he did not undress. He took from the curtained wardrobe a brown leather case, unlocked it, and lifted out a green ledger. He sat in the camp chair by the bed, opened the ledger, and stared at what he saw. It was in his own handwriting.

BOOK 1

GROVER BRAND

BRAND did not read his handwriting on the page, but stared across it at the wall.

Real harm had never come to Margaret, he thought. He did not think it would ever come to her: she was protected by goodness. He believed absolutely that the completely good are watched over. They suffer, he thought, but they are watched over. They do not really die young.

He was no longer completely good himself, and so was no longer entitled to protection, but Margaret was, and so he did not fear for her.

He loved Margaret, and in the space of four hours that day, while she was missing, presumably jeopardized, possibly harmed, not impossibly dead, he had forgotten her for two. He loved her and she him, to a point they were very close, and beyond that point the distance was unbridgeable. They had much, yet there was a hollowness beneath their feet. And it was he who had made it. And it was he who had made all their problems, or almost all, because he had married her for a selfish reason. He had not married her for love (though he loved her), nor for money, nor transferable fame, nor opportunity, nor even for vanity. He had married her because he wanted to get from her a true book.

He began to read.

THE BETWEEN-NOVELS JOURNAL OF GROVER BRAND

Talent is not moral but mystic. Not joyous but passionate.

Balls.

Who knows what talent is or is not?

On Margaret Dayton and talent: I saw two of her pictures after she came into Korbin's class at the university. Surprise: she *has* talent. A pure clear talent. Of course only very minor talents have purity and clarity. By their very nature major talents are complex, self-contradictory, and hence impure.

Still and all what she has, she has. A small talent but authentic.

How to *render* Margaret Dayton? How to make her exist?

All movie people are very unreal to me. Unreal and dull. She *appears* overwhelmingly real and far from dull. Though who can be sure.

To render her: get of course the way she fills the blue jeans. Banal but central. She has one hell of a behind. Get the behind. Get the scrubbed schoolgirl look of unmade fact. But remember a schoolgirl animated by sex. Almost permanent half-flush in cheeks and nervous trick of licking parted lips. Powerfully effective. Contribute to her quality. Manifestation of talent if you will . . .

She still doesn't exist. Always mess their hair, Mike said. *Her* hair neatly combed and bunned in back, though.

The Brand system: spill their purses.

So sat next to her and did next best thing: looked inside. Contents noted: great amount of loose face powder, bobby pins. Conventional lipstick. Two emergency Tampax (now she begins to become). Purse arranger. Great fantastic disarray. Ah. Now. Now she is coming into view.

Addenda to the Brand system: make them smell.

Her scent very pleasant. Clean fresh sweat mixed with perfume that seems harmless and then overtakes you. She has definite if light body odor, though, which is fine, it forever destroys antisepticness (is that a word?). Smell them and they throw a shadow–mixed metaphor but true.

She saw me peeking and looked, I swear, bewildered and embarrassed, by God *frightened,* instead of sore as hell. Got the guilties. Wrote her a note: "I am a writer. Need to look in ladies' purses for material." She smiled, to say I was forgiven, and then concentrated very anxiously on what Korbin was saying. She very very serious.

I do believe I am only one who knows who she is. Except Korbin: he looks meaningfully at her as he lectures.

She wears horn-rims most of time. Not dark glasses. Why nobody else has spotted her, yet. She not consciously seeking disguise I would guess, but not consciously looking like Margaret Dayton either. That old bit.

After Korbin stops she leans to me. What do you write? She whispers it still looking at Korbin. Novels, I answer. I name the last one. Oh, she says. Her eyes open a bit and she turns to look directly at me. You're Grover *Brand?* I nod. It always hurts not to be known. To be not only known, but instantly admired, man that is the golden glow. Clearly she has not only talent but taste. Not only taste but brains. Not only the this but the that. I suggest we have coffee after the lecture. She nods, and is well pleased, and so of course am I.

We sit in the sunshine, outside the sidewalk juice stand, America's sex kitten and a novelist not *quite* totally obscure. No one sees her, and of course no one ever sees a writer.

—What is a nice girl like you, I ask her.

—I want to learn.

—Learn what?

—Acting.

—Christ, you don't need to learn. *What* do you need to learn?

—An awful lot.

—You'll screw yourself up good. But I only started to say that. I do say, you think you can learn it here?

—Mr. Korbin is a genius.

—I wonder.

—When it comes to that what are you doing here?

—I had a professor who used to say, the way to understand the short story is to study the poem, the way to study the novel is to study the drama. I'm really studying the novel you see.

—You don't want to write plays?

—No.

—You could, you write wonderful dialogue.

Another shot of golden glow.

She: Maybe you're here to learn to write plays only you don't know it yet. I believe that, I believe people do these things and they don't know they're doing them. Only something *does* know and that's really why they do them.

—Identity search. Very large in the forties.

She looked puzzled at that.

—It could even be true, I say swiftly. What you just said. Keep it long enough and it'll come back in style.

—It's very true.

—Anyway I would rather die gradually at the hands of book reviewers than abruptly and finally at the hands of the drama critics. You don't like to die all at once, I found that out in a war. When the time comes you want to go slow.

—You wouldn't die, you're good.

—Good ain't nothing. I'm outside the establishment. I might not even *be* good at a play anyway. What I would like to be good at is poetry, only I wasn't. I started out as a poet.

—Why did you stop?

—I wasn't a good poet. At first I thought I just didn't have enough talent. Then I discovered I had a different kind of talent. The big thing about talent is to know what kind of talent you have.

—And you know. I think that's wonderful.

—No I don't know. I just work and hope one fine day. One fine day the light will go on and that will be it and I will know.

—It's that way with me. You'll know though.

—I'm not sure of it. The thing is to keep working.

—It's just that way with me.

When we say good-bye I know there is rapport, but I am not sure on what basis. All bases return to the first basis though.

On M. as talent: Mistake for Margaret to be here in classroom. Ignorance is biggest thing she has going for her. Too small, too spontaneous a talent to support a high degree of self-consciousness. Takes a big talent to support that.

Has terrific pressure on her already from other side. Commercial side. Could get caught smack dab in the middle. Squnched between commercial pressure (of pictures) and the workshop pressure. Four-thousand-fathom pressure of big *B I G* money against self-consciousness of formalism. Of book learning. NOT art vs. commerce. Bigger and more sinister; talent between its two natural enemies which are enemies of each other.

Why not use Dayton in this manifestation? Avoid writer, painter, composer as artist. Something more basic, more representative. The sex-bearer as artist.

Could be you are no longer between novels.

Would you marry a woman for a book?

You mean a good book?

Of course a good book.

For a good enough book I would marry an ape. A lady ape of course. Nothing queer about old Grover, yak yak yak.

All of us cherish an effigy of that magnificent self we would like to be. We hide it in a safe, furtively we slip it out for a peek, and on a good day we think we see a likeness. Then we put it back in the safe, and work or do not work at strengthening the likeness.

My effigy is called Man of Art. In caps. He sacrifices all of it to his work. His life. His self in its other aspects. And his humanity. Humanity in the sense of warmth, generosity, compassion, the most universal decencies. He would shoot his mother or his wife or even his daughter for the perfect work. Nobody can do those things of course, nobody I know, though there are some who have come close.

How close could I come? Not close, on that point of heartlessness I do not want to come close. Since I do not want to come close there, my effigy–made up only of my desires–could not come close either. So the effigy is flawed: even the perfect, imaginary Grover Brand is not perfect. But the effigy would at least be willing to sacrifice *himself* totally, he would have done so from the beginning.

Have I? No. Can I? No. I am too soft. To come close to that Brand of aspiration, I must practice an absolute ruthlessness upon myself. I have not practiced such a ruthlessness, yet. That has been what is missing.

Why am I moved to this at the thought of marrying Margaret?

You know why.

M. and I finally made it. Was beginning to wonder. She having kept me off these weeks with psychic pressure and of course I wasn't going to do anything but play it cool as cool (dated, that). Tonight in apartment she just said, are we ready to make love now? And I said, oh I think so. So we did.

Observations on M. in hay: Sweet. Tender. Not sensational. To be truly sensational woman must communicate something very like a sense of sin. At very least wild wonderful wantonness. With her it is natural and unthought about like breathing. Not unimportant, breathing is not unimportant. Done without big production, yet you die if you don't. Don't breathe that is. Same with Margaret and s-e-x. Or love. Very like Eve, before fall in *Paradise Lost*. It do have its idyllic charms at that. Depraved old Dad likes it a bit wicked though.

Margaret has a good mind if unsophisticated. She is awkward in discussion but receptive to ideas, deeply humble before them. To put it simply, she reads much better than she talks. Not a bad quality: She very much under the persuasion of Camus. Which is pity. She will be happy only in iron embrace of authoritarian church. Her emotions cry for deep satisfying ritual, and yet the absolute and final center of certainty.

She asks me the question of Camus and all true atheists: How can there be a God if what goes on does go on? If God exists, why doesn't he stop it?

—You suppose an all-powerful God, I say. Suppose there is a God and a good God but he is not all-powerful.

She looks at me indignantly. I have noticed that atheists will talk about only an *all-powerful* God even when they deny Him. It is as though they are in an argument they hope to lose. M. of course is not really an atheist or really anything but a searcher. Bow low to all true searchers.

—The trouble with Camus, I go on. He is very angry because he can find no totally powerful God. So he revolts. He says: such power as there is—The Absurd—is essentially evil. Only human goodness can be pitted against it. He is not really an atheist. He believes in the Devil.

She nods quite somberly.

—Now, I tell her. Adjust the semantics. Fix up the labels. Then you have a theology that is properly medieval and still fits Camus. For the Absurd read the Devil. Give the name God to the goodness Camus admits is in man. Then apply Camus's equation. The Devil is more powerful than God and tortures man. God aids and comforts as he can but is the lesser in power. He exists, helps men, but does not control.

—You believe that? she asks.

—Why not? I tell her. The system has at least theological rationality.

—You really believe it? She looks at me very intently.

—I just suggest it for those who have to have their symbols and many do. What I believe, I believe when men worship any benign

God they worship their own capacity for goodness. It is really provincial to object to the symbologies.

I have been playing Devil's advocate for her and find I have made certain resolutions for myself. It often works that way for me.

—What is goodness? she asks.

—Oh no. Not into that. You don't get me into that.

But natural goodness she has, more than anyone I have known. Question: Is it a limitation on experience to have natural goodness? I think it is.

Have been observing Korbin with M.: he has an angle. He spends a great deal of time with M., outside of class, talks to her as though she were putatively Bernhardt, or Geraldine Fitzgerald. M. takes it like sand takes to water: she likes it: she likes it an awful lot.

This of course intensifies pressure upon her though she does not know it. Yet. Pressure from side we will call formal, academic, workshop. Heightens drama of central, thematic situation. So I should be pleased. I am not. I bleed for her. I am not really tough enough to be writer I want to be.

Of course Korbin has an angle. It would be impossible for professor-director with only coterie reputation not to rise to dazzling lure suddenly offered him: one of great film names suddenly an adoring disciple. Would not be human if this did not start him scheming.

Certainly *I* not entitled to indignation. *I* am scheming, *I* have an angle, outsider would see it as far more reprehensible than Korbin's.

Yet I do not feel it so. I feel *pure,* even exalted. M. may produce my best book.

M. and I together at Korbin's apartment. Met Sylvia K. for first time. As material she far more interesting than he, as material I find her very interesting indeed. Get it over with: of *course* I would like to lay her. She is trim but not skinny anywhere, shortish but not short, hair black in one of those face framing bobs, a face more than vivacious, a New York face with a New York tension. What is in that face? Get it now before you know her too well to see it: shrewd shrill ambition, need to dominate, energy of definite pathological fiber (you're cheating, that not in her face, that in her quick hard movements: her body language), and intelligence, and sex. She a very intelligent and very sexy woman. She looks at you sexy: does she mean to: yes. Would she? Answer same as for everybody: given proper circumstances and effort.

Disappointing to find her such a doctrinaire *unreflecting* liberal. The New York religion is liberalism, and women more than men need undeviating dogma. All the stock postures on stock issues. If she were ten years older would bet she was a recanted card-holder. She only about thirty-three to thirty-six, however, so figure not.

She very clearly the animating force in that marriage. But K. is the talent. She manages his talent. Is she jealous of his talent? Honestly saw no signs of it. I would guess she supremely happy with situation, with management. Though not a-verse to di-version. Have already admitted would like to get into her pants. (Caught glimpse of them in fact as she sat: green to match dress, not cutaways but longish, gartered to hose: the kind of detail you need to *render* woman, to make reader see. I a dedicated investigator as always.) About K. later: he is as I say less interesting. I may have known him a bit too long: should have sketched him at once: you see things at very first you never see again.

To look at Korbin: almost an archetype, or a stereotype. Late thirties. About five nine. Dark brown curly hair, not black. Inevitable black horn-rims. Thoughtful intelligent face. What else in face? Have seen enough of it to be desensitized. Should have gotten it down at once. To me, now, his face a successful mask. Remember what I thought when I first saw him: intelligent then too of course, thwarted, faintly resentful, strongly egocentric. Man who *needs* disciples: the large world does not appreciate him sufficiently.

It fits. He has remarkable reputation without having had the unqualified success to round it off. I do not mean commercial success. He was supposed to be one of the best directors in college theater when he was at Iowa, then he had his workshop which provided a modest but serious competition for Actor's Studio, then he did that low budget 16-mm thing that was astonishingly like Cassavetes' *Shadows*. Give him his due: he imitates superbly. Precisely the kind of mind to do well in theater, at least in semi-creative areas of theater. There speaks arrogance of writer, of course.

In sum he is "hot" rather than "big"—"hot" suggesting great possibility, not yet achieved. He has never directed a Broadway play or a "real" full-length picture. This clearly is what gnaws, what makes him thwarted and resentful as noted. He has a reputation here and there as a genius, yet he has never *made it,* horrible italicized words. You can tell that M.'s open and artless veneration has set gears spinning behind horn-rims. M. after all *is* Margaret Dayton. I find that hard to remember.

His big article is "thrust." He has written a book about it, the book is a standard, and his "thrust" is quite baldly a different word for the "intention" of Actor's Studio. He has had sense enough to make it sound a little different. It isn't. "Thrust" is what character wants to do, where the play wants to go, and so on. K. has figured it all superbly, and writes very clearly and forcefully about it. Shows how "thrust" creates structure of whole play and also explosions in individual scenes. It is all in his book but I figure going over it more slowly in this class will make it stick, and *could* make me a better novelist. By sharpening structural and dramatic sense. Must never be too proud to learn.

Idle thought: suppose I got in box I see M. in? Threatened that is by doctrine and self-consciousness?

Not a chance.

M. of course wants to become better actress through K. He is very sharp on technique of acting, seeing it in terms of "thrust."

Did I mention, title of the course is simply Advanced Principles of Drama. It covers everything.

Margaret and I have decided to be married. Studio urges a production wedding, though of course it cannot do so with force of say fifteen years ago. She leaves it to me and I say why not. Time to practice what I preach: parochial to object to ritual forms if they are useful. Here clearly they will be useful, to her.

And how guilty is my conscience? What are ethics of marrying to get a book? Fine for the artist, for the artist they could not be better, but am I able to divorce me from simpler considerations of decency? No. I am not able. A fatal flaw for a writer, who should be after both more and less than goodness (a quote: from where? *Clem Anderson,* Cassill).

And of course it is not that simple, nothing is ever that simple, there is never just one reason for doing anything. What are *all* my reasons? Yes there is great affection, yes my ego is tickled, yes I know it will get me more readers, and after a fashion I absolutely love her. Not strong enough reasons to make me do it though: only strong enough reason is there is a true book in her and I am going to get it. And that I have seen the opportunity to direct absolute ruthlessness upon myself, though none of it must touch her.

Am I a monster? Of course. And absolutely not.

Ethical absolute here is clear: if I do marry her for my reasons I must never let her know. And be very particularly good to her, always.

M. and I at Korbin's apartment this afternoon, where he gives her lessons. Normally he would go to her: but he knows what he is doing: this way confirms guru and disciple thing. M. has prepared long scene from *Streetcar Named Desire*—the first big one between Blanche and Mitch.

She does it, not well.

No, my dear, no. Korbin most patient. Now go over it again. What does your character want?

M. tells him, she wants security.

What else?

M. puzzled.

She wants illusion too. You see, you must not lose sight of the complexity. What she wants is a very complex thing, *She* does not know how complex it is. But you, the artist, must know.

M. nods. She tries again, screws it up good.

This kind of thing very beyond her. My dismal fears are turning out.

Must note this: she studied that damn *Streetcar* scene half the night (she said). Did it again for K. Now: what she did was not Blanche Dubois as T.W. wrote her. Don't think she could ever get that psychotic sensitivity. But what she got was good, all of a piece, consonant with if limited by M.'s personality. Not Jessica Tandy but not bad. *Her* thing is there if Williams is not.

I watch Korbin. I see he is pleased. I do not know if he is surprised.

All he says is, "That was very good and interesting, Margaret." He does not talk like theatrical types in books: I myself have never met such types though am sure they abound.

Afterwards he and Margaret confer. He speaks softly, urgently, leaning toward her. She listens, her eyes wide, looking not at him but straight ahead, nodding.

What would you call that if you were to paint it? Messiah and disciple? This is Sylvia K. talking to me, very softly.

The question is, she said, which is the Messiah? You wouldn't paint it though. You'd write it. Wouldn't you?

Her voice is bland, her face blander, yet something suggests complicity between herself and me. Her body attitude? I make insufficiently clever answer.

I feel disloyal, vaguely. Only one wavelength open between her and me: she knows she excites me That Way. Is she moving from that to include me in some secret hostility against K–M learning situation? Which actually she encourages mightily. Her attitude apparently self-contradictory but not difficult to follow: she doesn't like it, but knows K. is on to a Very Good Thing. Hence her divided mind.

Honestly I do not share her hostilities, not even a little.

Later she congratulates M., kisses her on the cheek, runs her hand back and forth over M.'s back and does not take hand away. For a while.

K. not at all happy about marriage. Though he convincingly sincere in good wishes and so on, my writer's radar picks up his antagonism (writer's megalomania: everybody has radar). Easy to see: he does not want M.'s disciple-devotion and what it can do for him thrown off track by less worthy emotion. I understand: I sympathize: for thc first time I even *like* him.

I reassure him subtly: I am not the enemy: I *want* to see M. develop.

He much cheered and mollified.

Do not understand Sylvia's reaction to M. marrying me. Element of relief clearly one part of it, she clearly worried about growing guru intimacy between M. and her husband. Something else involved though: she is–this in part and obscurely–she is not altogether pleased. Her attitude toward M. enigmatic. Hostility, and tenderness, and possibly fascination–all submerged.

M. and I back from honeymoon in Honolulu (don't believe journal says we were married. Journal after all not diary or chronicle but spot-selected events and impressions that may help form book).

M. unbelievably good person. Generous, tolerant, good-tempered. Much too good for me. She also disorganized, sloppy, full of strange fears. Suppose there is no doubt I love her.

I am–no, I am not *content*. I have the satisfaction of doing the job, of obeying the imperative. I am making Margaret as happy as I can. And the unborn book feeds and grows wherever books wait to be born.

M. continually after me to do a play for her. She has no business doing a play. Neither do I.

Margaret Dayton, Movie Star, is not clearly visible in my wife. My wife does not walk like Margaret Dayton. The walk is the signature. M. walks the walk only when she is "on"–before cameras or otherwise. It is in truth only a technical device, she learned it dutifully, she uses it as device. The same for the breathlessly parted lips with the tongue caressing, the closed eyes and head back tilted, the pull of shoulders to dramatize the breast, the exhalation of ardent breath. I could account for Margaret Dayton the sex phenomenon by no more than half a dozen such devices. And the gift of her body. As I live with it, however, it is a body that moves aesthetic admiration rather than desire. It is too perfect for desire. It lacks the imperfection that makes low gamey lust. It does not touch the nasty nerve.

These are my own responses.

The devices that make her the love priestess–are they purely mechanical, or are they devices of art? There is no difference, of course. Not in the devices. The difference is elsewhere.

The great constant in her two selves–is it self and shadow? No, I think it is her two selves–is her imperative to love and to be loved. This, and her limitless charity, and her total incapacity to do harm willingly, are the heart both of M. my wife and the achieved Margaret Dayton–the character Margaret Dayton, Margaret Dayton the star.

The tension between this goodness, even timidity, on the one hand, and the contrived flamboyant sexuality on the other is what makes Margaret Dayton. She is in short her own work of art. Like all works of art she is made by the artist. The artist makes by joining what he is to what he has learned. Plus X. X, the final arbiter.

A specific:

Two weeks ago Margaret and I sit in the TV room playing gin. She wearing glasses, jeans, old shirt. I look upon her fondly, but I do not want it, I do not want her, called upon I could not rise to the occasion. At my request she runs *Redheads in Paris,* she has prints of all her pictures and projector mounted in wall. In the picture Dicky Clermont concentrated on her astonishing derriere as nobody has since. He shot it from above, below, the left, the right. Once I thought he was going to ram it into her (obviously he is like myself a behind man). Now, physically indifferent to M. of the flesh, beside me, I become inflamed by Margaret Dayton of illusion on the screen before me. Before the picture is done I cut off the projector and take her on the couch, struggling with the tight difficult jeans. I looked, I mean *really* looked, not at her wholesome flesh before (and under) me, but at her scorchingly erotic representation on film. And I am in a fever.

When it is over she smiled, possibly sadly. I am sure she understands.

Question: Is this a comment on art and actuality or on my own sexual neurosis?

Answer: Both.

Thoughts: The inflammatory is only the lesser part of Margaret Dayton but it is a part.

Was it, here, created by M. or simply by director and her cameramen using her body as raw material? It was created, in a sense, by all three, as everything must be on film. But I insist Margaret herself is the creative center, and I do not mean just her body.

One scene that shows her tension of opposites: in a picture with Mace Garrett, two rodeo cowboys play a hand of showdown to see who has her for the night. She consoles the loser with a touch on the cheek, a kiss on the forehead, and an unpromising enough line: "Don't you worry now, honey, tomorrow night's here before you know it." All of it is there: she is not earth mother but earth sister, with all taboos removed.

Is Margaret ambitious?

Clearly she could not have Made It without some ambition, and yet it is not at once visible. It is visible quite shortly, however. Her irremediable insecurity clutches fiercely at the shows of importance.

Her necessity to be loved wallows in being universally loved. So her engine is not an oversized ego but a stunted one.

This of course is nothing like all there is to it.

For herself, she is humble. But for her creation, Margaret Dayton, she has a pride almost savage. I have caught her speaking of the character Margaret Dayton in the third person, though not often.

Of one script—It's just antsy, it's not original. She needs something better.

—She?

—Oh you know what I mean.

At this point her ambition has taken on the edge of a craving for excellence. Hence the discipleship to Korbin. Hence her marriage to me—I represent something she aspires to.

It is a responsibility I wish I did not have.

M. and I have finished semester at Korbin's Theater Arts Lab. That is all for me, I do not know if I am helped or not. I mean of course in the writing of novels. Korbin now giving M. private lessons only. Declining all payment which shows astuteness. He after much bigger skins than lesson payments.

Korbin wants to do *Joan of Lorraine* at Pasadena Playhouse. Starring Margaret. I do not know whether to oppose or not. Am hung up most badly on my conscience here. I *want* her to do it, it most necessary and valuable to book to see exactly how she does make out. Yet I think it will hurt her. So I oppose it. She gently overrides me.

Question: If I marry her when all is said and done for book, why do I want to protect her from experience which will contribute to book?

Answer: I know she will not be hurt simply by marrying me. I fear she will be hurt by this *Joan* and other things and so *must* do what I can to shield her from them. Even though I know I cannot. I see nothing *finally* inconsistent about this.

M. declines scripts sent her by Globe for various reasons. Real reason of course is she wants nothing to interfere with *Joan of Lorraine*. K. has set it up.

Globe has suspended Margaret, who will not work anywhere until Globe contract expires. That in six months, about. She sees herself as renouncing commercialism by this. Sees herself as now committed absolutely to being serious actress.

I weep (metaphorically). The fact that I have expected this and have maneuvered myself a ringside seat does not diminish my concern and, almost, grief. Not at her loss of money. At what she may be doing to her clear, fine, slender talent which is so limited and yet absolutely her own. It has survived and even flourished in commercialism. I feel now that formalism, textbookism, academicism, call it what you will, is her great enemy.

And perhaps not. We will see.

That what I signed on for. Isn't it?

I purposely stayed away from rehearsals to see Margaret's *Joan* absolutely all at once when she opened. That was last night. And surprise—it is not bad. She gets by and a little more. Catches simultaneous awkwardness and sublime assurance of peasant girl very well. Projects also very well, the concept of sex transformed into mystic fervor. That really *very* good and probably not deliberate. She is weak on big speeches though and where absolute authority is required she does not have it. Nonprofessional's conclusion: doubt if she will ever have enough authority and control to carry a whole play in New York. But out here she is interesting and even respectable. If this had been filmed, and Korbin had been able to hold her hand and take her through difficult scenes a step at a time, she would have been a fairly good Joan, without apologies and with some aspects of brilliance. Period.

Some interesting, not at all simple things to think about. As trained and serious actress M. is not impossible. That is all to be said now, she is not impossible. This more than I thought could ever be said. When I stop to consider, it should not be too surprising: spontaneous and unique writing talents often, even usually, achieve something like adequacy when they are taken over by forces of conformity. What they lose is that essence of personality, that genius if you will, that is theirs alone and sets them apart.

Sometimes. This not a simple thing, at all. Many writers are improved, even *made* by formal training, and many others are destroyed. Who knows which will be which until it is over?

Maybe my view of M. pressed between opposing hostile elements is theatrical, sentimental. Maybe academic training *will* form her after all.

Did anybody ever play tournament tennis without intense instruction?

Only it isn't the same thing. Or is it?

Margaret pleased and rosy and shy over favorable local reaction (though not unmixed).

Did *you* like me, she asks.

God yes. I liked you.

Wouldn't it be funny if I made it? I mean really made it. Do you think I'll make it, Grove?

You made it a long time ago.

Hush now, I'm serious.

So am I.

But she does not understand.

Margaret very aglow with small success of *Joan,* very intensely involved with private studies with Korbin. Korbin has persuaded her to organize her own picture company. He has done so most artfully, by pretending to oppose it. Quite literally, she spends more waking hours with him than me.

Viewed from outside this situation would be most, most suspicious. Yet I am totally convinced it technically innocent and I am practically infallible on matters of this sort.

Famous last words.

If were suspicious of anybody would be suspicious of Nelson Glassgow.

M. told me, confessed is wrong word, they were lovers long time ago. He avoids situations of intimacy with her almost pathologically. She still a little in love with him I think, though this emotion so full of shades it should not be defined.

After some months:

What am I to M. now and she to me?

As I read in last entry, this kind of definition not healthy. All situations happily fluid. And definitions fix them. So should be avoided.

But not by writer.

Writer's sentence to be not healthy.

M. sweet, patient to me. I am I think considerate and tender to her. We love each other, more or less tranquilly.

Yet–we are less than lovers if more than friends.

Have I rejected her?

Has she asked for unalloyed love and have I refused it?

(Even a writer not required to think about everything.)

Yes he is.

Actually she has always been too deeply engaged with work to try for what she thinks she wants or what she doesn't know she thinks she wants.

At any rate our relationship now more or less level.

Dayton Productions announced with much tararara. Search for properties, O lovely word, has begun. A "property" is a piece of writing. The ultimate reduction of writer in this town, which is finally no town at all for writers.

Many months and nothing found for M. No "properties," that is, no suitable properties.

I resist importunities for screenplay–actually because I do not think I could do it.

Have not begun my novel–because do not yet know how it comes out.

About novel: Am I losing interest? Great danger there. Too much intimacy with materials worse than too little. For some writers. Must get relationships involving Margaret on paper–can I still see them?

They involve M. and me and Korbin and Sylvia and Glassgow. How about M. and me? We get along–warmly, peacefully, maybe contentedly, certainly incompletely. The 200-proof whang is missing, which unquestionably why we never fight. Has to be something very strong involved to produce fights. Why great loves seldom last (maybe they do, how do I know) while those involving softer emotions often make it.

Is there a scene that absolutely defines? Such scenes never really exist, or almost never–should I make up one? No, get the best you can remember exactly as it happens. The making up comes later.

One scene:

Margaret studying *View from the Bridge* and Arthur Miller's excellent essay on tragedy. It is K.'s copy of the play, which he annotated for M. (I looked at his notes–most perceptive–have I underrated Korbin?–probably).

I look over this fragmentary journal of mine. We sit side by side, most companionably, in fine house in Encino her money paying for (does my conscience hurt? Certainly not. My work more worthwhile than hers if not remunerative). We do not say a word but comfort and good will is there.

I look at her from time to time, she very intent, temporary lines in forehead, eyes squinted, mouth pursed.

She looking at me once when I look up.

Want a drink? she say.

No drink.

Hot chocolate then?

Good deal.

She goes to make it, her hand trailing across my shoulders as she passes, and comes back with two cups steaming on a tray. She very sweet as she offers it to me.

Not much. Is it?

Another:

She absorbed in work as I get ready to go to bed.

She: Do you want to?

Me: You're busy.

She: That doesn't matter. I'll do anything you want whenever you want.

Me: Put that damn book down then.

She smiles, stands, kisses me, and off we go.

I am sure there must be long conversations between M. and Korbin that have nothing to do with work, that are personal and perhaps intimate revelations. Yet I have no real picture of them. The only picture I have is the didactic one–Korbin instructing patiently, M. nodding with her eyes wide, her mouth pursed. There are words dropped like business, projection, tension, timing. And of course thrust.

I do remember one dinner. Korbin was telling funny stories, not jokes but stories about real people in the theater. They were funny;

he told them extremely well. M. in peal after peal of laughter. First time I have seen Korbin playful, and the first time I have seen him as less than fifty years old. Clearly he must have as many personalities as anyone else—clearly he and M. must speak of things besides their eternal, infernal craft. It is hard for me to call up such situations though. One does come. The two drinking hot tea with honey after a particularly long lesson. Korbin has declined a dinner invitation because he frankly does not feel like company. Sylvia is visiting in New York.

M.: How *will* you spend the evening, Max?

K.: I guess, I'll read some French plays and sip some wine. I just got a new batch of plays.

M.: You read them in French?

K.: Very slowly. Very, very slowly.

M.: What kind of wine do you like?

K.: Whatever's there. I don't know wines well, I don't care about them really.

(This exactly what I would not have expected him to say. Would have expected great show of authority on wines. Korbin is continually providing evidence he is not the stereotype I try to make him, I am continually surprised, and I continually reject such evidence.)

M.: Are you lonesome with Sylvia gone?

K. (smiling): I'll survive.

On Sylvia and M.—more complicated or is that because I want Sylvia to be more complicated? I suppose actually she is less complicated. Than Korbin.

She is powerfully drawn to Margaret, and resents her, and wants to use her, and wants various other contradictory things. One manifestation: she flatters M. shamefully and then claws her so swiftly, so artfully that M. does not know she has been clawed. Total pattern larger than any individual episodes. A couple:

Sylvia: Darling, you're more wonderful all the time. You're going to be a fine actress (pause) yet.

And: Ask Margaret, she's our reader.

After that one I tell her: Leave her alone, Sylvia.

She: What in the name of God are you talking about? Her snapping anger most convincing.

She likes to manage Margaret, she particularly likes to dictate her clothing.

Sylvia: Margaret, sweetie, that necklace is just, I mean, please *change* it, sweetie. And I really would suggest a different blouse, a different color.

Must admit her advice is generally good.

She likes to put her arm around Margaret, to kiss her arriving and leaving. Custom with many women. And yet?

But in contacts with me she knows no signs whatever of the latent. Her whole demeanor has that faint note of complicity, the unspoken hint that someday . . .

In conversations with the others, she invokes it: You two stay here and work all night if you want to—Grover and I will get ourselves to a motel. And so on.

All good clean fun. Yes indeed.

She knows she excites me and plays on it—an automated response for all women. She knows too I peek at her legs, and flashes once in a while on purpose.

Between Sylvia and Korbin:

A very strong cord there. In spite of, or rather as clearly evidenced by, the fact that most of their communication seems unspoken. This perhaps deepest indication of intimacy. A soft question and a nod for an answer, a word and a word. Limited dialogue, perfect understanding.

Wonder if much is going on there erotically? My guess is either very little or very great deal—what price intuition?

Between Korbin and myself, there exists the kind of truce, or tolerance, that exists between people who do not greatly like each other but who are too aware of the mutuality of their interests to let themselves dislike each other.

We exchange opinions on playwrights, absurd and unabsurd, their tricks of dialogue and so on, with careful deference to each other's expertise. He reads very few novels.

Nelson Glassgow shows himself infrequently, but he still a very important piece of situation. He and I get on, there is tension between him and both Korbins, particularly Max. I suspect he had been planning a separate company for Margaret a long time, and very very

very annoyed at suddenness and prominence of Korbins in picture.

There are depths under depths, memories stacked on memories, in thing between Margaret and him. M. seems imprecisely angry toward him, as though nursing an ancient indignity. She speaks little to him, and that coldly, and sometimes she flares out at him. She depends on him profoundly, though Korbin of course has cut into this dependence.

He clearly *was* The Man in Her Life. How much is left?

Plenty.

I think if he made determined true effort, she would leave me at once, though with some tears.

Glassgow is sardonic, irreverent, keenly intelligent.

I ask him, Were you really an English professor?

He: No. I was a part-time instructor.

Me: Why did you quit?

He: I was fired, they caught up with me.

He full of sharp aphorisms. One I like: I can't stand poor phonies. Rich phonies have their points, but I can't stand poor ones.

Clearly a man of parts.

No entries for many months, nothing central in that time to contribute to novel. Have not begun novel. Because do not know how it comes out. Should begin soon or may decide no novel there.

And no suitable "property" found for Margaret. Occasional flashes of tension between her and Korbin. She has even lost temper with me a time or two, most unusual for her generous sloppy charity.

Would like to see M. make peace with and return to Globe. Even if I should lose a novel by it. Try to steer her toward it without open suggestion. Those emperors of suggestion, the psychiatrists, are right: never break technique.

Glassgow has persuaded M. to do British picture to be made in France. Korbin against it, but his opposition melts totally when Glassgow gets him direction of it. This has taken much doing, clearly. And there is clause in his contract providing he can be summarily released if bankers not satisfied with his work as seen in rushes.

After long silence: Paris, practically alone, M. always fatigued after working day. She is at once perfectionist and acute self-doubter while working. Totally different personality: frightened, irritable, even tortured. Reasons for her tardiness and too-frequent psychically rooted illnesses.

Am furiously jealous of Korbin. And astonished. He and Margaret have *done* it. I have just seen second cut of picture. It is superb. A high comedy, with very gentle laughs, and a pathos he has understated exactly as he should. He has done *everything* exactly as he should. Astonishing thing to me is *he has not tried to make picture bigger than it can be*. One of final tests in any art, and one I never, ever thought he could pass.

M.'s character is a good-hearted beautifully blousy night club singer, American, who has affairs with and gives up some half a dozen men after putting their lives in order and restoring them to happiness. This character *is* M., of course. Korbin has seen it and defined her exactly. No mistake: the son of a bitch has gone and done it.

This to be a week of severe self-examination, for me.

Margaret and I want a vacation in Greece, I suppose the truth is I want a vacation in Greece, and after picture is cut we fly to Athens. Dull there. We visit islands in Cyclades and decide to take house on Mykonos. It about a hundred miles from Athens. All buildings are white, land is dry brown mountain. Very restful, though simple villagers not quite so simple as expected. The village like a Mexican small town but quieter. Back in hills honest-to-God peasants ride burros and lead goats, some women dressed in black like chorus of *Electra*. Margaret not abnormally tired, the picture unbelievably problem free, and she unwinds wonderfully and we decide to stay a couple of months. Island is semifashionable, with steady flow of tourists from all over Europe, but these not obtrusive.

Incredible color, line patterns here: black on blue on blue, white on brown on blue, many many others. Must write them. In passionate hurry to write them, to be *really* working again.

Have started a kind of between-novels novel, specific gravity very light but pleasure to myself very great. *Helen of Troy,* rendering Margaret lightly in the role. Theme: demigoddess of love has powers totally beyond her knowledge and control. Vaguely like John Erskine's little book way back there. Haven't read in fifteen years but remember as first-rate comedy of ideas. Would probably find dated if went back to it.

Book will not amount to much but I am enjoying it. Right of poets to relax in deliberately inconsequential works not only accepted but applauded. Why not equal rights for novelists?

Love getting pure visual images down as backdrop for narrative that is pure fantasy.

No more in journal until book done.

Book done. In not much more than two months. Would never have believed it. It a lightweight book but a good lightweight book.

Must record this for feel it important.

Finished book at ten and at eleven-thirty betrayed Margaret with a Greek peasant. A woman I mean—in Greece you had better specify. She was a maid who comes to us daily (M. had gone to the mainland for two days to shop). She about twenty-seven, thick bodied, heavy brown hair, tanned skin, face like a Disney Pan, undiluted by Slavs, Turks, or Franks. Told myself wanted a symbolic connection with apotheosis of ancient Aegean. Actually wanted gross and animalistic episode as counter to long cerebral effort.

Like this: she dusting in a room full of ninety-drachma busts. Ignored me studiously when I came in. When I said, "Hello, Nicola," there must have been something in my voice that told her. She looked over her shoulder and smiled in way I could not misunderstand. Never did it before, she never did. Eyes most meaningfully used. I came behind her and rested hand between shoulder blades. She looked at me again, kept dusting slowly. Very pretty, I said, or much pretty, in bad Greek. She said the same words in quite different intonation, kept dusting lightly. Let my hand slip down, she moves her dusting cloth lightly over marble, let my hand slip down farther. She stops, laughs softly, does not look at me while my hand keeps working.

I pull her erect, she stands quite still, I kiss her. She has a sweet kiss.

She laughs, a fine shine of white teeth, when I try to take off her sheath. Pulls it over her head in one quick strong motion and stands there laughing. Only in coarse cheesecloth pants and these do not stay long. Wonderful strong heavy *woman's* body. Big, unsagging breasts, belly full and strong the way a woman's belly ought to be, rich brown lovehair, smooth heavy thighs and calves. I kiss all her body as she stands, she makes no sound but soft laughter, and then I pull her to the red rug on the marble tile floor.

It is like swimming into a sea cave, the unchecked gasp of her pleasure is the surge of ocean, she comes to me like a spring tide.

She says words in Greek argot I do not know but cannot mistake. They as exciting as English equivalents and more simply *because* I do not know them.

The instant I saw her naked she was a hundred times more an incarnation of sex, for me, than M. has ever been. Why? M. is the universal love priestess, Nicola a Greek island girl, girl hell, woman. Maybe that is the answer.

What a lousy and wrong word is betray. I betrayed nobody. No possible harm if M. doesn't hear of it (now *there's* an original thought).

In New York after some weeks. M. liked book breathlessly on island, and Korbin and Sylvia like it unfakingly here. All three urge me to write screenplay from it. Why not? Grab every experience every chance you get. First rule for any artist. No. The second. First is that nothing counts but the work and all else must be immolated to it. Am I keeping that? Better not go into that. Better had.

Bought Lawson's book and Eisenstein's book and read both and started in. Wouldn't it be funny if this was real art form? Never thought of that, or rather never thought of that in connection with me. Camera moves from image to image as does novelist, that is novelist who knows what he is doing, and how many do. *Farewell to Arms* has sublime camera movement. Why didn't either picture just follow it the way it was?

In sequence of visuals am frankly imitating *Farewell.*

The picture made in Paris released simultaneously in New York, London, Paris, Rome–not I understand in absolutely usual procedure. Tremendous reviews in Europe and England, specifically on M.'s performance. New York reviews only fair, two even nasty. She weeps. Korbin furious–this one of those instants in which he becomes human. Why do they persecute her? he fumes. They don't of course. They simply cannot conceive she has transcended the stereotype of herself.

At work on screenplay in New York apartment on 84th St. (M. has total privacy in New York when she wishes it). Am learning from this thing. Am convinced it will make a better writer of me if I survive. Trick, always, is to survive. Korbin's here of course. Conferences with him. He is knowledgeable, pragmatic, yet aware, and is a real help. Have long since conceded he smarter than I credited him in beginning. He smart enough in fact to be maneuvering to get on as coauthor of screenplay. He ain't gonna.

Sylvia no longer excites me the way she did, she knows it, her conduct consequently subdued.

After nearly a year Dayton Productions is bluntly on its ass. No starts, no nothing. (Missing ingredient: one really sharp businessman.)

Feeling is that my screenplay would be too expensive to make for Dayton Productions, that a major studio ought to undertake it if anybody. Possibly too a desire for reassurance on its quality, that is its producibility (book will at last be published next spring). This the Hollywood syndrome: everybody wants confirmation of their judgment. (Thought: Is this not also the publishing syndrome, the critical syndrome, the universal syndrome?)

Glassgow in from Coast, limping slightly from his mishap: getting shot *in flagrante*. Happily only in the leg. He not only full of aplomb but is now representing his nemesis–where else could it happen? M. at first refuses to speak to him, then finally does so but is pure ice. Glassgow says the way to make *Helen* is have Globe make *Helen*–he can now approach Sidney Tate who has had stockholder trouble but is now safe. Temporarily.

Now that M. is finally speaking to Glassgow again, she can do nothing but berate him. She asks him if he has seen a certain play that opened in L.A. instead of Boston and he says no. And she is on him.

–I know, you've been *busy*. We all know how *busy* you've been, Nelson dear. We get papers in New York too, Nelson dear.–

And in a moment:–Did you get a purple heart, Nelson? If they didn't give you a purple heart you ought to do something about it. You really ought to.

And:–Maybe you can tell weather by your leg? Like the other old soldiers? Is that right, Nelson? Can you tell weather by your wound?

Glassgow cannot pass that:–Not by the leg, no. However, I can detect certain, phenomena, by a certain, stiffness, elsewhere.

M.'s cheeks flame, she glares at him, flounces off.

I suppose it is redundant to point out that she is clearly not over him, as the chroniclers of romance put it.

I am oddly undisturbed.

After great deal of negotiating Globe deal on *Helen* finalized. Pots of money for all. I find it supremely interesting that Glassgow has maneuvered Howard Sills in as executive producer. Korbin likes the stark quality of landscape on Mykonos for the picture, possibly because I used it as physical model in book. If logistic and financial problems can be worked out, which is to say if Greek government cooperates, Tate is willing to shoot it there.

First entry in many months. That I am willing to preserve. Have torn out several previous pages because they unimportant, only chronicle of personal despair, do not wish to see them. Am now optimistic again. Here on the island of papier-mâché walls of Troy, I have been swallowed by the monster but whole so to speak. I think. I hope. Have been trying to care for Margaret as best I can, but fear I have only limited talent in this direction. This is a tense, tearing time for her, it has gone on for months, it will go on for more months. Of course I see it as natural inevitable outcome of the pressure of forces between which she has placed herself. This was what I saw in the beginning, and so I am clearly biased. It may be much simpler: very hard work, very long picture, very great deal of money involved. Certainly enough by itself. Yet I insist on seeing M. as pushed by money on one hand; excessive self-consciousness, preoccupation with textbook, on other.

Meanwhile I rewrite dialogue for script almost daily, and I write nothing else. Sad fate for writer. Gloss it as you will, writer for American pictures is highly paid amanuensis for producer, or director, or producer-director. If writer is true writer *and* has emotional commitment to pictures, he *must* become producer-writer. No other way. I have no commitment to pictures. What I care about is the novel and only the novel.

Theoretically the screenplay should be absolutely firm before shooting starts. Within the framework of the fixed scenes, however, we are always polishing and sharpening. Just so we do not disturb production plan.

Korbin has inspirations that are sometimes brilliant and sometimes awful. Problem is to use good ones without unbalancing story, push him away from bad ones. Sills has excellent taste, remarkable facility for knowing what is at once commercially sound and not actually offensive to intelligence. He has few inspirations. Thank God.

Thought: Why is M. tensing up so here when she did so well in Paris picture? Korbin and what he represents same in each case.

Answer: So much more money involved here. The idea of bigness involved here. The size of the one also makes the other larger. Not a paradox: she is so afraid the lessons she has learned from Korbin will be swallowed up by money considerations that in her mind she makes the Korbin factor larger. So it will not be lost.

This too I have seen in writers.

M. has been shaky and she is getting worse. Seems perpetually on edge of tears, given to outbursts that come not from anger but fear. Have seen her whole body tremble in morning as she dresses. Have seen her come in at night, drop on bed, and stare, stare, wide-eyed at ceiling.

Is Korbin handling her badly? In all candor I do not think so. He very demanding on scenes but not unreasonable. To give him his due he has genuine, deep concern. I do think he is overdirecting though, which makes him even more an incarnation of the textbook (Caution: don't forget how well he did the Paris picture. Absolutely did not overdirect there). On this thing the thing is simply to turn M. loose before the cameras and let her *be* Margaret Dayton. I wrote it that way, even in the Industry a writer might know *something*.

My instinct tells me lit-tul Sylvia has a small pinky in M.'s shakes. Instinct hell: simple observation. Today M. blew a scene quite badly, six takes and still bad. Between Helen and Menelaus, difficult high comic irony. (My God, did I steal it from Erskine? I think I did.) As M. screwed it up, I saw Sylvia smiling ever so faintly, ever so enigmatically. Afterwards she consoled M. so sweetly, enfolded her so tenderly. What a wonderful thing is love set free of the fleshly fires.

Uh-huh.

M. most badly upset and wept in the hotel. I gave her aspirin, soup, and Nembutal, and now she sleeps deeply: no studying.—The hell with studying (I told her some time ago), you've already studied it, just do your work intuitively after that first preparation. Let your subpsyche sort it out overnight and before cameras do it intuitively. That's the way I write, writing after all has a *few* complications even if it is not the sublime art of acting.—Again my unfortunate unquenchable arrogance of craft: she understandably angered and rejected my advice.

That two weeks ago. Talked to Korbin, who stopped nightly skull sessions they had been having. He also hoping for improvement.

Yet no improvement.

Glassgow has indicated concern to me, and yesterday spoke to M. —Relax, Margaret, you're working at it. You don't have to work at it. Just relax.—

But M.—Oh shut up. Go find yourself a woman and a boat and get yourself shot. Just get shot this time by somebody that knows how to shoot.—And off she goes.

Glassgow to me—You see? What can I do?—

Me—What do you think I've been trying to do?—

Glassgow—Look, Brand, we've got to do something. She's completely screwed up, she's bombing every scene she does. Can't Korbin see what kind of shape he's got her in?

—I'm sure he does, I'm sure he's trying to reverse it.—I stop—You know I think Sylvia is doing no good. No good at all.—

—I never had any use for that broad—

We agree to stay in close touch.

Glassgow has a quality which makes almost everyone trust him. Possibly to his own chagrin. Probably to his own chagrin.

Talked to Mace Garrett today. When I was in high school he was one of the Great Gods of The Movies. No more: now a man in his mid-fifties with a still good but aging body and a fine worn smile that seems totally true. He is Hector, and is wearing a Trojan helmet with a long blue plume—a triumph of Globe's research department.

—Did these guys really wear these things?

—Absolutely.

He laughs and shakes his head.—What a way to make a living.

—Did you always want to be an actor?

—Good God no. I was a fighter, I just kind of fell into this acting thing.

—You like it?

—Where else can you make this kind of dough?

It is sad and hard to remember what Glassgow has told me: that Garrett thinks he is under sentence of death. He lives only to live through the picture, says Glassgow, his hundred thousand dollars will preserve other investments that will preserve the family he acquired so late.

But they are so often wrong about these predictions. Why should they not be wrong here? I shall *will* that they be wrong, and maybe they will be.

Garrett interests me profoundly. As material. As actor he is good workman only, yet he has talent, *is* talent. What talent? M.'s opposite—male sex figure? Not anymore.

His talent rather is a thing of personality, an unfaked intensity of looking at things, a commitment—to what?

His talent is his angle of vision? Yes. He has come to absolutely definite conclusions about the world, and keeps himself tightly gathered and in one piece as he faces it. A classic primitive existentialist. Question: Would this be a talent though if it did not come through in the way he looks and talks and moves?

Answer: No, it would not.

Left again with ultimate indefinability of talent.

Who *has* talent here? Tate, Sills, Korbin have remarkable skills, each of them. Do they have *talent* as I intuit it? Tate does I think, Sills and Korbin do not. Could not justify this judgment, it so intuitive as to be perverse. M. has talent, I have talent (I think), Garrett has talent, Glassgow has talent. Sylvia does not have it.

From this can we get a real definition of talent?

No.

Try.

Could talent be an absolutely personal unfaked way of looking at the universe—plus the ability to communicate it excitingly? Put it tighter: talent is an ability to show excitingly a unique and intensely held view of the world.

Not good enough—and yet a good beginning.

Terrible frightening thought: Do *I* still have talent or has it gone to simple skill? Is this why I resent Korbin? Because I see in him what I might become or have become? A clever and unbodied hand? Is he in the stinking end *mon semblable,* my mirror-self?

I do not think so. Indeed I might become him but not yet. Not yet. Will not admit it if I have but will hang on and *make myself not be him.*

Hanging on, making yourself be what you wish to be, is most of it or maybe all of it.

Margaret broke down today. Thank God here, with me, and not on location. It came on apparently abruptly and yet not really so. She frozen-faced at bedside coffee, God knows how long she had lain there staring at the dark, and frozen-faced as she fumbled into her clothes, and she spoke only in monosyllables. I suppose I sensed aspects of the catatonic but did not acknowledge them.

Then:

—I can't do it, I can't do it—she started—not wailing, not sobbing, keening is the word—she started keening in this long, low wind-cry and said over and over:—I can't do it, I can't do it.—

The four words. Over and over. Nothing else.

Margaret has a fever, I reported to Sills (company has island telephones on set). Doctor hired for picture came running. (He a very young doctor just through interning, residency, or whatever the hell is last step: wanted to rest and read after eight years of labor, he said. God knows he has had time, on the island so far he has only put on Band-Aids. Alas, he does not read Hemingway, Yeats, Conrad, James, Thomas, but *Not As a Stranger* and *American Journal of Psychology.*) M. quieted with aspirin when doctor arrived. Told him all of it, also said preferred Sills and others not know. He gave her hypo, said—That will make her sleep. If she does it again I have to tell Sills—Very fair, yea charitable.

I spend the day in the room with her. Drugged, she sleeps hard. Don't know what drug was but in afternoon she totally composed. When Sills and Korbin came by she quite cheerful.—A stinking twenty-four-hour virus—she told them—I've slept it away, I'll be back tomorrow.—

And then Sylvia. Who stroked M.'s hair, cooed, talked baby talk, and then said—We can go over your scenes right now, sweetheart, if you feel like it.—

No you can't, I said, you get out of here. Did not say it *quite* like that.

Find it difficult to remember Sylvia kindled gem-like et cetera in my pants. Resent her profoundly, distrust her profoundly.

It makes me sick and it makes me weep that such a generous easy-tempered girl as M. should be in this state. Have I done *all* I could for her? Yes, I have, or as close to all as I can come. The hot wire of guilt has scorched my conscience so that I have been twice as zealous in working to protect her. With the most self-flaying honesty I can say that.

At the same time, I am aware that my sense of obligation to the unwritten book has eroded. I care more about Margaret than the book. A great deal more. A fatal flaw. And I cannot even regret it.

This happened:

As I stopped at desk to check for mail, assistant manager said:

—Was your New York connection all right, sir?—

—What New York connection?—

—On the phone call, sir—

—I didn't call New York—

—I thought—he checks a pad—ah, that was *four*-eighteen (we are in three-eighteen). Mrs. Korbin—

Why is Sylvia calling New York? Family of course. Or a lover. Not my affair. Ha ha.

Why then have I set this down?

I *knew* he would deal. What was there in his face that made me know?

He is a displaced British colonial and has the unease of the displaced. The edges of his mouth are slack: I think this makes him look weak. His blue eyes are nearsighted and squint: to me this makes him appear defenseless and ashamed. He is very eager to please: the total of his face, to me, is amiable, insincere, afraid.

Later, in the elevator, after we have negotiated, the knowledge of his face strikes with a shock. In it truly is this: he loathes himself because he has been unlucky.

Because luck has kicked him he feels he deserves the kick. Because he feels he deserves the kick, he seeks to be kicked again. To be shamed again. So he shames himself.

All of this in a box inside a box inside a box in a locked vault.

This is the assistant manager. I paid him fifty down and promised him a hundred more if I can listen if Sylvia talks to New York again.

Today (in Margaret's trailer-dressing room) I find Sylvia with Margaret, open script between them, Margaret taut and scared looking, Sylvia sweetly expounding.

–Margaret, they're about ready for you on the setup I think.

She goes, Sylvia starts to go behind her, and I take Sylvia's arm with my left hand.

I hold her arm a moment. Sylvia's face turned to me is surprise. Past her face, through the open trailer door, I see Margaret's back in her brown cashmere coat going away.

–This is no time for romance, dear one, says Sylvia.

–I don't know what you're doing but you stop it–I tell her.

Her eyebrows tense.–What are you talking about?

–Sylvia, you stop it and you stop it now.–

Her face colors, I think I can feel the heat.

–Screw you, Brand. Anything I can do to help Margaret I will do and you can't stop me. She jerks her arm free, goes to the door and turns and says *self-righteously:*–I should think you'd want to help her too. But I guess that's asking too much, isn't it? I guess it's asking too much from a conceited writer snot like you.–

Down the steps she turns again and says with the serene malevolence of pure uncontaminated indignation:–You *writer!*–

Away she goes swinging her trim little behind. Self-righteously.

Does she think she means it?

At the instant I am sure she does. Whatever she is up to.

I hate her, and for the first time in months, I desire her.

Sidney Tate here. The Man. Himself.

Everybody knows why he is here. Picture has been costing too much, taking too long. The solvency of the studio is very nearly riding on the picture, and Tate's job is absolutely riding on it. As with Metro and *Ben-Hur,* Twentieth and *Cleopatra.* The picture that is the desperate, total gamble is the metaphor of these desperate years (I surmise). How they must all long for the safe decades of the film factory, which in retrospect must seem so distant, so flower-short, so sweet: the Industry's Camelot.

Tate's troubles, however, come from more than conditions. These indeed are menacing, but he himself is menaced by a more visible enemy: Vern McGaughey. McGaughey is a kind of raider, who gets hold of weak corporations and merges them for profit or collapses them and takes cash.

Story about McGaughey and Tate fascinating, at least fascinating to me. McGaughey supposedly embittered by Tate's consolidating him out of his own corporation a quarter-century ago. Entered present piratical career as result. Been after Tate at Globe for some time now, and damn near got him before. Both McGaughey and Tate, I gather, are incarnations of the appearance vs. reality principle. Tate is by appearance and indeed by reputation a most kindly man: yet his business eminence was founded on his skill and willingness with a hatchet. McGaughey has put more corporations out of business than any other of his piratical brethren: yet (according to *Fortune*) he is a charming fellow who frequently provides severance pay and organizes job searches for his victims.

If there is anything to the whispers, and there is always *something* to the whispers, his grand passion is his hate for Sidney Tate. Tate hate.

Tate's first two days he inspects everything: setups, the books, oh my yes the books, costumes, trailers, actors, extras including the Greek army—and the books, and the books, and the books.

This first tour with Sills only. Not even Korbin the director with him, absolutely not Brand the writer. He wears a business suit, I suspect he makes a great point of wearing a business suit, though it is most unusual on outdoor location. Moving about the set he looks most sober and grave. He seldom speaks, nods once in a while.

After five days—the word is—Tate has gone through shooting schedule for rest of picture and made changes that will save not quite one million dollars.

This largely done by cutting down on battle scenes.

This explained to Korbin and me jointly (to me as courtesy only, for as Mere Writer I have no real say).

Korbin objects violently:—This is spectacle. It is central to the picture and to the achievement of the picture and to the commercial success of the picture.

Tate:—It seems to me there is still all the spectacle you can possibly need. We can get it in one week instead of three, and have almost as much as before if we edit properly.—

Sills:—He's right, Max, I should have suggested that myself.—

Tate's silence says: *Yes, you should have.*

Sills blushes.

Sills has in fact done extremely well. Not his fault he is only tasteful producer and not a cost-controlling genius. Had Sills not done well out here, and had Tate himself not made the intelligent basic decisions, this picture would be beyond recovery. Costs are only a little past ten million—only? Only?—and picture should be brought in for seventeen or eighteen, twice the budget but still a feasible figure.

M.'s illness and bad performances which will have to be reshot will add (Sills told me frankly) more than half a million.

Again: Am I doing all possible? For her?

I think so. I truly think so.

I cannot help being pleased when Tate shows he is fallible, human.

Today he wanted to eliminate ships entirely, shoot whole Greek fleet from above in process studio. Would have saved $800,000. Oddly, I found proposal completely reasonable and Sills did not.

Sills opposed and convinced him. Said Tate:—You're probably right at that.—

It is to his credit that he conceded. Greatly to his credit.

How it must madden Tate that this is not a truly efficient business, that the top ten per cent of quality costs more than the bottom ninety.

Tate has had several long talks with Glassgow. Of course I do not know what about. But I have seen from a short distance Glassgow talking, Tate nodding. I have heard before that Tate has great confidence in Glassgow, and it is obviously true.

Astonishing how much confidence everybody has in Glassgow, whose great and abiding pride is his screw-it-all-to-hell persona.

Tate's coming has most seriously affected Margaret. Much more than Sills, he is the studio made flesh. Money made flesh. Huge money made flesh. She is frightened. I am frightened for her. I am desperately afraid I cannot pull her out of fear.

I tell her of course there is no need to be frightened:

—All you have to do is not do anything. Just relax and be you. Helen *is* you. I wrote this thing, so she is you.—

—I'm trying—she said—I'm trying.

—Don't try so hard. You don't have to try hard.

—All right—she smiles, if feebly—I'll try not to try.—

—Who's the greatest—(A game we play.)

—*You're* the greatest—

—Next to me?—

—*I'm* the greatest.—

I kiss her.—All right then, stop fretting.—Then certain other therapy.

Her scene that morning is first good one in weeks.

Now Margaret's *mother* is here, a week after Tate. Presumably to comfort and bolster daughter. Will it work that way? M. talks about mother almost not at all, I have surmised a Situation between them. M. greets ma dutifully but with something less than unbounded delight. And here, I am stuck—no, awed—by the fact that she is extremely handsome woman who looks decidedly under fifty and most decidedly bangable. Bangable as all hell. She very chic (of course on Margaret's money, and why not on Margaret's money?). Just as well she does not live with us.

I say to Margaret:—Your mother is a very handsome woman.

M. (remotely)—There are those who thought so. Mr. Nelson Glassgow thought so.

Me—What does that mean?

M. closes her face.

Me—Yes, you certainly have an attractive mother.

M. (suddenly angry)—If you're so goddamn antsy about my mother you just ask Glassgow. He can tell you what you want to know, he's had the full benefits.

So that is the root of the tender nerve.

This is the sequence: A long story conference this morning. Korbin shooting and so not present, but has voiced feelings most intensely.

Tate has ordered elimination of scene Korbin, Sills, and I believe to be key scene. Central to establishing Helen and reaction of Trojan princes to her. Tate wants to cut entirely, work important dope into scene before. Means total rewriting of two scenes, both scene before and after so naturally I am against. So are Sills and K.

Yet as I consider it I see it might be just as well. A big scene is lost, a better-knit continuity and faster pace is won. Considerable money saved.

Sills and K. against it. On principle I do not wish to side with moneybags against talent and friend of talent, but I say–Let's try it and see how it looks on paper.–

Who would ever have thought I could *write* with two people looking over my shoulder (soon three, for Korbin comes in)? Yet the quick draft is not bad, some weak lines I will work on alone of course. Sills and Korbin are almost satisfied and Tate is pleased.

And then the significant item:

As I approach Margaret's trailer, Sylvia comes down the steps. She is wearing a gray knit thing and moves well in it (I cannot help noting in the midst of fury).

We say nothing as we pass, but she glares at me, I think triumphantly.

And of course it happened. M. had a retreat this morning, retreat from reality, retreat better word than breakdown. And it was not such a breakdown as was the first: She did not go into apparent catatonia, nor hysteria. Just said dully–I don't feel like working today–And would not get out of bed.

Doctor came of course and repeated treatment.

–I'll have to tell Mr. Sills this time–he says–All about it, I mean–

(Apparently a company contract wipes out confessional sanctity of doctor-patient thing.)

–Don't you know he doesn't want to know?–

He looks at me, somewhat surprised, and I see it has taken.

I do not know whether he tells Sills or not. If he does, Sills will have to tell Tate, and he absolutely does not want to tell Tate.

A day later: I come in from location with M. and the assistant manager calls me over and M. goes up alone (I like his betraying unfrocked face so full of complicity).

–Tried to get you this afternoon, old boy (old boy has replaced sir since we became co-sinners). Mrs. ah Korbin called New York again. Delayed the call long as I could but couldn't get you.–

I swear.

—Got the name of the party though. Listened in myself. She was telling him about Miss Dayton's, Mrs. Brand's, ah, illness. Did not seem terribly sorry I must say.

—*Who* was she talking to?

—I have it down here. Have it all down.—

He goes to desk behind front desk and looks. Finds nothing and face grows worried. Opens one drawer, then another, then face panics, then opens last drawer. Goddamn him he has lost it. Face gets all broken up as he goes through pockets. Naturally fruitlessly.

Suddenly I am sure who it was. Like that.

—Would you know it if I said it?—

—Absolutely.—

—Was it Vern, McGaughey?—

Ecstatic, his face—Exactly! That's exactly who it was!—

—You're sure?—

—No doubt at all now that I've heard it. Vern McGaughey. McGaughey Enterprises.—

I give him the whole hundred. His face warmly, corruptly names me brother.

So Sylvia is a spy.

Not a spy. A saboteur.

In name of God *why?*

No, first what to do, then why.

Tell Sills? He will have to tell Tate and it *will* be in the fan. Still and all maybe I should tell Sills and Tate this second.

Out of question to tell Margaret—it would shatter her.

Tell Korbin? Absolutely. He may be able to handle the whole thing.

And Nelson Glassgow? Yes indeed Nelson Glassgow.

—You're sure?—says Korbin. Of course he knows I am sure but he repeats it:—You're sure?—

—There's no doubt.—

It occurs to me that he hates me, traditionally as one hates the bearer of bad news, and then I see that he is not thinking of me at all, that who he hates at that moment is his wife.

Like me he says:—Why? Why would she do it?—

Glassgow is instantly, explosively profane.—That bitch—is only openers. He reviles her for many seconds.

—What do we do first?—I ask.

—We get that broad out of here so fast, so fast—he cannot complete his metaphor. I have never seen a man more visibly furious.

—I see no need to tell Tate or Sills, do you? Just get her out.—

—Yes.—He puts himself in restraint an instant.—Just get her out of here.—He looks at me.—For Christ's sake, Brand. Why in *hell* would she do it?—

And that is the question. Why?

Now let us see what kind of perceptions *you* have. Why *did* Sylvia do it?

Obvious things first: she is jealous of M.'s relationship with Korbin. She does not envelop him as she did before M. He is not as dependent on her as he was before M. She is extraordinarily possessive of Korbin.

All true, but only part of a real reason.

Maybe she hates Margaret?

Why should she hate Margaret, her benefactor? *Because* Margaret is her benefactor. And is beautiful, successful, and famous. Not to mention generous and large-spirited.

Better, much better, those are what hate is made of.

She hates Tate or Sills? Impossible.

She's McGaughey's mistress? I doubt it. McGaughey is paying her? He couldn't pay enough, he couldn't begin to match the stake the two Korbins have in the success of this picture, and the success of Margaret.

Try again.

She is angry at M. because M. has reduced her husband's dependence upon her and indeed diluted the whole relationship. She is jealous because M. is superior, and resentful because M. has befriended and assisted the two of them. All of these things, and certainly more that I can't guess at, are compounded into a bizarre love-hate feeling for M. that seems to be overwhelming.

Summing these up, I feel my anger dissipating—has psychiatry abolished free will?

If it has, my books are lies.

Goddamn it, Sylvia *is responsible.*

I think.

And while Sylvia's perfidy or rather the knowledge of it ticks away, there comes another kick in the scrotum.

We have been rushing film to Alpha in Athens for processing and a first cut. Adequate facilities, faster and cheaper to send it there than New York or London. Globe has a top cutter and assistant on duty there of course. Then the print comes back.

In the hotel, Globe has rented a screening room: projector at rear wall, assortment of chairs, screen.

In a certain scene early in the third reel of four, I look at faces in this light. To my right: Nelson Glassgow's face, dour and set, Korbin's mouth turned down as though in pain. On two seats to the left Sills looks unhappy and shakes his head, next to him Tate's face absolutely blank, and between Tate and me, Margaret's face has tear streaks.

I press her arm. A moment later she gets up and leaves. I follow her. In the corridor she starts to cry and I get her to our room as quickly as possible.

Her scenes have really been quite bad.

In the room she sobs on the bed a long time as I try to comfort her.

In an hour, Sills calls: Come down at once.

–Later. Margaret's not well.–

He insists and I lose my temper.

I do agree to a conference the next day. I am angry with Sills and Tate. I am angry with myself because I have not averted the debacle, I am in fact angry with all.

I want to set this day down in sequence.

The events in the order they happened. It is important.

At conference, Tate, Sills, Korbin, Glassgow, and myself.

Tate most solicitous of Margaret. Says he does not wish to be indelicate but situation must be reviewed and resolved. He reviews it with absolute candor:

Almost all of Margaret's scenes are very bad, he says. They are so bad that the studio has only two alternatives. One is to replace Margaret immediately. The other is to reshoot the scenes.

He does not wish to replace Margaret. Replacing a star is always messy. And they have already paid Margaret a lot of money. Most important of all (and he is totally frank) they need Margaret in the picture to recover huge negative costs. No other star is big enough or available enough. Marilyn Monroe is dead four years, Elizabeth Taylor is tied up for the next two, and the two or three new ones are impossibly busy.

Now if the scenes are reshot: only close and medium shots need be done over, he says. They can be edited into spectacle scenes where necessary. Not many characters will be involved. The cost of reshooting thus will be considerable but not staggering.

–So–he says–it is in everybody's interest simply to reshoot the scenes. *If* Margaret can get herself together and do her best work or even an approximation of it.–

That, he concludes, is the issue:–Can she do it?–

–I am sure she can–I say–I have identified her problem and am sure it can be solved.–

After meeting Korbin overtakes me.–Sylvia is leaving the island tomorrow–he says, very shortly. His face looks hostile to me but it is probably only defensive. Sylvia after all has been only the final edge of the situation he created. He has to know it.

Glassgow catches me a little later.–What did Korbin tell you? Is that blank-blanking wife of his getting out?–

–He says so.–

–I hope it's not too late.–

–It's not too late. Of course Sylvia was only the point of it but at the end she made the difference. Korbin is straightened out now, and I think everything is going to be okay now.–

Certainly the first thing to do is to get rid of Sylvia, and if she is not gone by tomorrow, I will tell all of it to Tate and Sills.

The next thing to do is give M. a vacation if only a long weekend. In Athens: she loved Greek music and wine and nightclubs when we stopped there on the way out. With a rest, and Sylvia gone, and Korbin quiet, she might start swinging.

That is the sequence of the morning. I have no premonitions, rather do I feel more optimistic and hopeful than in months. The boil has been opened.

Korbin has changed schedule so Margaret has no scenes that day. I however have urgent changes to make in dialogue and must do them at once. I have coffee and a pomegranate for lunch and work on until done.

It is after four when I get back to the hotel. Margaret is not there.

Let me get the progress of my reaction exactly right. I am not even slightly apprehensive—at this point. I am not even curious.

It is not until six, and she still not back, that I feel the first uneasiness. Then I assume she is walking about the town, or on the beach.

Do I really know then? Is that why I do not at once go to find her? I don't think so.

I go to the bar and have a couple of glasses of resinated wine. I do not even think about her not being back. I honestly think I am not apprehensive at all at that point. I honestly think so.

And yet—

The instant I find the room empty the second time, I know the old old never to be mistaken jolt of pure disaster.

I rush out to the beach behind the hotel. The sun is down but the light has not gone: it is gray violet. I see the low black loom of islands shouldering out of a sea now gray, the white line of surf sweeping toward me. Stars are yellow against purple. No moon. I walk down the beach, at once tight with fear for Margaret, and lost in sea and sky.

I do not find her. I reject forms and colors, sternly, and go back to the hotel. Glassgow is not in his room.

Korbin is.

—Is Margaret gone?—he says.

—How did you know?—

—So is Sylvia.

We look at each other.

Brand looked at the last lines of his handwriting; he had written them the night before.

He stared at the last page, no longer reading, for many seconds. Then he closed the ledger and put it in the leather case. He did not lock it.

BOOK 2

SIDNEY TATE

1

NEVER BEFORE had fear been the driver; never had it held both reins and whip. Sidney Tate was sure he had been afraid no less than other men. But he had never committed himself and his responsibilities to a course of action because of fear. Now Margaret Dayton had forced him to do so. He felt that he had been ultimately violated in the most secret and inner recesses of his personality: he saw the virginity of his integrity as fatally impaired.

Tate knotted the sash of his flannel robe and moved heavily to the window. It looked to the coast and the sea. The breeze blew in strongly at forty-five degrees, faintly wet and bearing the stirring fresh scents that always rode the sea wind. Just below was the thick rind of white where the Aegean made surf at the rocky shore, beyond that the dark flat of water, and above the shadowed horizon the blueblack depths of sky and the scattered white points of stars. A black headland ran narrow and diminishing into the softer shades of the sea.

Tate turned from the window: he felt himself shut off from the promise he saw through it. He sat on the edge of the bed and invoked his old rule: assume the worst will happen and look at it squarely.

The worst that can happen is Haratunian withdraws the support of his voting stock.

If Haratunian withdraws his support: the worst that can happen is that Sidney Tate is removed from control of Globe-International.

If Sidney Tate is removed: the worst that can happen is Sidney Tate retires to the bosom of his wife and four children.

But he and his wife were not close though not hostile. His children were grown, and he would finish not as a winner but as a loser, not in triumph but in humiliation.

His deepest vision of himself would be shattered.

He knew that this vision should not depend on any event; he knew also that it did. Failure, failure for any reason, was for him the unremovable brand of incompetence. Incompetence would destroy totally *his* Sidney Tate.

He might have to bear it. But he did not want to. He would give almost anything not to have to.

He thought of what he had already given, and he moved away from that.

The situation was absurd: that a stockholders' battle and the destiny of a major corporation should balance on Margaret Dayton's attending or not attending a shipboard party. And Tate acknowledged that her attendance was all that was really required of him. Haratunian was one of the great satyrs, but he had his ethics, or rather his court rules. He asked only that Tate give him, in effect, an opportunity to, persuade, Margaret Dayton on his own. No more. Tate knew it was a reasonable request and a modest one–in the perspective of the powerful service Haratunian had done him and was willing to continue to do him. It would seem incredible to Haratunian that the president of the studio could not bring together its principal stockholder and its highest paid star in a purely social meeting. And yet Tate was confronted with exactly that failure: Margaret Dayton had refused him flatly.

Tate had known other issues, in more conventional corporations, to hang on just such horseshoe nails. He had known one major stockholder in an aircraft parts company to shift his support away from the president after an unfortunate afternoon on the golf course. He had known another to displace a chairman of the board who was unable to get him a membership in a men's club of purely local prestige in a small city.

Haratunian took his women seriously. And Tate took his request with absolute seriousness. Haratunian had saved both Globe-International as an operating entity, and Sidney Tate as its head. Tate knew perfectly that if he could not oblige Haratunian on a reasonable and decorous request, Haratunian would no longer oblige him.

When Dayton vanished, he had been unable to suppress a thrill of hope: her absence could be an out with Haratunian. But the radio telephone had not disguised Haratunian's impatience.

Tate walked to the dresser. From the top drawer he took a small electric coffeepot and a box of powdered milk. He heated water in the pot and poured it into a glass with milk powder. Then he poured generously from a bottle of Bristol Cream sherry into the milk, stirred, and began to drink.

This was Tate's only concession to sleeplessness. He declined steadfastly to take even the mildest sleeping pills, no matter how intense his personal situation. He always carried the electric pot, the Bristol Cream, powdered milk and instant coffee in his suitcase. The hot milk at night, the single cup of strong coffee immediately on arising were his necessities. He did not like to depend on others for what he required absolutely; he wanted to be as nearly self-sufficient as it was possible for a man to be.

Which was not nearly self-sufficient enough. He was humiliatingly dependent on Haratunian. And he was abjectly, impotently dependent upon Margaret Dayton.

He was more than sixty years old and he had never been in such a situation before. And he, accustomed to the grave and responsible uses of power, was powerless before a woman whose brains were in her belly.

"I wish I could go with you," Tate said across the breakfast table to his son. "I've really been very keen on it."

"I know you have. Maybe next week."

"I wish I could be sure. We seem to be living from crisis to crisis."

"You certainly do. Well. Delos will keep, it has for quite a while. And if you'll excuse me, I guess I'd better have at it."

"Of course."

Lawrence stood, fresh in khakis and engineer boots, and he finished the cup of coffee. He put it on the table. He was fairly tall and strongly built: his thick black hair was well combed over a firm clear face.

"You're sure old Globe-Int. won't need the jeep today?"

"Perfectly sure. There should be some perquisites with this job. After all."

"Good deal." Lawrence grinned at him, and Tate warmed with affection. "I'll get, then."

And he was gone, waving hand and light voice making a jaunty farewell.

Tate smiled at the door. His approval of Lawrence was without reservations. So too was his indulgence in it, which was one of his extremely rare personal indulgences. He permitted the approval to extend, moderately, to himself: he had done a good job. It would have been easy to spoil Lawrence and he had not done so. Now he gave himself unstintingly to the unreckoning pleasure of doing everything he could think of doing for his son. The race was done, the battle won: his boy was a quiet masterpiece of human engineering: brave, incorruptible, and cheerful–even kind to his father.

Lawrence was the youngest of three sons and four children. Tate had given both sanction and financial support to his academic career. "I'm glad we can afford a professor of history in the family," Tate told him.

"I'm glad you can too," Lawrence had said. "I'll admit one is a luxury."

Neither Lawrence, nor the two older sons, nor the husband of the daughter, had expected or asked for a job in Globe-International. They would not have received it. Tate had generously financed sons and son-in-law in their businesses. But he had moved against nepotism implacably when he came to real power in Globe-International: his toughness had helped Globe survive the crisis years when other major studios were collapsing or entering new fields. His toughness and his decisions had saved the studio.

Saved it so he could pimp for an Armenian billionaire: his mouth twisted.

He looked at the hard black shape of the telephone and returned to the realities of the day.

Was nine in the morning too early for a pimp to awaken his most prized property?

He tried. No answer. He called the desk and the set.

Margaret Dayton was still missing.

He dressed, in abstraction, and went downstairs. The black Citroën he had leased was waiting at the entrance. His driver, Harry Broncati, came up straight when he saw Tate and opened the rear door.

"Morning, Mr. Tate."

"Good morning, Harry."

Harry was a middleweight contender, once knocked out by Tiger Lou Flowers, who had been one of the technical advisers on the first *Kid Galahad* with Wayne Morris. Afterwards, he had hovered on the edge of the business first as a bit player, then as a bodyguard and driver for Globe-International notables.

He closed the door after Tate and started the car, then leaned backward and half-turned his head.

"Any sign a the dame, Mr. Tate?"

"No." Tate said it shortly.

"How can a big star like that just up and cut, Mr. Tate?"

"I wish I knew." Tate said it more shortly still. He did not like the ritualistic, and he felt false, camaraderie of the business.

"Think they'll find her today, Mr. Tate?"

Tate did not answer.

"I'll bet you guys got the whole Greek army looking for her, huh?"

"Not quite, Harry."

Well, thought Tate, privacy had been shattered by the announcement to the press. If privacy existed anywhere in this strange world, and he was not sure it did.

Sills was waiting for him at the gates in the walls of Troy.

"Have you heard anything?" Tate asked.

Sills shook his head. His face showed his depression and anxiety. "Nothing," he said. "Not one blessed thing. I've got two assistant directors checking everything on the island, and they haven't come up with a thing."

"The irresponsibility," Tate said. "It's unbelievable. It's more than that. A ten, almost twenty-million-dollar picture utterly dependent on the whims of one psychotic female. I mean utterly. Twelve years ago, I would have laughed in your face if you'd suggested it as a remote possibility."

"Obscene is the word," said Sills.

"How did it happen, Howard? How did we do it to ourselves?"

"Did we do it to ourselves? Yes, I guess we did. But not you and not me. It was done a long time before you or me. It was done in the beginning when the boys with the leggings and the caps and the barnyards in the orange groves decided the way to sell two-reelers was with the face and the name of the actor. The bind we're in, I mean the whole Industry's in, is the ultimate extension of that logic. We built the star system like Frankenstein's monster or that wooden horse out there and we're at its mercy."

"Yes," said Sidney Tate. "Yes we are. Absolutely."

"Once we could make them or break them. Now they can make us or break us."

"They can. They do."

"What can we do about it?"

Tate waved his hand: "Right now we can find Margaret Dayton and finish this picture."

"We'll find her."

"We damn well better, and that's the understatement of the decade."

"Isn't it though?"

And we'd better find her today because Haratunian comes in tomorrow. He said, "She's got to turn up sooner or later. Even Margaret Dayton can't walk out on a picture in the middle." He paused. "Yes she can. She can do anything if it's incredible enough. Well. Happy thoughts. I'll be around if you need me."

"Right, Sidney."

They parted; Tate walked aimlessly through the site of siege. For fourteen years he had been in the Industry (eternally the reverential capital, he admonished, in mockery), he had been a major power in it for all of that time, and yet he felt alien to it. It was really not his milieu; he was never at ease in its pandemonium and its bawdy. He wanted as much linear space between himself and its front lines as he could: his reality was the dark-paneled office, the eighteenth century simulacrum adjoining it that was the board room. In these places dwelt serenity, that prelude to decision and achievement; in them, the profligate gaudiness was as distant from himself as a corn dance from the grain exchange.

"A little more to the left, thirty-eight, a little more to the left, that's good. Come on up now, forty-five, come on up. Good, good, good, keep it there."

Tate looked up.

The voice came through a loudspeaker system: standing on a scaffolding behind the walls of Troy, the gaffer, the man in charge of lights, was placing his lights for an approaching scene. The lights had something of the look of howitzers, Tate thought: stubby black barrels on wheels.

A black-haired young man with a serious handsome face was positioning several of the Greek soldiers before the lights. He was calmly sure of what he was doing: Tate applauded him silently.

His name was Crasswell, and Tate had marked him for opportunity. Of course whether Tate could extend opportunity much longer was problematical, he thought.

At a lull, he came to Crasswell.

"How do you think it's going?" He asked it seriously and Crasswell answered the same way.

"You know how it's going right now, Mr. Tate."

"I don't mean right now, I mean what kind of a picture are we going to have?"

"We'll have a great picture if."

"If Miss Dayton finishes it? Don't be bashful, certain possibilities have also occurred to me."

"It can't help be a great picture, Mr. Tate. Dayton or no Dayton."

"I certainly hope it can't. With X million dollars down and X million to go."

"Dayton will get it back for us."

"If she comes back to us. Do you know what I've wondered, Crasswell? I've wondered if she's worth it or if any of them are worth it."

"I've wondered that too, Mr. Tate. But I guess they are, at least they are the way things are now, and Margaret Dayton is if anybody is. She's the biggest draw there is. Once I would have said the most valuable property there is only they aren't properties any more."

Tate laughed shortly. "They come closer to owning us. Now *why* is this quite attractive, moderately intelligent girl such a draw? Why is she? She is beautiful, but there are more beautiful girls in the cast of this picture. She has sex appeal, but there are girls on this picture with more sex appeal. Tell me, Crasswell. Why?"

Crasswell laughed. "Luck is always a good place to start."

Tate nodded.

"Then she has talent. It's not just that she gives the male public a world-wide erection, although that takes talent too, a lot of talent. These girls in the company that have more sex appeal, how many can make it show on film?"

"No argument."

"But her big thing is really something else. I'm not real sure how to put it. But when she's in front of the camera, I mean what the camera catches from her, is that she's real, she's like Chaplin's blind girl in *City Lights* or even Chaplin himself. Everybody identifies with her all at once, they know she loves everybody and everybody loves her. They feel she's taken a beating and she can still laugh and hope and love, and she's going to keep on taking a beating and she'll keep right on hoping and loving. It's a very great thing."

"The general view is, oh, somewhat different."

Crasswell smiled politely. His face had lost much of its candor: Tate guessed the young man feared he had gone too far, though Tate had asked for confidences. Now he drew Tate's attention to more than a dozen women clustered well back from the walls. As Tate watched, another approached them, suddenly switching her hips in a parody of a tart's walk.

"These are some of the camp followers," Crasswell said. "We shoot the big orgy scene today. You remember, early in the script, the night before the big attack. The warriors and their women."

"I remember. Kind of feast of the gladiators."

"That's right. It ought to be a good scene."

"It was a great scene in the picture we stole it from."

Crasswell looked at him quickly and laughed. "It sure was. *Demetrius and the Gladiators*. Those girls there we brought over, the rest are local."

They watched the girls, who were laughing loudly. One stood and posed herself in an extravagant attitude.

"They like to play whores," Crasswell said. "All of them do. I wonder why. Maybe it's the freedom of movement. Maybe they're working off repressions. They like it though."

"They seem to be enjoying themselves."

"The extras and the bit players always do. They think they're the real stars, I'm convinced of it. See that tall dark girl, that's Chryseis, the one that Agamemnon took from Achilles and got him sore."

"She's very Oriental-looking. Is she Turkish?"

"As a matter of fact, no. She's half Sioux Indian and half Chinese. Her father used to play the big chief in a lot of pre-adult Westerns and her mother worked in the wardrobe department at Globe. She photographs with a lot of voltage, I think we'll be hearing from her."

Tate nodded. Crasswell made the shop talk interesting.

"Mr. Tate."

He turned. It was Sills's secretary. She handed him a sealed envelope. He tore it open: the note was in Sills's own handwriting.

"No news of Dayton. Something of interest though from New York."

It was signed, Howard.

Tate put it carefully in his coat pocket. Haratunian's *Cerberus* should be only fifty or sixty miles away now. In a few hours it would be visible, the raked stack showing clearly over the horizon. He thanked Crasswell and walked toward the office of Howard Sills.

Tate reflected that his life had been committed to a quest for an archaic commodity: honor. He had sought his kind of success with single-mindedness, but it had not been the kind of success that could be achieved by the knife in the back, the rat's rush to each scrap of scattered cheese. He had wished himself above sordid intrigue and ordinary deceit; because of a series of circumstances, he had not had to engage in the demeaning struggles that almost inevitably marked a rise in corporation life. He had achieved power at a remarkably early age, and the concern of his life had been to build it with serenity, responsibility, and—the obsolescent word again—honor.

At this stage of his career of action, which was almost surely the last stage, he thought he had probably created those circumstances which moved him along the path of his clear if unformulated desire. We make ourselves, he thought, we choose the values of our lives without knowing it and make ourselves come true, and we never know we have done it until the making is finished and irrevocable.

And he had been fortunate, more fortunate surely than he deserved or always knew. For until he had set foot on Mykonos, he had come as close to that deep-locked picture of himself, he thought, as it was possible for a man to come. He had acted successfully, he had been virtuous and just, his honor and his dignity had been unassailable.

Until Margaret Dayton. Now at the end of his life in business, he was at her mercy. Hers and Haratunian's.

They had cornered him. Now his present, and cherished, portrait of himself must either be marred by himself or totally shattered by his great enemy: failure. He had opted for partial destruction: he would beat failure by delivering Dayton to Haratunian. Then he could leave the contest, ostensibly unbeaten, outwardly as he had always been. The violation of himself was not a large one, and certainly could not be seen, easily.

Maybe you were never permitted an absolute victory, he thought.

2

SIDNEY TATE was neither a showman, nor one of the royal heirs of Hollywood, nor what the Industry called a self-made man. He had come into it at the very top, borne upon his success as a physician to sick corporations. Globe-International had summoned him as president in 1951. His rejuvenation of what had been considered a hopelessly sick enterprise touched off "miracle man" epithets. He smiled, and was also half puzzled. He felt he had taken only the obvious measures, and wondered as always how his predecessors could have failed to do what he had done. ("Everything is clear-cut and simple to Sidney," one of his board members said to another. "He always sees the straight line and moves right down it. He's honestly puzzled when it's not that simple for somebody else.")

Tate had entered the world of corporations in the most conventional manner possible, as a junior line officer just graduated from the school of business administration at a Midwestern university. This was in 1922; the elaborate curriculum that marked the business academies of a quarter century later had not then evolved. He had studied economics, old style, and accounting. His father was an accountant, though not a CPA, and was head bookkeeper for a company that manufactured cardboard boxes, in a small city in southern Illinois; the job was neither very good nor very bad. Hugo Tate supported his family in middle-class adequacy that could manage, just barely, a membership in the town's only country club; by pinching he managed to send Sidney to Northwestern and let him join a respectable fraternity. He had never attempted to influence his son's choice of career; he was clearly well pleased when Sidney decided to major in business.

When Sidney told him of his decision, he nodded, approving, and, perhaps, seeking approval.

"I'm not surprised," he said. "I'm not in the least surprised and I may as well say frankly, I may as well tell you, I am pretty well pleased. Yes, I am pretty well satisfied. Wouldn't have stood in your way whatever you settled on, but this is good, substantial. Yes, I think you've made a wise choice." He stopped to light his pipe. He puffed, and the light from the hand flared up instantly to redden his pleasant anonymous features. He drew on the pipe again. "One thing I will tell you. Remember the heart of any business is the balance sheet and the books. The figures tell you the whole story, you just have to know how to read them. Whatever they tell you about the other stuff, what are they calling selling now, oh yes, marketing, whatever they tell you about marketing and all that, remember the whole story is in the figures. You have to learn how to read them. I hope you make a real study of accounting, in fact, I'd like you to get a CPA. Whatever firm you decide to go with and whatever end of it you finally settle in, get the CPA. I can help you with that, you know."

He did. Sidney Tate worked with his father closely for three summer vacations, and learned a great deal about reading figures.

Almost every evening, the day's work meticulously done, company time puritanically inviolate, Hugo Tate would instruct his son. Outside the tall thin windows, dusk would purple the sky, while the three-hundred-watt bulb on the long cord dropped its harsh yellow light on those two dark heads so close together.

"Now see this one." His father's voice was always patiently and pleasantly didactic as his slender and fastidiously scrubbed finger touched an entry. "What does it tell you?"

"It just tells me we sold twenty-three thousand one hundred and eleven dollars' worth of stuff in the Des Moines territory."

"Yes. It tells you that. Now how can you find out what else it tells you?"

"Well, I could check totals for preceding quarters and see if it's up or down."

"What else?"

"I could check totals for other areas and see if it's better or worse than the rest."

"Suppose it's worse?"

"Maybe something's wrong in that district."

"What then."

"Well, you check on it, you see what is wrong. Somebody does, anyway. Then when you see what's wrong you decide what to do about it. Then you do it."

"Suppose it's inefficiency in the office?"

"Then you get somebody more efficient."

"Suppose you see that the market has dried up, that maybe business has shifted and the office isn't going to pay its way anymore."

"You could try to create a new market." Sidney had just finished a course in advanced marketing at the university.

"You could." His father's disapproval was palpable: he could feel it. "If you were very lucky. But that's a gamble. The safe thing to do is move the office to a new area, a better one. Or just close it down. Never throw good money after bad, Sidney. There are times in business you just have to cut your losses as much as possible and accept them. Never forget that."

In those summers, Sidney felt his father was incurably, excessively cautious. But he was molded by these sessions more than he knew. He understood that his father was living vicariously in him; his father was making, through his instructions to his son, the top level decisions he would never have a chance to make. Sidney Tate had always felt great affection for his father. This perception increased it.

And during this time of instruction, Tate received his first clear vision of the Sidney Tate he wished to become. That ideal was born fifty years old, and more than a king. Tate the boy saw Tate the demigod in costly muted suitings and in neckties of somber richness: he saw him with snow-white hair worn like a diadem. The distant yet attainable Tate was almost completely visible: godlike in carriage, awesome in judgment, adamant in resolution, and yet–so far as possible–benign to and protective of the lower, only human beings. In the exercise of divinely ordered responsibilities, he was himself almost divine.

This master self was a comfortable if strongly guarded possession: he did not have to look at it often to feel his way toward it.

In those days, business had not yet begun its highly organized beat of colleges to find its future executive talent. But when he was graduated Sidney Tate found his own job, and a good one, with Sperry Flour. Sperry was a corporation somewhere between small and middle size, controlled but not wholly owned by the Sperry family. Its headquarters were in a medium-sized city in the Middle West. Tate had investigated it carefully; he knew the amount of capitalization, the annual earnings and dividends for each of the seventeen years since incorporation; the rate of growth. And he knew the ages of senior executives, and the number of relatives in the business. When he stepped from the train, he did so in complete confidence that he was taking hold of a future. After his six months of rotating assignments, he was moved into the office of the treasurer. He was a special assistant without title but with very real responsibilities. He understood then that he had been marked for treasurer, and in the not remote future. The title of assistant treasurer came within the year.

With it, came a quite formal elevation in his personal relationships in the company: it was as though he had been a noncom and had received a battlefield commission. Alfred Sperry, who was president and chairman of the board, called him "Tate" instead of "Mr. Tate" with a precisely measurable increase in warmth.

Ellis Sperry, the younger brother and executive vice president, alternated between "Tate" and "Sidney," with slightly more overt and slightly less precise cordiality. George Wharton, the treasurer and a first cousin, invited him for cocktails and dinner.

He had been on first name terms with Wharton for a long time. Wharton had the diffident charm of the man who knows himself weak, and seeks to atone for it by amiability. Almost from the beginning, he had shyly sought Sidney's approval, as though he were the subordinate. He was slender but with a belly, almost bald on top with long blond hair on the sides that was extraordinarily light in color for his age, and mild blue eyes that had a certain keenness behind the gold-rimmed spectacles. He was Sidney's introduction to that phenomenon which he was to encounter frequently in years to come: the fairly close relative who is neither a real outsider nor yet genuinely within the power circle of a family business.

When he offered congratulations, Sidney was sure they were genuine, and they warmed him.

"This isn't exactly a surprise, Sidney, as you well know. But I am delighted. In fact, I think we had just better have a little drink on it. No, don't look so shocked, Sidney. I don't mean now. How about coming for cocktails and dinner Friday, tomorrow?"

"I'd love to."

"Fine. Let me give you the address."

Tate went by taxi to the Wharton house. It was February: snow made heavy patches on lawns and sidewalks though the paved streets were swept. In his long tweed coat, Tate felt the cold. His feet were numb inside his shoes and galoshes when the cab stopped. The meter was $2.80: it pained him to pay it.

The house was two stories tall and white. Snow quilted the dark roof whitely. He rang the doorbell. The door was opened by a blonde girl with a pleasant and indeterminate face.

"Hello," she said. "I'm Georgia Wharton. Come on in before you freeze."

His eyes moved directly to the wood fire in the grate, then he saw the room was large and heavily if quietly furnished: he instantly felt its solidity.

Wharton came to shake hands. "Hello, Sidney. This is an overdue pleasure." He steered Tate to a plump woman sitting in a deep chair. She smiled and extended her hand as he introduced her as Mrs. Wharton.

"We've heard so much about you."

He was seated by Georgia Wharton.

She asked him, "Do you like our city?"

"Why yes, I like it very much," he lied. "I had some fraternity brothers from here, they helped me get acquainted."

"What house were you?"

"Kappa Sigma."

"That's a nice house. Dad's Sigma Chi. Everybody in the family is except his cousins. They're Yalies, nothing so vulgar as a fraternity. The Black Cat and Bones, my dear."

"Georgia," her father said from the other side of the table.

"I shock Dad," she said. "I'm not supposed to take the exalted name in vain."

After dinner, Tate found himself alone, briefly, with her.

"What do you do for amusement?" she asked.

"Sometimes I play squash. Mostly I work."

"I might have known."

"What do you do?"

"I don't do anything. A few good works, the Junior League and a couple of charities. I haven't done anything really since I came out a couple of years ago."

"Did you have fun?"

"I kind of had fun. It's a lot of stuff but Mother and Dad were set on it. Dad more than Mother. I would have liked it better if I had been better looking."

"Oh come on."

"True. Most of the others were better looking than me. Not all of them though."

"Not many of them . . ."

"You don't even know. That's exactly the right thing to have said, though."

When Tate was leaving, she said, "You've been getting away with this isolation much too long. I'm having a thing next Sunday. Can you come?"

"Absolutely."

That winter, he saw a great deal of her, and it was by her choice. She invited him to several parties, and he responded with concerts and the theater when touring companies were in town. He wondered why she sought his company. Though he was a presentable commodity, he was without local position and he did not believe she was drawn by a strong physical attraction. He decided she felt superior to him and as a consequence was completely at ease with him. She was a nervous girl, with marked feelings of inferiority, and he understood that any situation in which she found assurance would appeal to her. He liked her, but was not excited by her, and never went further than a decorous good night kiss. He thought she preferred it so.

"You are a funny one," she said one night after he brought her home from a concert. "I never went out with a man before who didn't think he had to try to seduce me as a matter of male pride. Don't you have any male pride?"

"I'm using the slow approach. After a sufficient period of time you want to seduce me. I read it in a magazine."

"Well, I'll tell you, it's working a little bit."

"Naturally. The magazine said it would." He wanted to move away from that ground. Getting involved with Georgia Wharton was not something he wanted to do. He did not want an awkward factor introduced into his business relationships, he felt that any drift from the level of perfect decorum would have been a betrayal of her father, and he was not drawn to her.

"It's positively ungentlemanly of you not to even kiss me like you mean it."

He saw he was not going to escape that, at least. So he kissed her firmly and energetically and withdrew.

"Goddamn you," she said coolly.

"That's not like you."

"What do you know about what's like me? I think you're a goddamn prig, I don't know why I care about you."

"You don't care about me that way. We're good friends."

"You don't know what I care about."

She seized and kissed him, she opened her lips and drove her tongue at his. He did not let himself respond, he did not really want to because she was not an object of desire to him, and then she touched him, fumblingly, but effectively, and quite abruptly he did desire her.

At that moment, almost as though he were an observer at a clinical distance, he was astonished at the suddenness and intensity of his hunger. She had been very nearly a disembodied personality to him: sexless, passionless, antiseptic. Now he knew how feeble were all contrary arguments when the conflagration was really going. He was aware of the heat of her body: it was itself a physical force. Her cheek burned against his.

"No. Don't do that. I don't want that. Yes I do."

"We've got to go somewhere," he said.

"No we don't. We can't go anywhere. Just kiss me. Don't do anything but kiss me."

He kissed her and his hands pressed her.

"This is like incest to you," she said. "You've been thinking of me as a sister."

"You're no sister."

"You know that now."

He released her and moved away. "No we can't."

"Because of my father?"

"Yes."

"I'm not his wife, I'm his daughter. You're not betraying anybody."

"We shouldn't."

"We're going to."

"Yes. We're going to."

He kissed her and began to unbutton her blouse. "Suppose your father came down."

"He won't come down. I never have before. You'll take care of me won't you darling?"

"I'll take care of you."

Her arms fought for his body and her mouth for his mouth. He knew that he, himself, did not really exist for her, that he was a surrogate for years of desperate fantasy. Oddly he did not mind. He felt himself borne on the exaltation of her pure, impersonal passion.

"I never thought this would happen to you and me," he said.

"I know you didn't."

"Did you?"

"Maybe."

"Come on. Did you?"

"Yes," she said. "I thought it would. I thought I would make it happen."

"I didn't know you ever thought about me like that."

"I picked you. You were responsible and gentle."

"Picked me?"

"To be the first. I was so tired of being a virgin. Everybody thinks Georgia, she's such a *wholesome* girl, she wouldn't get *involved* in anything. Well I'm not wholesome, I want to get involved, I'm tired of everybody making me Big Sister or Little Sister."

"And I was handy." He did not say but thought: and not in your set and therefore not apt to be embarrassing.

"Not just that. You're you, I wanted it to be you. Oh I'm not saying I'm in love with you or anything, but it's not just because you were convenient."

"Thanks."

"Come on now. You aren't going to tell me you're in love with me."

"No."

"But you think I ought to be with you, don't you?"

He felt himself blushing, and they both laughed.

"Of course you do," she said. "It's all right. I don't hold it against you. You're very sweet and very kind and very very capable. I may fall in love with you. Does that make you feel better?"

"Enormously."

"Do you think one has anything to do with the other?"

"So they say."

"I think they're crazy. Maybe they can happen at the same time but they're not the same thing. Do I look very different?"

"No. I think of you differently though."

"That's good. I didn't like the way you thought of me before. Don't I really look any different?"

"You look sexier. Somehow."

"Somehow."

"I've got to go. Come here."

"What are you going to do to me I hope?"

"I'm going to kiss you good night and get out of here."

"Oh pooh. Well. There'll be other nights."

"Yes there will."

"Good night darling."

Their affair continued through the spring. If her father suspected, he gave no sign. In May, Georgia told Tate she was pregnant, and the June wedding was a large one.

It had never occurred to Tate not to marry her. He suspected that he would have married her anyway; he suspected, too, that he might have brought the situation about without acknowledging it to himself. Do you always do what you most profoundly intend? he wondered. Is there some secret engine in the mind that propels you where it wants you to go?

He was not sure, then, and he was never sure.

Tate knew George Wharton was pleased at the marriage. And he was aware of a discreet but massive shift in his status in the company. He had not married the boss's daughter, for George Wharton was no power, but with perceptive delicacy and at a distance, he had at least formally entered the family. He knew that the combination of his now proved ability and the modest, distant connection was approved by Albert Sperry. He also knew that had he been either more assertive or less able, it would not have been.

Wharton retired in 1925, and Tate became treasurer formally. He would have been treasurer if he had never married Georgia Wharton, and he knew it, but as the husband of a fairly close cousin, his role was larger and had more possibilities. He knew that, too.

Either Georgia was mistaken about her condition, or an imperceptible accident occurred. Their first son, Sidney III, was born sixteen months after their wedding, and the second, Robert, fourteen months after that. The years between 1925 and 1928 were otherwise unmarked by any overtly dramatic events. Sidney's influence in Sperry steadily mounted the slope of importance, but remained well outside the limit of policy consideration.

In those years of early maturity, Tate almost succeeded in denying his awareness of that Tate to be achieved. He had tried to hide the master form from himself, and to convince himself he had forgotten it. To indulge any fantasy was to daydream. A serious man did not daydream. He might plan imaginatively, but he did not daydream: he was concerned with the fact and nothing but the fact. Yet the Tate of his desire was always ahead though in shadow. The Tate who breathed had already formed himself on the one who did not.

In 1928, Sperry acquired options on two other plants, one in Texas and one in Kansas. Sidney advised against it.

It was mentioned to him as a possibility by Albert Sperry after the two of them had discussed the third quarter's report in his office.

Sperry nodded his head at the sheets and pushed them an inch away with his finger.

"Sidney, what would you think of our expanding our production facilities right now?"

Tate understood the question was a courtesy. "The grosses are certainly way up," he said. "They'll never get much higher with our present facilities."

"No. And I think we ought to look ahead to expansion, and the business climate being what it is, I think we ought to go ahead right now. How do you see it?"

Sidney breathed twice. "It's a question of reading the signs, of course. Certainly they give every reason for optimism at first look and even at second look. But quite frankly I fear some aspects of the picture. I think we're in the middle of a funny kind of inflation, not so much money as general economic activity. Stocks look way overpriced. The gross national product doesn't in my opinion justify what's happening. My own instinct at this time suggests caution. I appreciate your asking."

"You're very cautious for a young man, Sidney."

"Yes, sir."

"Well, I'm very grateful for your opinion, of course, but we're pretty well decided to go ahead with acquiring the two plants."

"It'll probably work out extremely well. As you say, I'm a very cautious man."

"Caution certainly has its place, Sidney. I'm glad we have one conservative man around."

Alfred Sperry did not entirely ignore Tate's misgivings on the expansion. Sidney learned, later, that Sperry had been enough impressed by his short argument to limit the enlargement of facilities to a little more than half of what he had been strongly considering. He bought the two new plants, but only those two, and he made the down payments out of the cash reserve. He did not mortgage the home plant to pay for expansion. This fact, in the end, made it possible for Sperry Flour to survive 1929 and 1932. This, and the president who succeeded Albert Sperry: Sidney Tate.

The last week in October, 1929, remained in Sidney's memory with the distorted, fragmented super-reality of a death in the family or the end of a love affair. The time defined itself in jerky newsreels of image and motion: the dark-bodied newsboys brandishing their black and white doom, the faces frozen in pale immobility that somehow transcended fright and the voices frozen with them. The newspapers, always newspapers, eternally open to the New York Stock Exchange quotations. The fall of footsteps acquired a quality that Sidney never defined to himself, but ever afterward, when he heard a single, slow passage of footsteps in a dimension of otherwise perfect silence, he felt dread of an unseen but always approaching disaster.

The third day after the first drop, Sidney's door swung inward, violently, and a flushed and distorted face thrust toward him. It took a part of a second for him to recognize his secretary.

"Mr. Tate they want you. In Mr. Sperry's office. Something's happened to him Mr. Tate. Something bad's happened to Mr. Sperry."

He was already on his feet and running down the corridor.

In Sperry's office he saw first the ring of bodies surrounding the desk in a swirling, unpurposed movement. He thought it a crowd; as he burst through it, he saw there were only four people: Sperry, Albert Sperry's two secretaries, and his administrative assistant, Slaymaker.

Albert Sperry sat in the chair at the desk, his head far back and feet straight ahead. His eyes were open, and his lips altered in recognition of Sidney. His hand pressed at the center of his chest.

"Lift him up on the desk so he can lie down," Sidney said.

Sperry smiled gracefully and embarrassedly at Sidney. "Terribly sorry," he said.

The next time Sidney saw Albert Sperry was in a private room at St. Catherine's Hospital, and there were only the two of them in it. Sperry's bed was elevated slightly: the white of his pillows and sheets backgrounded his head for a portrait. Every company should have a president who looked like Albert Sperry, Sidney thought. Or rather, every company should have a president who incarnated one of the standard designs as well as did Albert Sperry. He was one of the very best types: in his sixties, a week after a coronary, his face was pinkly smooth and unlined, his hair as thick as it had ever been and superbly white (he *had* to use bluing) and the only word for the half-delicate precision of his features was aristocratic. He was of a type fiction or films would instantly have assigned to New York or Boston instead of the Middle West.

Now he was smiling, gently, ironically, at Tate. "It's only a coronary, Sidney, a simple honest coronary, I'm just walking wounded. This week I have read the obituaries of *six* people that I knew personally, I mean I knew well, and they have all contained the delicate phrase 'died suddenly.' A splendid euphemism, don't you agree?"

Sidney smiled. "I'm glad you don't need it."

"It's partly your doing, my friend, that I don't need it."

"You wouldn't have needed it under any circumstances."

"No, I don't think I would. However, we have some problems. We are in one hell of a shape, of course, but at the same time, considering what has happened to everybody else, we are in pretty damn good shape. Does that make sense to you?"

"It's exactly the way I would put it."

"Sidney, you remember what you said, that we were having a funny kind of inflation and some kind of shakedown was coming? I thought you were wrong then, though not completely. Well, I think you're right now. I think what happened on the big board is just the beginning. I think we are in, I mean the country is in, for a very tough time."

"So do I."

The fine head nodded. "You were right on the first count and you're going to turn out right on the second, I wish you weren't. However, our problem right now is survival. Can we survive?"

"Yes."

"How?"

"Retrench, retrench, retrench. Sell off these two new plants if we can, if we can't, accept the foreclosures. Work hard to keep our present markets but simplify the services. Cushion every phase of the total operation that we possibly can and combine jobs wherever we can. Schedule production as close to actual orders as we dare. We'll survive."

"Not all of our people will."

"The company's first obligation is to survive. It can do a lot for a lot of people if it's alive. It's no good to anybody dead."

"You're a tough man, Sidney. I'm glad you're on our side."

"I'm not tough. I have to work at it not be a softie."

Sperry laughed as though he enjoyed it.

"As I said, I'm glad you're on our side." His laughter stopped, and his face returned to its smooth gravity. "Sidney, you're taking over as president. Any objections?"

"None if you have none."

"I have none, believe me. Some problems, yes. Oh my yes, I will have some problems. My brother will understand but his wife won't, and neither will our sister. But I have the fifty-one per cent and Ellis will vote his with me anyway. As you say, the only real problem is survival. Sidney, you'd better leave me now. We'll work out the details tomorrow."

It had happened. Tate had achieved his desire before he was thirty: he had entered top management. And he felt no elation.

He did not know why, but he felt unreal, unsatisfied, and even frightened. He did not know that it was because–standing at last in the posture of the master Sidney Tate–he felt nothing like what he had imagined that Tate should feel. He was concerned with a task and little else, and he was weary of it before he began it. For it was to wield an executioner's axe.

3

THE morning's mail was waiting for him in the customary three piles: urgent, immediate, and deferrable. On top of the immediate pile was *Newsweek*. The date on the cover was April 9, 1937. A penciled note was clipped to it: *Have you seen this? J.* The other side of the clip was placed at "Business and Finance," and he opened the magazine to the article about which he had received five telephone calls the night before.

"Into the St. Louis offices of the McGaughey Paper Co. last week came a kindly and courteous surgeon. He is Sidney Tate, 37, who heals faltering corporations by therapy that can only be described as drastic. Tate's official entrance apparently confirmed rumors that have been circulating quietly but persistently for many months: that McGaughey Paper is in bad trouble.

"Tate insists he is a doctor rather than executioner. He is proud of the fact that in the last decade, he has saved almost a dozen companies from the terminal illnesses of liquidation and bankruptcy. 'Sometimes you have to amputate a leg to save a life,' he is said to have said. If he didn't say it, he should have: the Tate treatment is severe. It is also simple and unvarying: retrench and consolidate. So far it has always worked–for the ailing corporation. But many personnel, presidents as well as clerks, have been prescribed right out of jobs and into the street.

"Tate's career as specialist began after the 1929 crash, when as its 29-year-old president, he kept Sperry Flour alive by selling off secondary plants, combining operations, offices and jobs, and reducing staff to little less than bare essentials. No caricature efficiency expert, Tate always seeks the fundamental problem, and usually finds it at the highest level of policy. Directors seldom bring him in unless a situation is desperate; when they do, the top brass rattles. He went on leave from Sperry to perform similar services for several other corporations, and finally resigned active management of Sperry to move around to trouble spots. (He is still on Sperry's board.) The Tate operational method has firmed up solidly: he goes into the beckoning corporation for a flat salary and stock participation—sometimes as president, sometimes without title—and he has nearly absolute authority. When, and if, he feels the corporation is sound again, he resigns executive direction but remains on the board. Concerns to which he has ministered include Adams Aircraft Parts, Rawson's Baby Food, Iowa Mills, Passjen's Knit Wear, and Flamingo Foods. He has never had a bankruptcy, and though two of his corporations (Passjen's and Flamingo) went into liquidation, their stockholders made a profit.

"His only failure (not an absolute one) was in book publishing. Brought into floundering Chapman House in 1935, he returned all his salary and stock after two weeks and quit. 'This isn't a business,' he reportedly said; 'I don't know what it is, but I do know one thing it is not. It is not a business.'

"Sidney Tate is an important figure in American business before forty. But strangely—possibly because of his conservatism and caution—he has almost never been called a boy wonder.

"McGaughey Paper could turn out to be his toughest chore. Insiders speculate that a collision between Tate and Vern McGaughey, president and founder, may well be inevitable. The two men are opposites not only in personality, but in business philosophy. Where the conservative Tate seeks success in consolidation and cutting costs, the aggressive McGaughey wants to expand, and expand, and expand. His penchant for forward motion has carried him from his beginnings as the sole owner of a foreclosed paper mill fifteen years ago to his present eminence as a large (recently a controlling) stockholder in five corporations, now subsidiaries of McGaughey Paper. Yet one group of stockholders feels that the same aggressive willingness to take the calculated risk that brought McGaughey ahead, may well be the source of the company's present difficulties. This group speaks of too-rapid expansion, insufficient capitalization and excessive risk.

"It is not a small group. With proxies, it could now control a majority of stock in McGaughey Paper. For rugged Vern McGaughey, who used to insist that he control any corporation in which he is active, is known to have sold large blocks of stock in recent months for reasons described as compelling. Now that the directors have extended their invitation to Sidney Tate and Tate has accepted it, a small war in St. Louis seems imminent."

Tate flipped the magazine closed with his forefinger and pushed it away from him. He looked up suddenly to see his secretary's eyes on him. She quickly looked away and he felt his face heat. He was annoyed and embarrassed by the article. It was not downright inaccurate but it was overdramatic and sure to be troublesome. The situation at McGaughey Paper was bad and was going to be worse. It was unfortunate that it had been exploited by a clever journalist. He had always distrusted the press, and his few recent encounters with it had made him distrust it more. He conceded that government was a legitimate concern of journalism; business was a completely private affair.

"That will make a mess," he said heavily, ostensibly to the girl sitting near him, pad ready for dictation. "That will leave us with a real mess."

"Is it really that bad, Mr. Tate? I thought it was rather nice."

"I doubt if McGaughey will."

McGaughey *was* a problem. His aggressive heavy-footed restlessness was indeed the root of the company's difficulties. Quite simply, these were that too much money had been spent and not enough had come in. McGaughey had taken profits from the parent company and the subsidiaries it controlled, and had used it all in the building of a personal empire in the communications field: chain of radio stations in Missouri, Tennessee, and a daily newspaper in Dallas. Of course, he had only made the down payments (which were large) on the radio chain and newspaper, and so was even further extended. With luck and time, they might be solid properties. But McGaughey had gone through practically all his capital reserve to buy them, and had left his other companies dangerously low on operating capital. Consequently, they were exposed and in trouble. A week's study of their books had told Tate, too, that they were loose and inefficient in organization, and expensive in operation. It was a classic send-for-Tate case and would have to be resolved in the classic Tate manner: by the selling off of properties, consolidation of functions (including the merger of two of the companies), and by the removal of the president.

Tate knew he was moving with unusual deliberation towards the final solution. It was not only because he disliked McGaughey so thoroughly. It was also because McGaughey imparted to him an unreasonable feeling of personal guilt, which he could not deny. Always he felt regret when he faced the fact of his casualties. But in other situations, any sense of guilt was instantly and automatically overcome by the knowledge that he was expending the few to save the many. Consequently, he could honestly say (to himself) he did not feel guilty. Now, McGaughey made him feel guilty. He did not know why.

On his first encounter with McGaughey he had felt it all: the instant antagonism of one natural enemy toward the other, and the inexplicable, wholly ungirded-for twinge of self-reproach.

McGaughey had been at the airport himself to greet Tate and drive him into town. As Sidney came down the ramp, he recognized the other from business magazine pictures: tall, without overcoat, a daring brown hat angled on his head. Even at fifty feet, he gave off a vitality as palpable as the scent of a large animal.

Never, thought Tate, had he seen the condemned make it a point to greet the hangman. So McGaughey would be working all the way, maneuvering to avoid disaster until he was literally buried by it. You had to admire that—Tate thought.

McGaughey's handclasp was firm, his smile warm and intimate, and Tate again knew the instant of admiration: he *was* pitching, all the way. This close, his physical vitality was almost overpowering. His tanned face was ugly in such an attractive way that it became uniquely handsome. He was about forty, and Tate was reminded of a picture of Franklin Delano Roosevelt as a candidate for the vice presidency in 1920.

"Glad to see you, Tate. I know what a damn nuisance it is to fool with these so-called limousines, so I drove out myself. We'll have a good lunch somewhere."

"That's awfully kind of you, you shouldn't have."

"Nonsense, my pleasure. Come on, let's get your bags."

His energy blew Tate forward and into the railed enclosure. The bags came out quickly. In moments, McGaughey was behind the wheel of his car and Tate on the seat beside him. Both the interior and engine of the automobile whispered "money." Tate felt the pleasure of its power as McGaughey accelerated on the highway.

"This is a fine automobile," said Tate, who drove a Buick. "It's an expensive car, isn't it?"

"It's a Cord."

"It's a damn fine car."

"I've had it three months, it's a hell of a car. You see how it rides, it handles like a sweetheart, and it'll do an honest hundred and twenty."

"You've driven it a hundred and twenty?"

The Rooseveltian face creased into a grin.

"Couple of times. There's a five-mile stretch on the road to my house that's as lonesome as a salt flat."

Tate had come to a conception of McGaughey from a study of his balance sheets. It was in that instant confirmed. And Tate was not only shocked at the audacity of a man who would drive a car a hundred and twenty miles an hour; for the moment, he envied it.

He said nothing, and let McGaughey carry the entire burden of conversation. This indecorous, tasteless meeting was entirely his affair: let him do the sweating.

If McGaughey was sweating, he did not show it. All the way back to town, he carried on a cheerful monologue, broken only by the minimized and absolutely required assents from Tate. He covered, Tate thought, everything under the sun except the tangled affairs of McGaughey Paper.

"Do you know St. Louis well, Sidney?"

"I used to know it fairly well. I daresay I'm out of touch now."

"Fine, then I'll be your tour-master. Any objection to the Hunt Room for lunch?"

"No objection." Sidney was surprised and a little amused: the most expensive place in town was hardly the choice to impress a hatchet man with one's economy and sobriety.

Again, he resented and admired McGaughey's impudence. He could understand, increasingly, how that impudence and charm and great animal energy had propelled McGaughey so far, so fast. He could also understand how it had driven him into his present trouble.

And he was aware that he envied McGaughey those very attributes he deplored.

In the Hunt Room, McGaughey checked his preference and ordered the drinks. "One martini, extra dry, with Beefeater gin and Martini and Rossi vermouth. Daiquiri with light Bacardi rum." The daiquiri was for Sidney, who found that drink less of a blow to judgment than a martini.

The drinks came. "Two more right away," said McGaughey. Sidney opened his mouth to speak. "Come on," said McGaughey. "You don't want to work today."

"Don't you?"

"No." He smiled at Sidney. "And that is a hell of a way to impress the new boss, isn't it?"

"I'm no boss."

"Of course you are, Sidney. Shall we finish the minuet and get down to cases? What are you going to recommend for McGaughey Paper?"

"McGaughey, I just stepped off an airplane. I'll be here studying the situation for months before I'll be able to recommend anything."

"Come on. You studied our books for a month before you got on the plane and you're Sidney Tate." The smile was markedly Rooseveltian: surely he cultivated it. "You know damned well what you mean to do. You know every hole in any corporate structure, you know every loose end that can be tied up or damn near it, and you know what you want to do about it. Now what is it?"

"I have some thoughts. I won't know if they're sound or not until I've been here awhile, and I prefer not to discuss them."

"You won't even give me your working hypothesis?"

"I haven't said I have a working hypothesis."

"No, you haven't. Let me have a guess then. Let me guess you're going to sell off my newspaper and radio stations."

"I can't stop you from guessing."

"I'll keep on guessing. I'll guess you want to merge two of my little companies and sell all my stock in another."

"You're the one that's saying it." Tate was surprised: he had tentatively decided to do just that, and he did not think it obvious.

"Well, I won't ask if I'm right, you wouldn't tell me." He smiled again. "But for the sake of a hypothetical discussion of a hypothetical situation by two hypothetical partners, let's just say you have. It would be a mistake, Sidney. All of it. And I can show you why."

Tate did not say anything.

"All those properties I just bought are making money right now, Sidney. We can make payments on the stations and paper out of revenue."

"They've drained your capital reserve and you've already borrowed right up to your limit. Suppose something went wrong, McGaughey. Anything, any little thing. Do you realize what a hole you'd be in?"

"Suppose nothing goes wrong? In ten years, we'll own a good-sized newspaper and a nice fat radio chain."

"In ten years you'll have made down payments on as many other newspaper and radio stations as you can scrape out of capital reserve and cash on hand. Won't you now?"

"You're very discerning, Sidney. I probably will."

"Uh-huh."

"But don't you see the possibilities, Sidney? Don't you see them? In ten years we'll have a real communications empire. In twenty we could be almost as big as the Chandlers or McCormicks."

"And in three you may be flat on your big fat bankruptcy."

"That's a chance. You have to take some chances."

"It's a wild gamble and I don't have to take wild gambles. How about that plastics corporation? It's been losing money since you got it."

"When it starts making, it'll make big. Right now we've been concentrating on research and development, just getting ready."

"There are other plastic outfits that have been doing a hell of a lot of research and development *and* making money."

"We have two very big things we've been concentrating on Sidney. Very big. When things start moving with them, they'll move like an earthquake."

"Mmm-mmm."

"It's the truth."

"McGaughey, you aren't situated to think of maybe and tomorrow. Your problem is survival and survival right now. That's why your board sent for me."

"Okay, Sidney, let's turn up the cards. You think we'll collapse if we don't cut way back right away, you and that cinchy Barton group. Well, I just happen to think we'll make it, and if you look at the balance sheet, even you will have to admit we've got a damn good chance. Now this is my proposition, you let me keep the paper and radio station. Let me keep the plastics company for eighteen months, if it's not on its own by then I'll drop it. I'll merge those two appliance parts firms right away."

"No. Not unless I come across something to change my mind and I don't think I will."

"Ah. Ah. There I think I can be of some small service. In changing your mind, I mean. You see, you didn't let me finish. What I was going to say was, you let me go ahead along those lines I outlined and half my stock in McGaughey Paper and all subsidiaries is yours. Except your voting rights, you have to sign over voting rights to me."

"My God." Nobody had ever gotten close enough to Tate to try to bribe him before. He realized at that moment that he had fancied, with self-congratulation, that nobody could have. "McGaughey, I'll say one thing for you. You've got brass."

"All right. I've got brass. How about it?"

Tate laughed. He laughed harder, the tension of the encounter suddenly dissipating in McGaughey's ultimate absurdity. He saw the confidence and self-aware charm slip from the other's face, and lines showed between his eyes.

"No. I must say I'm honored, but no thank you."

"The offer stays open."

"You don't fool around, do you McGaughey?"

"No." He was very serious. "I don't fool around and I never do anything halfway. That's an awful good deal I offered you. You think about it."

"It is an awfully good deal and I don't need to think about it. No."

"So be it. Sidney, if I may suggest, the deviled turkey steaks here are marvelous."

That lunch had been a month ago. After it, he avoided all further private conversations with McGaughey.

Until now, when at almost the very moment his decision had become firm, this unfortunate notoriety descended upon the whole situation. He had planned to tell McGaughey of his recommendation today, before making the formal report to the board. Now, decorum and tact prescribed that he postpone that encounter. He decided to wait another week.

But two hours later, his secretary came in and said apologetically, "Mr. McGaughey would like to see you. I told him you were on long distance. Shall I ask him to make it another time?"

Tate sighed, his preference for diplomacy, such as it was, had miscarried. He would have to get it over with at this worst of times.

"No," he said. "Bring him on in."

McGaughey strode in with the vigor that was almost but not quite theatrical.

"Sidney."

"Hello, Vernon."

"You've been quite a stranger lately, young man." McGaughey's glance touched *Newsweek*. "I see that you see that we are at war. Very interesting article, eh?"

Sidney looked at him levelly.

"I guess we are at that. Of course we are, Sidney. You make up your mind yet? Officially?"

"Yes. Yes, I have."

"What's it going to be?"

"Just about what you figured."

"Including the replacement of the president?"

"I'm sorry."

McGaughey nodded, "Have you given full thought to that deal I offered you?"

"I haven't needed to."

"I wish you had. I wish you would. We could do an awful lot for each other."

Sidney said nothing.

"So you're going to kick me out in the street."

"Come on, McGaughey, that's pretty damn melodramatic. You've still got forty per cent of the stock, you know."

"Yes, I have less than fifty per cent of a corporation I founded."

"You can fight it out at the stockholders' meeting if you want."

"You know I've already lost the proxy fight. Don't you?"

"Yes."

"Then you must know my only chance is with you."

Tate was annoyed and embarrassed; personal appeals in business matters always embarrassed him; they were sentimental, gauche, and indecorous. In his embarrassment he sought refuge in cliché. "Business is business."

"Business is what I'm talking about, do you think I'm asking personal favors for Vernon McGaughey? If you let me keep a free hand, this company will wind up with more money than it ever hoped to see. You take my offer, so will you. You can do the company, the stockholders and yourself a great big service all at once. Just by saying yes."

"McGaughey, you're making me very angry."

"Look, Tate, don't you see what this is? This is a classic collision between bookkeeping and creative business. If you listen to the clerks, you never go ahead. The man with the imagination, yes and the brains and the guts to go ahead, is what makes business. Listen to the bookkeeper long enough and everything dies."

"That is one of the oldest fairy tales there is, McGaughey, and I'm sick of it. There is one way and one way only for a business to survive and that is to make money. You have been losing money, and now you drag in that worn-out imagination alibi. I won't buy it."

"No. You won't buy anything I'm selling. You're kicking me out after I founded this company. My brains and guts and imagination created this outfit, and now you bookkeepers are taking it away from me. That's really what you are, Sidney, a bookkeeper. Just a bookkeeper. I'm worth all of you put together for just one reason: I create."

"McGaughey, try to act like a grown man."

"But I've learned something, Sidney. I mean I've really taken it in. The guy who creates always gets shoved out. He's always the loser. The guys who wreck come out on top. And that's you, Sidney, a wrecker and a bookkeeper. Well, I'm going to do a little wrecking myself for a while. It's a lot easier than building. An awful lot easier."

"Good luck."

"I don't need your luck. Maybe our paths will cross again sometime, Sidney. I won't forget."

4

"It will be a challenge to you, Mr. Tate. A challenge. That appeals to you, ah?"

"It appeals to me, but I'm not sure it appeals enough. The entertainment business is absolutely new to me. I'm sure it has a whole set of considerations that are unique to it."

"It is not that different, Mr. Tate. You make a product, you sell the product. I grant you there are the headaches. There are headaches any time you work with artists, Mr. Tate. But finally we are businessmen dealing with other businessmen. We have problems that are purely business problems. Our present management has not solved them. We ask you to solve them, Mr. Tate."

Mr. Green gestured impressively with both hands. His blue eyes looked brightly out of a smooth pink face; his head was bare on top and heavily fendered with white. He was slightly smaller than middle-sized, and wore a dark gray suit, a white shirt with wide-spread collar, and a silver tie with a small pearl pin. Tate thought the most notable element of his appearance was the cherubic aspect of his face. Yet he was renowned for piratical ruthlessness, and he was the captain of a group which had recently acquired control of Globe-International Pictures. He wanted Tate to be president of Globe-International.

Tate was living that year, 1951, in a large twenty-year-old Georgian house in University Heights in Dallas: he had been brought in to reorganize Granville-Yost Cotton Co. He liked Dallas and he liked the business: Granville-Yost was a cotton factor with international operations. And the problem had been interesting and only mildly difficult. He did not find Mr. Green's proposition particularly interesting, and he was faintly uneasy at the prospect of dealing with a commodity so intangible as entertainment. His very brief experience in book publishing had been traumatic. He had already decided not to accept the offer: he had not said so that afternoon only because he always used all available time before taking any big decision. The financial terms offered had made this decision a big one.

It was early twilight when he turned the Sedan de Ville into the driveway (now in Cadillac country, he had relinquished his Buick, with regret). Georgia was waiting for him in the living room, already mixing the one Scotch and water he permitted himself before dinner. As he entered, she turned and came toward him, presenting the glass and her face for a kiss. He accepted both and sat down.

"There's a letter from Sidney," she said. "He passed the Latin all right."

"That's a relief." Sidney was the oldest, and was at St. Andrew's.

"Isn't it? It was the one bright spot of the day. The luncheon was ghastly, I came home and the new girl had done everything you could think of wrong, and Lawrence is coming down with flu or something. What's happened to you?"

"Nothing that I know of. I was offered a chance to go into the picture business."

"Picture business? Movies? How exciting."

"Not necessarily."

"It sounds exciting. Would you be a producer or something?"

Tate laughed. "I would be president of Globe-International Studios."

She was impressed.

"They have a balance sheet problem," he said.

"Are you going to take it?"

"I don't think so."

"Good."

"You'd object to it?"

"Have I ever objected to anything? I just have some kind of impression that they are pretty awful types in that kind of thing. Bad grammar, bad manners, funny clothes, awful women. I've always heard that's the way it is."

"Some of the finest people in Dallas murder grammar and wear clothes that would be very funny in New York."

"That's different. And everybody we know in Dallas has lovely manners."

Tate sipped his Scotch. It suddenly occurred to him that he might take the job.

"I'm glad you've decided against it. Maybe we can stay here awhile longer."

Tate did not answer. He glanced at Georgia's face. Her features were still pleasant; they had become worn. Her generous mouth had always been her only really individual mark; now faint lines running from its corner to her nose gave her a blurred aspect that suggested permanent fatigue. She had not grown fat, and her body was not unpleasant; it had never been truly exciting.

Remembering her early passion, directed with splendid, impersonal ardor at himself only as the faceless instrument of its fulfillment, he was awed again at the erosions of time and pain. After three children, she had lost, almost suddenly, her once overpowering desire. Or perhaps she had only lost her desire for him—the thought was sudden and faintly jolting. However, their passages were infrequent, and not welcomed by her. Tate had taken no mistress, and he found his wife's reluctance annoying. But no more than that, he realized. Looking at her over his glass, he found himself wondering what it would be like with other women. As though he were watching himself from a certain distance, he noted he felt no guilt.

"It's very attractive financially," he said. "I haven't decided absolutely I won't take it."

Three days later, he called Green and accepted.

Tate found his transition to the Industry considerably more complicated than Green had suggested. But not, finally, impossible. Once he was able to view the flat circular cans with the spooled film inside as "product"—which was what its manufacturers called it anyway—he felt he was in possession of the total equation. It turned out that he was not: there were unbelievable contradictions and impalpables.

Yet he saw the first move at once, before he saw anything else. He sold off part of the Globe-International lot in Beverly Hills for twenty million dollars, and ended a cash and credit shortage.

After study, and mistakes, he discovered what he thought was the handle to the package. It seemed so simple that he could scarcely believe it had not been seen before, or acted upon before. It was that the television series had made obsolete and replaced the "B" picture, and that the habit audience had become the television audience. He almost feared his diagnosis because it seemed so obvious: finally he decided the Industry had not accepted its basic premise because the Industry did not wish to accept it.

He committed Globe completely to a big and expensive program of television development. And he accepted the other truth of the new age, one that all the Industry had been willing to accept. This was that only extraordinary and costly full-length pictures could make money.

By acting upon those principles, and by his experience in consolidation and cost cutting, he terminated Globe's balance sheet problem in two years. He did it quietly, and as nearly anonymously as possible, but after his second stockholders' meeting, he was an ordained hero.

He was never one of the Industry's spectacular figures; from the time he took over at Globe-International, he was one of its most powerful.

Tate's hair had gone gray, not white, and this was an unrecognized disappointment. Otherwise his appearance was much as he had fancied it when he was young enough to permit himself the weakness of fancy. His carriage and his clothing were almost as discreetly regal as he had seen them in those indulged days. Only he accepted these and all trappings without thought. He did not think about any of his prerogatives. They were there and automatic, and of course he would be incensed if they were gone, but as a matter of will he freely dispensed with them. Now, Tate the ideal existed only in responsibility and the perfect exercise of it. That Tate acted always with a dignity so much more than perfect that it suggested divinity; he wanted no gratification but perfect performance.

At that point, the Tate he wanted to be, was indistinguishable from the Tate that he could tell others saw. At moments, in fact, he knew the supreme pleasure of his life: the oneness of what he thought he was with what he knew he wanted to be.

He was at this high plateau of his life when he met Eve Morrow. He was then fifty-three years old and, for the first time, genuinely restless in his marriage.

Whenever he had to consider it, which was seldom, Tate was irritated by a canon of the motion picture: that the man and girl "meet cute." It was his observation that all romantic relationships —whether they ended in liaison or marriage—began at society's conventional points of contact. He met Eve Morrow because she moved next door.

The Tates owned a house on Beverly Glen in Beverly Hills which cost only $225,000. This was a small figure for a power of Sidney's standing, and the house represented the absolute minimum to which he could acceptably descend. While the years of the palaces were done, Sidney knew more than two dozen executives or producers whose houses cost more than a half-million, and he was sure there were more. Still, he knew that his house was regarded as appropriate to the Tate configuration: solid, not only unostentatious, but calculatedly anti-spectacular.

An architect lived on one side of him, and the board chairman of an electronics company on the other. The architect, berserk at smog, decamped to Newport Beach. A few weeks later, moving vans announced new occupants.

Tate was informed by his wife, "I couldn't contain my curiosity, I called the realtors," she said. "All they could tell me was the house was leased to a Mrs. Louis Morrow."

"A widow?"

"Or a divorcee. She has two young children, I've seen them all in the pool. I'll call on her when she's had a chance to get settled."

Two weeks later, Eve Morrow came for dinner. She offered Tate her hand as his wife introduced them; he found it firm and not at all soft.

"It's nice to have you in Southern California," Tate said.

"It's nice to be in Southern California, I think." She had a pleasant unforced smile.

Tate put her age at about thirty—perhaps thirty-two. If he had been in any other business he would have guessed twenty-eight, but he had learned enough to make him wary. She was fairly tall, about five six or seven, she had dark blonde hair and wore it long, and against the white linen of her dress her arms and shoulders were light smooth brown. Her body was athletic rather than voluptuous in the severely fitting white dress; her bosom was not exciting, but her legs were extraordinary.

Tate's man mixed them all martinis.

"What brings you to the village?"

"Ennui really. My husband's executors bought some Southern California real estate and that was the excuse. It was just an excuse. I wanted to get out of Philadelphia."

"You don't like Philadelphia?"

"Let's say that all at once it was getting awfully monotonous."

So she was a widow, with money. There had to be a lot of it. Sidney knew what a big house in Beverly Hills leased for.

"How long do you plan to be with us?"

"I don't really know. It depends on so many things. Like how my children like it and how I like it and what I can find to do to pass the time."

"We'll have to do something about that last."

Her son was nine and her daughter six, she said. Her husband had been killed in an automobile wreck the year before. He had been a captain in an artillery regiment, having been Yale ROTC, and he had fought all nineteen months in Korea without a wound. She had stuck it a year and now wanted a new place.

"All at once I was sick of the same places and the same faces, I'd just had it."

He watched her face over the dinner table; it made altering patterns of warmth. He decided she was a more mature and authentic version of what the Kelly girl at Paramount was supposed to be.

He looked away from her and saw his wife looking at him and forced himself to smile. Had he done that to avoid an appearance of interest? He wondered.

She returned their invitation, they had her at a small dinner party, and Sidney began to see her swimming every afternoon as he came home. She had made certain adjustments in the landscaping, and one was the removal of a hedge which had blocked the view from, and to, her pool. As he turned into the driveway,–it was his pride that he always drove himself–his eye immediately lined to the oval of turquoise in her yard. A white-capped head bobbed on the green, a brown figure in a white suit bounded on the long board. Across the silence he heard only the bombombom of the board as she sprang, and the splash of water.

Sometimes she did not see him, sometimes she saw and waved at him, and one afternoon she called, "Why don't you two come over for a swim and a drink?"

It happened that Georgia had just left the house. Sidney went alone, in trunks and a white terry robe. He paddled lightly in the pool and he watched her dive. Finally she wrapped herself in a half-length white robe, took off the bathing cap, and shook out her honey hair. It was wet at the ends. She smiled at him as he watched her. Her face was clear and flawless but not soft.

"Think we've earned a drink?" she said.

"You have. I'll have one anyway."

"Good for you. Martini? Vodka martini?"

He started to ask for Scotch and water. He said, "Fine, make it vodka."

"I'll mix them. No, stay where you are, I really want to. I want to impress you."

He watched the splendid brown legs under the rough white cloth as they moved away, and as they stopped at the bar at the other end of the pool. She came back with the drinks, he looked from her legs to her face, and saw she was smiling. He felt himself blushing. She dropped her hand on his shoulder as she handed him the glass.

Every afternoon, he waited for the sight of her in the pool. When he did not get it, he felt deprived. Occasionally, he and Georgia would join her, and sometimes dripping in the white suit, she crossed the two yards to their pool.

In August, Georgia's sister-in-law became seriously ill, and she went to her. The day after his wife left, Eve gave Sidney dinner.

She was wearing a silver hostess gown: Sidney had never seen her in anything but white before: her hair was elaborately dressed on one side of her head, and she was grave and quiet during dinner. After dinner, in a sitting room off the pool patio, she put records on the stereo.

"Want to dance, Sidney?"

"I certainly do."

She opened her arms to him. He took a dozen steps, stopped, and slid his left arm behind her back. She leaned backward and looked directly at him, then she closed her eyes, he drew her to him, and he kissed her. He felt the firm shape of her body through the metallic fabric. His leg was between hers, their heat suddenly encasing him, and her breasts crumpled softly against his chest.

She checked him, then came to him again, and her mouth opened wide against his. She pressed herself closer, twisting, and she moaned faintly.

"Is it what you want, Sidney?"

"Yes."

She led him out of the room, down a carpeted hallway, to a door at the end. She opened it and he followed her inside.

The light from the pool came weakly through the window between the half-closed drapes and thinned the darkness to faint visibility. In it, her body lost its brownness, and was white.

"Could I have a cigarette, darling?"

He lighted it for her, and saw the orange ash pulse in the dark.

"I've wanted this to happen a long time," she said.

"So have I, I'm afraid."

"You mustn't feel guilty."

"I don't feel guilty."

"You do, a little. But this doesn't have anything to do with anybody else. It's purely personal."

"I hope so."

He heard her laugh.

"Is there anything I can do for you?"

"You've done it."

"I mean anything special."

"No."

"Are you sure?"

"Yes." He stopped. "No."

"Tell me."

"Put on the white bathing suit."

She turned her face into the pillow and he saw her shoulders quiver. He touched her shoulder miserably: he had made her cry, he thought. She lifted her head, her face was contorted, and then he saw it was contorted with laughter. Her body shook with laughter. He was angry.

"You asked."

"I certainly did and I certainly will. It's wet though, will that matter?"

"No."

"Maybe you'll like it wet," her lips touched him lightly, and he felt the bed move as she left it.

Every night his wife was gone, they were together. He did not go again for dinner, nor did he, any more, join her in the pool. Each night at nine o'clock he walked through the two yards to the shadow of her house, and tapped at the door that connected a small patio with her bedroom. She would let him in; by midnight, he would be gone.

At fifty-three, Tate knew little of physical love beyond the straightforward and uncomplicated thrusts of a settled marriage. Eve Morrow taught him how unimaginative he had been.

She officiated at their rites not like a priestess of the mysteries, but like a sensible and good-humored counselor at a Sunday School camp for Main Line boys and girls (which indeed she had been). She directed Tate with the easy efficiency of the matron of upper suburbia.

She knew well, and was not bashful about knowing, any number of games and devices, most of which involved a high degree of visibility: she liked the light on. She made him parade before her nude. She performed strip teases for him—so professionally that he was astonished. And she required that he take her in costumes that varied from the white bathing suit to her blue fox coat.

Yet she avoided wantonness. Her wholesomeness was not impaired; rather, it was more sharply marked by the contrast (to Sidney) between her activities and her attitude toward them. She would be in the middle of her strip-dance, the *Bolero* beating softly on the high-fi, and she would smile at him not lasciviously but gaily: *isn't this fun? look how well I can do it?*

Later, she might say, "Come over here, darling," candidly and casually: "No, no, darling. Like this. See?"

And, "Be still now. This is the executive position. You don't have to move at all."

Tate had thought his fires were out: he was surprised how her relaxed art kindled them. He also had an uneasiness which he knew was unsophisticated but which he could not check.

Was it *right* for her to kneel so casually and openly before him, naked, in the *light?* Was he *normal* to be so excited as she walked back and forth before him on spiked heels, her thick blonde hair shining between the prongs of her garter belt?

He was sure she loved him deeply. And yet she clearly regarded sex not as love, nor as anything that had much to do with love, but as a fine merry game which lovers could play.

His wife did not come back in two weeks, nor in four. They had the freedom of time, and freedom from complication.

They never went to Palm Springs, which was a cliché, but twice they spent short weekends at Santa Barbara, a hundred and twenty-five miles north on the coast. They registered in separate rooms. From her window, they could see the thick Pacific blue vanishing in haze on the west.

The second time, after breakfast, she said, "Sidney, can I have a screen test?"

"A screen test," he looked at her. "A screen test?"

"Sidney you innocent, what do you think I moved next door for? Damn you, don't you dare look betrayed. Don't you dare. It makes no difference at all, now."

"All right."

"Thank you. I don't even know if I want it anymore. But I came out here to see what might happen and I want to see. I don't think I'll be any good, I just want to see."

"I'll set it up for Wednesday."

"You're a love. Please don't be mad."

He stayed away from the set while the screen test was being made, and did not see her at all while she was on the lot. The next day, after it was printed, he saw it in his private projection room. She was not bad, he was surprised that she was not bad at all, but she was not nearly good enough. Her assurance became affectation, and the camera pinched her nose and cheekbones together in a way that made her less than pretty.

He told her.

"It's kind of a relief," she said.

"It should be. You aren't enough of a bitch to make it. You have to be a real bitch, a little bit less or maybe a little bit more than human. If you were what you would have to be, I mean to make it in this business, if you were that I never would have cared about you in the first place."

"I guess that's a compliment."

"You don't have to guess. It is."

When his wife did come back, two months after she had gone, Sidney saw that she intuited changes. He was certain that she would soon perceive what the changes were. He did not want to cause her pain, and so he found it easy to slip into deception.

After she had been back a week, he set his face into a moderately troubled look and said to her, "I'm having serious trouble. Maybe you can suggest something."

"I certainly will if I can."

"It's the Loomis picture. The two of them split up in the middle of it, they aren't speaking now, and she's trying to seduce the director, I think out of spite. He looks like he's ready to commit murder. It's a mess. Everybody on the picture is so tense they're doing badly. I don't know what to do."

That was all true, if overstated. He saw she accepted it as cause of his preoccupation, and he felt the attack of self-reproach. But his face remained guileless, in its false candor. He was shocked at his own capacity for deceit—he had never viewed the ritualistic dissembling of business as deceit.

Later, alone in his study, staring unseeing at the mimeographed pages of white script, of a super-Western, he considered the situation. He would ask Georgia to divorce him. (He would be generous, of course.) It would astonish the Industry. Careful Sidney Tate, wouldn't you know he was up to something? The stuffy ones always fool you. Yes, he even gave her a screen test.

There was one thing. One small thing. He hadn't asked Eve, yet.

He left his office at noon, and met her at an apartment he had rented on Laurel Canyon. In the afternoon, he said, "I want us to get married."

"Sidney. You only think you do."

"I know I do."

"No you don't. You just think I'm your last chance. When I came along you were thinking life had passed you by, you weren't really alive and you'd soon be dead. I was the life preserver, I was all of it, and you latched on. Sidney, I love you, I'd do anything you wanted me to do, marry you or anything else if you really wanted it. But you don't. I'm an adventure to you and you'd better leave it like that."

"We can't go on this way." He did not know what a banality he had committed until he heard his own words, and he blushed.

"I didn't know they were using that line this year, either." She smiled, "Darling, I'm going back to Philadelphia. Vice is not for you. That's a joke. I know it isn't vice, all too well."

"I don't want you to go back to Philadelphia. I want to marry you."

"Sidney, I wasn't lying, I'd marry you in a second if I didn't know it was the worst conceivable thing for you. Forget about that and come here and make love to me, now."

She did go back to Philadelphia, but not immediately, and there were other afternoons, other importunities. When she left, he knew a sense of loss very like death. And he knew a total, flooding relief.

Georgia never hinted that she knew.

5

IN THE MOST difficult years of the studios, Sidney Tate had found the handle to survival and had held it firmly. Though he felt he had only perceived the obvious, he had set a pattern: operating revenue from television and large profits from large pictures. Then in the early sixties, when others who had learned from him were flourishing, he had difficulties. The difficulties became trouble. Tate's career had been built upon solving the balance sheet problems of others;

for the first time in his life, he had a balance sheet problem of his own; unbelievably, he found himself in jeopardy.

His bad luck was of a very simple kind. Three pictures supposed to make substantial profits had had substantial losses.

A big Broadway play, bought and made with a great deal of money, had been rejected by the public. A super-Western founded on the Jason myth had also foundered on it; it was the first Western since *The Gunfighter* to lose money. These accounted for his first annual deficit, it was not great, and it had no great consequences. Yet it shook Tate's halo. And when his real trouble came, the next year, he lost his halo entirely.

The danger came from a picture called *The Admiral's Lady*. It was supposed to recover the losses of the other two, and Tate's sanctity. Instead, it looked more and more like his nemesis.

It was based like two earlier successes on the Lord Nelson–Lady Hamilton story. One of the great male box office stars had demanded the direction of the picture as his price to play Nelson. Sidney had paid it uneasily, but he had paid it.

Looking backward, he permitted himself no excuses. It was the only major error in business judgment he had ever made, but he had made it, and he would pay for it.

Marlow directed a splendid picture and gave a splendid performance. But his caprice and administrative incompetence doubled the original budget. And though its chances of ultimately getting back more than the fourteen-million-dollar negative costs were good, it left a deficit at the end of the fiscal year that could not be deferred. Tate had been as unassailable as St. Peter: suddenly he found himself mortal and vulnerable.

Even after the most adroit accounting procedures, the Marlow picture left Globe-International with a five-million-dollar loss for the year. Globe paid no dividends the last quarter, there was a heavy volume of selling, and common shares dropped from 91 to 78 before they firmed. Then they suddenly dropped two more points and, as suddenly, firmed again.

After the last quick drop and stabilization, Tate was more than suspicious. He paid for, and demanded, the very best intelligence service he could get, and a young man from his broker's office had some answers quite quickly.

"We've pretty well established that one particular group had bought up fifty thousand shares," he said. "It's headed by a man named Vern McGaughey, you probably know about him. He's a raider in the most obvious way, he specializes in getting control of corporations and then sells them out and takes the cash. It's an old tactic but it can still work. He's worked it pretty well so far. As I said, I'm sure you know all about Vern McGaughey."

Tate laughed. "I fired him once, years ago."

Pearson looked at him sharply.

"In a reorganization," Tate said. "It was his own company, McGaughey Paper. He was pretty sore."

The young man did not answer. Tate said:

"I guess maybe he's still sore."

"Maybe he is."

"Fifty thousand shares is more than I've got."

"I know it."

"It's better than thirty per cent of the common."

Tate picked up a ballpoint pen and dropped it softly on the edge of the desk.

"McGaughey. Vern McGaughey." He dropped the pen and stood up. In a quite different voice, he said, "I'd better get ready for the proxy fight."

"I'm sorry, Mr. Tate."

"Be sorry for McGaughey."

Tate had seen proxy fights from close range, but because of the unique pattern of his career, he had never been a principal. He accepted such wars as part of business as it was conducted, and yet he felt that management lost both authority and dignity when forced into a public eye-gouging. The hypocritical courting of the small stockholder, the hat-in-hand soliciting of the large investor was faintly shameful to him: such scurrying disturbed the tranquil air in the temples of decision.

Yet he knew when he heard "McGaughey" what he was in for, in fact he had known before the Marlow picture was finished what he was in for, and he committed himself to the struggle completely. He put a staff of a dozen men on the campaign, and he personally talked to the substantial shareholders.

After three months, which was one month before the annual stockholders' meeting, he did not have enough proxies. But, his information told him, neither did McGaughey.

Tate had acquired through options, bonuses, and purchases across the board 15,000 shares of Globe common, which was a shade under ten per cent of the whole. He was able to speak unqualifiedly for half a dozen principals who together owned about twenty per cent. He needed proxies for another 31,000 shares, to have his majority, and he could obtain only 7,000. He had about thirty-eight per cent of the votes, and his information gave McGaughey thirty-three per cent. Some five per cent of the stock would be unvoted, of course. The rest–36,000 shares, twenty-four per cent–was owned by one man. And he was uncommitted.

Tate looked again down the list of large investors. All had a percentage figure at the left. Except for one, all had a T or M on the right. The unmarked name was Haratunian.

Haratunian was an Armenian of great and shadowy wealth–"just another Byzantine billionaire," somebody had said, as a joke. Though not so elusive as the elusive Mr. Hughes, he was not an easy man to locate, and he was a genuinely difficult one to confront. Yet he was Tate's hope, and quite possibly his last one.

Haratunian spent much of his life aboard his 200-foot motor vessel, the *Cerberus*. His communications equipment was said to exceed that of Navy ships designed solely for the direction of large-scale amphibious operations. From the *Cerberus,* Haratunian managed, closely, a system of holdings supposedly so intricate that even his accountants could not codify it completely. His long trips at sea had the obvious advantage of making it impossible to subpoena any of his scattered records. They also made him a very difficult personage to meet face to face.

In an air age, the range of his appearances was not startling. But their unexpectedness was. He might dock in Honolulu (or anchor three miles out if he were in a delicate situation with the U.S. government), receive the press instantly and affably, and be a highly accessible, gregarious figure for weeks. Then he would vanish as completely as though the blue heave of the Pacific had closed over the raked single funnel of *Cerberus*. He might not be seen for months, except by wandering steamers and obscure ports in the distances of the world, where he had excellent arrangements for meeting the needs of himself and *Cerberus*. Sometimes his favorite private aircraft, a refitted PBM, would drop upon a capital of the great world to take aboard certain fashionables. It would discharge them at the lowered gangway of the *Cerberus* on some glistening sea on the other side of the world. Days, or weeks, later, the PBM would once more glide steeply out of civilized skies and release them–sometimes exalted; sometimes shaken, but never tranquil. So it was said.

It was probable, Tate thought, that the services of an unemployed minister of propaganda and the petty cash outlay for an Ibn Saud were required to maintain the exotic mystery which was Haratunian's vanity.

His beginnings were prosaic enough in truth: his father had owned a shipping line and he had inherited it. The past could not be concealed and careful biographers knew it: yet much that was printed and said suggested he had been born on Mt. Ararat without visible parentage.

Now his wealth ranged from Bolivian tin to Iranian oil, and was linked by one of the world's largest cargo fleets. As it had grown, so had a corpus of Haratunian apocrypha: some might be true. But which?

Tate reviewed it. Haratunian was richer than J. Paul Getty. He was not so rich. He was a civilized internationalist; he was a global brigand. He was urbane, he was foul-tempered; he was kind, he was cruel; he was imaginative, he was animalistic.

He was one of the great satyrs of his time; he had long periods of monastic asceticism.

He was a Communist–he was looking for new Hitlers to back. He controlled every government in the Near East, including Nasser's –Nasser would not allow him in Egypt and he was in danger of assassination in any Arab country.

He once had hosted a symposium on ethics conducted by a renowned philosopher, while in the not at all distant background a troup of Arab nymphs swayed lasciviously to a Bach arabesque.

He supported a clinic in Libya for the treatment of indigenous eye disease. He helped rebuild Saint Stephen's Cathedral in Vienna. He had once thrust a lighted cigar into a singularly vulnerable section of a great soprano: she never before or since sounded a truer high C. He had been one of the backers of the Irgun in their fight against the British in Palestine. He maintained residences in Miami, London, Vevey, Tangiers, and Buenos Aires. He was on intimate terms with Somerset Maugham, Winston Churchill, Bourguiba, the Spanish Pretender, Queen Frederika of Greece, the Marquis de Cuervas, Gian-Carlo Menotti, Elizabeth Taylor, Cantinflas, and Joseph Kennedy.

However, there was nothing in the least apocryphal about his holdings in Globe-International. They were twenty-four per cent. So far, he had never demanded a voice in management, or given a proxy, or even attended, personally, a stockholders' meeting. Perhaps he was awaiting a decisive moment, Tate considered. Perhaps Globe-International was simply not high on his list of urgent activities. Or perhaps he simply viewed his stock in a motion picture company as a useful tool in his womanizing. Whatever, it was to him Tate must turn. The McGaughey raid had placed his business life directly in the hands of a man he had never seen.

Tate had to find Haratunian before he could solicit his help. He prepared himself for a long and perhaps frustrating attempt. It turned out to be magically simple. Tate simply picked up a telephone, dialed the number of the Los Angeles office of the Armenian-American Shipping Company, and quite shortly was speaking to the manager.

"This is Sidney Tate," he said. "I am chairman of the board of Globe-International Pictures. If it is at all possible, I should like to see Mr. Haratunian at his earliest convenience. If that isn't possible, I'd like to talk to him by telephone."

"Yes, Mr. Tate." The voice was courteous and completely American. "Let me see if Mr. Haratunian is available. I'll call you back, sir."

He did so in less than an hour.

"Mr. Tate, would it be convenient for you to join Mr. Haratunian at sea, sir? You'd have to plan on being gone three days."

"Yes," said Tate.

"Fine. Mr. Haratunian's plane will pick you up at Long Beach Airport at eleven o'clock tomorrow morning then. If that's satisfactory, of course."

"Yes," said Tate.

He saw the ship, clearly outlined and black against the flat silver-blue of the Mediterranean, only when the plane started its downward glide. He watched her enlarge blackly, then lost her as the plane circled. He did not look again until he felt the soft bump of the floats touching and saw through the glass the hull, gray now, rushing toward and then crawling past him alongside. He was climbing a ladder to the deck, receiving the salute of an officer in white, and following the officer forward along a passageway.

The officer knocked on a door. Tate noticed his hands were cold. Behind the door a voice called something, the officer opened the door and stood aside, and Tate walked in.

Just inside the door he stopped. His eyes moved between two white bulkheads to a gray metal desk at the end of the room. Suspended above it was a gyrocompass repeater. To the left, the room angled sharply into an L and disappeared. It was the sitting room of an ascetic, or a working sea captain, Tate thought.

He was disconcerted at finding himself apparently alone. Then—theatrically he thought—a figure materialized from the edge of the L and came toward him.

"Mr. Tate," said Haratunian. "It was so good of you to come."

Tate felt his hand surrender under the other's grip. He looked into a deeply tanned face that surprised him with its delicacy: the mouth was full and sensual, the cheeks lean and high-boned, and the eyes dark brown and intent. The head was bald, clean-shaven, and tanned to the same ruddiness as the face.

"Not at all. I'm delighted we were able to arrange a meeting."

The full mouth smiled beautifully; the eyes, Tate decided, would be perpetually watchful.

"I can't tell you how sorry I am to put you to this inconvenience. I simply couldn't get away myself. Was your trip quite comfortable?"

"Extremely comfortable, thanks."

"Splendid. Come have a seat in my sitting room, I use this part as an extra chart room. I command the ship myself, you know."

"How extraordinary."

"Not really. I am a licensed master."

He led Tate around the corner of the L. Passing the table, Tate noticed one chart tacked precisely in place, and parallel rulers mounted on a movable compass rose. Behind the L were a leather chair, a bed without headboard, fixed to the bulkhead, and mounted on the right wall, a red and a blue and a yellow telephone. Tate's eye returned to the bed and studied its placement: he remembered all the stories of surprised officers in pleasure craft converted to wartime purposes.

In the stories, the officer would discover a button and press it, and the floor under his bed would revolve to bring his bed alongside another bed in the next stateroom.

"It's quite true, Mr. Tate," said Haratunian. Tate turned sharply, and felt the heat in his face. Haratunian smiled. "Look." He went to the bed and touched something. Tate watched the bulkhead, bed, and Haratunian swing inward as though on a turntable, and he was staring now at a smooth, light green bulkhead. He heard machinery hum, and watched Haratunian and his bed swing back toward him, and the green bulkhead swing outward and vanish as the other came back into place.

"Well," said Tate. "I never believed it."

"The unforgivable thing about clichés, Mr. Tate, is that they end up being true." Without a change in voice or posture he said: "Why did you come twelve thousand miles to see me?"

Tate had no doubt that Haratunian knew why. "To ask your help."

"You mean my proxy."

"Yes." Tate was not surprised. He tried to match the other's directness. "Will you give it to me?"

"Perhaps. What will you give me?"

"What would you like?"

Haratunian smiled. "Control."

Tate started to say: *I don't see how that can be arranged.* But he did not. Haratunian would know how it could be arranged. He said, "What particular plan did you have in mind?"

"Your stock and mine together come to about thirty-four per cent of the common." Haratunian spoke almost negligently, his wide finger traced courses on the fixed chart. "There is another eighteen per cent that is said to be more or less available. I will buy it. But I will need your stock to have control."

"I want to keep it."

"You can keep it. Just so you sign the voting rights to me."

Tate did not want to sign over his voting rights. He did not wish to exchange one executioner for another. What was gained? Time, he answered. Does any condemned man turn down a stay of execution because it is not a pardon? He had received another proposition like that once. Where? From Vern McGaughey.

"You would remain in your present capacity, of course," said Haratunian. "I contemplate no changes in your organization."

That was just the thing to have said, Tate thought. But he would fight as long as he could and win as much as he could.

"Would you guarantee not to liquidate the company?"

"I make no guarantees that impede the conduct of my affairs."

Tate understood the many men who had reason to hate Haratunian.

"If it's going to be liquidated, I might as well let McGaughey liquidate it."

"I make no guarantees." Haratunian had swung the chair so he faced not Sidney but the round port in the bulkhead on his left. His light brown face was smoothed of all lines and of all expression; his chin tucked downward and made the suggestion of a fold of skin beneath. Sidney saw he was presenting a practiced and calculated aspect of Olympian aloofness, and he wanted to laugh. Yet it was not an occasion for laughter.

"And I make none for the company without some assurance." Tate decided he would not give in on that point, even though he knew that he might, consequently, lose everything.

Haratunian's chin elevated several degrees; his mouth pursed; God, he suggested, was not moved.

"If you can assure me personally that you will not liquidate unless extraordinary conditions arise, I will be satisfied."

Only Haratunian's lips moved and his voice was soft. "Who will judge what are extraordinary conditions?"

"You."

He swung suddenly in the chair and his face, sharp now, bore on Sidney. "It will be understood that I and only I am the judge of such conditions?"

"It's understood."

The hard face suddenly smiled, dazzlingly. Sidney, who knew the smile was premeditated, was nevertheless dazzled.

"I think that is very fair." He extended his hand. "I assure you, Sidney, I have no idea of liquidating your company, or of interfering with your decisions. On most matters."

"I'm very pleased," said Tate.

In two hours, they finished their planning.

"Would you like to leave right away, Sidney?" said Haratunian. "I can get you out immediately but I really think you ought to spend the night aboard. Or longer if you can, much longer."

"I'd like to very much," Tate lied.

He stayed two nights and days. Haratunian was a charming, more than perfect if supremely exotic host. His affability was so marked it became almost deferential. Yet twice, in giving instructions to his secretary, a not so young man in blue blazer and white slacks, he showed himself capable not simply of temper but of instant and deep malignancy.

"Beirut wants to know what to do about the wildcat company that is trying to come in," the secretary said on one occasion, lingering respectfully inside the door.

"Do? Do for the love of God?" Haratunian's eyes opened very wide and his face distorted in fury. "Ruin the bastards, that's what do. Ruin them, by God."

Tate was impressed. Later it occurred to him that the scene had been staged, so he would be impressed.

Haratunian had three young Italian women on board. They did not eat with Tate and Haratunian, but were summoned for conversation after meals. The first evening, someone tapped on the door of Tate's stateroom. He opened it and the most attractive of the three came in. Her name was Nelda; she was lush, plumlike, and faintly overripe.

He understood that Haratunian had ordered her to visit him. He also understood that if he sent her away, he would offend Haratunian. He gave her a drink, a blanket and a pillow, and showed her the sofa. Her eyebrows drew together, then she shrugged, and smiled.

The morning of the third day, Sidney boarded the plane for his return to Los Angeles. After takeoff, he could see Haratunian on deck, waving.

Sidney checked into the Waldorf-Astoria three days before the stockholders' meeting. He came alone and he took only a sitting room suite. He called the reservation desk to see when Haratunian was expected. No reservation was held in that name, the clerk said. Sidney was not surprised: an incognito would accord with Haratunian's mystique. Still, he wished Haratunian were on hand. It had been Haratunian's decision not to give Tate his proxy but to appear and vote his stock himself. In that way, he said, they would avoid the deadline for filing the proxy. Also, he felt it would be more demoralizing to the opposition if he appeared suddenly and backed Tate personally. Tate agreed that it would be more dramatic. Privately, he felt the proxy would be more decorous. Yet he really had no choice.

Now, in his hotel room with the confrontation nearly at hand, he could not stifle a nervousness about Haratunian. Suppose he didn't make it? Of course he'll make it, Sidney answered himself sternly. But suppose he doesn't? Suppose he doesn't?

He knew he would remain nervous until he actually saw Haratunian at the meeting. He accepted his uneasiness as a fact and resolved to live with it for three days.

He shaved, showered, dressed, and went to the coffee shop for an early, quick dinner. He was on his soup, spooning it carefully, when someone sat at his table. He looked up at Vern McGaughey.

McGaughey looked more like Franklin D. Roosevelt than ever.

He said, "Hello, Sidney."

Tate said: "Do sit down. How are you, Vernon?"

"The question is, Sidney, how are you?"

"I'm fine."

"Are you now? I hear it differently."

McGaughey's face was smiling, triumphant, and virtuous. *Virtuous* by God, Tate thought. And looking into McGaughey's face, Tate saw the mind working: McGaughey was getting honorable, long-delayed, and *just* revenge on a scoundrel who had betrayed him.

At that instant, Sidney not only found it impossible to dislike McGaughey: he felt a keen and profound sympathy for him that was almost affection.

Sidney said, "You don't want to believe everything you hear, Vernon."

"Oh I believe that, Sidney."

"Suit yourself."

"Haratunian wouldn't come through, would he, Sidney?"

"You seem to have the answers."

McGaughey was happy. He wore like a mantle the air of a virtuous man who has fought his way to ultimate justice. His conviction of his own justice was as palpable as his necktie. Sidney not only liked him. He pitied him. He said, "You still think I shafted you, don't you, Vernon?"

McGaughey enjoyed that. "Want me to let you off the hook, Sidney?"

"Why not?" Suddenly, he wanted to give McGaughey his moment, or part of it. He did not want to take it all away. "How about letting me off the hook, Vernon?"

"I've waited twenty years to hear you ask that, Sidney. Come on. Ask again. Tell me why I should. Come on."

"I've already asked you."

McGaughey laughed. At least once in his life he has been happy, Sidney thought. At that moment, he felt a genuine fondness for his oldest enemy.

"Uh-uhh. No, Sidney. I am not going to let you off, I am not going to let you off, I am not going to let you off."

"All right," said Tate. "I asked."

That was on a Monday. When the stockholders' meeting opened Wednesday at eleven o'clock, Sidney Tate had not seen nor heard from Haratunian. He had not seen nor heard from him by the beginning of the treasurer's report, and he was more than nervous.

McGaughey was seated about two-thirds of the way back from the front row. He was flanked by half a dozen cohorts, and, slightly less openly, he still had the look of righteous triumph and anticipation. His seating position was strategic for the asking of questions: heads would turn toward him, he would be seen as well as heard. He had plenty of experience at that, now, Tate thought. And where was Haratunian?

When the treasurer finished, McGaughey was on his feet. Detachedly, Sidney admired his appearance: he was virile, handsome, commanding. And where was Haratunian?

"I should like to put a question to the chairman," said McGaughey. His voice was ringing and clear. It was a voice for men to follow.

"Very well, Mr. McGaughey."

"Does the present management have any defense for the five-million-dollar loss for the last fiscal year? Does it not seem to management that this is an appalling loss?"

"It was explained in the report, Mr. McGaughey, that the debit will eventually be amortized by anticipated receipts from *The Admiral's Lady.*" Where was Haratunian?

"I say that is false, sir. I say to you, sir, that you have conducted the affairs of Globe-International with incompetence and impropriety."

Had Haratunian betrayed him? "It is your privilege to suggest what you will, Mr. McGaughey. Management stands on its record."

"I put it to you that that record is a disgrace. I put it to you that a full-scale inquiry into the affairs of our company is in order." The ringing voice paused, then climbed dramatically. "I put it to you that a new management is in order!"

There was handclapping from scattered sections of the room. McGaughey paced his eloquence well, Tate thought.

He said tonelessly and calmly, "You may propose such a new management when we come to election of officers, Mr. McGaughey."

"I most certainly SHALL!"

The scattered applause sounded again.

Tate willed his face and his body into serenity as he continued through the agenda. He understood now that Haratunian had betrayed him. Perhaps he and McGaughey had been allies from the start. He smiled, naturally and affably, while he surrendered to the hatred of Haratunian, and of himself who had trusted Haratunian—yet he had lost nothing by that trust, for he had already lost all without it. Though now he was naked against the public humiliation of defeat, and that was only minutes away. He considered, almost mildly, how he might escape from at least that, and rejected every route of flight as obscene. He would take his beating stoically; he could do no more.

"The next item on our agenda is election of officers."

Haratunian was walking down the aisle.

Sidney was suddenly aware his mouth was open. He closed it.

Haratunian had a remarkably graceful, gliding walk: it carried him forward until he reached the front row of seats. His large brown eyes arced upward and met Sidney's guilelessly; his mouth curved to suggest an irony shared.

Tate understood that few had recognized Haratunian, and he could not keep from looking quickly at McGaughey.

McGaughey was surprised and uncertain. He was not yet afraid.

Haratunian had stopped at the end of the aisle, still standing. His athletic, not large, body somehow suggested great magnitude.

"Mr. Chairman." Haratunian's voice was faintly theatrical.

"Mr. Haratunian." Tate recognized him, calling his name with unusual clarity.

A swell of whispers rolled through the room.

Haratunian said, "I wish to express my support of and confidence in the present management of our company. I wish to announce my intention to vote 36,911 shares, approximately twenty-four per cent of common stock, for the present officers."

He sat down, looking at no one.

A movement in the seats caught Tate's eye. It was McGaughey, leaving.

An hour after the meeting had adjourned, Tate sat in the living room of Haratunian's suite, which was one floor above the meeting room, and listened to Haratunian.

"I hope I did not cause you any nervousness, Sidney."

"Well, I was a little nervous."

"I am so sorry. I thought it better this way. To surprise them completely. I am so sorry I surprised you nearly as completely."

"I had complete confidence."

"There was no risk actually. I have been here since two days before the meeting even though I did not think it best to contact you. And I had this small device to keep me informed of the progress of the meeting." He moved to a small speaker, unconcealed upon the table. "It is affixed somehow to the speaker's microphone. So you see, Sidney, I really was not exposing you. You were under my protection all the time. I am so sorry you were worried though."

I wasn't really worried, Tate started to say. He thought better of it. He did say, "I must confess I was worried."

He saw amusement, if that was what it was, in Haratunian's brown eyes. "Never worry, Sidney. Promise me you will never worry. Life is much too short to worry."

6

TATE had been back on the Coast for five days when Nelson Glassgow came to see him.

Tate and Glassgow had a special relationship which had never made money for either but which both enjoyed. It came from the fact that neither had been really absorbed by the Industry, Tate decided. Tate glacially disapproved of its minuets: Glassgow mocked them as he mocked himself. Each understood the other's attitude: the understanding made for a reciprocity of confidence.

That day, Glassgow greeted him with clearly unfaked pleasure. "I'm glad you made it, Sidney."

"So am I." He did not like to have his problems public knowledge, but they were public knowledge.

"What's ahead now?"

"The same. Some television, some big pictures. Nothing in between."

"That's the way it is now."

"That's the way."

"How would you like to have Margaret Dayton for a big picture?"

Tate looked at him sharply, but his voice was casual. "I don't really think so, Nelson. She's so expensive since she left us."

"She is that. Well. I guess I'll have to take her somewhere else."

"Of course," said Tate. "She may not be as expensive as I've heard."

"Oh, I'm sure she is. She's very expensive. I'll see you, Sidney." He got up.

"Sit down, Nelson. What does she get?"

"A million dollars."

"I mean what does she really get?"

"A million dollars."

Tate exhaled.

"She gets it, Sidney."

"I know she gets it. I'll admit it. It's still immoral."

"It's obscene. But it's obscene that we live in a society that finds its gods in actors if you'll pardon the expression, instead of philosophers or poets or talent agents. However. Those are the conditions that prevail and we have to adjust. The Romans worshiped chariot drivers."

Sidney tapped on his desk. "Actually, she could even be worth half that. Given the right picture and the right budget and the right everything else."

"Suppose I brought you the right picture and the right everything else."

"Which you just happen to represent?"

"Which I just happen to represent."

"Director and writer and supporting cast?"

"No. Director and writer and producer."

Tate laughed. "All cheap?"

"Cheap enough. A million for Dayton and two hundred thousand for Grover Brand and one-fifty for Max Korbin and one-fifty for Howard Sills."

"Don't tease me, Nelson. It's been a trying day."

"Sidney, you know this is a very very good deal for you."

"Oh yes. Oh my yes."

"You know it is. Brand–"

"Brand. Brand is Dayton's husband, and he's never written a screenplay or any kind of a play. Korbin. Korbin has directed one art-house feature and nothing else. Sills." He stopped, he liked Sills. "Sills has had a little bad luck lately."

"That's why his price is down."

Tate looked at him.

"You know what he's done," said Glassgow.

"I know what he's done lately."

"He's had as you say a certain amount of bad luck. Anybody can have bad luck, Sidney."

Tate got the thrust. He smiled with no particular joy. "From here in I want to be surrounded by only lucky people. I don't care how good they are. They just have to be lucky."

"Well. Howard doesn't have to be part of the package."

"But Brand and Korbin do. Right?"

"Indeed right."

"You know you're way high but we'll talk about that later. Now let's talk about the story. What have you got?"

"Helen of Troy."

"Don't tell me you've signed Homer."

"No, I'm afraid he's still public domain. I just represent the talents that can make him explode."

"Of course." Sidney ordered his face into polite, faint, visible skepticism.

"Ah, Sidney, you know I do. One love goddess bringing flesh to another. Why Sidney, you old skeptic, it practically documents reincarnation."

Glassgow's speech had an edge of irony that derided himself: he appeared to live in a permanent state of self-mockery. Yet Tate knew him for a very hard bargainer.

"All right, Nelson. I'll confess I'm titillated by the possibility. Where does that take us? There is as you know a great deal involved."

"I know it," said Glassgow. "I know what's involved, Sidney."

"The big picture is shooting craps. Shooting craps, by God." Tate almost never used the expletive. "You lose on one and you try to double up on the next to get it back and you lose on that one and you double up again. And if you lose on that one. Well you know what three big pictures have done to me."

"I do know," Glassgow spoke soberly. "Maybe this could be your answer, Sidney. I honestly don't know but maybe it could. Take your time and check everything out. If you're truly interested after you take a look, I won't take it anywhere else for a while."

"I'd like to see something on paper besides the *Iliad*."

"How about a screenplay?"

"On spec?" Tate was astonished.

"You could call it that." His hand dipped, brought up his attaché case. He took from it a blue manuscript half an inch thick. "And you know what, I just happen to have it with me." He shoved it across the desk to Tate.

"Well, by God," said Tate.

"Let me know what you think of it."

"No blank verse, I trust?"

"No blank verse."

Sidney called Glassgow two days later.

"I like it pretty well," he said.

"I thought you might."

"I have to check an awful lot of things out."

"Nobody else will see it till you make up your mind."

Tate had his conferences and studies. He decided that the picture should be made for seven million dollars, and added two as a cushion. As reports came in, the project seemed increasingly feasible. He called Haratunian.

"I have the greatest confidence in your judgment, Sidney," said the voice in his ear that started ten thousand miles away. "I would never interfere with you or question your decisions in the slightest. Not while you are making money." And he laughed merrily.

He reached a tentative agreement with Glassgow for a million for Dayton and Brand's screenplay from his novel, one-fifty of it for the writing, and the rest to her. She was willing to take less if his screenplay were used. Sills was to get a hundred and Korbin one-fifty. On the grounds that Margaret wanted him, Tate also accepted as co-star another Glassgow client, Mace Garrett. Garrett had been one of the great male stars of the Gable-Flynn era; he was still a useful name.

Sidney held the two-year-old De Ville in the outside lane of the Ventura Freeway uncoiling into the heat haze and smog of the San Fernando Valley. He saw COLDWATER CANYON NEXT TURNOFF, slanted properly into the exit lane, turned off and under the freeway, and headed south toward the Santa Monica Mountains, a brown wave against smog-yellow sky.

He was going to call on Margaret Dayton, whom he had never met, as protocol to the already completed signing of contracts for *Helen of Troy*. Nelson Glassgow had taken them to her and returned them to Sidney. Twenty or even fifteen years ago, Sidney thought, she would have come to the office, borne by chauffeured town car, and an army of flacks would have memorialized the event for headlines if not for history. Now, after the fact, he called upon her, and did not in the least mind it. He had suggested lunch at Scandia. Glassgow had insisted that Dayton wanted to entertain him. Tate suspected that the agent feared she could not be on time anywhere else, and he suspected that the fear was entirely justified: Dayton had a reputation for pathological tardiness. Yet Tate was beguiled by the chance to see her at her best or worst, and he could not smother his pleasure at saving Globe the hundred-odd dollars that lunch for four at Scandia represented. Old cost accountants never die, he thought, they just become board chairmen.

He was on the right street now if street was what you called it: a thin curving pavement winding among long low houses guarded by massive greenery and spaced a quarter-mile apart. Three- to five-acre estates, $200,000 to $300,000 he estimated. For Margaret Dayton, such a setting was temperate. He found the number on one of two brick posts at the entrance to the driveway, turned in, and parked.

As he walked toward the doorway, he could see the house itself for the first time. It was beige-pink adobe, trimmed with dark brown wood. Described to him, it would have seemed cloying; confronting him, it was tasteful and handsome. At the door, he pushed the buzzer and stepped back. He heard chimes inside, and waited. No one answered. He pushed the buzzer again hard, twice, and heard the chimes again: no answer. He turned his wrist: seven minutes past three o'clock and the appointed hour. As his finger moved toward the buzzer once more, the door opened and a girl in blue jeans and a yellow handkerchief over her head stood in the doorway.

"Good afternoon," he said. "Mr. Tate, to see Miss Dayton."

She looked at him strangely. He felt uncomfortable.

"Miss Dayton is expecting me," he said.

"I'm Margaret Dayton," she said.

She extended her hand and he took it. He was suddenly aware that he was staring at her. She released his hand. "Come on in," she said. "Gee, I guess the time kind of slipped up on me. It does that every once in a while."

"That's quite all right."

He followed her into the house. She led him down a thickly carpeted hallway, and into a pine-paneled, not-large room. One wall was shelved and full of books, the one next to it had a built-in television set, and against the third was a couch covered with brown naugahyde. A book lay open on the couch, cards lay on a coffee table, with a cup and saucer beside them.

"Have a seat." She wiped her hands on the front of her jeans. "Would you like a drink? Or coffee or something?"

Tate sat on one end of the couch. "Tea would be fine."

She went to the door. "Ma-ry. Ma-ry."

Tate watched her face in profile. If he had seen her on the street, anonymous, he would never have recognized her.

He heard her speaking. "Mary honey, would you bring in some tea and those little, you know, cake things? Thank you honey."

She came back into the room and looked brightly and expectantly at Tate. Her unpowdered face shone. She is actually plain, Tate thought, she is plain and pleasant looking and no more.

He had run her last three pictures in his projection room at the studio, and had been convinced that whatever else she had, she was one of the most beautiful women alive. He made all allowances for her costume and still was unable to fuse the image on the screen and the cheerful-faced girl in blue jeans.

"Nelson's supposed to be here," she offered.

"Yes."

"I don't know where he is, he's supposed to be here. Gee, I'm sorry the time slipped up so."

"Don't give it a thought."

"I get interested in something and the time just slips up."

"Of course."

"I was reading this book, this Faulkner book. It's the one where the colored nurse kills the baby to bring them together. Does that really seem reasonable to you?"

"I can't say that it does." Tate had not read it. He picked it up and looked at the title: *Requiem for a Nun*.

"It doesn't to me either." She brought one hand almost to her chin and clasped it. "Why should she do that? I mean there are lots of other things she could have done, she didn't have to do that."

"It certainly seems illogical."

"That's the thing about so many books and plays too, they do these things that are supposed to be so significant and profound and everything and they don't make sense. Do you think all that stuff makes sense?"

"Well—" Tate was feeling more inane by the minute.

"Tolstoy always makes sense. When he says they do something you believe they do it. You know who else makes sense, most of the time anyway. Tennessee Williams. His characters may do real kooky things but you *believe* them, you believe they do them. You know?"

Tate nodded.

"Blanche Dubois, now I understand her. To me Blanche Dubois makes sense. She's a kook and all but she makes *sense*. I'd like to play her sometime, on the stage I mean. Do you think I could play her, Mr. Tate?"

"Why not?" said Tate desperately.

"I guess I'm kind of a kook myself. I've decided you have to be a little bit of a kook to have any personality. You know?"

Tate inclined his head.

"But I'd rather be the kind of a kook I am than some other kind of kook. I did Blanche in a scene at Max's Theater Arts Lab and to tell the truth I think I bombed. Everybody said it was fine and all and I'm pretty sure I bombed. Still I know I *could* play her."

"Of course you could." Tate found his entry into the conversation. "And you'll play Helen of Troy magnificently, too. We're going to make a great picture."

He felt specious as he spoke, the falsely hearty exploiter, and yet he could not find a real point of contact with the girl. He did not know what he had expected; whatever it was she was not it.

"I hope so. Grover wrote a wonderful script."

"Yes, he did." Tate was grateful for a chance at honesty. "He's a wonderful writer."

"He's got to grow up though before he can be a really great writer. Understand, I tell him that all the time so I'm not putting him down to you. Sometimes I think that's my mission maybe, to make Grover grow up and get some sense and be a great writer."

"The experience of the picture will be very good for him. It'll enlarge his horizons considerably."

"I liked his script. I like everything he writes but sometimes maybe it gets a little too, it doesn't make sense. I like this though. Nelson says *Helen of Troy* is right in line with the Dayton image. Nelson is always talking about the Dayton image, the Dayton image. Sometimes I say myself screw the Dayton image, but he's right I guess. And you really like things like that, you say screw them and all that, but you really like them. I mean, you're a girl and everything, so why not be good at it? Where the hell is Nelson?"

"I was wondering myself."

"Like, as, I said you just better go ahead and be good at what you have to do. He was supposed to be here a long time ago."

"Maybe he was detained."

"Maybe he had a wreck or something. Wouldn't that be *nice?"* But she did not look as though she thought it would be nice. "He drives so fast," she said–almost fearfully, Tate thought. Then she said, "The lousy bastard."

Her relationship with Glassgow did appear to have its interesting aspects, Tate thought. He said, "I'm sure he's all right, he's just been held up somewhere." He knew now that Nelson Glassgow had never intended to come, not on time.

The phone rang. She stood and walked to it. In the flat heels, she moved with a rolling, purposeless gait that had nothing of the Dayton walk in it. "Hello," she said.

Tate saw her body stiffen. She said, "Oh, it's you," and he heard her voice change. It was not simply harsh but brutal. "I have just one thing to say to you. I want those prints back and I want the negative back and if I don't get them I'll cut your heart out and don't you think I can't. I want you to give them to Mr. Glassgow right away. Don't you sell another print. I don't know. He may give you something if he feels like it. I'll damn well give you something if you don't give them to him. You have them there by tomorrow or I'll have you in jail. You hear?" She hung up.

Her face was angry, and neither pleasant nor plain, Tate thought.

"That son of a bitch," she said. "Prop man. He took some candid shots of me when I was fooling around on the set dancing and just fooling around. That was fine, you understand, if he can get some good shots and sell them to a magazine that's just fine, I'm glad to see him make some money. But, well, you see, to tell the truth right out I just didn't have any pants on that day, and I forgot about it, and a couple of the shots were, you know, embarrassing. Embarrassing hell. They showed just everything. If he had given me the pictures I would have given him a thousand dollars without his asking, but no, he had to peddle them around. Well, I get them back or he goes to jail. I've got *that* all worked out."

Tate cleared his throat. He had felt the blood in his face since she said "pants."

"Very trying experience," he managed.

"Not particularly," she said coolly, "just annoying. Anyway, I'm sorry you had to listen to it and let's forget about it. Where is Nelson? He was supposed to be here an hour and a half ago. He promised."

She called Glassgow's office again and was told, apparently, that he was on his way.

"Damn him," she said. "He's a bastard. Mr. Tate. Can I ask your advice about something?"

"Of course."

"I need your advice on what kind of present to give my husband. What kind of a present would a man, a man that age, like? He's thirty-four."

He's already got it, Tate wanted to say. But he said, "I don't know. What do you give a handsome young novelist who's got everything?

I would guess it depends on the occasion and how much you want to spend and so on. What is the occasion?"

"I guess kind of an anniversary. We've been married six months."

"How much do you want to spend?"

"I hadn't thought about it."

"Well, you could give him a sports car maybe."

"He's a lousy driver, he'd kill himself in a sports car."

"How about—" Tate stopped and thought again. "How about a special leatherbound and embossed set of the works of his favorite author?"

"You mean his next favorite author. *He's* his favorite author. It's a wonderful idea though. I'll get his books fixed up with gold letters and Joseph Conrad fixed up with silver letters and that will make him very very happy. Mr. Tate, you are a genius. I can see why you run Globe-International."

She came to him, put her arms about him, and kissed him quickly and lightly. "You don't mind if I kiss you, do you? It looks like I already have anyway."

She stepped away and Nelson Glassgow walked into the room.

"Hello, Sidney, hello, lover."

"Goddamn you," said Margaret Dayton. "Knock next time."

"Sorry I was late, my car conked when I was trying to get it started."

"You're a liar."

"Yes, I am." Tate looked at him sternly, and he smiled back. "I thought you two should get acquainted. But I have the boys outside, with cameras and you had better expedite into something glamorous. I mean now."

"Merde," said Margaret.

"You've been reading again," said Glassgow.

"You ought to learn how yourself." She left and slammed the door.

She had bristled at Glassgow from the instant he came in. Was there some grievance between them, or was she simply in love with him, or both? Tate wondered. Then he remembered a recent difficulty of Glassgow's and thought he understood.

"It took you long enough," said Tate.

"I told you. I wanted you to get to know her."

"I don't want to know her, I just want her to make the picture."

"Come on, Sidney. If she doesn't move you, you're a sick man."

"How about you?"

Glassgow flushed. "I have a long term and highly profitable *business* arrangement with her."

Tate smiled gently.

"I'm going to get the photographers," said Glassgow rapidly. "They're your still men, by the way. Judson let me have them." He left.

He returned a few minutes later with two men in sport shirts. They and Tate acknowledged each other.

"Sit down," said Glassgow. "You could have a long wait."

But they did not. Margaret Dayton entered, and she had not been gone more than fifteen minutes.

For the first time that afternoon, she looked like Margaret Dayton. Her red hair was flowing and impeccably disarranged and full (it had to be a wig). She was in a tight white sheath that fitted incredibly (though there were no visible traces a girdle had to be involved). And her face was, Margaret Dayton's face. The cheeks had been just touched with rouge; the mouth had been painted in that famous, exploited half-pout. But Sidney knew the real phenomenon: she had set her face into the expression, and her body into the movements, of the character she played who was called Margaret Dayton. It was an old Hollywood story, attributable to dozens: the star was not recognized on the street when she did not wish to be, and when she wished to be, moments later, she was inundated.

Margaret Dayton, the character, moved forward in a muted version of a stripper's hard-heeled stride, the points of her heels striking the floor just hard enough to produce an interesting action within the sheath. Her head was tossed back, the lips parted in the Dayton pout: she was one of a million publicity stills suddenly become flesh.

"Just like that, Miss Dayton," said one of the men.

She stopped and set her body, one hip thrusting slightly outward, the chin elevating to a point just safely short of caricature. Her tongue licked her lips, they glistened wetly, parted, and the quick white bursts of bulbs shattered Sidney's eyes.

"Insurance shot."

She drew a breath, tightened her lips, opened them, and the flashes came again.

"Now you and Mr. Tate looking at the script or something."

"I want my husband in that one," she said.

Tate saw the photographers exchange looks: who is *he?*

He said, "Mr. Brand wrote the screenplay. We must have him, of course."

"I have to get him," Margaret Dayton said. "He won't let me put an intercom in his studio."

She hurried out, though still in the Dayton walk, and Tate thought he had never seen anything more provocative, than the action under the white sheath going away.

He glanced at the photogs, who were visibly containing their annoyance, and he heard one murmur to the other:

"A *writer*. Jesus."

Margaret Dayton returned, on the arm of a compact, medium-sized young man. He wore a brightly flowered sport shirt, his hair was blond and rumpled, he was in his early thirties, and he acknowledged introductions shortly.

"I'm sure this is awfully important," he said. "I was working."

Margaret Dayton looked at Brand with the most visible pride and pressed his arm with her fingers. In that moment she looked very shy; it came to Tate that truly she was very shy.

Glassgow and Brand smiled ironically at each other, and Tate thought the situation among the three was not uncomplicated.

"Mr. Brand is a very famous novelist," Tate said to the photographers.

"Nobody ever heard of him," said Brand. But the glance he gave Tate was appreciative.

The photographers posed them, the flashes were interminable, and then the photographers were departing in bored, competent, union-girded aloofness.

"Well," said Glassgow. "I guess we're really in business. Want a drink, Sidney?"

"Well. Maybe a symbolic drink?"

"Margaret? Grover?"

They said yes.

Margaret Dayton helped him fix the drinks. They raised the glasses, Brand just barely, and drank.

That had been two years and four months ago. He remembered it as vividly as he remembered anything in his life, and he wished, fairly, badly, that it had never, ever, happened.

7

Sidney Tate wandered alone and unnoticed through the soldiers and technicians in motion about the Trojan horse. Could they all be engaged in purposeful activity? he wondered. Perhaps . . . perhaps. And yet most of them seemed to be dashing forward and backward in motion which existed for its own sake and which turned ultimately back upon itself, motion which had no purpose except the annihilation of purpose—or of time. He sighed: think how much more it would cost in California, he directed himself, and felt better. But not for long. Not even for a moment could he truly forget The Question: where was Dayton?

At the moment of crisis, Tate intuitively and unhesitatingly turned to a man who was not in his employ: Nelson Glassgow. He had done so before, and now he admitted that it was in Glassgow that he placed his ultimate confidence. Howard Sills had theoretical status as producer; Max Korbin was, also theoretically, her Svengali; Octavia Dayton was her mother; and Grover Brand was not only her husband but her writer. Yet, now, when he felt himself shadowed by catastrophe, he wanted Nelson Glassgow who was only her agent.

No one knew where Glassgow was. Tate knew: he went into town after him.

Harry drove slowly down the pocked gravel road that became the only village street big enough for a car. The bumps were hard even through the Citroën's air suspension: Tate got out of the car with relief when the road ended in front of the blue flag that marked the walk-up post office.

He lost himself three times in the maze of paths between close white walls, then he found the tall white steps that led upward to the Mykonos house of Nelson Glassgow. Like all Mykonos houses, it was really an apartment, an upper floor, and on either side, its walls were also the walls of adjoining houses. Glassgow lived, officially, at the hotel: he kept the house for special occasions, of intensely varied sorts.

The key was in the lock, how like Glassgow, and Tate turned it and walked in. In a tiny hallway, he met a smell of closeness and airlessness: he knew it was because the villagers kept the windows almost closed against the high Mykonos winds, or the great heat that came when the winds did not blow.

In a small living room he found Nelson Glassgow sitting on a couch surrounded by women. Actually there were only four: a plump brown-haired woman who might have been French, or German, or Greek, or American, and who looked sleepy but serene; two blonde, unmistakably Gallic girls; and a dark-haired young woman in a print dress who was Slavic-Greek or Italian-Greek and who was five or six months pregnant.

Glassgow looked up at him and smiled. "Hello, Sidney."

"Good morning, Nelson," he said sardonically. "You mustn't take Margaret's situation so bad. I mean, you mustn't worry about it so. Life does go on."

"A wake should be jolly, Sidney."

"Oh my *yes.*"

"Actually this is part of my investigation."

"I had no doubt of it."

"It's really not *quite* as good a party as it looks . . ."

"I *am* sorry."

"We met the French girls at breakfast on the waterfront, I had the feeling they were trying to tell me something. The young Greek lady who is rather largely pregnant is my landlady."

"That does relieve me."

"She owns the property, it's the women who own property on this island because their men are always at sea. Her man is at sea."

"She must be lonesome," said Tate with awesome self-control.

"I'm sure she is. Would you like me to arrange a lay, Sidney?"

"Nelson!"

"It's all right, nobody has the English but us. I understand the pregnant lady is thought by many to be quite exceptional, I couldn't say myself."

"Nelson. I need you." Tate said it seriously.

Glassgow's face was suddenly different, and Tate had seen no intervening stage of alteration. It had been glazed with drink and Glassgow's self-deriding merriment: then it was clear and sharply alert.

"It looks like she's really gone," said Tate.

"Really gone?"

"She's your client, Nelson."

"You'll remember I pointed out a Dayton deal had its problems as well as its rewards and nobody, not me or anybody else, nobody could guarantee her absolute punctuality and reliability."

Tate did not remember but he let it pass. "Nelson for heaven's sake don't get defensive. I am not blaming you, I am asking your help. We can't stand any more waste. Do you know how much we're over budget?"

"Five million?"

"Seven."

"Let's get going," said Glassgow. He stood, incongruously graceful in his soiled clothes, and patted the Greek girl on her belly: the gesture somehow escaped lewdness. He said something in a language strange to Tate, the girl giggled, and he followed Tate to the door.

Going back to Troy from the village, holding the jarring stone street that became the coast road, the Citroën took them through the town. Through his window Tate watched the seaward side of the town go by. Like all island towns, it was built long and thin and close to the sea. The houses were tall and thin and with dark windows stood like white dominoes on end. Along the street were citizens in ten-year-back European clothes and loose peasant clothes and ensembles of the two. It was a one-way road. Harry stopped to let pass a stooped old woman with a black shawl over her head, leading two donkeys with full burlap packs on their backs. The road left the town behind, held close to shore, cut inland sharply to miss a jut of rock, and cut back again.

"You have no leads at all?" Tate said from his left side of the back seat to Glassgow.

"None of them checked," said Glassgow. "I have lines out."

Tate nodded. He looked from Glassgow to the road twisting ahead. It ran between brown stone walls and was still only wide enough for one car. Coming into a sharp curve, Harry blew the horn and almost stopped, another horn sounded and he did stop, and around the curve came a very old bus with dust behind it. It would be the Plati Gialos bus returning from the beach. Harry backed into a space off the road and let it pass, then started ahead.

Tate looked back at Glassgow. Glassgow's head had tilted backward and sunk into the deep Citroën cushions, his eyes were closed, and his breath came in deep audible regularity.

He looked exhausted from his inquiries, Tate thought.

For no visible reason Glassgow's head snapped forward with a start and his eyes opened. Tate watched him remembering, wildly, for one instant, where he was.

"Tired?" Tate asked with compassionate irony.

"My all for my clients." It was not worth a smile and Tate gave it none.

"Go back to sleep," he said.

Glassgow looked at him gratefully and let his head fall backwards again. Tate looked at the sunlight on the upturned face, past the face to the wall sliding by the car, and over the wall to the hard brown earth crossed by a network of small walls. Beyond all that was the sea. The engine hummed smoothly; Glassgow snored softly.

Tate was thinking of what should be done, everywhere, that day.

The Citroën turned from the road to dirt tracks on the plain that was location, passed parked cars, tents, Quonsets, and stopped in front of a Quonset marked *Production*. He touched Glassgow gently on the arm.

They went straight into Sills's office: Sills looked no happier than Tate felt. Tate took the Silex on the hotplate and poured coffee into a white mug. Glassgow drank all the coffee, lowered the mug and refilled it, and drank again.

"Think you'll make it now?" said Tate.

"Now there's a possibility."

Tate's face considered a smile, briefly, but did not make it, and he heard his face and voice fill unforcedly with the heaviness of his authority.

"Let's see just exactly where we are. What's the status report, Howard?"

"We've got three assistant directors going over the island and our craft union people are helping them. We had to send some cables to the union offices in town on that one. I've given the chief of tourist police a–consideration, and I've promised him another if he turns up anything. We've checked the regular boats to the mainland, nothing, any small aircraft in and out, nothing, we've alerted the various agencies at Piraeus and Athens, nothing yet. We're left with three possibilities. One, they're somewhere on the island, they went off on a jaunt on the island and they got lost. Two, she and Sylvia went on a boat trip in one of these caïques and something happened to the boat. We've got the Greek coast guard, whatever it is they call it, out there looking, and I chartered a couple of helicopters from Athens yesterday as you suggested, Sidney, to make our own search. They went out late yesterday and are back today, we're in touch but nothing yet. If they're out there floating around, they'll be found, and if the boat went over, well they're drowned by this time. The third possibility, Nelson, is that your client has run out on the picture."

"Yes," said Glassgow. Tate watched him try to focus a mind that, visibly, did not want to focus. "But I'm certain Margaret hasn't run out on the picture. She's erratic but she never ran out on a picture in her life. I would guess what's happened is she just took herself a little unannounced vacation, maybe two or three days. I know it's a lousy trick but she may have felt it was necessary, she may have felt she was right on the edge of a breakdown."

"Why didn't she come to us?" said Tate.

"You know Margaret and her fears."

"Yes," said Tate, not sympathetically.

"If she's in Athens or Piraeus we'll find her," said Sills. "Crestman and Arthur are coordinating our check in both places."

"Very good," said Tate. "Your whole strategy is very good, Howard." It was a carefully considered award.

"Thank you, Sidney."

Looking at their faces, it occurred to Tate that three men had spoken of a female motion picture star for three minutes and had not once referred to her as *the cunt*. In certain other contexts, this would not be simply unbelievable but miraculous.

"Another possibility of course is suicide," said Tate.

They looked at him.

"But Sylvia's being gone too rules that out," he said.

"It doesn't rule out murder," said Sills.

"We've considered that," said Tate. "It's possible. What's even more possible is that they're out of Greece completely."

"Do you think they've had time?"

"Oh, yes. They could have gotten out of here on a boat the night before they were missed, and gotten out of Athens on a plane the next morning before we started. My own feeling is that either has happened, or they've been done very serious harm." He spoke flatly and looked steadily at the others. None spoke for a moment.

"Let's assume the worst," Tate said. "Suppose she's dead. Where does that leave us with the picture?"

"Nowhere good," said Sills.

"Can we finish it? You know as well as I do the insurance doesn't begin to cover us."

"We can *finish* it. It won't be the same picture but we can finish it. Whether we can recover negative costs with Margaret's biggest scenes lost is something else."

"I will not equivocate about my primary responsibility here," said Tate. "My primary responsibility is to the stockholders whose sixteen-odd million dollars we have spent. I'm concerned about Margaret's safety but my first responsibility is to the stockholders."

"Of course," said Sills.

"Mine isn't," said Glassgow. "My responsibility is Margaret Dayton, and I mean to find her, and I mean to have plenty of help until she is found."

Tate said, gently, "So do we all mean to find her. But we have other things to think about, too."

Glassgow subsided. "Of course you do. I'm sorry."

"It's all right," said Tate. "The point is we can finish the picture without her though admittedly with serious losses in content."

"The losses will be very serious," Sills said. "I don't want to give you a falsely optimistic estimate, Sidney."

"Nor do I want onc. But if she *is* dead there's nothing we can do about it. Point two." He called through the door in the plywood. "Laura, may we have the tape, please? Point two is we have some very serious survival problems of our own."

A slender gray-haired woman brought in a tape recorder, set it down, and left at Tate's infinitesimal nod. Tate watched Glassgow reflexively assess and discount her for sex.

"Laura's recorded some of the short-wave stuff from New York." Tate's finger pulled down the switch, he watched the spools turn, and heard the tiny reproduction of the reproduction of a voice:

"Whatever happened in Asia today, for most of us the big story is, whatever happened to Margaret Dayton? The impulsive picture star disappeared yesterday from the scenic Greek island where

Globe-International is making her newest picture, the twenty- or thirty- or forty-million-dollar epic, *Helen of Troy.*"

Tate exaggerated a wince. "It seems Margaret just went and *vanished.* She worked day before yesterday, didn't show up yesterday, and a hurried and harried search did not produce her.

"So of course the rumor merchants have been having a *wonderful* time. The European press has come up with some remarkable efforts. Try these"–the voice chuckled tinnily: "Margaret's eloped with her costar Mace Garrett. She's deep sea fishing with a young Greek poet. The mysterious Balkan billionaire Haratunian–there really *is* a Haratunian–has whisked her off the island to his yacht somewhere in the Mediterranean. Albanian Communists have kidnapped her. Greek revolutionaries have kidnapped her. Turkish reactionaries have kidnapped her."

"I missed those," said Sills softly.

"And–prosaically enough–she's walked out for more money. Publicity stunt? Reporters assigned to the film say ab-so-lute-ly *not.* The Globe brass is more than concerned. And well they might be. For Miss Dayton's *adventure,* has touched off reverberations right here in New York. And mighty ones they are.

"A major stockholder in Globe-International is crying for the immediate execution of everybody connected with the picture. His name is Vern McGaughey. He's famous–corporation-wise as they say–for shaking things up. He's been accusing Globe president Sidney Tate of inefficiency ever since the *Helen of Troy* budget began its celebrated climb. Before that, he tried unsuccessfully to depose Tate at the annual stockholders' meeting last year. Here's what he has to say about Helen's latest misfortune: 'Another result of the most grossly inefficient management ever inflicted upon a modern corporation. Sidney Tate–' "

Tate snapped it off. "You know the situation as well as I do. I have to keep Haratunian with me to hold off McGaughey. If I lose Margaret I lose Haratunian. If I lose Haratunian I'm out. If I'm out Howard is out and all my other people are out. This is what is involved."

He looked from one to the other and said with his elegant irony, "I'm highly susceptible to any solutions."

"Does Octavia know anything?" said Sills.

Glassgow said, "She says no and I don't think she's lying. I think we should talk to her again though. She might remember a remark or something, one thing that'll lead to another thing."

Sills looked at him quickly and Tate did not look at him at all.

"If you would," said Tate easily. "It would be very neighborly."

BOOK 3

OCTAVIA DAYTON

1

THE DOOR opened: through it Glassgow faced a soundly shaped woman in a blue dressing gown: her features had much of Margaret's in them but were not a replica. They were mature yet unlined; her hair was more brown and less red than Margaret's; the sweep of gown about her hips and its close fit about the bosom showed the full detailing of her figure. She stared at him with a suddenly humorous and divining face.

"Come in, Nelson," she said, and her hand dropped from the doorknob and she stepped back from the door to let him enter.

"Are you all right, Octavia?"

"Reasonably. Are *you?"*

Octavia Dayton studied him with concern. His lean face had a heavy beard shadow, though it was morning, and fatigue was heavy upon it. So, too, was something else: memory.

She moved away from that.

"Have they learned anything?" she said.

He shook his head. *"You* don't have any ideas at all?"

"None at all. She doesn't confide in me, you know. These last few years she and I have not been exactly close."

"I know."

She looked at him with the quick shaft of humor. "You should know."

"There's never any one cause, is there?" he said.

"Of course not."

She walked in front of the window and back, and stood against the light.

"You know Sylvia's gone too," he said.

"I guess there's no doubt they're together?"

"I have no doubt."

"Where could they go? I mean really where. This is all so stupid."

"It is."

"Margaret's not stupid."

"No. But she's, let's say she's easily influenced."

"You think Sylvia?"

"I have no doubt of that, either."

"Why?"

"I don't know."

"*I* certainly don't."

"She didn't let *anything* drop? Think hard. Anything about how she felt or what she wanted to do or anything? It wouldn't be direct."

"As I told you, our relations have been rather, formal. All she's spoken of that I remember is how tired she's been. You know how things are with us."

"When are the two of you going to get friendly again? This is foolishness, you know."

"Darling, *I* do know."

"Did you ever think you'd have problems like this that day you came to the pet shop?"

"I was sure I'd have all kinds of problems. I was also sure some of them would involve you."

"And so they did."

"So they did."

She smiled, he embraced her lightly, and before he moved to the door, he patted her derriere too quickly to give offense.

"Take care," he said. "I'll keep in touch."

"Please do. Good-bye, Nelson."

The door shut behind Glassgow, and Octavia walked to the window. Her view was of the sea and of the point of the island: a sweep of dark mountain into blue space. She was more frightened for Margaret, much more frightened, than she had shown Glassgow. For a moment he had shifted her focus. She felt the layered reproach she always felt for any pain which came to Margaret, and she felt, resentfully, that her sense of guilt was unreasoning and unjustified. She had always been Margaret's servitor, she thought; indeed, a large part of her life had been lived for Margaret instead of for herself. In all particulars of performance—she thought righteously—she was blameless; on the profound level of decision and will she knew in her heart she was guilty as hell. She *had* put Margaret into the picture business.

It did not seem long ago. Nothing seemed *very* long ago. Nothing at all.

She remembered the many persons she had wanted to be in her life, and how she would settle for one: a woman imperfect, forgiven, and loved. That seemed as distant as the most incredible fantasies of her girlhood.

She put her hand on her breast, shivering in the wind that blew through the window from the sea. It had happened so fast, she thought. Everything happened so fast. Things began and things ended and suddenly your life was half over and you wondered where it had gone: you had torn off half your only sheet of paper and you had not written enough on it. You had not thought long enough or hard enough about what you would write on it, and you had wasted it more from carelessness than anything else. You simply had not concentrated. Perhaps in the end it was a kind of laziness, and that was the worst crime, or sin.

Sin, for she did believe in sin. And yet her life to look at it would not seem a lazy life at all. She did not know how she could change it, she was not sure what she should have done differently. And absolutely none of it seemed long ago at all.

2

OCTAVIA DAYTON came to California in 1946. She had arrived in New York in 1940 from her place of birth—never in her most despairing moments did she call it home. That place was London, England. She was the daughter of a cab driver, and from her earliest awareness, she had lived simply to escape her beginnings. She dreamed of being superbly beautiful, superbly glamorous, and superhumanly safe. She knew of only two conditions that made such an offer: royal princess and movie star. The first was closed even to fancy. She settled for the second, and prepared herself by reading fan magazines.

She did escape by an older method: she got pregnant.

She did so at nineteen: she was then a waitress in a Liverpool pub. She was just fat enough to be buxom, she lived in the rough warm world of men and drink as though it were an element of nature, and her virginity had been abdicated years before. She had left London with an able-bodied seaman off a Cunard ship when she was seventeen, and had been pleased enough to stay in Liverpool. She had always hated London.

The instrument of her deliverance wandered into her pub half-drunk, on a rainy evening early in 1940. His name was Charles Dayton, and he was an ensign in the United States Navy, which was then in the war but not officially.

He had been graduated from the Naval Academy the year before at twenty-four, slightly older than his contemporaries. He had been an enlisted man, a signalman third class, and after a competitive examination had entered the Academy at twenty, the maximum allowable age. On graduation, he was assigned as communications officer to a 1630-ton destroyer. When the Navy began to escort convoys, the destroyer ran from New York to Liverpool and back.

Dayton was a young man addicted to loneliness, and his identity had been essentially fixed by his years as an enlisted man in the peace-time navy. Gentility made him uncomfortable: he moved as if by gravity to the low and the companionable. On his evenings of liberty, he usually wandered alone through the belts of gaudy in the ports of the world. He had a stolid capacity for empathy that both made him welcome and protected him, if imperfectly, in those places without law.

Octavia had seen him two nights before, but had paid him no special notice. "Nice looking," she had categorized him; she categorized reflexively every man on whom her eyes fell. This was her second best.

He sat not at the bar but at a table, slow and faintly unsteady and grave.

"What'll it be, ducks?" she said briskly, routinely flirting. She had already noted that he was an officer.

"Whiskey. Whiskey soda."

"No Yankee whiskey, love."

"Okay. That's okay. Scotch whiskey. And. Soda."

He was holding himself erect with a visible effort.

She served him.

"You. Are very pretty," he said.

"Who cares?"

"Why I care. I. Have to take you out and show you who cares."

She had never been out with–her euphemism–an officer.

"I don't mind," she said.

There was nowhere much to go when she was off. They wandered a bit and then he checked them in a walk-up hotel. She did not object. But in the room, lying on the bed beside him, she kept space between them. He made fumbling efforts to close it but was too drunk really to care and was snoring as she pushed him away the third time. In the morning, she was briefly awake as he dressed, and awake again as his hand shook her shoulder.

"Keep the room," he said. "I'll be back this afternoon."

He was, shortly after noon. She had awakened half an hour before but was still in bed. She heard the door open, turned her head on the pillow, and saw him, already inside, close it. He stood quite still for a moment, in the blue and gold uniform, the raffish white and gold cap, looking down at her. She thought he was quite handsome, more handsome than she remembered.

"You look very nice," she said.

He smiled and did not answer. He took off his cap and set it on the dresser. He took off his coat and hung it carefully over the back of the chair, smoothing and adjusting the shoulders. Then he turned to her.

"Ain't you got nothing to say for yourself?" she said.

He smiled, sat slowly on the bed, and fell upon her.

It was not rape, quite. She fought him silently and furiously, not threatening to scream, not scratching, but twisting and striking with all her power. He overcame her; she was astonished at the hardness of his arms, for he had looked soft. He took her with a methodical driving violence that seemed insatiable. She begged him to stop, she tried to push him off, then she submitted entirely.

When he finally had spent himself, she–aching up her belly, trembling in her muscles, bruised, shaken and sobbing–was more his than she had been anybody's. And she was already thinking of a future. She did not go back to her job that night. He kept her in that room, and for four days she left it only when he was not present. Except for the one night he had the duty, he arrived each day about three o'clock, and left the next morning at six. They quit the room only for dinner and did not stray far from the hotel. The district, like the hotel, was cheap, and each day she decided indignantly she would demand the posh dinner she deserved. Daily she rehearsed the speech: "You can bleeding well show your appreciation by taking me to a bleeding good place. I ain't no Piccadilly Circus whore, you know, I'm a decent girl, you can bleeding well show your appreciation, you can."

But at evening, she did not care. The fifth day, he himself proposed a meal at the Adelphi.

She said little, listened to him order, and ate with embarrassment but greedily. She was already engaged with another prospect. Her vision of herself had shrunk: what she wished to be above all else was safe. The only clear thing about the vision was that she, it, was permanently beyond and immune to poverty. She determined to make him marry her.

She wasted no time. In bed in the hotel, she told him:

"I'm scared. I missed today. You been careful like you said?"

"You're damn right I've been careful."

"It's likely all right. Happens like this sometimes."

"It better be all right."

"It's likely all right."

"Octavia."

"Yes ducks?"

"Don't try anything."

"I don't know what you mean." She made her voice weepy. "I don't know what right you got to talk to me that way. I been nice to you. You got no right." She pretended to cry, and quite shortly, she was crying.

She said nothing more that second week. She knew that at that point she had no weapons to hold him except memory and desire, and she worked hard so they would both be strong: he would go to sea but he would also return.

"When you got to go back to sea, love?"

"Don't know," he said shortly.

"You mean you can't tell me, don't you? That's all right, I know about them things. Can I write you?"

"Why not?"

"I ain't got your address, that's why not."

He wrote it for her: a ship and a post office.

One day he did not appear. When he was not there the next, she knew he had gone out. Bloody foolishness, she thought: if she were a Nazi agent she'd know now he was gone and he might as well have told her in the first place.

Laboriously, she wrote him a letter a week. Intuitively, she made it no more frequent. And she wrote not of love but of pleasure.

In her second letter, she wrote, "Everything is all right now. Nothing to worry about everything is fine."

That ought to do it, she thought.

She had found another job at another pub, effortlessly, two days after he left. At some prompting of her intuition, she remained chaste, although she was transiently pawed by the sailors she served. Sometimes she went out with one, and let him have certain intimate caresses with his good night kiss. But, technically, she did not betray Dayton.

"I'm being true to me love," she would say. She acted not from obligation but from prudence. Though she could not have said why prudence was gratified by her abstinence, she felt vaguely but certainly that it was.

Of course Dayton came back. Of course he came to the place she worked–she had told him where it was in every letter.

She was standing at the end of the bar, placing tankards of beer on her tray, and after she had turned and was approaching her table she saw him sitting against the wall. He was looking directly at her and grinning. She smiled at him, gestured that she would come to him at once, and served the beers. She was faintly, astonishingly, frightened. She could feel her body accelerating.

She walked to his table, aware of his eyes cataloguing her shape and movements. She wondered what he would say.

He said, "Hello."

"Hello. I can't talk to you now. I mean I can't sit with you or nothing. You look just wonderful. Are you all right? Can I bring you something?"

"Bring me some whiskey," he said. "You look pretty good yourself." He looked at her very closely. "Good enough to eat." He smiled. "What time you off?"

"Twelve."

"I'll be waiting."

"Wait a block down or so. That way. We ain't supposed to go out with customers."

He nodded.

Two sailors had waited for her outside. They fell in with her and asked how about it Tavvy, let's have some fun. She laughed and said no. They followed until Dayton stepped out of the shadows. She took his arm, and the sailors left.

"Friends?"

"Oh no, they was just having a little joke. Most of the chaps are always having their jokes."

"Uh-huh."

"Did you have a bad time out?" she asked him.

"Rough weather, hard to sleep. That's always bad. I don't mind anything if I can sleep. You can't sleep, it's bad."

"Oh poor love. I'm so sorry."

She stopped and touched his face with her hand. He kissed her and she brought her body to his.

Finally he was able to stop a cab and they went to a hotel (a good one this time, she noted with satisfaction). He had already checked in. She had planned it very carefully, and part of the plan was that she would not tell him her lie for several days. In this week—he going back to the ship for eight hours every day, she awaiting him as before—she executed various stratagems so her lie finally would not be a lie.

"You remember what I told you before?"

She was aware of his body tensing. "What you told me?"

"You remember, I told you I missed. Well I missed again and I never did come around and I went to a doctor and he gave me tests and things and he said that it was all right. He said somebody had gone and got me with child all right. Course I didn't tell him it was *you* or anything."

"I told you." His voice was flat. "You know I told you."

"What do you mean you told me? I don't know what you're talking about, love."

"I told you not to try it."

"I don't know what you're talking about."

"You're no more knocked up than I am."

"What do you mean knocked up? What're you talking about?"

"I mean goddammit, I don't think you're pregnant."

She giggled. "Is that what it means? Over here when somebody knocks you up they wake you up in the morning. You know? Knock me up about seven. Knock me up early. Like that. It's very different, what?"

"You're a little liar."

"I wouldn't lie to you, love."

"You're a little liar but okay. Okay. How much will it cost?"

"How much will what cost, love?"

"Oh-oh. So that's it."

He said nothing more, and she felt a danger in his silence that frightened her.

She was not surprised when he did not return that afternoon or the next. She had already made her plans. The third day of his absence, she arose at nine o'clock, washed all vestiges of makeup from her face, put on a white dress, and went to the docks. She asked directions as she needed. She expected stern challenges by armed sentries; she looked for barbed wire fortifications. Yet all that impeded her was confusion: no one knew where the destroyer was moored. She proceeded from informant to informant for almost four hours before she came to it: a lean knife-nosed ship painted two shades of gray, a blue pennant at the bow whipping thinly against a lead-colored sky. The three sharp-edged white numerals on her side were the same as those on the sheet of paper in her purse: she did not need to look. The ship was smaller than the others she had seen that day: she trembled alongside the pier, held captive by thick doubled lines. A long gangway ran at forty-five degrees from the deck to the pier. At the head of it, on deck, stood a sailor and an officer, both in blue uniforms and white hats. She looked closely and was relieved to see the officer was not Dayton. Still she trembled; she was full of fear and doubt. This was her chance, she admonished herself, maybe her only chance, and she commanded herself to approach the gangway on legs that quivered with weakness. She started up it, her heels striking the boards like an unrhythmic drummer, and the sailor turned to face her. She saw the pistol in the holster at his side and felt an addition of fright. He permitted her to take one step off the gangway and no more.

He looked at her, fully and directly, and she was aware of the tightness of her dress at her breasts and hips. She knew what *he* wanted, all right. His stare answered, impertinently, that he knew what *she* was.

Yet his voice was not unfriendly: "You want something?"

Now was the time. "I want to see your commanding officer, that's what I want."

"You ah you got any kind of appointment?"

"No, I got to see him, that's what I got."

"Now I just don't know about that." His eyebrows contracted, olympianly, and the officer in the billed cap materialized at his side.

"What is it, Goblanski?"

"This ah this young lady wants to see the captain . . ."

"Oh does she? What do you want to see him about, Miss?"

She was frightened by his hard and accusing stare. "That's a personal and private matter."

"I see." The officer and the sailor glanced at each other quickly. The officer almost smiled; the other raised his eyebrows and then one shoulder, elegantly.

"Would you excuse us a moment, please?" They moved away.

She saw the officer had one wide and one thin gold stripe on his sleeve. That would make him–she groped–a leftenant junior grade.

She heard the sailor say, "trying to put the bee on somebody, somebody must have got to her . . . trying to make one of our guys take the fall."

She did not understand the leftenant's answer, then, she heard ". . . have to take her to the skipper anyway." She could hear too the quickened beat of her heart; she drew as deep a breath as she could draw. She saw the sailor shake his head dolefully, and the pair came back to her.

"I'll have to know your business before I take you to the captain," the leftenant said.

"It's personal and private like I said."

"I'll have to know."

"Well then it's about . . . I hope to see him about, a man on board this ship."

"What about a man on board this ship?"

"I have to see him, that's all."

She saw herself seduced, pregnant, and helpless before a hostile universe of men. She was as sad as if it had been true: she felt warm wet paths on her cheeks.

"All right. All right now." The leftenant was frightened. "Come on now. I'll take you to see him, just get yourself together."

"I can't help it." She sobbed, openly and in sweet pleasure. How hard were men, how cruel was the world, how brave was she! She brought her handkerchief to her eyes.

He left her, returned, and led her down a passageway. She followed like Joan of Arc.

He knocked upon a door, got an answer, opened the door and stepped aside as she entered. She heard the door close behind her and she was alone with a gray-haired man whose blue sleeve bore two and a half gold stripes.

He was a small man and dry of juices. He looked at her coldly. "Sit down. So you claim one of my men got you in trouble?"

She dipped her head. Under his dry and unsympathetic eye she had no desire to weep, and she felt not the pleasure of self-pity but fear.

"All right." His voice accused her. "Who do you say it is?"

"I don't *say* who it is, it is Ensign Charles Dayton is who it is. He left me."

"Mr. Dayton?" He looked at her in astonishment. "You mean, that is, ah, you, you had a relationship with Ensign Dayton?"

"Yessir I had relations with Ensign Dayton and he . . ." she searched, found, and said in triumph, "he knocked me up."

The captain cleared his throat; the cracked tan skin of his cheek took red tones. "Ensign Dayton?" he said quite mildly. "You're sure?"

She looked at him and understood that he did not like Charles Dayton.

"Tell me about it," he said, reassuringly.

She understood that he did not like Charles Dayton at all.

She told him.

It was twilight when Dayton returned to the room. On the bed, in the deep gray light, she heard the key in the door, and she closed her eyes and heard the knob turn, the door open, and close. She felt him standing there and was afraid. She kept her eyes closed.

"So you went and did it," he said.

She pretended to resist the first thrust against sleep, and moaned.

"I told you not to do it," he said.

She opened her eyes, simulating the return to awareness. "Why hello, love. Didn't hear you come in."

"How did you know he hates me?" His voice was a single hopeless tone.

"Who hates you, love? What you talking about?"

"He's always hated me because I was an enlisted man. How did you know?"

"What you talking about?"

"Anybody else would have thrown you out. But I had to draw a captain that hates me."

"I didn't mean to do nothing bad to you."

"You know what he said, he said I could marry you or take a general court for conduct prejudicial and for fornication. So I got a choice. I can ruin myself slow or fast."

"I meant you no harm, Charlie. It's just I have the child to think on."

"You don't have any child in you. Even if you do. That could have been taken care of."

"I never meant you no harm." She was crying: now that her thought had become act, and existed beyond and separate from herself, she was terrified of it. But she could not let it go.

"You just meant to get yourself a pigeon. And you did. Now I'll tell you how it's going to be. I'll marry you however they do it outside of church here, before whatever they call a justice of the peace, and I'll give you an allowance, and after the kid is born I'll divorce you. If the blood tests say it's mine I'll provide for it. If not I won't. That is it. That is it period. Do you understand?"

"No that ain't it. You got to get me out of this bloody country before the Germans start bombing it. You got to get me to New York."

He looked at her, reckoning. Then he shrugged. "All right. That's no skin off. I can divorce you in the States easier than I can here."

"You promise? You'll get me to New York?"

"If you don't make me any trouble, I'll get you to New York."

The requisite number of days after Dayton got the license, they were married by a Registrar of Marriages.

Outside the building, Dayton stopped a cab, put her inside, and gave the driver the address of the hotel. From his wallet he gave her a bundle of notes. "I'll see you sometime," he said.

Back in the room, she wept. Then she stopped crying and felt triumph for the first time. She had done what she planned as she planned. Almost. Only she was not really pregnant. If she had a child by him she could hold him forever. She liked Dayton and had been more than excited by him. She would like to be an American officer's wife, she could improve herself. It was a shame she hadn't really conceived. But it was too late now; he would never touch her again.

She found herself abruptly exhausted. The tensions of the week clubbed her together and at once. She took off her shoes and stockings and dress, fell on the bed in her slip, and dropped into a deep sleep.

The light exploded and waked her.

"Hello bride," said Dayton's voice. It was thick and blurred. "How's the little bride?"

He stood, heavily, just inside the closed door, and light fell on his face under the twisted visor of his cap. His face was glazed; he smiled, ponderously.

"Got to check the bride out, haven't I now? Course she's already checked out but les see how it is legal."

He threw his cap to a chair, came to the bed, and took her brutally. She understood he needed to hurt her for what she had done, and she let him. When he finally slept, his body pinned hers to the mattress. She circled him with both arms, smoothed his hair, and kissed his forehead.

3

IN LESS than a month, she was on a Swedish passenger ship bound for New York. When she boarded, she suspected she was pregnant; five weeks later, tests at the Brooklyn Navy Yard hospital made her sure. She was convinced it had been the last time: Charles, finally, had kept her from being a liar.

Navy housing found her a small apartment near the Sand Street Gate. She wrote Charles the address, then found herself dropped into an isolation almost absolute. She had known loneliness deeply, but never solitude, and she felt herself fragmenting under its impact. She was not secure as she had hoped to be secure. She had made herself safe, after a fashion, by marrying Dayton. But she did not *feel* safe. She saw she was finally trapped by her externals: her ignorance and its instant visibility. She would have to change it.

She conscientiously tried to "improve" herself, but was not sure how to go about it; she settled for reading *Life* and the *Reader's Digest* and seeing a motion picture every day.

One day she saw a picture made in England in which Wendy Hiller played a Cockney girl. Octavia felt a wave of hostility and homesickness as she watched the character Eliza. Leslie Howard took her over, in the picture his name was Professor Higgins, and he taught her proper speech, and she became a lady.

She was out of the theater before three o'clock, and rushed to a telephone. She called the Yard and asked if there was anybody in charge of education and all that, the operator gave her the Education and Training Service office. A young man's voice answered, "Training, Yeoman Saperstein."

"I'm a navy officer's wife," she said. "Where can I learn to talk good American?"

She heard a long moment of silence.

"I said where–"

The pleasant young voice said, "Why don't you try the speech department at Brooklyn College? Let me tell you how to get there."

The class in remedial speech was not at all the way it was with Leslie Howard and Wendy Hiller. After the first two weeks, she did not think she was speaking better at all. Yet she persevered, and wrote Charles what she was doing. He wrote in return a short but not hostile note, and one day his voice was on the telephone and he appeared himself in the late afternoon. His ship was in for a Navy Yard availability, he said. It was the first time she had seen him in the two months she had been in New York.

She opened the door to his knock and kissed him timidly on the cheek. He embraced her lightly, and awkwardly patted her shoulder. She understood he had decided to maintain a truce until he could alter the situation.

"You're thin," she said. "Did you have a bad time?"

"Bad from the weather. The weather's always lousy in the Atlantic in winter. Hard to eat and hard to sleep."

"Must be awful not being able to sleep."

"It's no fun. How are you? You look different."

She giggled. "You know I'm different."

"I mean beside that."

"Am I? I don't know how."

"I don't either, but–. How are those lessons on whatever they are?"

"I don't know. I guess I'll always be a London girl."

"No, I can tell a difference. Not much but it's there."

"I'm glad."

The only bed in the apartment was a double bed. In it, beside her, he said, "I don't guess."

"Oh, yes," she giggled, the second time that day. "It's all right for three more months, doctor says."

His ship was in the Yard for seventeen days. In that time, he was never angry nor rough with her. She did not know what it meant; now she was simply grateful for such gifts as came her way.

He went back to sea and did not return for another two months. When he came back, she was herself aware of a marked change in her speech. She could talk for minutes without slipping into her London accent.

"You're doing well," he told her. "I'd never have believed it."

"I'll do better."

He was in the Yard one more time before the baby was born. He did not see Margaret until she was almost a month old.

"She's beautiful," he said. He held the white-dressed infant in the air. "Beautiful."

She saw the cloud on his face.

"She's yours, love. But get the tests. I want you to be sure in your own mind."

He looked away and rubbed his chin with his hand.

"I want you to," she said.

"I'm–"

"You have to to please me."

He did. She saw he was enormously pleased to know with certainty.

"Were you sure?" he asked her.

"I haven't been with anybody since I started with you."

He blushed.

"When do you want the divorce, Charlie?"

"There's no hurry on that. Better for everybody if we let it ride for a while."

"Whatever you want."

4

SHE had to discontinue the course at Brooklyn College for several weeks. Then she exchanged baby-sitting services with a Chief Petty Officer's wife one night a week and resumed the remedial work. Her instructor advised her to take a correspondence course in composition; she worried through it with great difficulty.

She had won part of what she had wanted for herself—or become a fraction of what she wanted to be. But now she wanted more, or wanted to be more. She wanted to be Dayton's wife genuinely and totally: she wanted him to love her. She already loved him.

He was in and out of the Yard every six or eight weeks, and was good to her. One day between his returns, she knew that he was not going to divorce her, and she went about the apartment singing. She did not think he knew it yet.

In the fall of 1941, she extended the arrangements with the Chief's wife to two nights a week and enrolled at the college in the freshman literature course and in advanced speech correction. Most of the speech work consisted of private sessions with the instructor; between them, and with a certain merriment, they decided she should have an Oxonian accent.

After the shock of Pearl Harbor in December, her life was much as it had been the year before. Charles's schedule was almost the same; he told her he was running no more risks than he had run for two years.

By the spring of 1942, her native accent could have been detected only by a professional; the Oxonian that replaced it was passable.

By the fall of 1942, two years after she had come to New York, she had completed four semesters of speech correction, work in remedial writing and reading, and had passed (without credit) the freshman courses in composition and literature.

In January of 1943, Dayton was transferred off the ship and assigned to the commissioning detail for a 2100-ton destroyer under construction in Philadelphia. For the first time, he took her to a ship's party, at the officers' club in the Philadelphia Yard, and she began to see other wives. They were a widely dissimilar lot, and she was accepted routinely. She knew that a totally new phase of her life had begun. She was not only happy in love returned; she had the low-keyed but permanent exaltation of having made herself—almost—what she wished to be. Even on the day-by-day roller coaster of her spirits, she never lost that exaltation.

The three months in Philadelphia were easily the happiest in her life. The destroyer was commissioned and sent to the Pacific. Octavia and her baby went across continent by train, to live and to wait on another shore.

The ship went into San Pedro for a short and final availability before she went to the forward area. Octavia and Charles stayed in the Hilton Hotel in Long Beach for the two weeks he was in port.

From their window they could see the harbor, which was red and green and yellow lights moving slowly across the dark.

"I don't want to divorce you, Tavvy. I mean ever."

"I've known that for a long time, Charles. I love you very much."

Three days later, he was gone. She received awkwardly tender weekly letters from him. She wrote him more frequently than that and read the newspapers and tried to guess where he was. She found a duplex in Long Beach and was able to support herself and Margaret on the two hundred and twenty-five dollars a month Dayton sent, which was almost all his salary. It was not easy.

The letters came, and she knew he was in motion across the Pacific: he wrote once of a "big damn flat blue circle with just us and our friends at the center of it. That's all there is days at a time."

In June, 1944, the attack on the Marianas—Guam, Saipan, Tinian—was in the headlines.

She read these with the same fear ordered into numbness as she had read all the others for almost a year. She had no shadow of a premonition; yet when the telegram came it was as though she had been waiting for it. It was a day before she could cry; then she broke so completely an alarmed neighbor called a doctor.

When shock dulled, and she had performed the duties of survival, she found he had left only the ten-thousand-dollar service insurance. It was enough to keep her and Margaret for about two years. She went to an employment agency on Hill Street and told her story frankly.

The square-jawed woman behind the desk looked at her appraisingly. "Why don't you try modeling?"

"I don't know how."

"There are places to learn." The woman opened a directory and flipped yellow pages.

Octavia paid a three-hundred-dollar fee, went to a modeling school for six weeks, and began to make a living. She was too full of body for marked success in a business that made a fetish of bone. Still, she did far better than she would have done in New York. She was not sought after, but she had steady activity in bathing suits and catalogue dresses for unstarved women.

"You were born out of your time, Tavvy," a lean flat-nosed photographer told her at Malibu one day as he posed her looking to the sea. "You're the best looking woman I work with. The thing is you look too much like a woman. It's the skinny ones get the cream."

"Don't I know it."

"You're the best looking, don't let anybody tell you different," he said. "When are we going to shack, Tavvy?"

"To tell the absolute truth, darling, I don't *really* think we are."

She became addicted to the oldest narcotic: activity. She understood, by steps, that she had lost her hard-won self. She felt, not that she was exactly nothing, but that she was something like nothing.

Margaret was three years old. Octavia left her at a day nursery for working mothers that offered overtime sitting service into the evening: she often worked late on beach jobs, although she had not yet begun to go with men again. One Saturday, it occurred to her that she had not seen her daughter awake for five days. She wept, but could do nothing to alter the situation. She tried to make up for it by flooding Margaret with attention on weekends, and knew it was not enough.

Some days she felt herself in a badly imagined universe, that had no link to reality. Neither she, nor her daughter, nor walls nor floor nor sky, existed except in a gray fantasy that was not even her own. One such day she stood in the doorway of their small living room and looked at her daughter bent over dolls on the floor. That moment, the child had nothing at all to do with her. It occurred to her that she did not love her daughter enough, perhaps not at all, and she could only try to feel guilt. Not seeing her, Margaret said to the doll, "I be your mommy, doll, I take care of you." And Octavia felt a rush of affection: the walls, the child, and she herself were at once totally real. She ran into the room and picked Margaret up.

5

FOR MONTHS after Dayton's death she did not want the company of men. Then she wanted it very much. But she imposed a discipline upon herself; she did not "go out" with any man until a full year of her mourning, and penance, had passed.

Then she had relations with the first man she dated, on the first night she dated him.

He was a male model, colorlessly handsome, egomaniacal, dull. She did not care for him, but let him have her simply to terminate one state of life and begin another.

"You needed that, hon," he told her afterwards.

"Oh go to hell." She started to cry for no reason she knew.

She did not see him again but resumed what she came to consider as a normal life. She had a succession of intimates, never professing love, and never taking a new one before the last had been discarded. She had loved Dayton, and did not think she would love anyone else. Yet she had a deep capacity for pleasure and coolly enjoyed her possibilities for variety. She did not neglect Margaret, either willfully or carelessly, for her work or her men, and still the necessities of her days were such that Margaret was neglected. On days she worked, she was able to have breakfast with her daughter, and then she did not see her again until after dark. She never went out until Margaret was in bed, and still their time together was measured in minutes.

On the days she had no jobs, she was over-solicitous and Margaret was nervous from the change and cried. Octavia did not know what to do except get married, and she did not want to get married, and she particularly did not want to marry any of the men who might have wanted to marry her. One who did not want to marry her but who brought a massive change to her life, was Walter Button.

Earlier in her life she had retreated to the external fantasy of becoming a "movie star" as though it were a narcotic; now, on the very spot where the miracles of becoming were wrought, she took not one step in the direction of the Industry. She was afraid. It was one thing to dream over fan magazines and chocolates; it was quite another to present one's self at the door. Economics finally drew her to the outermost of the concentric circles: another model took her to Central Casting and the extras' union. Sometimes she worked as an extra when she had no action modeling. She went to evening classes at a "dramatic school," and tried to get some parts with lines. She was not successful.

This situation changed when she met Walter Button. Button was a producer of B pictures inside the apparatus of one of the largest studios. She met him not on any of her picture assignments but at a party in North Hollywood given by a still photographer for whom she sometimes posed. Later, she learned Button was a regular at the photographer's parties: he had acquired three or four mistresses at them. Button was a muscular, fat-padded, gray-shocked man of about fifty. He was almost a stereotype, except that instead of a European accent he had a Southern hill twang.

He was almost ugly but she found him not without magnetism. Since she was between companions, since she felt a liaison with him would be not unpleasant and clearly advantageous, and since his ponderous glances made his wishes evident, she decided with no particular effort she would accommodate him.

He paid her a lumbering compliment.

"I know, I ought to be in pictures."

"Now that's just where you ought not to be. You look just too plain nice to go through all that, honey."

"Just where do you think I ought to be?" She teased him, having already made up her mind.

"Now I'll just have to tell you bout that. You ought to be protected, is what you ought to be."

And so she was. She accepted him in her bed not immediately but shortly. He put her under a studio contract for six months at $350 a week.

But he threw her only an occasional one- and two-line part, and she perceived that she was supposed to be delighted with these and expect no more. She also perceived that one of the reasons she had been selected was that he believed he would have no problems with her: she was not a contender for real roles.

Looking at herself in her seconds-long appearances, she had to admit that she seemed nondescript. She photographed not badly but less well than she looked: she showed no signs of being an actress. It would be different if she were properly presented, if she herself were serious—or so she insisted to herself.

And Button could present her properly; she was determined to make him. It was his practice to come to her apartment about nine, after Margaret was safely asleep. One evening, she met him at the door with the sweet daiquiris he liked, instantly loosed his tie and opened his collar, and pulled a stool to his chair for his feet.

And she told him, from his lap, "Lover, you're a handsome, handsome man."

He pulled his head back and looked at her. "If I didn't know you so well I'd swear you was after something."

"I'm always after something, you brute, I'm after pleasing you."

"Uh-huh."

"What I, am, after, is to please, you."

"That's mighty nice."

"When people are crazy about each other they ought to do all they can for each other. Don't you think so?"

He closed one eye and looked at her with the other. "Why sure," he said. "Sure I do."

"You know you'd do something for me if I asked you and if you could."

"Sure I would."

"I know it too, sweet, and I know you wouldn't be mad if I asked you to do a teeny favor for me."

"Oh I wouldn't be mad."

"Promise?"

"Promise."

She traced a design on his cheek with her finger.

"Well, I read the script of that Western, you know, *Hanging Ground,* and I thought . . ."

"What *did* you think, baby-boo?"

"Why I thought, I just thought, sweetie, now Octavia could do that woman."

His voice was tender. "Is that what you thought, baby-boo?"

"Yes indeed, I read it and I thought I know I can do it, I know I can. And I wondered, would Baby think I was abusing his affection if I asked him to let me."

"Is that what my yummyyum wondered?" He murmured in a tone of infinite tenderness.

"*Would* you think I was abusing your confidence, lover?"

"Course I wouldn't. Course not."

"Oh. Oh you mean I can? You mean I really *can?* I'm so happy I don't know what to say!"

"You bitch," he said casually, and without moving her from his lap he slapped her twice. She cried out. "You conniving bitch, don't you ever mess in my business again, you hear me?"

She sobbed, and got off his lap.

"You hear me?"

She sobbed again. She was standing with her back to him.

"Well now that's understood, we don't want to have no more unpleasantness, do we?"

She was crying steadily and did not answer.

"Come over and give Daddy a big kiss."

She did not move.

"Come over to Daddy and we'll have ourselves a party."

She picked a magazine from the coffee table and hit him across the face with it. She swore at him with words she had not used aloud since she left England, and she finished, "It'll be a bloody day I have a bloody party with you you bloody fat bastard."

She came at him with her nails. He grabbed her wrists and slung her to the floor.

"My goodness," he said mildly. "You sure get riled up."

"I'll rile you you bastard. Get out of here. Good. Bye. Get out, get out."

"Wait a cotton-picking minute now. You want a stinking old part all that bad, I just might let you have it."

"You're a liar."

"Oh no, I'll give you a try in it. Some conditions though."

"Conditions?"

"We got to have ourselves a party right now. *Right* now."

He cast her, and she learned all her lines in advance in two days. She practiced various deliveries of each, she worked hard on her body movement, and when she saw the third day of rushes, she knew she was no good.

"It's pretty bad, isn't it?" she asked Button.

"I wouldn't say that."

"Do you want me out?"

"Certainly not."

"Come on now. Don't you want me out? Really? I won't be angry."

"It's just you don't photograph as good as you look, Tavvy. It's that way with a lot of people."

"I know it."

"It ain't your fault. I know you worked hard. It's just what that damn camera does."

"Thank you for the chance." She kissed him lightly on the cheek and ran to the women's room and cried.

6

SHE stayed with Button almost two years and acquired a certain status as his official mistress. He renewed her contract at the six-month option points, and she continued to appear in the one- and two-line parts: the contract kept her from being a whore.

Also, she had more time with Margaret. Yet Button's demands were sometimes precipitate, and created tensions between herself and her daughter. One weekend, when she had promised to take

Margaret to Catalina, Button demanded her presence in Palm Springs.

Octavia told Margaret, who was nine, and watched the child's face close against her.

"Sweetheart, I don't want to not keep my promise. This has come up, they have to shoot some scenes, Mommy has to work. You see, baby? I have to work. I have to work to support us, and I can't always work just when I want to."

Margaret's face stayed stubborn and closed.

"Don't you see?"

"You're a promise breaker. You promised you would and now you won't. You're a promise breaker."

Out of guilt, Octavia responded defensively. "You ungrateful *bloody* little girl. You serpent's tooth."

Margaret's face altered into curiosity. "What's a serpenztooth?"

"It's what you are. No it isn't. I know you're disappointed baby. I was rough with you because I felt so badly about calling our trip off and because I can't help it. I don't want to be a promise breaker."

"All right."

"We'll go on a weekend soon. I promise."

"All right."

And they did, though it was six weeks later.

Her relations with Button had settled into comfortable tedium when she met Howard Sills at a party, to which Button took her. She had been introduced to him before, she had seen that he was interested in her, but she had never had a real conversation with him. That night, at the party in Westwood, she found him by her side.

Sills was several levels higher in the hierarchy than Button, though his luck was on a down curve. He had been the Crown Prince at Globe-International but had lost that eminence when he went to war: he was still a major figure though no longer connected with a studio. He looked like the most desired stereotype of college president: with prematurely white hair, a keen gaze, and a certain loftiness of carriage.

He was standing beside her when she turned suddenly, struck his elbow, and spilled his drink on her dress. He made ardent apologies, insisted he pay for either cleaning or a new dress, and as they talked, she was aware he desired her.

"Walter is a very lucky man," he said.

"What do you mean?"

"Everybody knows everything out here, my dear. If you and Button ever come to the parting of the ways, I know some very beautiful places I'd like to show you."

She laughed. "Is that an offer?"

"It most assuredly is."

Still teasing: "I'll remember."

It was two days later that Button set her free, and she was neither surprised nor displeased. Yet the manner of the ending infuriated her.

"Baby-boo," said he solemnly, "we been friends a long time."

"I do hope so."

"Sometimes, sometimes in people's lives the time comes when they got to be different *kinds* of friends."

She laughed quite pleasantly. "You mean you're throwing me over, Walter?"

"It ain't that way at all."

"What way is it?"

"I told you, the time just comes."

"And it's just come for us, is that the idea?"

"I feel real bad about it, baby."

"For depriving me of yourself? That's awfully sweet of you darling, but I really will try to survive."

"You'll be fine, baby. And you know what, I know somebody that thinks you're pretty great."

"Well goddamn you. This does make me mad. I am *not* an item of merchandise."

His cheek quivered above his jawbone.

"This certain somebody is just pretty crazy about you."

She understood. "Oh. Oohh I see, I really do. Sills has ordered you to pass me on, isn't that it?"

"It ain't like that at all."

"What is it like then?"

He said nothing.

"The hell with both of you."

But she didn't hold to it, and she knew she wouldn't even as she said it. She refused to reply to Sills's telephone calls; then one evening she answered the doorbell and there he was: white-haired and handsome. He greeted her with exquisite courtesy and she let him into the apartment with only a tremor of hesitation.

He came straight to it. "Mrs. Dayton, I'm terribly sorry if I've offended you. Would you mind telling me how I've done so?"

"I'm not an heirloom, Mr. Sills. I won't be passed on."

She expected him to deny he had pressured Button. He did not.

"Mrs. Dayton, I wanted you to be my close friend, my best friend, and I wanted that so badly that I was willing to do anything to make it so. I make no excuses. I hope you'll understand and forgive me."

"You make it very difficult to be angry with you."

"I don't want you angry with me."

7

HER YEAR with Sills, actually it was somewhat less, could have been a rerun of her two with Button except the dialogue was better: Sills was an extremely cultivated man. He was also a careful one, and he never took her to a public function. She became pregnant by him, he arranged a legal abortion in Mexico, then he became nervous and moved discreetly out of her life. And generously—his present was a savings account with five thousand dollars in it.

Her next friend was an aging Hungarian director, that lasted six months, and the one after that was the vice president of a lesser studio. Before she fully realized it, the pattern of her life had been established: she was successively, and comparatively virtuously, the mistress of almost important men.

Sills would have given her a serious screen test, but she was still full of her failure. She not only did not ask him but brushed off his casual offer. The vice president of the little studio thought she could make it as a character woman, usually playing the other woman, and he persuaded her to another test. But that was bad too and she dismissed her chances for good.

Once she knew she did not and would not have it, a hardness that had not been there before set in. She started taking lovers on the side, not many but she made no bones about taking them, and they were all young. Suddenly all of the men who really excited her were young. She was thirty-one and most of her life she had been drawn to older men. Now she found herself attracted to men twenty-two, twenty, eighteen.

These were part of the syndrome of her restlessness, and did not assuage it: it had its roots not in desire but disappointment. She felt not simply a failure but a shadow: she scarcely believed in her own existence. As well as lovers, she began to take lessons of all sorts, guitar and painting and sculpture, and at all of them was a talented amateur. She sang, accompanying herself on the guitar, rather better than she did anything else, but she preferred to paint. She could lose herself in painting. She had the temperament and impetus of a real painter, but not the talent, and she knew it. She decided it was her curse to be semitalented at everything.

She had made up a dozen Octavia Daytons, but she had made none of them come true. She could not invent a self she could become; she continued to feel herself substanceless and without shape. She slipped into what she called "zero periods" for days and sometimes for weeks. In these, the handles on her life—her child, her home, her lessons, the bit work she still did—she could scarcely touch. Yet she had developed conscience to such a high degree, where Margaret was concerned, that her attention to her daughter never wavered. In those periods when she had to force it, it was more rigorous and more consistent because it was not spontaneous. She knew that Margaret knew the difference. Still, she was sure that she and Margaret were better friends than most mothers and preadolescent daughters.

Margaret started to menstruate when she was eleven. "It's the climate," a friend told Octavia. "Mine started when she was ten."

When she was thirteen, Margaret was fully developed and fully aware of boys. Octavia remembered her own youth and feared her daughter would be promiscuous: God knows she would come by it honestly.

She decided not to permit Margaret to date until she was fourteen, she would have preferred sixteen but knew she couldn't enforce that without storms. And she had to let Margaret go to junior high school parties, where boys and girls danced, and sometimes (she feared) were left much too much alone.

When she was in the eighth grade, she came home from a Halloween party with a look on her face that Octavia recognized at once.

"Did you let some boy kiss you at that party?"

"Oh no."

"Don't lie to me. You let him kiss you. Didn't you?"

"I—"

"I said don't lie to me. What else did you let him do?"

"What do you mean?"

"Did you let him touch you?"

"He had to touch me when he kissed me."

"Did he touch you here?" Octavia gestured.

"Oh no."

"Did he put his hand up your dress?"

"Mother!"

"I have to know these things, I have to protect you. I don't want you getting yourself pregnant, not yet I don't."

"I wouldn't do anything like that. What makes you think I'd do something like that?"

"Girls seldom plan to. Look. Let a boy kiss you if you like him, if you really like him. Don't let him do anything else."

"I won't."

Octavia laughed, with tenderness and exasperation. She knew she was bucking not only simple biology but heredity. "I know you will find that very difficult to believe, but I actually do know what I'm talking about."

"Yes, mum. I do believe you, honest."

Margaret was sixteen when Octavia decided, or became aware that she had decided, to direct her toward the Industry. It was her own lover of the moment, not her lover-protector-father but the illicit young one in which she was indulging herself, who brought the recognition to her. His name was Carlos.

Octavia was painting Margaret nude in her bedroom. She was absorbed in her brush work, thinking Margaret made a very satisfactory model, when the girl screamed a small scream, flung her arms across her breasts, and ran flat-footed through the doorway into her room that adjoined.

She turned from the easel and saw a handsome black-haired Mexican in the doorway.

"Damn you, you knock. Whoever gave you the idea you could come charging in like that?"

"I thought you did."

"Well my dear boy, don't you ever do it again, do you hear?"

"Who was that anyway? Marilyn Monroe?"

"She's pretty, isn't she?"

"You better believe it. You never did say who she was."

"I told you I had a daughter." She had not told him her daughter was physically grown though, and she had managed their earlier meetings so he had never seen Margaret. Her motives were simple: she had wanted to seem as young as possible.

"You're kidding," he said.

"Oh no."

"You ain't old enough to have a daughter like that."

"For that remark, I just may not shoot you."

"Geez, I wouldn't of said all that if I'd of known it was your daughter."

"That's all right. After all—there's no reason why my family shouldn't be as attractive as anybody else's, is there?"

"Not when you put it that way."

He thrust his arms toward her, and after a glance at the closed door to confirm her privacy, she came into them and surrendered for an instant. She felt pleasurably the slide of his palms upon her buttocks and then she pushed him away.

"That's enough for now, my boy. Restrain yourself. Carlos, is she *really* that, that pretty?"

"I wouldn't fool you, lover."

8

THREE WEEKS later, she came home from a weekend in Palm Springs with her protector, another director—and of less importance than the one who had gone before. It had been a trying three days, he had become abusively jealous and then impotent, and she was confronted nakedly with what she had been able to gloss before:

that the caliber of her men was on a down curve. She looked forward to a satisfying weep when she got home.

The light in the dining room showed through the window. She found her key in her purse, worked it into the keyhole, and found the door was not locked. Warn Margaret, she thought, and stepped inside.

Margaret was not in the room, she was probably asleep, and Octavia took off her shoes so as not to wake her.

She tiptoed to the hallway and heard Margaret tossing on her bed. I'll look in, she thought, and turned out the hall light, and opened the door to see, in the faint light from the street, her daughter on her back on the bed with a man between her knees. Neither saw nor heard her. She perceived the exact phase of frenzy in the thresh of bodies, recognized Carlos's dark head, and she heard Margaret moan. The moans were a sound without source: "Oh, oh, oh, oh," and then suddenly sharp *"Oh oh"* and belonging absolutely to Margaret.

Octavia did not scream, or seek a weapon to kill Carlos, or do any of the things that she would have expected to do, before.

What she did do was tiptoe into the living room, pick up her shoes, and tiptoe out and down the stairs. Then she put her shoes on, went to a bar in the block, nursed one bourbon for an hour, and went home. Margaret was asleep and alone.

She called Carlos to the apartment the next day when Margaret was in school.

She did not come out of the bedroom until she heard Carlos knock, come in, and call out to her. Then she walked straight through the doorway and said at once, "You son of a bitch if you touch her again I'll kill you."

His amazement was very creditable. "What you talking about, Tavvy?"

"I saw you last night. I *saw* you you bastard, and I still don't know why I didn't kill you then. I will next time, do you hear me?"

He understood she *had* seen him. His face lost color and he looked frightened, and his fright made him look much younger even than twenty-two.

"I'm sorry, Tavvy. It just happened. I swear I'm sorry, it just happened all at once. You know how those things happen."

"I know how they happen and I know how pretty boys can get themselves killed."

"I guess you want me to go away."

"No." She looked at him coolly. "You have your uses and I'll keep you around but don't you come near Margaret. Don't even come around when she's in the apartment. You better understand that."

"I understand, Tavvy."

"Carlos."

"Yes, Tavvy?"

"Was . . . Could you . . . Was she a virgin?"

"I swear I don't know, Tavvy. She could of been."

"Did you, wear anything? Tell me the truth, damn you."

"Tavvy, I . . ."

"So you didn't."

When he was gone, she took a single-edged razor blade, made a cut in her arm safely away from the vein, and held a sanitary napkin to the cut. She took the napkin to her gynecologist.

"Margaret's bleeding in the middle of her cycle. I think she ought to have a D. and C."

The gynecologist examined the napkin and raised his eyebrows at her. But she knew him to be a most helpful man if total decorum were maintained, and he proved his helpfulness again.

Octavia told Margaret only that the doctor felt she should be examined. Afterwards, her urge was to upbraid her daughter in a satisfying scene. Then she resolved to say nothing. She kept that resolution somewhat less than an hour after she brought Margaret back from the clinic.

In the apartment Margaret said, "What was that for?"

Octavia had decided on gentle aloofness and mystic intimations of reproach. The first words she said were, "That was to make damn well sure you aren't pregnant after that episode with Carlos, that was what it was for."

Margaret's face froze.

"I saw you." Octavia could not stop. "I saw him administering his tender attentions."

"You saw me."

"I came in and saw you and that Mexican inside you, that's what I saw."

Margaret's face changed.

"You stood there watching. All the time."

"Not all the time."

"You're my mother and you stood there watching."

"Don't you say that. Don't, you, say it. I did not *stand there* watching. I came in. And I saw you. And I got out because I thought that was best for you."

Margaret looked at Octavia.

Octavia slapped her.

"Don't you dare look at me like that. I DID NOT WATCH YOU, you bloody little whore."

"Please don't call me that."

"That's what you are, oh you've tasted it, and you'll be back for more, and you've turned into a bloody little whore."

"If I'm a whore maybe I got it from my mother."

Octavia slapped her again.

Margaret put her hand to her cheek. "I shouldn't have said that, I'm sorry."

"No you shouldn't have said it you little bitch, you are a bloody little bitch and I've done everything for you and now you turn into a whore."

"You don't look very nice when you talk like that."

"Get out of here." Octavia was screaming, all she had been holding back since she opened the door in the dark had started to rush out and she could not stop any of it. "Get out. Get out."

"All right," said Margaret.

Octavia screamed, and ran into her bedroom. She locked the door, dropped on the bed, and her mouth made sounds into the pillow. Her body shook hard, and harder, and harder still, and she thought, this is what it is to be hysterical. Then she passed into open relieved weeping, then somewhere in that she slipped into unconsciousness. She came back and knew it was much later: *I fainted,* she thought, then *no I just cried myself to sleep*. Then she remembered, and surrendered to total shame.

She had done things she could never do. Only she had done them. She would acknowledge error to her daughter, she would apologize totally. She should have offered understanding; she had hurled hysteria. She felt unjustified for the first time in her life.

She walked to the living room in her rumpled dress and stockinged feet.

"Margaret." Her voice was timid. There was no answer.

"Margaret?"

She went into Margaret's room, saw the folded white sheet of paper propped against a lampstand on the dresser, and picked it up.

"Mother–I have taken sixty dollars from your purse and got out like you said. Will pay you back when I can. I should not have said the thing I said to you and I am sorry for that. Margaret."

Octavia sat down on the bed. The paper fluttered to the floor. She stood and walked into the front room. She picked up the telephone and put it down.

She did not want to embarrass Margaret, Margaret was sure to come back in an hour or two, she should not call the police. Then she thought that she had left home for good only a year older than Margaret.

She picked up the phone, dialed Information and then the police, then a tired voice in Missing Persons said, "Okay, we'll put out an all-points on her."

She went down the outside stairway and to the sidewalk by the street. It was dusk; the street lights had not come on. She stepped from the sidewalk to the street. She looked at the dark gray strip of asphalt narrowing between the closing lines of green-topped palms, under the smog-dark and starless sky. Then she looked the other way. No difference, nothing. She had not really expected to see anything. She went back to the apartment.

Before midnight, she had to call her doctor. He came and gave her barbiturates. Margaret did not appear the next day, nor was she heard from, and the next night the doctor had to sedate her by injection.

He was about to hospitalize her when a telegram came. *"Am all right will write Margaret,"* it said. It was sent from San Bernardino.

Missing Persons advised San Bernardino and that was that as far as they were concerned.

Margaret's letter came the next day. She had a job, she said, she was fine. She would come to see her mother in a few months if her mother wanted her to.

Octavia was dressing to drive to San Bernardino when she collapsed. She had been feeling warm but thought it entirely emotional: suddenly her legs would not hold her and she was very hot. She fell on the floor, then crawled to and pulled herself upon the bed. When she was strong enough she called her doctor. He came, decided it was virus pneumonia seriously complicated by shock, and put her at once in hospital. Three days later she was able to write Margaret care of General Delivery, San Bernardino. It was an imploring letter: Margaret answered with the address of the grocery store where she worked. But it was three weeks before Octavia got out of the hospital and a week after that before she was able to drive.

9

SHE found it with only a little trouble: Vito's Grocery, on a side street in the rind of San Bernardino near the highway.

She sat in her car a moment. She felt very cold and found she had to gather courage. Through her window she stared across the close low roofs of the city to the dark mountains peaked in white in the clear washed blue sky. They increased her fear, she did not know why. She shivered. Then she got out and slammed the car door. She heard her own high heels on the walk, as though from a certain distance. Then she pushed open the screen door.

Margaret was checking items and ringing amounts on a cash register. She did not see Octavia, who stood for a moment just inside the door. She did not see her until the customer was gone. Octavia came to the checkstand.

Margaret's face lighted, and she smiled, then she looked timid and embarrassed.

"Hello, Mom."

"Hello, darling."

Awkwardly they kissed.

"Are you well now, Mom?"

"I guess. Are you all right?"

"I'm fine."

"I've been so worried about you." Her hands were ice. She swallowed and flicked her lips with her tongue. "I'm so sorry. I can't tell you how sorry I am."

"It's all right now."

"Please. I'm so sorry."

"It's all right Mama. Really."

She was relieved to find she would not cry after all. "Well, let's go home."

"Mama. There's something I've got to tell you."

"Oh? Tell me then."

Margaret looked at the canned tomato section on the shelves to her left.

"I'm married."

Octavia looked at the same shelf of tomatoes: Del Monte, she noted. Next to it were canned peaches, then pears, then instant coffee jars.

Try it now, she thought, maybe now you can talk. She said: "Married?"

"Yes, Mama."

"Who are you married to, Margaret?"

"Vito."

Octavia looked again at the bald-headed and moustached Italian who was now looking across the store openly at them.

"Vito," said Octavia. "I see."

"Vito," Margaret called. "Come meet my mother."

Vito came to the checkstand.

"Vito," said Margaret nervously. "This is my mother."

"Glad to see you," said Vito.

His brown eyes looked at her directly and keenly. The muscles in his face were firm and tight: Octavia thought it a hard face and maybe a cruel one, then he smiled, and she felt almost easy.

She said, "How are you, Vito?"

"Vito gave me this job the day after, the first day I came to San Bernardino," Margaret said.

"That was very kind of him."

"Vito is a very kind man," Margaret said.

"I'm sure he is," said Octavia. "I'm sure he is."

"I love Vito."

"Margaret. You go get a soda or something while your mother and I have a talk."

Margaret glanced at him, and left at once.

"Mister—" said Octavia.

"Stefano."

"Mister Stefano, you have been kind to my daughter. I am going to assume you wish her well, and I am going to assume further that you want to do what is best for her."

Under his clear brown gaze, she felt herself falter.

"Don't be scared, Mrs. Dayton," he said, and smiled again. "I'm not going to hurt you."

She understood completely how a girl raised without one could make him her father.

"Mr. Stefano. Margaret is sixteen years old."

"I know that."

"I want her home, Mr. Stefano."

"That might not be so easy." He spoke to her gently, as though explaining something difficult to a child. "We got married in city hall."

"Not in the church?"

"Not in the church." He said it reluctantly and she knew she had won something.

"We have to have this annulled, Mr. Stefano. I say this in all appreciation and gratitude for your kindness."

"It might be best if Margaret was married. You think of that?"

"She's—you mean she's pregnant?"

"No. I don't mean that. I just mean she's a woman, sixteen years old or not."

"I, see what you mean. I still, feel quite certain, it's best she return to me."

"You want to ask Margaret?"

"No. She'd probably want to stay."

He nodded.

"It's not what she wants, it's what she ought to do," said Octavia.

She felt the edge of his look again, and then saw him nod.

"All right." His voice had authority and decision, as did the planes of his face. "An American girl, maybe you're right. I think you are right. Take her home, Mrs. Dayton."

"Thank you."

In her experience, strength joined to generosity was not absolutely rare but it was rare enough: she was grateful.

"You let me have a little talk with Margaret now, Mrs. Dayton, then you take her home."

She kissed a worn brown cheek and fled.

10

OCTAVIA was not going to let Margaret's last year in Franklin High School go by default. "I suppose you can figure you're a big girl now," she told her daughter. "But you're going to finish school whatever you do."

"I want to, Mom."

Now she let Margaret date almost as she would, and asked only ritual questions. Margaret decorously gave her no visible reason for distress. Octavia suspected she was receiving certain biological attentions from time to time, but said nothing. Margaret was not a virgin and she *had* been married. Decorum, now, was really all that could be expected, and was in fact all Octavia asked.

The relationship between the two of them was warm, perhaps warmer than it had ever been, and stable. Octavia was convinced she wanted to be only a "good mother" to Margaret, whatever that was. And a former protector, the head of the small studio, now an independent, gave her a real job as receptionist. She had accepted herself, she felt, and she studied the possible courses for Margaret.

The events that followed Carlos's sudden entrance upon mother painting, daughter nude, had obliterated the first thought it produced in Octavia. Now that thought returned fully formed and strong: Margaret should be an actress in motion pictures. A star. The word no longer awed her. She understood now that a "movie star" was a manufactured product, most but not all of the time the end result of the skills of others. She understood too that most of the factory had been dismantled. But not all. Not quite. Though the studios were past their great days, though they no longer produced stars on an assembly line, though the Industry lived off the big names it had fabricated one and two decades before, something remained. The plant had not stopped entirely: it still made one or two stars a year. Octavia was convinced Margaret was material for it.

She was certain this conviction came from Margaret's astonishing body: in the coldest appraisal, Octavia thought it the most extraordinary body she had ever seen and she felt Margaret's face was pretty and expressive enough not to fail it. Octavia was not aware of something else: Margaret was surrogate for her own ambitions which she thought long extinguished.

"How would you like to be in pictures?" she asked Margaret one Sunday afternoon.

"Gee I don't know, I never thought about it, I guess I'd kind of like it. Is there anybody that wouldn't like to be a movie star?"

"I didn't say star, I just said in pictures. They are not the same thing, believe me."

"I suppose I'd like that all right too, just being in them I mean. But you know I can't act, they never even gave me a part in the class play."

Octavia said a very succinct word.

"Mother!"

They both laughed. Since the marriage, annulment, and those events that had led up to them, Octavia no longer felt committed to parental perfection: she relaxed. The job had been done. It could have been somewhat better, she thought, and it could have been a great deal worse. Now she had another job.

"I think we ought to have a good talk with Hal," she said. Hal was her protector, a still-working director who had known much better years.

"But Mother, what on earth makes you think I could do anything at all that way?"

Octavia made a rising sweeping gesture with her hand that indicated all of Margaret. "That," she said. "All that."

Margaret blushed.

"Walk around for me, dear," Hal said.

Margaret walked around the room on high heels, her cheeks deeply colored. Watching her, Octavia was awed at the sexuality her daughter incarnated. She had dressed Margaret for impact, and had done it skillfully, but seeing her daughter, quite suddenly, as Hal must see her, she was more than impressed.

She watched the long line of movement that started at Margaret's waist and went to her ankles.

"Ah-hah," Hal said. "Ah-hah. It may be a very good idea."

"What should we do?"

"Do?"

"Should I send her to the Pasadena Playhouse, or UCLA, or L.A. State, or where?"

"You send her anywhere like that you ought to be shot."

"Why? What do you mean?"

"I mean that formal training bushwah would play hell with her pizazz. Pizazz is what she's got. If you mess with it, you might kill it."

"She's got to have some kind of preparation."

"Send her to one of those places where they never heard about dramatic values and where they just teach her to walk and talk. That won't hurt her. I know a couple."

"Do you think she has a good chance, Hal?"

"Nobody has a good chance, you know that. The biggest part of it is being in the right place at the right time. But if her pizazz comes through on camera, yes, she does have *a* chance."

She sent Margaret to a school for adolescent actors that Hal recommended. She knew that the school was low-level, but she checked elsewhere, too, and satisfied herself that it could at least teach Margaret to walk and to talk.

"I know a couple of agents who specialize in young people," Hal told her. "I'll be glad to line her up."

"I want Nelson Glassgow to handle her."

"Nelson Glassgow? He'll never touch her."

"Won't he?" said Octavia.

On the telephone Glassgow was abrupt to her, then all at once relenting and almost kind. She wondered why. She was suddenly intrigued at the prospect of meeting him quite apart from the desire to make use of him for Margaret. She tried to pull together as well as she could the strands of the Glassgow myth: he picked out the sharp talents before anyone else identified them; representation by Glassgow was a guarantee of a kind of success; he did not care about money because women not his clients supported him; he was a literary genius who was too lazy to write; he had been a big professor at a big university in the East and had been kicked out for knocking up twelve co-eds in one year; his only office was a pet hospital.

If a small part of it were true he was a very interesting man, she thought. And the part about the pet hospital was certainly true, for that was where she was to meet him, with Margaret.

Inside the hospital, she wrinkled her nose from the strange new smell. Her hand on Margaret's elbow, she worked her way to where they had been directed: stacks of orange crates that made a kind of cubicle. At the end of one stack she stopped, and stood indecisively. A man suddenly materialized at the end of the stack.

"Mrs. Dayton? I'm Nelson Glassgow."

"How do you do?"

He was not an aesthetically handsome man. He was fairly tall, six feet and no more she guessed, he was moderately slender, he had heavy black hair, a lean face, and a prominent nose. The face was mobile and showed a snapping vitality, even in those brief movements of his body that she saw, there was a rapid urgency. His collar was loose, his tie was pulled to one side, and there was an ink smudge on the line of his jaw. Octavia thought he was one of the most attractive men she had ever seen.

He was antagonistic in conversation. "Do you want her to be caged? Like that?" He jabbed his finger toward a sleeping ocelot. And later, suddenly, after it seemed she had almost won him over, he said brutally to Margaret:

"Take off your clothes. I want to see what I'm merchandising."

She made her own bluff. "Do as Mr. Glassgow says, dear. He is Hollywood's most distinguished agent."

She saw he was surprised.

"That won't really be necessary," he said with sudden and surprising gentleness. "I wanted you to get an idea of what you can expect." To Octavia, quite differently, he said, "All right. If I don't handle her someone else will. I'll get out the contracts."

"I'll have my lawyer look at them tomorrow," Octavia said, and felt that she had at last made one real score.

In her car, on the way home, Margaret said, "He's kind of funny."

"He has a big reputation."

"He's still funny. I like him."

"I guess I like him, too."

11

THAT was how it had started, and it had started a long time ago. Now, in her room in a tourist hotel in Mykonos, Greece, Octavia was remembering not that first meeting but another. She had an enduring affection for Nelson Glassgow, and a physical pull toward him which, too, had lasted.

The number of different affections and attractions which one person could hold at once was unlimited, she thought. So were their shapes. It was perfectly possible to be in love with two men at once, or three, or four. The shape of each feeling would be different, and they would not be equally strong, but they could exist at the same time. Nobody liked to admit this, but it was true.

She was still fuzzy from the Nembutal. She had been badly worried the night before. She feared for Margaret, and she had gone to sleep only with a second capsule. Now she was so slack she almost had to summon concern by an act of will.

She went into the bath, took a hot shower and then a cold, and felt clearheaded and sharp as she dressed. Worry settled upon her immovably, and she felt relieved: without it, she would have felt that she did not exist.

BOOK 4

NELSON GLASSGOW

1

Glassgow heard the lock jump as he closed the door, and he started down the hall with the heat of Octavia's flesh still in his palm. She still touched the nerve: he would never deny it. The days unseized were a stronger weld between them than the single achieved encounter: they were a wistful mutual loss: what joys we could have had. And so on. Gone forever. Nothing was gone forever. Glassgow walked ahead in the open passageway of the hotel.

He had bases to touch, he was a man who gravitated to the strange and strangely placed, and now these might serve him. He found one such in a hotel room with its door open. This one was running a vacuum cleaner.

He saw her profiled: in dirty white cotton dress, bent over the vacuum, white handkerchief tying back straight black hair. Her brown face was dried to make age unfixable: she could have been forty, or sixty-five.

He stepped into the door. "Sweetheart," he said. "Nicola."

The vacuum stopped, she straightened and turned, and she smiled with teeth and gaps in not quite regular alternation.

"Swee-hart," she said, and she giggled, for with him she was coy.

She had the words of English, they all had the words of English. He had talked to her out of true interest, and had flirted with her and given her money out of a desire to be liked, which swam close to the surface of his arrogance and which he felt to be obscene. Also he felt she might be useful.

Now he touched her chin with his forefinger: he had started to slap her behind but decided not. "Nicola my sweetheart."

She shrilled a laugh, tooth and gap. "Swee-hart."

(What embers in that dried head, what hopes. Regrettably he could offer only consolation and a jest. I would if I could, baby. Really I would.)

What he did give her was a bill. "You love me?"

"Lav you."

"You know the beautiful young lady? Beautiful. Lady."

She knew.

"Do you know where she is?"

She did not know.

"Did you see her two nights ago? See her. Two. Nights." Fingers.

She hadn't.

He sighed. "Swee-hart," she said. He patted her hip and departed.

Next the bar.

He had already talked once to Narchos. Narchos was to have been listening for him. Narchos wore French moustaches and a Western bar jacket, white. Glassgow wished him more exotic: he was grateful though that he was a linguist.

Glassgow paid for the resinated wine with a large bill and left the change on the counter. "Did you hear anything?"

"I think the man, Kimon, you know him, he has a café. I think that man has something to tell you."

Importantly and conspiratorially: oh Christ he wants to make a production.

"When will I find him?" said Glassgow importantly and conspiratorially.

"Today, tomorrow. He comes in his place, he comes out."

Glassgow put another bill on the bar and left, as conspiratorially as he could.

The hotel was a series of multiple, modern bungalows built on rock very near the sea. Glassgow walked between the bungalows, through an arch in the low stone wall around them, down a wide packed strip of dirt. He turned right, away from the sea, and started through the white hallways that were the streets. He passed open doorways and saw through them Greek women chopping vegetables, he stepped carefully to avoid donkey dung on the solid white stone, he passed shops with woven shirts displayed, and he passed a small grocery. He came to a very tiny square that was more of a clearing. On one side was Kimon's Café. Mr. Kimon wore a white shirt and a three-inch wide, hand-painted necktie. His face showed his pride was his cunning: said it: *don't you wish you knew what I knew*. He spoke English rapidly and badly.

Yes, he had seen the women. The woman in the pictures and the other woman. It should be worth something (Glassgow gave him a bill). They had looked in several windows on the street, and had gone in and out of shops. They had gotten into an automobile driven by a bad man with a broken nose (Glassgow recognized Harry). The car had driven away. He had not seen them again. When had it been? It had been (counting on fingers) four days ago.

Two days before she was missed.

Glassgow thanked him and left.

A headshake too from the bloody aproned man at the fish stall where the piers began. The smell of the harbor, never absent, came over him amplified and huge: marine life dead and alive counterpointed by rotting wood, old canvas, potatoes, flour, wine, human excrement, diesel exhaust and other perfumes.

On the south side of the harbor was a very long street. Along it were many open air cafés, at this hour most tables empty, and many shops. Glassgow wandered in and out of them and learned nothing. He checked, again, at the offices of three shipping companies and learned nothing. Then he walked back to the hotel. From its one telephone, at the desk, he called Sidney Tate with the news that he had no news.

Feeling light-headed and unbodied from sleeplessness, he moved to his bungalow and up the stairs, each step a separate effort observed from a distance.

His key missed the keyhole twice and then found it. He opened the door with the deliberation of a drunk or very tired man and stepped into the room.

He felt himself inside a hallucination: *is this me? Of course not.* He had made up this weary Nelson Glassgow, this man looking for that woman had nothing to do with *him*. A mistake had been made. For the time it took to close his eyes and open them, he thought he might disintegrate that Glassgow with a breath and make a new one. It seemed quite possible.

He did not believe any of it, any of it which had brought him to Mykonos, Greece. It had all happened to somebody else.

2

Nelson Glassgow had come to Southern California in the late 1940's, not to found a career but to drown one. To him, dutifully distended with received wisdom, that patch of earth was the world's great delta of Nada: it pleased him to fancy at the time that he was choosing the moral equivalent of rational suicide. Later, and not much later, he had to acknowledge that this was megalomania. At no time was he really a serious candidate for self-liquidation.

What he wanted was its exact opposite: a total suspension of value, a perfect liberation from the responsibility of responsible action. A Camusesque suicide, and that was the only kind he could consider, carried exactly those responsibilities of choice which he wished to reject.

In Southern California, he did not find what he did not know he wanted. He found something else.

A girl years younger than himself had pointed him towards it with one unambiguous statement.

"I would do just anything for an A."

He still remembered the day, and well, with confused but durable affection. In shirt sleeves, he had been sitting before the gray metal desk. On the desk top was a rubber-banded sheaf of ungraded papers. At one side of the desk stood the girl, whose name he had forgotten a month after, but whose shape, satisfactorily composed and artfully displayed, was to remain clearly in his mind fifteen years later. Not her face; he remembered that as interesting but could not see it. He did remember she had dark blonde hair and wore gold-rimmed glasses. The glasses were her most provocative feature.

"I would do just anything for an A," she had said, and looked at him.

That was when he had been a college English teacher. Not *quite* a professor. But he had taught in a college classroom, and he had been happy—happy?—there. But what good was happiness et cetera. That was another time the malignancy had gotten him, and it got him often. It spurred and scored from inside, and it stood outside and mocked and appraised. At the same time. He had been a good Sartrist then. Man makes himself. The will creates its own values and moves toward them. But that was before he recognized the inside-outside devil that disrupted the handiwork of his will. That devil was his most intimate self and hence his worst enemy.

The day the girl asked for her A, Glassgow was a half-time instructor in English at a state university in the Middle West. Not a teaching assistant. He thus had more status: he made $1,500 a year instead of $900.

He had come to the university from Columbia, where he had taken an M.A., on the strength of a friendship between his major professor and the chairman of the English department. He had gone to Columbia straight from the army, where he had been regimental clerk and had never seen combat, and where safety had left him feeling guilty and incomplete. His headquarters had been in Paris at the end of and immediately after the war, and he had attended, without credit, two courses in French literature at the Sorbonne. After he was separated, he spent three weeks at his home in a small Illinois town, then went to Columbia, then to the university in the Midwest. After two years there, he had completed his course work on the doctorate: he needed only to pass the comprehensive and write the dissertation, which meant he was halfway home. He was well into his dissertation: it had started as a seminar paper, had been intensified and expanded for his master's thesis, and was going to be intensified and expanded again for the Ph.D. He got great pleasure from the mileage he had squeezed out of it: he felt he was at least winning points from the system. The paper was on Sartre's influence on the American novel in the late nineteen-forties.

He could worry it into a dissertation in three months. His only problem was the medieval and anachronistic torture of the comprehensive examination. Two of seven candidates had passed it the semester before, and now he had it to look forward to. He prepared for it and taught two sections of *Understanding Literature,* a course required for graduation. On that possibly fated day, he was lecturing on *Heart of Darkness,* and he had the incident with Litvak which, perhaps, started it all.

Litvak was a sullen-faced, dogged young man who bore his imperceptions like a banner. His hand went into the air, stayed there, and Glassgow stopped. "Yes, Mr. Litvak?"

"How do you know that's what that means?" Litvak said. "I don't see anything in it that makes it mean that. I don't see that the hippo meat has to be anything but stinking old hippo meat."

"The story is about corruption, Mr. Litvak. The hippo meat spoils, which is to say it becomes corrupt, and then it suggests and prepares for the discovery of the corruption of Kurtz which is to come."

"I don't see that at all. I don't see that it's anything at all but stinking old meat."

Glassgow, fighting for sweetness, explained again.

"I don't see that," said Litvak.

Glassgow abandoned sweetness. "In the words of another great artist, Mr. Litvak, if you don't know what it is, you better not mess with it."

"I don't think you are answering my question, professor."

Glassgow felt the devil jabbing.

"If you come around after class, Mr. Litvak, I will draw you a picture." The jabs came harder and Glassgow knew he was going to do something. "It is against my academic philosophy to let retarded students slow a class unduly."

The class laughed. Litvak flushed; his fat face looked sullen and righteously miserable. Glassgow felt ashamed, and triumphant. It was a cheap and unfair exploitation of classroom power. Yet the jerk had it coming.

He finished his lecture, remorseful and annoyed at Litvak's wounded, pouting misery. He would have to make it up to him somehow. After class, a knock came on his office door, he called "Come in," and a dark blonde girl with gold-rimmed glasses entered. He recognized her as a face in a rear row; now he noted she had an interesting, attractive body.

"I have a problem, Mr. Glassgow."

"Ah?"

"I need an A in this course."

"You do have a problem, Miss—"

"Garson. Karen Garson. I need it to graduate. If I don't get it, I won't have the grade points."

"Well. There isn't really much I can do. I guess you'll just make it or you won't, isn't that right? About all I can do is suggest you study hard."

"I don't know if I can study hard enough," she said.

He looked up at her.

"I would just do anything for an A," she said.

And there it was.

He looked straight in front of him and tapped a pencil on the side of the desk. "An A. Well. Let's have a look." He reached into a drawer and took out his grade. "Miss ah Garson wasn't it. Right now"–he turned her grades out with his finger–"you figure at a good strong B." The real figure was C. "So you need an A to graduate."

"I have to have it," she said.

He looked up at her and their eyes met. He was still under thirty, and she was more than twenty.

"Perhaps we can work out an extra project of some sort."

"That would be wonderful."

"Perhaps an extra paper or something."

"Oh, I'd love that. I really would. I'd just be so obliged."

"Tell you what, I've got another appointment now and I'm snowed the rest of the day. Now I have an evening office hour, so why don't you just drop in then? About eight. I think we can work something out."

"Oh, I hope we can."

They did. Two days later he got a call from the secretary of the English department. "Mr. Ball would like to see you right away."

"There's this young man Litvak," Alex Ball said to him. He did not look at Glassgow but at a point in space just forward of the desk.

"I have to tell you he's got a case. I *was* a little hard on him."

Ball cleared his throat. "That isn't exactly. Ah. This is, about something else."

"Oh?"

"Litvak says he saw you out with a young lady, ah, Wednesday night."

"I do sometimes go out with young ladies. If they have enough money to take me."

Ball gave the point in space serious attention. "He says this young lady is in your own course."

"He seems to be a talkative young man."

"He said ah he says you took her to a roadhouse."

"I didn't know the word roadhouse was still active in the language."

"Mmmm ah, he says the two of you had several drinks there."

"On my salary?"

"He says," Ball cleared his throat and studiously avoided meeting Glassgow's eyes. "He says after the two of you finished drinking you took her to one of the cabins in the back. He says he saw the two of you ah enter and the lights go out and remain that way for some time and then he saw you come out."

"That reminds me of a story, Alex. Punch line is 'Nevair to know.' Do you know it?"

"This is serious, Nelson. Now I have to ask you, I don't want to dignify his charges but it's part of my job, you appreciate that, I have to ask you if it's true."

He thought: if I have learned one thing in twenty-eight years it is: always plead not guilty. He said: "Absolutely and categorically not."

Relief showed on Ball's charitable, sagging face. "You formally deny it then."

"I deny it most formally, absolutely, and categorically."

"Thank goodness." Ball shucked his official manner with heavy relief. "I certainly thought you had better judgment than to whore around with your students. What got into this punk Litvak?"

"I gave him a hard time the other day. Not hard enough for this though."

"Well he's got no corroboration so you've got no problem. I had to go through the formality of questioning you without telling you that, of course. The little bastard did put it in writing, though, so I'm afraid you're in for a full-dress confrontation of the all-university ethics committee. It won't be pleasant but it won't harm you permanently. I'll be with you all the way." He looked keenly at Glassgow and Glassgow knew that he knew all that he wanted to know. "Just don't change your story on me."

"No story to change. He's a little liar."

"Of course he is," said Alex. "He's a vindictive lying little bastard."

That was on a Friday. The meeting with the ethics committee came on the following Thursday, which was swift turning for the wheels of academe. The committee consisted of three full professors, elected, and the president or his representative, ex-officio. This case was not worth the president's time or that of the dean of the university, Glassgow noted. The president's representative today was Cowper, the dean of arts and sciences. Goody Cowper, the English teaching assistants and instructors called him. His teaching field had been early American literature. He was in his middle fifties, was plump and short, and had an infinite and quivering capacity for moral indignation. Much of this was directed at overt manifestations of heterosexuality. Years before, Cowper had tried to remove *For Whom the Bell Tolls* from a freshman reading list and the instructor who put it there from the university. The faculty had beaten his brains out on that one, and he had been in very bad odor for a long time. However, he had been most sympathetic and understanding in the case of a history instructor caught in a police trap, and he had recovered a certain amount of cartel. He was a very useful man to uphold the banner of morality before legislative investigating committees and lady fascists beyond the menopause. He had a splendid platform face, formed by the heavy pursing of the mouth into a stern and infantile moue, and by the downward pull of fuzzy eyebrows. He looked (someone said) like a year-old baby in chief justice's robes.

He fixed Glassgow with his best hanging-judge-of-the-nursery stare: anyone feckless enough to be accused–it declared–was worse than guilty. Glassgow gazed back, he hoped innocently.

The hearing was at two in the afternoon in a seminar room. Glassgow was seated at one end of the table and Lawrence, the chairman, at the other. Cowper sat on the chairman's left, Stornes and Broncati on the right. Lawrence was in philosophy, Stornes in political science, and Broncati in foreign languages.

Lawrence had a grave, warm face which could turn puckish or awesome instantly. Today he had it set in professional aloofness. So, too, was his voice.

He said: "I think perhaps we might get started. The purpose of our meeting as you know is to consider certain, charges, made against Mr. Glassgow. These charges are contained in a letter from a student named Richard Litvak. Litvak is a student in Mr. Glassgow's Understanding Literature, a general education course I believe. He charges Mr. Glassgow with having relations with another student, a girl, in the same class.

"Now there is no prescribed procedure for a hearing of this sort and I think we might move right into it with a reading of Litvak's letter. Is this satisfactory to you, Mr. Glassgow?"

"Entirely." Glassgow inclined his head.

"Very well. The Litvak letter is addressed to Professor Ball as chairman of the department of English. 'Dear Doctor Ball: On the evening of Wednesday, April 11th, while passing the side door of South Hall, I saw Mr. Glassgow and a young lady emerge from the side door of South Hall. I happened to be there as I was returning from the library about eight o'clock, having prepared my extensive university assignments which I normally do at the library [Glassgow saw Stornes and Broncati smile at each other] and as stated I saw Mr. Glassgow and the young lady emerge from the door. I recognized her as a fellow student in the same class as myself taught by Mister Glassgow and knowing this is improper I considered it my duty to follow for evidence to present said evidence to authorities. They got into yellow convertible which was property of young lady and drove on highway toward roadhouse known as The Dove. They sat very close together and after stopping and parking outside roadhouse appeared to be kissing and so on.' "

(Lawrence's lips moved upward slightly; he quickly restrained them.)

" 'They entered roadhouse and sat at table and I entered bar where could not be seen and observed for evidence which believed to be my duty and which had no choice but to regretfully perform. They had several drinks of alcoholic beverage and Mister Glassgow put hand under table and appeared to be quotation fooling around end of quotation.' "

(A tiny and smothered explosion took place at the end of the table. Broncati lowered his head and raised it instantly, his face fiercely austere. Lawrence smiled, gently, and then went on.)

" 'They had many alcoholic drinks which I knew is against college regulations to have with students. Parenthesis Naturally I was forced to order drink in bar to continue investigation but did not, underlined, drink parenthesis closed. After more quote fooling around unquote which made them get very excited, Mister Glassgow having hand under table and kissing student twice he went to desk where cabins rented and came back and accompanying student went out in back. Following from a distance because it was my duty, they went into cabin and turned on lights but I could not see anything and turned off lights and it was dark.

" 'I could not naturally hang around in back but returned to bar and watched and after about two hours they came out and got in yellow convertible and departed.

" 'This is a truthful report which I swear to be the truth and feel it my painful duty to inform authorities. Very truly yours, Richard Litvak.'

"There is a postscript," Lawrence said. " 'Had to order several drinks to continue investigation but'—and this is capitalized—'DID NOT DRINK.'

"That ends the letter," said Lawrence. His face was masterfully incommunicative.

Glassgow looked at the other faces: Broncati's was sternly devoted to duty except for his mouth, which twitched upward uncontrollably. Stornes's was smiling, candidly and openly, but with no undue amusement. Goody Cowper glowered and his lips made a small trumpet.

One certainly for, one certainly against, and two undecided, Glassgow thought. It would depend on Lawrence. Which was, after all, the way he had figured it at the outset.

Lawrence said, "We have a letter from the chairman of the English department. If the committee has no objections, I will read it and make it part of the record and we will have completed the reading of all written communications. Does the committee have any objections?"

The committee had none.

Lawrence read: "Members of the University Committee on Ethics and Professional Practices, G. L. Lawrence, Chairman. Gentlemen: I have discussed this matter with both Litvak and Mister Glassgow and, in fulfillment of my own responsibilities as chairman of the English department, I have made my own investigation of Litvak's charges.

"They are uncorroborated and in my considered judgment, untrue. I have recommended to the dean of student activities that an intensive psychiatric examination of Litvak is strongly desirable. This letter, of course, is in no sense an attempt to influence the judgment of the committee, but is for your information only. Sincerely, A. M. Ball, Chairman, department of English."

Well bless you Alex, thought Glassgow. Above and beyond.

"I must point out that this is not evidence at all in any legal sense," said Lawrence. "And it should have absolutely no bearing upon our own investigation and findings. However, our proceedings, while hardly informal, are nevertheless somewhat more flexible than those of a court of law, and I am going to accept the letter as part of the file on this case, if the committee has no objection."

None, and a point for our side, Glassgow thought.

"Now this committee has such a small corpus of procedural precedent before it that it is creating precedent almost every time it meets," said Lawrence. "We have examined such written communications as bear upon the, matter, under consideration. Perhaps our next step is to hear directly, from the, principals. I have Mr. Litvak waiting in another room. If it is your pleasure, we can now call upon him."

Bring him in, the committee murmured. "Bring the boy in!" trumpeted Goody Cowper, and glared at the defendant, if defendant was the word.

It was the word, thought Glassgow.

Lawrence left the room and came back with Litvak. Under the black-rimmed glasses the boy's face was frightened and much whiter than Glassgow knew it. Looking at him, Glassgow could feel no anger but only commiseration. Poor little bastard, he's so scared and he wishes he'd never gotten into this, and I wish he never had either.

Lawrence put him in a chair at one side of the seminar table, halfway between himself and Glassgow.

"Would you identify yourself, please."

"Sir?"

"Would you . . ."

"Oh. Richard S. Litvak."

"And you're a student at this university?"

"Yes, sir."

Litvak's voice quavered and Glassgow could see the muscles in his arms working. He was probably clenching and unclenching his hands under the table.

"Mr. Litvak, your letter has been read to members of this committee. Serious charges, I must say, extremely serious, are made in it. It is the function of this committee to evaluate those charges. I must tell you you are fully responsible for those charges and if they are found to be frivolous, unfounded or irresponsible, you yourself face quite grave charges. Is that clear?"

The white face bobbed. "Yessir."

"Very well. Do you wish to affirm again the contents of your letter?"

"Sir?"

"I mean do you wish to stand by it?"

"Oh. Yessir."

Lawrence was not making things easy for Litvak, which was as it should be, and yet Glassgow's sympathies were directed to the frightened boy who was now (perhaps unwillingly) committed to Glassgow's destruction.

Lawrence nodded curtly. "Now you say you saw Mr. Glassgow and the student coming out of a door in South Hall. What door is that?"

"East door. It's in the letter."

"Will you please speak louder, Mr. Litvak?"

"East door." Litvak apparently realized he had almost shouted it and cowered.

"And what time was this?"

"It was after I left the library. I guess it was about seven-thirty maybe."

"You say eight in your letter."

"Seven-thirty is right."

Lawrence frowned slightly. "The two are not the same, Mr. Litvak. Which *do* you mean?"

"Between seven-thirty and eight. I guess it was closer to eight."

"I see." Lawrence would have made a superb attorney, Glassgow thought. His attitude was clear, and firm: charges had been made against a faculty member by a student. They would be scrupulously explored, and if found to be true, the faculty member would be held accountable. The burden of proof, however, was entirely upon the accuser. So was the responsibility for convincing the committee. All presumptions were on the side of the accused. They were all against the accuser. He could have asked for nothing fairer, thought Glassgow. And yet he felt the curious sympathy for Litvak.

"And what do you wish to say you saw there?"

"Well. Well then they got in this cream-colored convertible."

"Are you sure about the color?"

"I guess so. I *think* it was cream-colored."

"You say in your letter it was yellow."

"Well, a color like that, yellow or cream-colored, something like that."

"You're quite sure?"

"It was something *like* that."

Lawrence's face expressed disapproval, and Glassgow knew he intended it to. He led Litvak through a rehearsal of what the boy had said in the letter, and Litvak floundered and sprawled as he followed. Glassgow listened to him tell the truth with such confusion, contradiction, and uncertainty that the truth became unbelievable. There were moments when Glassgow disbelieved him, and Glassgow *knew* it was so.

By the time he was describing what happened at The Dove, he had lost all credibility.

"You say you saw improprieties committed at the table?"

"Well. Mr. Glassgow kissed her and then put his hand under her dress it looked like, and then she leaned back and closed her eyes and—"

"I think that'll be sufficient Mr. Litvak. You say you witnessed improprieties."

Jerked by questions, Litvak finished his story. He contradicted himself three times on the angle of vision from his position at the bar, and he admitted he consumed part of the drinks he ordered.

"Does that mean you lied in your letter?"

"Oh no sir."

"Oh? Now how is that? In your letter you say in capital letters DID NOT DRINK." Lawrence's voice sounded the capitals, with a faint hint of irony. "Now you say you did. You have to be lying one time or another, don't you?"

"I didn't. I meant I just drank a little because I had to. I didn't mean to lie or anything."

"I see. Now was there anyone with you who can corroborate your story?"

"Cor–"

"Who can back you up. Who saw the same thing–"

"I. I guess not."

"So it's your word against Mr. Glassgow's, isn't that right?"

"I guess it is."

"That'll be all, Litvak. I *think* you'd better wait in that other room."

Litvak fled.

Glassgow felt genuine compassion for him; still no one had *asked* him to write that fool letter. Now he knew he had won the committee simply because Litvak had lost them. All he had to do was complete the formalities by denying everything and he would be officially exonerated and Litvak would be out of the university. So, too, would Glassgow be, he suspected, but not immediately.

"Would you mind having a seat, Glassgow?" said Lawrence affably.

"Not at all." He sat in the chair.

"Well," Lawrence said diffidently and gently. "You heard Mr. Litvak . . . Is it true that you had improper relations with a student?"

"No," said Glassgow.

Then he was aware of–rather than felt–the jabbing. And he saw it.

Before some clear interior eye, there suddenly appeared a Doré woodcut from Dante. A body lay flat on the ground. Its naked rump extended grotesque and tempting into space. A three-tined, deep-thrust pitchfork rose out of its flesh. Leaning on the handle of the pitchfork was a short pot-bellied devil who stared on the carcass and grinned, devilishly. The face of the carcass stared outward at the beholder: it was pained, polite and curious. It was the face of Nelson Glassgow.

To the committee, Glassgow said, "No, I had no relations of any kind with her."

Lawrence nodded, faintly but approvingly.

Something flipped the woodcut off: another came on. Now the pot-bellied devil on the up-rumped carcass had his own arms raised and his finger pointing downward, a gesture to a line of sibling devils watching gleefully from the background. Glassgow's face was discreetly uncomfortable, most courteously inquiring.

"Mr. Glassgow, did you have any kind of personal relationship, I mean a quite proper one, with the, student, in question which might, say, have been misinterpreted?"

Again the picture flipped. Now the devil had leaped into space to throw all of his weight on the fork. His stubby widespread legs planted at right angles to the handle. Glassgow's face was slightly more pained, but self-consciously decorous.

Glassgow said, "I had no personal relationship with her of any kind." Glassgow's eyes fell upon Goody Cowper, whose face was, quite suddenly, remarkably like the face of the devil.

Lawrence nodded understandingly. "One last question and I'm sure you appreciate I must put it to you as a formality. Have you committed any breach of ethics, of any kind, with the student in question?"

"Absolutely not," said Glassgow. "Most absolutely not."

In a new picture, the devil twisted the fork.

Glassgow said, "All I did was screw her."

In the last Doré woodcut, the small devil sat on the ground, his hands across his belly and one leg in the air and howled with merriment. In the corner of the frame, Glassgow's face looked discreetly inquiring.

Though it was midsemester, Glassgow was off campus within five days, and in Los Angeles three days after that. He had three hundred dollars in traveler's checks and no plans.

3

WHEN he came to Southern California, he told himself he had picked his spot because he considered it symbolically appropriate: he was rejecting academe for Gehenna. He had no course of action formulated; the current of circumstances could take him where it would. Later, he decided that quite apart from his awareness, some deeper understanding had driven him to a divination of what he was, or what he wanted to be. At the time, he felt only that he was correctly obeying an obscure intuition.

He spent two nights in an old, cheap hotel downtown on Fifth Street and moved to an old cheap apartment house in a declining area on the eastern margin of Hollywood, just west of Vermont Avenue and south of Melrose.

He would do something in the film industry, of course: that was part of his repudiation of the old. Like many English professors, he had intended, imprecisely and fuzzily, to write–as soon as he got the Ph.D., as soon as he obtained tenure by publishing scholarly articles, as soon as he made associate professor, as soon as his life was two-thirds over.

Now–he told himself–I will really do it. This has all been most fortunate. I will write for television.

A small ad in the Sunday Times demanded: Are YOU ready for television? He enrolled; the writing course was taught by an exhausted playwright; yet Glassgow was impressed at the high quality of instruction. He admonished himself that he must not throw his intellectual weight around; he found quickly that he might have a certain difficulty doing so. Half a dozen young men in the class knew as much about dramatic literature as he did, and considerably more about dramaturgic theory.

And–he decided, when plays were read to the class–they were more talented.

This group of literates began to have drinks at a tavern on Melrose after class. The most gifted was the least articulate–a short chubby boy named Johnson, who wore an apologetic black moustache, and was meekly silent during the table pronouncements. Glassgow and he became friends. Glassgow read what he wrote, and saw that it kept getting better and better.

"When are you going to quit this nonsense and write a play?" Glassgow asked him. "I mean a real one."

"I couldn't write a real play. This small-scale stuff is my speed, I know my limitations."

"You don't know a damn about your limitations. Of course you can write a play."

"All right, tell me one to write."

"See now," Glassgow had read Sartre's *The Flies* that week, honing his French and it had sent him back to the Agamemnon trilogy.

"Take this young guy. He's been away from home a long time, see, and now he's back. There's something he's got to do, get his girl or save somebody or kill somebody or something. All the way through he's trying to decide what he really ought to do while the bad guys are after him and everything. He finally decides and does it and gets clobbered for it. But he defines himself when he acts, see. So we got tragedy loaded with affirmation. Like it?"

"I like Hamlet every time I read it."

"That's not Hamlet; that's Orestes. You see? Everything starts somewhere else."

"You're right. You know, I might play around with that."

Johnson wrote three versions of *The Flies* aimed at two television anthology shows. He got them read at MCA and William Morris; the television departments of both companies asked to see more of his work but felt these plays were too "complex" for the medium.

"Hell with them," said Glassgow, handing back the Morris letter. They were in his shabby apartment. "I'll sell them for you."

"You got to be an agent even to talk to anybody."

"Well hell, so I'm an agent."

"As of when?"

"As of as soon as you lend me five bucks to get some business cards printed."

It amused him to list on the card the address of a Hollywood pet hospital he sometimes visited.

He started the Johnson scripts on the rounds of the programs which might use it—his card with the pet hospital address accompanying. One story editor asked to see Glassgow.

"This Johnson thing is terrific," he said. "Only it's got too much balls. The brute truth is the medium can't handle that much balls. Now he cuts the balls off, we'd probably take it."

"What would you want him to cut?"

The editor told him and said, "That doesn't leave much, does it? Name of the game, I guess."

"Name of the game," said Glassgow. "I'll see what he says."

Glassgow thought Johnson ought to make the changes and persuaded him to do so. "You can't care too much about what happens in this medium because you're always going to be castrated. Pick up the cash in TV and save the best for the live theater."

Johnson agreed. He wrote several TV scripts quite rapidly, Glassgow sold most of them, and then Johnson stopped everything else to try the play. He had been outlining it for some time, and he finished a draft and a revision in less than three months.

It was set in a Southern town, the bad man was a racist plantation owner, the Orestes figure was a wanderer in love with the bad man's daughter. He came back to town and refused to leave in spite of what was done to him.

"This is it," Glassgow told Johnson. "Just don't let anybody talk you out of it."

"You handle it for me."

"You'd be cutting your own throat. I'm not big enough to get a Broadway production for you."

"I want you to handle it."

"I'll see what I can do, and if I can't do anything, you take it to one of the big ones. Okay?"

"Fair enough."

The routine procedure would be to send the script to one of the big agencies in New York, and the agency in turn would show it to established producers. Alternatively, Glassgow could go to New York himself and show it.

He calculated the odds against getting production for a new playwright, and followed neither of the ritualistic courses. He sent the play instead to Nora Lyon.

Nora Lyon was one of the screen's great exfoliations of sex in the late nineteen-thirties. In a famous cover story, a national magazine had named her forever, or at least for ten years: The Love Princess. Her luck had held through the war and for a year or two after, and it was 1949 before the Industry's divining rods showed her on the downgrade. Three pictures made in desperation were unsuccessful and she finished it off with a monumental scandal: a gangster well elevated in the hierarchy was shotgunned to death through her living room window. After that, she had gone into a long seclusion, and when she tried to come out of it, she found she was a historical figure.

The strongest female role in Johnson's play was that of an aging, alcoholic socialite hoping pathologically for a return to past glories. Rereading the script after what might or might not be his divine inspiration, Glassgow saw in her scenes not an imagined character but Nora Lyon.

He sent her agent a script and–violating protocol–one direct to her. He was always intuitively fearful that gears would not mesh.

He received the script back from the agent in two weeks, with an inked note: "Nora likes but says not for her." Glassgow refused to accept it. With a certain amount of difficulty, he obtained the Lyon address, it was on Benedict Canyon, and he went, unannounced, to see her.

He was prepared for rebuff but found none: a straw-haired butler in a double-breasted sack coat took his card in, returned, and led him through the house to the pool area and the enclosed cabana.

Inside the cabana, Nora Lyon was half-reclining on a long chaise. A pile of bound manuscripts was on the floor beside her. She wore a one-piece black bathing suit, her black hair hung loose to her shoulders, and black horn-rimmed spectacles were propped on her nose. She took them off with her left hand, smiled at Glassgow, and extended her right to him. He approached, took her hand, and smiled down at her.

"Hello," she said. "I'm awfully glad to see you. It was so good of you to send me the play."

"I couldn't have done anything else, being as excited about it as I was. I only wish you had liked it better."

Glassgow felt nervous and awkward and was furious with himself because of his awkwardness. He had the intellectual's genuine contempt of motion picture "personalities." Yet Nora Lyon was a goddess of his youth, ravished by him in a hundred adolescent fantasies, and now she was incarnated into quite healthy flesh before him. First responses endure: he was awed by her simply because he had been awed by her when she was young.

She was smiling faintly, as though she were not unaware of her Pavlovian effect. "I liked the play enormously," she said. "I just didn't think the character was for me."

His eyes remained fixed upon her; he did not think he could have looked away from her if he tried and he did not particularly wish to try. Her body had the smooth heavy curves of the well-conditioned mature woman, her skin was deeply and evenly tanned, and her face was so taut and free of wrinkles that a face-lift had to be responsible. He knew her to be fifty-one; she looked thirty-seven.

She smiled faintly at his long glance, and he understood that she welcomed it.

"I thought she was for you. I've been rereading the play and in her scenes I can only see you."

She laughed pleasantly. "I'm not sure that's flattering. She's a has-been, a drunk, and the next thing to a nymphomaniac."

"She is also a woman with a tremendous range of emotions and I see you as the one person uniquely capable of bringing her to life."

"Are you trying to hustle me for the backing, Mr. Glassgow?" She smiled in perfect good humor.

"I certainly am, but what I'm telling you is the absolute truth."

"I don't know whether you mean that or not but it *is* the truth, I could play the hell out of that woman."

"I know you could."

"I don't mind telling you I was very strongly tempted."

"Why don't you then?"

She smiled at him patiently, and spoke to him didactically.

"Don't you see, the public would identify me with the character. You know what the character is. And you know or you damn well ought to know what my particular problems are. After what happened to Steve in my living room, they think I'm an underworld figure, and all I did was sleep with the man twice. Anyway, that's why I can't."

"I think you're wrong," he smiled at her. "As you say, I'm hustling you."

"I wish you had had better luck hustling me. I like the part, I like the play, I like you. But I can't take the chance." She offered him her hand again. "I am grateful to you for thinking of me, and it was good of you to come out."

"It was my pleasure, and it was good of you to see me."

Having lost it, he walked to the door. And then he decided to try the truth in its ultimate cruelty.

"You are a goddamn fool," he said, and watched her eyes open wide and her mouth harden. "You've had the love princess business. You've *had* it. You are on the ash heap and the only way you'll get off ever is to come on new and different and better. You've got to be a fine actress or you're nothing and this is the best chance you'll ever get." She had swung her tanned legs over the chaise and was crouched on the edge of it, glaring at him (he thought) as smoky-eyed as Medea. He changed his voice. "You're a great talent and a beautiful woman, maybe more beautiful than when you were twenty-five, but in a damn different way and you have to accept the difference. You take what you have and you decide to use it the way it can be used and you'll exist again. What you are is what you decide right now."

She ran the few steps toward him, her white teeth bared by her lips, and she swung an open hand at him. He caught it at the wrist, and then her other wrist the same way.

"You son of a bitch," she whispered. "You mean crummy lying son of a bitch." She tried to break free and he gripped her tightly. They struggled in a silence broken only by the wrenches of her breath.

"I'll kill you you lying son of a bitch."

He felt the heat and then the solid flesh of her body as they wrestled (*my god, this is Nora Lyon and your leg is touching hers*), then he pulled her close, his thigh defined every line of her firm belly, then he pushed it between her thighs and heat took his body unconditionally. Still holding her wrists, still drawing her against him, he kissed her.

She bit him. He felt blood in his mouth.

"I want to make love to you," he said.

She spat in his face.

"I've wanted to make love to you since I was twelve years old."

"You're a bastard."

"You're the most exciting woman in the world."

He had touched a nerve, as a button. She had been straining violently against his grip, hate coming out of her toward him like a physical substance. When he said those words, her arms relaxed, the struggle was over, and he knew it. When she smiled, it was in triumph, and her low caressing voice was the voice of conquest.

"You're bleeding, darling. We'll have to take care of that." She touched his mouth with a finger and then brushed it with her lips. "We can't have you bleeding." She took his hand. "Come along, darling." He followed her along the edge of the pool and into the house.

Three of her bedroom walls were mirrors. She smiled at him, and he was aware his mouth was open. She pointed eyeward with one finger, and he looked and saw the ceiling too was a mirror.

She kissed him, blood exploded in his ears, and she started to loose his tie.

4

SHE backed the play entirely. ("A Broadway play costs half as much as a quickie picture just so it isn't a musical," she said.) They ran it at the Oval Theater on Melrose for three weeks and worked it over. Then they took it, with her and the putative director, to Margo Jones Theater in the Round in Dallas and worked it over again. It was a well-tested, shrewdly revised play when it opened in New York, and it was a solid hit. Out of it came three careers: those of Nora Lyon, Johnson Johnson and Nelson Glassgow.

Now Glassgow had an identity: he was the discoverer of Johnson Johnson, and his office was a pet hospital. He knew the value of a perverse image, and cultivated his with a fair amount of amusement. He artfully created a small legend: he seldom wrote letters, he met clients only in cafés and bars, he did not care about money but was only interested in furthering brilliant talents. He adroitly picked up fashionable European directors and players who were not quite stars, he searched out five young television writers and he took on a careful culling of young American actors from the workshop theaters. Representation by Nelson Glassgow became a certification of unique talent, though not necessarily an earnest of commercial success.

His public personality, also, was that of the attacker, the smasher of sacred objects. If he had been a first-line importance, he would not have been endured and he knew it; as a figure of the second rank, Glassgow the iconoclast was not simply tolerated but admired and even liked.

His need to attack was not in the least feigned. Once, long ago, he had been convinced that somewhere was the one, true Glassgow, waiting only to be discovered. Because he could not find that one, he tore himself, and because he tore himself, he needed to tear.

He would have liked it better if he had been required to manufacture a Glassgow, rather than to find one. He would have made a wise and balanced man, swift in debate but not quarrelsome, brave in his causes but not belligerent, not a compromiser but skillful in binding together factions, powerful but discreet in action.

Quite different was a phantom Glassgow whose outlined shape he tried to fill.

That Glassgow was always at war, never to be attacked because always attacking, invulnerable in the armor of constant thrusting motion. His climaxes of pleasure came not from simple destruction but in unwarned shattering demolition—always of the unjust. He never paused, nor slowed, nor tired.

Glassgow of breath would not have described the phantom, but he fleshed it remarkably though incompletely. He armored the jelly of his vulnerability with permanent motion and attack. But his conscience was implacable if desperately concealed: almost always, his targets were either abstractions or himself. Still, the process of shattering sustained him—whatever was shattered.

He had been a talent agent for five years and was firmly established in his small but singular fashion, when Octavia Dayton came to him by appointment at the Valhalla Pet Hospital in the early afternoon of an April day in 1957. She had not been entirely unknown to him when she requested the audience: she had achieved a fragile notoriety for her succession of lovers, some well known, and for her desultory and unsuccessful efforts to establish herself as an actress. Glassgow had seen her at parties: she was not a call girl or in any sense a professional, but she was known to be discreetly available if for the right people at the right time.

When she called, he had tried to put her off as kindly as possible. As she persisted, he became half as brutal as he tried to make the world think him; "For God's sake no, no. Mrs. Dayton, I handle only serious people."

She swallowed the insult. "This is about my daughter, Mr. Glassgow. I really think she has something to offer you."

"I don't represent children."

"She's seventeen."

He was surprised that Octavia was old enough to have a seventeen-year-old daughter, and astonished that she should admit it. He agreed to see the two of them at the hospital, breaking two rules.

They entered at the exact stroke of two; they had waited outside for several minutes. Glassgow received them in his aperture at the rear of a large room filled with the hospital's caged patients. Dogs barked raggedly; monkeys screeched in a pattern.

Octavia Dayton was of an age and presence that stipulated she be called a handsome woman, instead of pretty or attractive. Glassgow put her at forty; later he learned she was then two years short of it. She had dark red hair, a ripe, serviceable, and carefully girdled body, and a fullness of face that suggested abundant gratification of many appetites. She was manifestly gripped in the tension of her ambitions, which Glassgow despised. Yet her eyes and mouth had between them a certain candor and hard self-appraisal that went far toward redeeming her, for him. He regretted his insult on the telephone, and so greeted her very courteously.

"It was kind of you to come here," he said. "I have an awfully tight afternoon or I would have come to you."

"Here is fine," she said brightly. "And this is Margaret."

The first quality of Margaret Dayton that exposed itself to Glassgow was shyness. She was tenderly and miserably shy. She blushed when he offered his hand, and she looked away; he felt both warmth and a strong gratitude toward her.

The next thing about her that came in was that she had, possibly, the most exciting body he had ever seen, or perceived, for she had an effect that went beyond the visual and the aesthetic. He was physically aware of it, and he felt a trace of shyness himself. It was as though sex were some huge, visible cargo which she was compelled to carry and which had a tangibility and aspect that embarrassed both her and the beholder.

All of this came to him before he said, "Hello, Margaret."

"Hello," she said, and looked away, and touched her lower lip with her teeth.

"How serious are you about this? About acting?" Glassgow asked.

"Mother wants me to."

"Do you want to yourself?" he said sharply.

"I'd just as soon," Margaret Dayton said.

A big dog began to bark loudly. Glassgow gestured at the cages and spoke to Mrs. Dayton. "Is that what you want for her?"

The dog stopped barking and Octavia Dayton's answer was half-shouted and loud. "I didn't hear you."

"Do you want her to be caged?"

"I'm afraid I don't know what you mean."

"Look at those cages. Cats and dogs, monkeys and parakeets, there's even a perfumed hog and a jaguar in the back. They're fed, pampered, and many of them will be behind bars forever. Is that what you want for her?"

Mrs. Dayton smiled sweetly and repudiatingly. "You're so, vivid, Mr. Glassgow. I know you don't really equate a dramatic career with a cage."

"Don't I?" He turned on the girl. "Do *you* want to be caged?"

"No."

"Why don't you forget it then?"

She glanced at him and then away and did not answer.

"Do you want to be a big success? Is that the idea?"

"I don't care about that particularly."

Glassgow laughed shortly. "You begin to interest me. If you don't want success you'll probably get drowned with it. If you really hate it, you'll wind up the hottest property in town."

She looked at him gravely.

For no reason Glassgow felt faintly guilty.

"I'm fooling of course," he said. "I think. The truth is this business calls for a lot of work. You haven't given me any reason to believe you'll do it. Will you?"

"I'll work."

"Because your mother wants you to?" he said quite gently.

She colored; her lower lip went deeply under her white teeth.

"Margaret," said her mother dangerously.

Nelson Glassgow felt his devil jabbing and he did not want to push him away. A banal line from an old and banal picture came to him. He said, "Take off your clothes. I want to see what I'm merchandising."

He had wanted to see how far Mrs. Dayton would go. She said cheerfully, "Do as Mr. Glassgow says, dear. He's Hollywood's most distinguished agent."

He looked condemningly at Octavia Dayton. She smiled back in total agreement with his judgment of her, and in defiance of it.

Margaret looked at him much as he had looked at her mother.

"That won't really be necessary," he said softly. "I wanted you to get an idea of what you can expect."

He turned again to Octavia. "All right. If I don't handle her someone else will. I'll get out the contracts."

"I'll take them to my lawyer today," said Octavia, sweetly.

When the two had gone, Glassgow stared in abstraction at the distant wall of cages. He had never represented any talent which was not almost ostentatiously artistic. Whatever luck Margaret Dayton might have, he considered, she was not and would never be a self-conscious artist. Yet she had stirred him, and not simply physically. There was a sweetly pathetic thing there; she had made you feel she was born to love and to suffer for it. Not quite. Rather, it was that she needed love badly, and, somehow, communicated the need strongly.

"That's why I signed her," he said aloud. In adjoining cages, monkeys screeched.

5

GLASSGOW learned Octavia Dayton had exposed her daughter to one of the "dramatic schools" for youngsters, where she had learned to speak understandably and to walk smoothly. She had not learned much else.

Nelson Glassgow did not want her to learn much else. He had more than an intuition that too much training would inhibit her personality, and alter its unique emanations. Yet there were minimal techniques she had to master. He worked her into the company at the Oval Theater; he was sure she would learn much of what she needed to know there.

Octavia Dayton had not bothered him the first few weeks after the signing of the contracts. She telephoned him four days after he put Margaret in the Oval and he returned her call, that time. He did not return any of the dozen she made the next week, and one morning she caught him at the pet hospital.

He was standing in his cubbyhole opening and reading letters and he looked up and saw Octavia Dayton, silently smiling. She was in a green dress that fitted to show the well-conditioned maturity of her body, and wore a sharp green hat over her red hair. Glassgow was furious at her intrusion, and thought, again, that she was an extremely desirable woman.

He greeted her: "Goddamn it, I have no idea of returning your stupid calls. I won't waste my time on your stupid goddamn calls."

"Are you so sure they're stupid?"

"You're her goddamn mother, of course they're stupid."

"I just want to know what kind of progress my daughter is making. Is that so bad?"

Glassgow grimaced.

"She is my daughter."

"She's my client and I don't want you interfering. However," he raised his hand in a gesture of concession, "I'll telephone you once a week and let you know what's going on. In return you stay out of my hair. Okay?"

Her mouth pursed; she was good-humored and defeated. "All right, Mr. Glassgow. You've a bargain. I won't call you, you'll call me." She started out.

"Did you really go to Oxford?" he called after her.

She stopped and turned. "I went to Brooklyn College." She smiled. "The accent I was born with was Cockney. Good day, Mr. Glassgow."

Watching her walk away, handsome, firmly shaped by her girdle, looking ripe rather than middle-aged, it occurred to him that he would rather sleep with her than anybody he knew.

Glassgow maneuvered to get Margaret a series of two- and three-line parts at the Oval. They were not demanding, but they did accustom her to simple body movement before an audience. And they gave her practice in the delivery of simple lines.

Without conscious intent, she did remarkable things to these. Her high voice and self-conscious delivery would isolate the line from the passage, almost, and the solemnity with which she spoke it gave a fine comic impact. This was intensified and counterpointed by her physical voltage. Her walk continued to say she was pure sex—and was embarrassed by it.

Glassgow saw, he thought, the shape of her public personality: the ingenuous comedienne with sex appeal she did not understand; a younger, more beautiful, perhaps more complicated Marie Wilson.

Sometimes he came by the Oval to watch her in the workshop.

When he did, he would take her to a juice bar two blocks away, and discuss her progress. With her, he always felt vaguely ponderous and didactic, and he covered this by an excess of his insulating skepticism.

She always accepted his pronouncements without dissent, looking at him with her docile, but disturbing, gravity. He intuited she had a feeling for him but he rejected the knowledge. One afternoon, after she finished rehearsal in a three-line part, he came from his seat toward her on the stage. Waiting behind the stage, he saw a young, blond, sideburned actor strut to her. He said something, Glassgow heard her answer, "I can't today, Mr. Glassgow wants to see me." She looked at the young man with sympathetic regret, and Glassgow felt himself injured, and angry.

At the juice bar, he brought two cherry-banana-papayas to the table in the patio off the sidewalk. They drank, and he heard himself asking, "Who was your friend?"

"My friend?"

"The actor back there, the blond guy."

"Oh. He's a boy."

"I see–he's a boy."

"His name's Johnny Roberts, he calls himself Dirk Roberts."

"Romance?" Glassgow said it with the palpable false joviality that he hated.

She looked at him with her clear, green eyes. "Johnny is a homosexual."

"Oh." Glassgow submerged in a sea of idiocy.

"Johnny uses me for a shoulder to cry on. He's having a very unhappy love affair, he's in love with the boy that's got the lead in *Glass Menagerie* next week. Johnny says that boy is so promiscuous and unfaithful, Johnny gets sick he gets so jealous."

"Oh, I see." Inanely, he drummed his fingers on the table. "Don't they, those, the homosexuals, upset you a little?"

"No. I like them, they're sweet. They kind of gravitate to me."

"Be careful."

Her eyes touched his again. "Mr. Glassgow, I'm not all that innocent. I've been married."

"I didn't know that." He felt the blood in his face.

"It was when I was fifteen. Mother had it annulled. He was an older man. I ran away from home and married him and Mother caught up with me and had it annulled."

"For a young girl that's quite an experience."

"I didn't marry him for experience, I liked him."

"Were you in love with him?"

"No."

He saw she was ready to tell him anything else he wanted to know, and reflexively he moved away from intimacy. He said lightly, "Experience is supposed to be great for an actress, though sometimes I wonder. I'm glad you didn't get hurt."

She stared at him steadily, and he saw that she knew he had rejected a kind of offer. "Vito didn't hurt me," she said.

He did not go back to the Oval, nor see her at all, for almost a month. He did not see her because he was afraid of her. He was afraid she might upset the careful balance of his life.

At that point in it, he was poised on a small peak of self-acceptance: the Glassgow who decided and appeared to attack, he found satisfactory though not admirable. He had never planned that Glassgow consciously, but he had intuitively selected the master form for him, and he had not been badly served by him. He had forgotten, almost, the vulnerability which that Glassgow had to guard.

The day he admitted he feared her, he asked her to meet him in the juice bar after her class.

He bought Live-Longer specials: guava and strawberry juice, blackstrap molasses, yogurt, wheat germ, and—Glassgow's contribution—high protein powder. He told her:

"I think the Oval has about served our purpose, I think maybe the thing to do is to try to move you right away. I don't think you'll ever be an actress in the formal sense, but you've got something bigger, and you know most of what you need to know right now."

"Whatever you think, Mr. Glassgow."

He called on Howard Sills at the Globe-International Picture Corporation lot in West Hollywood. Glassgow knew that before his day, the stages had been filled with big budget and B pictures shooting. The day of his visit, casts were at work on three television series. Not a single full-length was in progress.

Glassgow knew Globe had three pictures shooting on location in various parts of the world, but none were at work on the lot. This was the Sidney Tate design that had saved the studio a few years before: a very few big location pictures, as many quick, economical TV projects as possible. It had occurred to Glassgow that Tate had simply perceived that the TV series had filled the place of the old B picture. Now it was easy to see. It had not been so easy when Tate saw it, he reflected.

Sills was on Stage Three, watching interiors of his own series, *Barbados Run*. Though a series, the stories were presented in what was essentially an anthology framework: they were linked by the character of a handsome young American captain and his schooner, *Rainbow*.

Glassgow stood beside Sills on the corner of the stage, well back from the camera area. They watched a blonde actress admit tersely that it was really she who shot Mr. Overseer, who reneged on his promise to take her away. Her older but understanding husband took her in his arms and, ecstatic with new understanding, they faced the police inspector. "He was a rat," said the inspector comfortingly, "I don't think she'll get a day more than twenty years." The wife and husband beamed at each other and that was it.

"We fade into Noel on the ship and then the ship sailing away for the fade-out." Sills smiled wryly. "A real classic, huh?"

"I've seen worse," said Glassgow.

"Oh yes," said Sills. "That's the great consolation in this medium. You've always seen worse." Defensively, still humorously, he said, "Honestly, some of these have been good, about as good as you can get in TV. One out of five is good, two are fair, and two are pretty bad. We get the most favorable fan mail on the bad ones, of course. What are you selling me today, Nelson?"

"A girl." Glassgow told him about Margaret.

"Octavia's daughter?"

"Yes."

Sills looked thoughtful. "I may have something. When can she get over?"

"In half an hour."

Sills heard her read and said yes, then later he said no, then a week later he said absolutely yes.

In an episode which was double first cousin to Maugham's *Rain*, she played a young tart who was responsible for the degradation of a powerful American businessman. She undulated through the picture in a tight print dress, not speaking a word until the end.

Then she spoke one line: "You're nothing but a *pig,* Mr. Crawford."

Margaret pronounced it, almost, "peeg." She stamped her foot and turned and flounced away, the camera centering on her swaying derriere. This was the final scene—except, of course, for the signature fade-out of *Rainbow* and her handsome captain heading toward the horizon.

The episode was thoroughly housebroken, all concerned thought: it was well within the established limits of the medium's expression. Yet it touched off a reaction which had few counterparts in commercial television. Newspaper editorials expressed concern at the dangers to public morality implicit in "sensation-seeking TV." A Congressman from Tennessee cited the episode on the floor of the House and demanded tighter FCC control.

Those in the television-motion-picture complex were astonished, and puzzled.

"It looked tame enough in script," Sills said to Glassgow, over drinks at Scandia one afternoon. "All she did was walk around and say that one little line."

"That's all she did."

"Then why the press, I wonder."

"Howard," said Glassgow. "If Margaret Dayton walked up to a counter and asked for a drink of water, if she did it on camera that is, the public would think they had seen her ravished."

Sills looked thoughtful.

Three days later Sills called Glassgow to his office and offered Dayton an old-fashioned, long-term contract with options.

Glassgow scanned it. "You can't hardly get that kind no more. How come, Howard?"

"We believe in her."

"It would seem so." Glassgow looked at him with some amusement. He was perfectly aware that if Globe had believed in her tremendously he would have been talking to Sidney Tate. "You have to be kidding about the seven years."

"It's the standard contract."

"Three years."

"Five."

"Three is it. I won't tie her up any longer than three, Howard, and I'm not bargaining, I mean it."

The contracts were revised for three. Glassgow brought them to Margaret for signature.

Margaret and Octavia Dayton lived in an apartment house in unfashionable Hollywood, off Santa Monica Boulevard. It was not too far from the place Glassgow had lighted when he first came to town. This one was pink and full of angles and lines, with the inevitable swimming pool in the court. That was where Glassgow found Margaret Dayton.

Approaching, he saw a bony blonde girl stooped over a small boy in the shallow end, and a white-capped head moving over the water at the other. He stopped well back from the edge and waited for Margaret to recognize him. He saw her contorted face under the cap as she swam toward him, the mouth opening on the follow-through of the stroke to breathe, and her eyes changed from vacancy to awareness as they touched him.

She stopped at poolside and rested her arms on the edge. He was recording their unmuscular firm smoothness as she said, "Hi." She was not quite panting but breathing deeply.

"Hi, Margaret."

She came out dripping in a one-piece green bathing suit that might have been her skin. It was cut conservatively, covering more than most, and Glassgow thought that it was perhaps this modesty that made the effect so overwhelming.

"How are you?" she smiled at him, still drawing breath deeply.

"Fine, I've got great news. Let's sit down somewhere." He felt constrained; since that day at the juice bar, their relationship had been mildly formal.

"Okay." She pulled off the white cap and shook out her red hair, picked up a huge white beach towel from a table by the pool and draped it over her shoulders, and then led him to a wrought-iron table and chairs.

"I've got a contract with Globe-International," he told her at once.

"Why that's just fine, isn't it?"

"You might say that. You might even say it is very goddamned good."

"Well, I guess it is very goddamn good if you say so. I don't know much about it."

He was instantly pacified, and he even felt a vague self-reproach for his sharpness. "That's what you've got me for," he said. "You aren't supposed to know. Anyway. We've got a three-year contract with Globe, naturally with options, and they say they have plans for you. I don't know, maybe they do, but I'm always mistrustful on principle."

"You certainly are." Her red hair, loose and uncombed and streaked with ropes of dampness, swung above her shoulders.

"Be glad, dear, that's one of my functions, to be mistrustful. Still and all, I'm convinced this is progress."

"I guess it's because of all that fuss they kicked up about *Barbados Run.*" She suddenly parodied herself. "You're nothing but a *peeg,* Mister Crawford!"

"That's the reason."

"Oh that makes me so mad, that just makes me furious. I didn't do anything except say that one old line and they all got so worked up and everything."

"You'll have to get used to it, Margaret. You'll always make people react very strongly one way or the other. It's not something you can change, and you shouldn't want to. Now. Here's the contract. Read it very carefully tonight, ask me any questions you like tomorrow, and when you're satisfied, you can sign."

"Are you satisfied?"

"Absolutely."

"I'll sign them now."

"You will like hell. I don't want you signing anything before you study it, no matter who tells you it's okay."

"All right."

"For heaven's sake don't look injured. I'm trying to protect you."

"I know that, Mr. Glassgow. I'll read these and send them to you. Did you want to see me about anything else?"

Her voice was grave and studiously without intonation. He regretted he had spoken harshly; as a consequence, he spoke harshly again. "That's all."

"If you'll excuse me I'll dry off then."

She told him good-bye and left. He watched her back in the green suit as she went up the outside stairs to the balcony of the second-floor apartment. She opened a door and closed it after her. He dropped his gaze and recognized her big pink purse on a chair: she must have forgotten it. Beside it was a book. Automatically he checked the title: *The Plague* by Albert Camus.

His eyebrows drew together and he raised his head to stare at the door through which she had just passed.

He got the signed contracts by special delivery, two days later.

6

MARGARET had many parts in Globe television pictures that year. Each was small, but vivid: they gave her enough scope to make an impression and enough time on camera to do it. All were essentially the same part she had played in the false *Rain*.

She had only feature billing. But something quite extraordinary began to happen. More pictures of her were beginning to appear in magazines and newspapers than of any other Globe television personality. A health magazine ran a layout of her exercises, and listed her rules for figure control (Glassgow had gotten them from a Vic Tanny instructor). A man's magazine ran a two-page fold-out of her, with nudity artfully simulated. Shot after shot appeared in newspapers. Both Glassgow and Globe's publicity department were impressed: they knew the efforts each contributed did not begin to account for the volume of exposure.

Glassgow called on Sidney Tate one day with an attaché case full of published pictures of Margaret Dayton. "I've been aware of this," Tate admitted. "In a way, it's very impressive." He dropped the two-page picture on his desk and nudged it backward with his finger.

"It's more than impressive, Sidney. You know your publicity people haven't expended anything like this kind of effort on her."

"I know that."

"This has happened damn near by itself. Does that suggest anything to you?"

"It suggests Miss Dayton is compellingly photogenic."

"I thought it might suggest that it's time to make her a star."

"She isn't star material," said Tate.

The two looked at each other across the desk.

"You can't mean that," said Glassgow.

"I do mean it. She is not and will never be a star. She has a certain appeal and she should prosper, for a while. She has neither the talent nor the strength of personality to be a real star."

"After this press reaction, how can you say that?"

"Nelson. Do you remember Toby Wing?"

"Vaguely."

"For several years in the thirties, she was the most photographed girl in the Industry. I myself never remember seeing her in a single motion picture."

"Margaret Dayton isn't Toby Wing."

"I wasn't suggesting that she is. I just wanted to point out to you that it takes more than newspaper pictures to make a star."

"I won't crowd you, Sidney. I'll simply hope you change your mind."

"Good. I hope I'll always be able to change my mind. If I ought to."

Annoyed at Tate, and at himself for partly sharing Tate's reservations, Glassgow took Margaret to Scandia that night. It was the first time he had taken her anywhere except the juice stand. Her pleasure at his attention showed in the color of her face and the animation of her attitudes; this frightened him a little: he was not sure why.

After dinner, they drove out to Malibu to a café on the edge of the water. She drank Cuba Libres rapidly, and he raised his eyebrows as the third came to the table.

"I better be careful or you might take advantage of me. Would you take advantage of a girl that had three drinks, Mr. Glassgow?"

"Only if I had the opportunity."

"Suurre. Sure. Sure you would. That I would have to see, Mr. Glassgow."

"Nelson."

"I prefer Mr. Glassgow. It's much more sterner. More stern. Mr. Nelson Glassgow. Very stern Mister Nelson Glassgow."

"Absolutely."

"I think you don't like redheads Mister Glassgow. I think you have a thing, you know, in reverse. I think I am getting tight and had better shut up."

"You're fine, don't worry about it."

"Don't wor-ry about *it,* Mister Nelson Glassgow will take care of *every*thing."

"You're right, you better shut up."

"Yes, *sir."*

She was meek and quiet. Glassgow tried to look out the window but could only see the reflection of light in the glass. He heard the surf, well out, and then the surge of water on the pilings beneath.

"Could I have another drink?" she asked him.

"Do you want to get drunk?"

"I think so."

"Have you ever been drunk?"

"No."

"Maybe you ought to then." He ordered more drinks, and watched her face glaze, not too slowly, as they progressed.

"That's enough," he said, half an hour later.

"I'm not drunk."

"Yes you are. I don't want you to get sick with it."

"I'm not drunk."

"Let's go home."

He paid. She put her arm through his and walked with only a slight uncertainty. He felt the soft heavy thrust of her breast into his side, and was aware and ashamed of the heat rising to his face.

He turned toward the beach and south again when he hit Malibu Road. He could hold it for three miles, out of Coast Highway traffic. He drove very slowly and leaned across Margaret, herself leaning against the seat, eyes closed, head bare, the white curve of her throat a foot from his lips in the dark. He rolled down her window so the air would come to her.

"I'm not asleep," she said.

"I thought you were."

"I'm just drunk."

"You're just a little drunk."

"Drunk enough."

"Enough for what?"

"To tell you. I'm in love with you, Nelson."

He drove on. Between the houses he could see the dark slab of water and its white edge of surf.

"No you aren't," he said.

"Yes I am. Don't worry though. I'm drunk enough where we can forget it and it'll be like I never said it."

He did not say anything. He touched her hand, awkwardly, and brought his back to the wheel.

She was in a deep sleep when he came to her apartment house. He saw no lights: so Octavia was out. He picked her up, she felt tremendously heavy, and walked stiff-legged to the door. He worked his fingers beneath her and turned the knob, it came open, and he was relieved at the convenience and angry at her carelessness. His arms straining, he walked through an open door, and lowered her to the bed inside. He slipped off her shoes, worked the cover free of her body, she murmured complainingly, and he put the covers over her.

Wondering if she was really asleep, he tiptoed out.

He did not see her for a time for he was very busy, and for her. Weeks later, he did persuade Tate to make a loan-out of her to a young director named Ricci, who was producing his own picture in New Orleans. It was a very low cost picture, budgeted at $225,000. Margaret played a stripper in a Bourbon Street nightclub who fell in love with an eighteen-year-old busboy. Ricci, the young director, had modeled it carefully after certain films by Vittorio De Sica, and it had De Sica's fine naturalistic surface.

Margaret had some incisive scenes: the early love passage between herself and the boy where each tried, inarticulately, to communicate; a strip sequence in which she danced explosively and chatted between turns with a friend at a ringside table; and a walk through the streets of the French Quarter with her face showing a marvelous mobility and warmth.

It was that scene which made a believer out of Glassgow.

He saw it for the first time in a projection room at Associated Artists, which had helped capitalize the picture and would distribute it.

To a degree that might have surprised Sidney Tate, he had secretly shared Tate's conviction that the girl had neither the drive nor the desire to become a star. As he sat in his seat while the lights went on after the screening, he was convinced that the very absence of pathological drive was her uniqueness and strength. Since that uniqueness happened to be fused with an incredible body.

He made his farewells, walked to his Lancia in the lot, and drove to the pet hospital.

He pulled into his place behind the building and turned off the motor. He sat still a moment, then turned it back on, backed the car out, and headed for the Globe-International office in Beverly Hills.

His chances of seeing Sidney Tate without an appointment were extremely bad. Yet the ball fell into the slot: he not only was able to see Tate, but got in almost at once.

He asked Tate if he had seen the picture.

"I saw it," said Tate noncommittally.

"Do you still think Margaret won't make it?"

"That depends on what you mean, make it. I think she's already made a nice little place for herself."

"You know what I mean, Sidney. Are you ready to make a star out of her?"

Tate looked at him directly. "No."

"You're absolutely convinced she doesn't have it."

Tate hesitated. "I'm not absolutely convinced of anything in this business. I still don't think she's star material."

"How about releasing us then? She's only got a little more than a year to go on the contract."

"Why should I?"

"Simple fairness." Glassgow wondered as he said it if there were another man in the business to whom he could cite fairness as a reason. "You aren't going to do anything very big for her. I think I can do better elsewhere on the strength of this picture, but I have to do it right away."

"Do you have any nibbles?"

"No." Glassgow had decided long ago that any course other than honesty would be fatal in dealing with Tate.

"And you really think you can make her a big one?"

"I'm certain of it."

"All right. You can have the release. I don't mind telling you that if you had three years more on the contract you couldn't have it. One condition."

"What is it?"

"If she does take off, she'll do a picture for us."

"Deal."

So Margaret Dayton became a free agent, and Nelson Glassgow had to do something about her immediately. He was sharply aware of the urgencies: she was balanced on a knife edge. She was "hot" in that she was rising and was a mobile, unfixed element. She had taken a certain amount of ground in Ricci's surprising but not sensational picture, and she now had to expand what she had won or lose it. This was the point: she would either move ahead or fall back. There was no middle ground, and Glassgow knew it. What happened in her next picture might define the shape of her career.

He had to find the opportunity before he could fight for it.

He invoked all his sources of information and assistance, those acknowledged and those secret. It was in public print, however, that the word came. One of the queens of the columns wrote: "Kip Beaumont, reported set in Dickie Clermont's *Redheads Prefer Gentlemen,* has withdrawn, for reasons unknown."

7

HE read it over coffee, canceled his morning appointments, and drove to the American Pictures lot above Highland. He had clearance, and the entrance guard waved him inside. He parked, recognizing Clermont's red Facel Vega, in one of the strips, and went to the big corrugated iron building that enclosed Stage Fourteen.

Of the twenty stages on the lot, only that one was in use, and Glassgow reflected that this was symptomatic of the Industry's current anemia. Several cars were parked in the executive lot, but there were even more empty slots.

In the spaces of concrete between the corrugated barns and the white stucco office buildings, Glassgow saw only three workmen. Clermont's picture, *The Parisian Way,* was the only one shooting on the lot, and was the first one to shoot there in three months. It was not an American picture but belonged to Stanish Productions, which operated within the corporate framework but had its own identity.

The Parisian Way was farce with music. It was the kind of picture associated with Clermont: as a Swiss director working in the French industry in the 1930's, he had made a reputation in high comedy. "The Clermont touch" was famous–for a while. He was in the Ernst Lubitsch–René Clair–Billy Wilder circle of fashion, and he had come to Hollywood on the strength of it, in 1938, and had never left. The signature of his work–a very fast cutting between close-ups, comic sex symbols (once he had used a cannon firing to indicate the act), and a deft, funny use of dramatic irony–these had long since soaked into the general resource of the Industry and no longer defined his work alone. His poised and air-light art had hardened into formula a decade before. But he practiced it ably, and was one of the most commercially successful directors in town–or out.

Over the first door of the big building was a lighted red bulb. Glassgow opened the door, heard a blare of music, and tiptoed through dim light behind a huge backdrop. Properties were scattered along his path: an old car, movable lamp posts, fireplugs.

He came from behind the backdrop and saw the action more than fifty feet in front of him. Inside a simulated café with the forward wall removed, many people were dancing. Cameras on booms thrust toward the dancers. From the distance Glassgow saw the beret that was Clermont's trademark, above the canvas back of a chair. In the big open space behind the cameras many people were standing and some sitting. Most were workers in the technical departments, some wore makeup.

He tiptoed through them and stopped just behind Clermont. He saw the set was a simulation of a working class French café and the dancers were Parisian stereotypes. The music came not from a band but from a big jukebox at the far wall. The dancers were twisting, the derriere of one pretty, heavy blonde shook in the very eye of the camera.

"Cut," called Clermont, and made a gesture with his hand. The music went off, the dancers lost motion in a grotesque suddenness. The blonde turned, smiled at Clermont, and parodied wiping sweat from her forehead.

"Don't waste all the footage on that behind." Clermont said it to a cameraman, but made the joke for her. "It's not worth it."

"I hope it's worth it," she said in good humor. "It's the only one I've got."

Clermont chuckled, then called loudly, "Take ten, everybody." He pushed back the beret.

"Hello, Dickie," said Glassgow.

Clermont took him in with a half-turn of the head and a glance. "Nelson." His tanned face had heavy seams running from his nose to his mouth, and elsewhere was entirely smooth, though sagging. Glassgow had thought on occasion that he looked a heavier, less sensitive Gide.

"How is the picture going?" said Glassgow.

"I think we're going to get a real good picture out of it, Nelson."

"What I saw looked fine."

"Oh that was nothing, we've got some really great stuff in the can." Clermont had cultivated American vernacular, and it was overlaid with a still strong French rhythm.

"How is the one you're casting shaping up?"

"Which one? I'm mixed up in three."

"The redheads one."

Clermont looked at him keenly. "You selling me somebody, Nelson?"

"Margaret Dayton."

"Who is Margaret Dayton?"

"Dickie, come *on.*"

Clermont smiled. "I hear she got herself a pretty good picture."

"She's got herself a hell of a picture. Haven't you seen it?"

"I go to two kinds of pictures, my friend, the ones I can't avoid and my own."

"You ought to see this one. I'll get a print and bring it over, tonight if you want."

"What kind of part you want for her?"

"You know what I want, I want the Kip Beaumont part."

"Nelson, you really think I put a green kid in that part? I got to have a name."

"Just look at the print, Dickie. That's all I ask."

"It's a waste of time. You know I got to have a name."

"I'd appreciate it very much if you'd look at it, Dickie," said Glassgow softly.

It translated as: you owe me a favor. Glassgow had taken a young mistress off Dickie's hands by getting her a role in a TV series shooting in Hawaii.

"All I ask is that you look at it."

"Okay. Okay. Bring it over at nine then."

They ran it in Clermont's projection room that night. In the light bouncing back from the screen, Glassgow studied Clermont's face during Margaret's walk through the Quarter. All he learned was that Clermont watched the picture intently.

The running over, the whirr of the projector silent, the lights on, Clermont said:

"She's pretty good."

Glassgow said nothing.

"Anyway she had some good direction in the picture and she can take direction, that's what counts."

Glassgow nodded.

"The problem is, like I said, I got to have some names to carry the picture. I got Fran Donald in one of the woman parts, if I get Jim Morris for the man, I could maybe think about your girl. The whole thing is I got to have at least two names."

"I appreciate that."

"I'll tell you, I think I could get something pretty good out of your girl. But the whole thing is the names, you know that."

"Doesn't anybody care about making names any more?"

Clermont grinned. "To tell you the truth, no. What do you want for this little girl if it does work out, anyway?"

"Star billing and thirty-five thousand."

"Star billing?"

"She had it in the Ricci picture. As far as I'm concerned that established it. It can be the last billing but it has to be star."

"It's fine with me, I don't have nothing but goodwill, you know that, but the other stars will probably raise hell."

"Not if you put them first."

"We will have to see. I'm not the producer, I'm the director, but we'll see what happens."

"You aren't making a mistake, Dickie."

"Now I like your girl fine but we'll have to see what happens."

That was it though not all of it. For four weeks Glassgow sweated and schemed, Clermont got Morris for the male lead, and then took Margaret. Glassgow got a compromise billing for Margaret as "Also starring." He was almost satisfied.

He told her about it at nine-thirty in the morning over coffee at the breakfast bar in her apartment. He had found her in the pool: now she was wrapped in a white terry pool robe, seated on a bar stool next to his, red hair streaked with water. She listened silently, nodding her head, white teeth clamping lightly on her lower lip.

"This is the most important deal we've had." He wanted her to be aware of what was involved, and yet did not want to frighten her. "Whatever, they call it, it's a starring role in a big-budget picture."

She nodded again.

"Does it scare you?"

"Oh no."

"It would be damn strange if you weren't a little scared."

"I guess I am a little scared."

"Great, that's how you ought to be. What do you think of it otherwise?"

"It's all right."

"I wonder how you survive without that pathological ambition."

"What do you mean?"

"Most girls in this business would leave their husbands, abandon their children, kick out their parents, or fornicate the length of Hollywood Freeway for this. To you it's just something else you have to do. I think. I suppose this is why I scheme so hard for you."

"If you scheme, why should I?"

"Why indeed?" He stared at her. She was smiling now, regarding him boldly, and he knew that what she had told him was as clearly in her thought as it was in his. *I'm in love with you, Nelson.*

"I repeat, I wonder how you survive?" He tried to move around the solidity of that memory. "Yet you aren't surviving, you're exploding. You *have* to like some of this or you couldn't do it. What about it do you *like?*"

"I like it when I'm working. You know, talking or doing something in a part when I'm somebody else. I can make everything very clear to myself when I'm somebody else." He saw she had forgotten him, for the instant. "Everything else makes me kind of sick. I don't mean really sick but I just don't like it. You know?"

He nodded.

"But I like to work, if it's something I like. Like the girl in that New Orleans picture. I liked her, and I liked to *be* her, when I was her I could make everything come out all right for her. Once I start *being* somebody, somebody else, I like that."

"I think you'll like your character in this picture."

"I guess I will. I like most of them." She looked fully at him and her face altered. "I had a lot of fun that night."

"So did I." Her eyes were wide and still directly on him, and he turned his from them. "Do it again some time."

He moved quickly into a discussion of Clermont's temperament and the peculiarities of the stars. Then he left. He was not quite sure how he felt as he drove out to CBS on Fairfax and Third, on a mission for another client.

American was not going to send *Redheads* to Europe for location. A special unit was to pick up background footage on the Continent, notably in Paris, but the picture would be shot at the plant in West Hollywood.

Margaret Dayton had advanced to a totally new plateau of pressure, and Glassgow was concerned as to how she would cope with it. The studio publicity department, skeletonized though it had become, had worked hard on the picture from the moment casting had begun. Before shooting had started the major columns had given important space to Margaret's assignment and to her capabilities and this of course was a result of the studio's effort. She had been widely photographed for more than a year, but was experiencing for the first time the impact of an intense and calculated campaign by a major studio. She had several interviews, some television appearances, and the volume of newspaper pictures increased. She remained quiet and docile, but Glassgow was fully aware of a new tension within her.

"Does all this bother you?" he asked her one night.

"I get a little nervous sometimes."

"You'll be surprised how quick you get used to it."

"I don't really mind now."

Glassgow had decided to stay away from the set the first week of shooting. She had to adjust to the situation, and she had to do it alone. He would only retard the adjustment, he thought, and do her ultimate harm if he were too solicitous. He called her the evening of her first day at work.

"How'd it go?"

"All right I guess."

"Any problems? Everything all right with Clermont?"

"I *guess* so."

He was apprehensive but let it pass. "I don't think I should be on set for a while. I'll be out next week."

"All right." She sounded very tired.

He reined himself tightly the rest of the week. The next Monday he was on the set in midmorning. He met Clermont at a coffee urn.

"How is my client doing?"

Clermont motioned him away from the urn to a space of privacy. "I have been wanting to talk to you about that, Nelson. She is not doing."

"Oh?"

"I had planned to call you today. I want her out. We'll pay her money all right but she has to get out."

"For Christ's sake, what are you talking about? You know what she can do, that's why you picked her."

"As I tell you she is not doing it. She freezes. I get nothing out of her. She should be in one of your school class plays. She gives me nothing."

"I don't understand that. She's never done that before."

Clermont shrugged. "A big picture, high standards, some are too spoiled to adjust to high standards. See for yourself."

He did not go to Margaret, but watched her next scene from the fringe of observers behind the cameras. She was supposed to thwart the advances of a Frenchman with apparent artlessness: Glassgow saw she was terrified.

"Miss Dayton." Clermont dramatized his exasperation. "Please Miss Dayton. You are vivacious. You are playful. You are sexy but in a playful way you understand. Try it again, please."

She was bad again.

Clermont's face was red.

"Miss Dayton. Will you show some animation please? Will you please please please act just a little bit, huh?"

Margaret ran off the set.

"You see?" Clermont turned to Glassgow.

"Dickie. Could we talk privately a minute?"

They went into the frame cubbyhole that was his office.

"Goddamn it Dickie, don't you see she's terrified?"

"I see she is wooden and headstrong and spoiled."

"You don't see a damn thing. She is not headstrong, she is not spoiled, she is simply terrified of you. Don't bully her for God's sake, reassure her."

"I am accustomed to handling my own actors, Mr. Glassgow."

"And I wouldn't dream of interfering. But I want you to know she's afraid of you."

Clermont's face was a study in mollification, impatience, and a sly pride.

"No reason for her to be afraid of me, no reason for anybody to be afraid of me. However, I will try to assuage the feeling of the child and perhaps indeed she will do better."

Margaret had a converted trailer for a dressing room, as did the other stars. Glassgow walked with Clermont to the steps and door.

"I'm sure you'd rather talk to her alone," said Glassgow. Clermont inclined his head.

Glassgow stood a few feet from the window of the trailer and pretended to read *Hollywood Reporter*. He heard the waves of Dickie's voice rising into occasional comprehensibility.

"Wonderfully. Musn't worry. Only pretend. Son of a bitch. Doing fine. In my hands. Great. Great."

Glassgow walked from the trailer to the edge of the set, a hundred feet away. Ten minutes later he saw Clermont return. Clermont gathered a group of technicians about him and spoke earnestly.

Glassgow started to go to Margaret but thought better of it. He waited, glancing occasionally at a dozen takes of a scene between two Frenchmen.

He saw Margaret standing well back near the big wall. He asked a question with the lift of his eyebrows. She smiled faintly and nodded all right.

Clermont finished the scene and dismissed the players. He saw Margaret, walked over to her, and brought her to the set with his arm around her.

"Are we going to kill them, darling?" he said when it was all ready. "You bet we are going to kill them."

Margaret laughed, very quickly, and Glassgow saw her teeth bite into her lower lip.

But she was much better in the scene, which was to say she was much less frightened. Her quality showed itself to a degree, but insufficiently. Yet a small explosion of applause followed Clermont's "Cut!" and Glassgow, surprised, turned to see it come from those men who had huddled with Clermont. Then he understood: Dickie was a fiend of astuteness once he got an idea.

Dickie said to Margaret, "Sweetheart, that was it, that was perfect. We don't need any more on that one. You were only great darling." Abruptly he turned his attention to an assistant director hovering by his chair. "Let's get set up for Scene Fifty-three, same set."

Glassgow rubbed his upper lip with his fingers. He suspected that, much later, it would turn out that one camera had a malfunction and the scene would have to go again. But Dickie's benevolent deception had done its job: Margaret appeared to have lost her fear.

He looked at her standing by Clermont, who had risen from the chair. She was laughing naturally, red was in her cheeks, and she clearly was in the grip of a pleasurable tension.

8

THE DAY AFTER Margaret finished the picture, Glassgow came to dinner in the Daytons' new apartment on Beverly Drive. Octavia made drinks: Sauterne and soda for Margaret and vodka martinis for herself and Glassgow. She was wearing a superbly fitted cocktail dress, and he felt the heavy impact of her physical presence.

Glassgow thought what he had often thought: that he would rather bed Octavia than her daughter. Of course business tabooed her, and of course he could no more take Margaret than his own daughter, if he had had one, yet the speculation, the comparison, had its interest.

"Take it, Svengali." Octavia thrust the tray with the glasses toward him. She smiled at him swiftly and perhaps cryptically, as though she knew what had passed through his mind. And of course she did, he thought. Women intuit the excitement they set off. For that matter so do men. He took the glass.

"Cheers," said Octavia. "A girl doesn't finish her first starring picture every day."

"It's just also starring," said Margaret.

Octavia snorted.

"The word's around it's going to be a big one," said Glassgow. "Have you seen any of the rushes?"

"I have," said Margaret.

"How were they?" said her mother.

"I thought I was pretty good."

Glassgow looked into his martini and one side of his mouth twisted slightly upward.

"I'm not as good as I was in the New Orleans picture but that one has more to it."

"Don't you let Dickie Clermont hear you say the other one had more to it."

"Nelson, I'm not really a damned fool."

"No you're not."

"She is tired," said Octavia.

"What she is is hungry," said Margaret.

They went in to the table, Margaret served steak, salad and potatoes and Octavia poured wine: Chateau Rothschild 1955.

After dinner Octavia said, "Well I'm off to Vegas." She turned to Glassgow and added very swiftly, "A big party of us are going up."

"Have a ball," said Glassgow.

"Perhaps I will." She looked at him and it was he who colored. It was he, also, who wished he was going to Vegas, with her.

When Octavia had gone, Glassgow sat in the armless chair in the living room while Margaret poured him brandy. Her breasts pressed his shoulder, he was sure deliberately, and he felt the too-familiar desire to shatter things. He fought it, then capitulated, then took the brandy bottle from Margaret's hand and set it on the coffee table and pulled her down to him. He kissed her, and not stopping, turned her body and drew her to his lap. She moaned, slid her arms around him, and opened her mouth to his.

He thought: I have done a very stupid thing.

But he had done it, and he had bought everything that came after.

"Please love me, Nelson," she said.

"You're a child." But he wanted to shatter—even if he shattered his own safety.

"No, I'm not. You have to stop thinking of me as a child. I'm not a child and I am in love with you. Sometimes I think I'm going to break up I'm so in love with you. Please love me back."

"I love you." He wondered how much he was lying and decided: not completely.

"Do something about it then."

Her body was shivering, and he undressed her very slowly.

Later, in her bedroom, he said, "I hadn't meant to do this."

"I know it. I seduced you."

"No, you didn't."

"It's just that I'm in love with you."

"That's an idiotic expression. Let's get out of here."

"Where are we going?"

"Anywhere."

Anywhere was Laguna. They checked into a motel on the beach at two o'clock and arose at noon. A low cloud ceiling threw the sky, sea, and beach into shades of pearl.

They walked along the beach. It was half-deserted for the day was Wednesday.

"Do you suppose you're my father figure?"

"When did you learn that?"

"I just learned it. Do you suppose you are?"

"Let's not work the incest bit too hard."

"Are you going to leave me when we get back, Nelson?"

He watched the sand carefully. "I don't know. Be best for both of us if I did."

"Please don't."

He watched his feet as they pushed lightly in the sand. "I doubt that I will."

He didn't. To his own incredulity and shock, he found he was in an affair of the dimensions he had fled so long: it was a kind of a "love" affair. Margaret loved him, he permitted her to do so, and he denounced himself for his dishonesty. He insisted it was dishonesty, perhaps too strenuously (he considered). Had he permitted himself to admit he returned her feeling—genuinely, not paternally, not commiseratingly—his image of himself would have been shattered. Yet he was profoundly engaged: before he had completely registered the fact, he had glided into a strongly welded relationship with Margaret Dayton.

He did not spend all or most of his time with her. He had other clients and much work. Some days they did not meet at all. Their routines were unpretentious. Sometimes she would be waiting in his apartment when he came home in the late afternoon. Sometimes, then, they would kiss and go directly to bed. Sometimes they would have a drink, go to dinner, come back and go to bed. Sometimes, even, they would not go to bed at all. Less frequently, Glassgow would pick her up at her apartment, and they would drive far distances in the Lancia: to Santa Barbara, Tijuana, Palm Springs, once to Morro Bay at the southern edge of Northern California.

Glassgow felt that he was cheating. He was getting the benisons that being loved conferred: worshipful companionship and a fine bed. He was not giving full return. Yet Margaret was happy and perhaps, he thought, this was the design she wanted. Perhaps she had wanted it and had made it come true, exactly as it was.

"I'm cheating you," he told her once.

He was twisting the Lancia through brown hills on Doheny Drive. It was a hard-bright, hot afternoon, the smog rolled away by a strong west wind. "I don't, I'm not giving you what you really want."

"You aren't cheating me."

And so he let it go.

He was uneasy with the situation. Frightened of it. He had lost succcssfully the memory of the hurts, but the fear of them had shaped him: he had tried to make himself so he would not have to undergo them again.

His failure to become completely the Glassgow he had selected, not quite awarely, was the exact measure of his failure to protect himself completely. The gap between the two Glassgows had been an entrance for Margaret, and for pain, and now the achieved Glassgow, who had turned out to be the not quite achieved Glassgow, was about to fall.

She did not work for two months. He was convinced that *Redheads* was going to make her very big, and he wanted no lesser efforts to follow and to take the edge off that success. So for two months, he was the center of her life, and joined to her in a deepening, and to him dangerous, intimacy.

Then the picture was released.

It had had two premieres, one at the Egyptian in Hollywood and one in Oakland. Both were successful, and American decided to take it to the Music Hall in New York.

They ordered Margaret to go with it. She told Glassgow she didn't want to go without him.

"I can't. I'll be tied up now for weeks with the MGM contracts for Johnson's new play."

"Couldn't you do what you have to do over the phone?"

"The real thing is I shouldn't be seen with you, I mean it shouldn't be noticed that we are et cetera."

"I don't see why."

"At this particular point you have to register as young and single and unattached. The public doesn't really expect virginity but they don't want to know exactly what's happening."

"I think you just don't want to go."

She cried. She cried, too, when he drove her to Burbank to catch a jet to New York. She cheered somewhat with excitement of departure. A girl in American's publicity department was going with her.

She kissed Glassgow good-bye.

"You won't change your mind and go?"

"I can't. You'll have a ball anyway."

She stopped on the gangway, just outside the door, and waved at him.

Glassgow knew what was coming, he had a conviction of Margaret's success that was almost mystical. He knew from contacts in studio publicity that *Life* and *Look* had layouts on Margaret that were ready to go if the picture took off.

"They asked us," said his friend. "But naturally we're going to take advantage of the break and give Margaret Dayton plenty of attention. If the picture takes off and so on."

It took off. *Redheads Prefer Gentlemen* opened to praise, even, from some of the New York critics. The theme of this more literate criticism was that Dickie Clermont had made his best picture in fifteen years; he was in full possession, again, of the perception and timing that had made him one of the Continental masters of high comedy.

But to the mass media, it was Margaret's triumph. A two-page layout broke in *Life; Look* had four. *Playboy* had timed, with the release, another center pull-out of Margaret, now a discreet two garments removed from nudity. The fan magazines were demanding interviews as soon as she returned, Glassgow was told, and American's publicity and advertising departments made suitable adjustments to the *Redheads* campaign.

They shuttled Margaret to big cities for openings. When Glassgow picked her up at Burbank, six weeks after he had left her there, he knew it had happened: Margaret Dayton had made it.

9

SHE kissed him, hard, as she came to the railing for visitors, and he wondered how much it had changed her.

Not much, he decided.

In the Lancia, she sat as close to him as she could get, the length of her leg pressing hard and warm against his.

They had been on the telephone many times, always it had been she who called, and Glassgow did not have the sense of a real separation.

Her head tilted back against his arm. Her eyes were closed, and her face, though unlined, had a droop of tiredness.

Suddenly she opened her eyes and smiled at him. "I'm home, damn you. Take me somewhere and love me."

It was ten in the morning.

He drove to his own apartment in Beverly. Somewhat after two in the afternoon, all at once full of velocity, they rushed to Long Beach to catch the steamer to Catalina. Through the weekend, Glassgow looked for signs of success-corruption but she showed chiefly fatigue and harassment. She was almost impervious to glory, though happily not quite. He had decided he must leave her as lover—though absolutely not as agent—and her unalterable, cheerful subordination of herself to him made it hard. He decided to postpone telling her, and it was not until two weeks later that he could bring himself to do it.

"You've got to get rid of me," he said. "I don't mean as your agent."

She looked at him blank-faced.

"What are you talking about?"

"We have to stop this and be just friends. I'm limiting your development."

"What do you mean you're limiting my development?"

"I'm taking too much of your time and much too much of your attention."

Her face was still trained on him, set, her eyes wide.

He said, "You've got to follow your luck. You only get that luck once."

"What are you talking about?"

He had to smile.

"Don't you really know what's happened? You've made it. You've made it big."

"I don't care about all that."

"You will. You will more than ever if you lose it now you've had it." He stopped and touched her shoulder.

"Look. I've seen it happen before. You've made it but you haven't nailed it down. To nail it down you have to work harder and concentrate harder than you've ever done in your life. That has to be your life."

"Concentrate on what?"

"On being Margaret Dayton."

She looked at him in a kind of bewilderment. Or, he thought, shock.

"You can't ease up," he went on. "Now is the one time you can't ease up. You can't give it any less than all of yourself."

"Give it, give what? You are talking pretty damn crazy, did you know it?"

"Margaret. It's over. It has to be."

"Don't you love me any more?"

"Yes. I love you."

"But you're not in love with me, is that it?"

"I feel about you the way I always have, and you know how that is."

"Well screw you and screw your advice and screw everything." She began to cry. "Screw just everything." She bawled and he pulled her head to his chest and tried to comfort her, paternally, with his hands on her back.

"Nelson." Her voice was suddenly meek and muffled against his chest. "You really want us to break up?"

"We have to, baby."

"I don't want to."

"I'll still be around." He tried, dismally, unsuccessfully, to joke. "We have a contract, you know."

She cried loudly and he kept his arms around her, awkwardly. He did not leave her until she had composed herself, almost.

The step taken, he had thought that he would not see her for a time, and that when he did, they would be very different quantities to each other than they had been. Yet she was waiting in his apartment a week later and they tumbled into bed with no firm effort otherwise on his part. It happened twice more. He consoled himself with a line from Remarque: "The best way to break off with a woman is to sleep with her occasionally."

It was with a sensation of anticlimax that he finally made the emotional break good by going to Europe himself.

When he returned, he carried on all his business conversations with her by telephone. She accepted it. He managed to avoid seeing her for a month, and when he did, it was in a conference with four other people. The break had firmed, it was good and necessary, and he denied, almost successfully, his sense of loss.

He fulfilled his role of agent precisely during the two pictures he had signed for with American. They were alone once and she looked at him directly, in a clear communication, but he turned away.

She went through several publicity romances of no significance (though she *had* to be doing something with some of the men), and he thought the half-public rumors about her and Mace Garrett were of the same cloth. He thought, too, they were extremely ill-advised. She had just been cast in a picture with Garrett. Garrett was also a Glassgow client, and Glassgow had worked for months to get him and Margaret in the same picture. Once the Prince, once a huge name in the business and still a star, Garrett was fifty-four. In the Industry, he was famous for one idiosyncrasy, he tried to have, not necessarily an affair, but at least one session, with each leading lady.

Glassgow, feeling certain twinges, drove to location in Arizona and made himself inconspicuous for a morning, before he announced himself. He watched Margaret and the gray-templed Garrett holding hands as they watched a scene. He saw Margaret's face lift provocatively to Garrett, and he was certain Garrett had had his token. It was nothing to him, of course—yet he felt physically ill. Hours later, he spoke briefly to Margaret and drove back to town the same day.

Less than a week after, he was awakened by his doorbell. He was sure it would be Margaret, though he did not know why. It was.

She was wearing slacks, a green kerchief was over her head, and her face was dirty. He stepped back from the door, she came in, and she fell into his arms and began to cry. She cried it out, or almost out, and said, "That son of a bitch. That crummy jerk son of a bitch."

Glassgow did not probe. He knew Garrett as one of the few likable actors in town. He was also one of the randiest and he must have figured any female in the business knew what she was doing.

He stroked her shoulder and she began to cry again.

The picture was done, and he did not have to send her back to Arizona. When she left him, she said she was going to drive to a health ranch in Tecate, Mexico.

That afternoon, he drove to the pet hospital. The chattering and howling mocked him: he decided the hospital had outlived its usefulness.

He could not work. They had come at last: pain and fall. He knew that he had been waiting for them, it was not even impossible that he had secretly craved them, though he thought not. The armor had been no armor at all when it counted. Margaret had penetrated it. Now he had fallen.

He had feared to need her too much, and because he had feared, he did need her too much. He wanted to cry to her to come back, that he would take anything, be anything.

But he did not.

He went back to the apartment, decided not to eat, then went to the Crescendo on the Strip to hear Mort Sahl. He never did. He sat at the bar instead and began to drink Scotch and water. He realized, suddenly, that he was drunk and was furious at himself: he, Nelson Glassgow, was committing a cliché.

He was absurd, he thought. He had left Margaret. He could not expect her to wear a chastity belt after he left her. He had accepted that she would have other men after he left her. It was irrational that he should feel such loss.

He looked across the bar to his face in the mirror. It looked silly. He went to wash it and walked back with the elaborate precision of the loaded. He sat and a woman said behind him, "I'll buy you a drink or take you home, Mr. Glassgow. Whichever you like."

He turned his head about and upward to look at Octavia Dayton. Through his dullness he saw she looked very smart, was smiling, and had concern in her eyes.

"Buy you one," he said. "Pleasant coincidence."

"No coincidence. A friend saw you and called." She sat down and said softly, "You're rather tight. Let me drive you home. I don't want you in any mess."

"I'm all right."

"Please let me drive you."

To his own surprise he surrendered at once. "All right."

She drove him not to his apartment but hers.

"You can sleep in Margaret's bed, she's not here you know, and I'll take you to get your own car in the morning. That seems simplest."

"No pajamas." That sounded extraordinarily funny to him.

"You just might survive that. Margaret's bed is in there."

"I'd rather sleep in your bed."

"You're tight."

"I *would* rather sleep in your bed."

"I know you would, my dear. You love Margaret but you'd rather sleep with me."

"How did you know?"

She smiled. "It won't make any difference where you sleep, not tonight."

She was right. In the morning, she brought him a pitcher of water and a pot of coffee. She looked very wide awake and ripely desirable as she set the tray by his bed. He drank the water and considered that he might not die. After the coffee, he was sure he would not.

"Toothbrush in the bath," she called from the kitchen. "Went out and bought it for you."

After a shower, and a breakfast of scrambled eggs and steak, he felt astonishingly well. He stood up from the table. "That was great."

Already standing, she threw him the same ironic tender glance. "You do look better."

"Oh I am better."

They stared at each other for many seconds. She opened her hands and beckoned him. "Come to mother." She opened her arms and said, "Come to mother now."

He moved into her arms: then she took his hand and led him to the most profound pleasure he had ever known.

Three hours later they were both sitting at the table, again. He had finished his cigarette and was smiling comfortably, nothing but comfortably, at Octavia when he heard the front door close, and high heels thud on the carpeting coming closer, and of course he knew who, and of course there was nothing to do, and what did it matter now anyway?

He was watching the door with alert detached interest when it swung inward and showed Margaret, red hair and blue slacks.

She stopped. She looked down at Glassgow, then Octavia, then Glassgow. "Excuse *me,"* she said, and the door closed behind her.

Glassgow listened to the silence.

"She didn't say *continue,"* he said.

Octavia looked at him across the table.

That had been two years before they came to Mykonos.

10

In the room in the hotel on Mykonos he let his trousers fall, stepped out of them, left them on the floor. The shirt dropped two feet from the trousers: he was aware of nothing but the profound, so-familiar, bleary, bleary fatigue. And a great sweeping annoyance at Margaret that somehow could not peak into anger. She meant well: she always meant well: that was her first and final weapon.

Thinking of her, he thought of an infinity of shapes of her, one behind the other, no one exactly like another. The first few were clearly visible if each less so; behind them, the ordered file of Margarets receded face by face into a wavy line of shadows. The one in front, today, was Margaret Furens: jaw set, eyes indignant, she had righteous flashing reasons for violent idiocy. *I have rights. I have some rights.* And so she wrote a check, or denounced an Importance, or walked out on a picture.

And yet she meant so well. And she was not stupid: he had a profound if narrow respect for her intelligence. But she was criminally rash and imprudent.

He himself had the reputation of being a rash man and an imprudent one, and yet he knew that for a long time his rash and imprudent actions had worked for him. Not always, but always for a long time.

At the heart of each of his violences was a core of calculation. Even when he did not immediately acknowledge his purpose, ultimately it faced and winked at him.

Not always, but always lately. Once it had been quite different.

Had he become a mature man or a charlatan?

Goddamn Margaret.

He just managed to turn down the blankets of his bed, and pull them to his chin after he dropped into its softness. He had feared that he might not sleep: he need not have.

BOOK 5

MACE GARRETT

1

HE closed his eyes, opened them, and lay with them wide open, checking himself awareness by awareness, as though he were still a professional athlete, which he had not been for thirty years. He decided it had been neither a good night nor a bad one: he had not slept enough to feel really well and he had slept enough to get by.

Turned carefully to face him, the wristwatch on the bed table said six-thirty-two. Arithmetic: he would stay in bed until seven. He had learned long ago not to bounce out: let the metabolism crawl ahead by the inch. He had time to sleep another hour even, his call was not until seven-thirty, only he knew he would never make sleep now. He went through the relax drill anyway: squeeze a little more physical rest out of it. His body could function remarkably on rest without sleep, even at fifty-six, even with the thrombus on the left atrial wall. It was his mind that was colored black by a lack of sleep.

He would have a hard day today, because now all days were hard. Margaret gone did not mean a rest, it only meant a change. They would shoot around her.

He would be in the chariots today. He would not really have to drive them of course, they had stunt men to drive them, but he would get lurched around. They had a device like the electric horse in the gym that rocked and rolled the fake chariots for the close-ups, and Garrett was going to be bucked and he might get sick from it.

"I hope not," he said, and then knew he had said it out loud.

"Where the hell is she?" he said, still out loud.

He was certain she had not abandoned the picture. He had known those who abandoned pictures, they were instantly abandoned themselves in the great age of the studios, and Margaret was not one of them. He could not believe that anything bad had happened to her either. It could have though. The types in the hills looked hard enough for anything. Maybe not though. Maybe they were the salt of the earth. Who could tell. Margaret was just up to some foolishness. He hoped so, he liked Margaret, that was not a good enough word. But he had to worry about his hundred thousand dollars, he would not get his hundred thousand dollars until the picture was finished. It would be finished though, Margaret or no Margaret, he would get paid Margaret or no Margaret, what he had to worry about was whether *he* finished the picture.

What a jerk he was to worry about himself when he should be worrying about Margaret. Margaret had got him the picture and the price. Still, everything depended on whether he finished the picture. For the first time in his life the life of someone he cared about depended absolutely on him. Lives. He should not think about that, he needed the rest and he should get it while he could. Or try.

He thought about Arlene, and then he was not thinking about Arlene but about Hilda, and then he suddenly was aware he had come out of a doze, and then he was aware of what was now, for him, and for that time of day, an extraordinary circumstance.

Shall we smuggle it into town, your lordship? You better get up before that gets you in trouble.

He got out of bed, it was seven-fifteen, he felt much better than he had forty minutes before. He washed, came back, took off his pajamas, and looked at himself full length in the mirror, partly from vanity, partly from the coldest professional interest. He had no belly though he had fat over the kidneys. The muscle separation was still good. The deltoids and pectorals that had been his trademark were big and still firm. He looked nothing like fifty-six if you stopped at the neck. Above the neck. Well. A shave would fix some of it above the neck. The morning bristle was gray, all gray, he could not dye that but he did not have to. The thrombus of course did not show.

Still facing the mirror, he did the Charles Atlas exercises the doctor had shown him decades ago when they were dynamic tension instead of isometrics. He did them slowly, avoiding a rush of the heartbeat but making the muscles define themselves as they worked against each other.

Then he put on the white terry robe and went into the bath to shave with a blade. With his heavy gray he could not use an electric. He shaved, showered, dressed in slacks, sport shirt and jacket, and when he checked at the mirror again he looked not only like a forty-five-year-old man but a well one.

He opted for breakfast from the location kitchen instead of the hotel dining room, and went to one of the Globe cars on the street in front of the hotel. The driver was Harry, the old middleweight: as part of a deal with the Teamsters, Globe had brought four drivers over and hired Greeks for the rest. Globe did not have to bring the drivers but found it good labor relations.

Harry opened the door from the inside and Garrett got in. "Come aboard, champ," said Harry.

"How they hanging, Harry?" he said.

Harry started the Citroën smoothly, swung into the one-way street, and shifted gears. "They still looking for Margaret," he said.

Garrett understood Harry was pleased to be authority. "She'll turn up," he said. "Don't you figure?"

"Sidney Tate don't look so sure."

"Well hell, the front office has to look like they're worrying to earn their dough."

"You think she'll be in today?"

"I expect her in before dark." He wished he did.

Harry made doubting sounds.

He diverted Harry to boxing talk, and made ritual responses while he watched the country go by. Before coffee, he was half asleep and the rocky brown shore and blue sea spinning backward outside his window faintly hypnotized him. At Troy, he drew coffee from the urn into a plastic cup and drank two cups of it as he stood watching the company move to the start of the day's work. Two hundred yards in front of him, the Greek and Trojan armies faced each other indifferently. Assistant directors moved between them bearing electric megaphones, and Garrett heard the electronic rasp of these without distinguishing words. Crews were tugging cameras into position on wooden tracks. A cluster of crew and cast continuously moved and re-formed about the coffee urn. To the right of the urn and a hundred feet away were the toilet trailers: men came up and down the steps constantly. There was less traffic among the women.

Breakfast for the crew was finished, the portable kitchen was formally closed, but Garrett could still get a special order out of it. When that was gone all of it would be gone. Come on, he bucked himself, you're getting a hundred thousand again, anyway for this one. You know why, something answered.

At a wooden table by the kitchen, he ate his scrambled eggs, dry toast and grapefruit, three hundred and fifty calories, all he could have, and went to makeup. Margaret had makeup come to her, so could he, he supposed, but the hell with it. They only put the base on him anyway and he could have done that himself.

After makeup he went to his dressing room to put on Hector's armor. The dressing room was half of a trailer: a bunk on one end wall and a mirror on the other and two small straight chairs between. He dressed, leaving off the heavy breastplate and helmet, and sat in one of the chairs and read a week-old copy of *Film Daily*.

A knock on the door and Nelson Glassgow came in. He raised his hand in greeting, swung the other chair around, and sat with its back toward him and his arms upon it.

"How you feel?" Glassgow asked.

"Good." It was only half a lie. He was grateful for Glassgow's steady concern. His agent had been zealous in watching his health through the picture, and his watchfulness did not flag now, when trouble over his truly valuable property, Margaret Dayton, understandably might have forced all else from his mind.

"Anything on Margaret?"

"No."

"Sylvia. I never trusted Sylvia."

"Me either. I can't see Margaret running out on a picture though."

"She wouldn't run out on a picture. Oh she's a little nuts all right but no just walking out, not telling anybody yes or no or kiss my ass. Depend on it it is lit-tul Sylvia's work and when I get my hands on that mother."

"It might be pretty nice work," said Garrett factually.

"Not for me."

Garrett looked at his watch. "I got to go. You ought to have one client anyway that's early."

"You better believe it. I'll go with you and show the flag."

Garrett put on the breastplate but did not lace it and carried the helmet in his hand. The tall plume of the helmet nodded with his steps. "Let's stop a sec," Glassgow said, and they went into the Quonset marked PRODUCTION.

Sills and Tate were sitting at Sills's desk.

Over an alpaca blue cardigan Sills's handsome elegant face showed deep traces of fatigue. Fatigue showed too in Tate's neat stern features but more guardedly.

"News?" said Glassgow, and Tate shook his head and Sills said "No," at the same time.

"We'll have some today," said Sills.

"We hope," said Tate. Garrett looked at him: pressed brown suit, fresh white shirt, looking neat and calm and massive (though he was not massive, he was not even big), and if Margaret *was* out of the picture, Tate was out of everything.

Tate saw him looking. "Did you ever go off in the middle of a picture, Garrett?"

Garrett started to say, "I was never even late," and checked himself: Margaret was not only a friend but a benefactor. He said instead, "When you have a big woman star you have lots of, sensitivity. I've never seen them any other way and I've seen them all."

"Not many are this, sensitive."

Defending Margaret, Garrett said, "They're all bad news," and then understanding he had not supported her at all, said miserably, "Margaret, she's more responsible than most of them." He looked at his watch, said "I'm due outside," and left swiftly as he could.

He was real helpful, he was. Yes he was.

He was sympathetic to Tate and Sills and Korbin and Glassgow, he was sorry for Margaret wherever she was, but the only thing he could truly and deeply care about was whether he made it himself.

If he did, Arlene and her baby would be taken care of. He would meet his obligation on the San Diego County development and in two years his piece of that had to be worth half a million. He would have his insurance paid in advance for another year and that would keep them until it was time to liquidate. The San Diego thing and a little cash, and someday a tax refund, was all he had out of the ten million dollars he had made. And he did not have the San Diego deal nailed down, not yet. How does a man go through ten million dollars? Why it's no trick at all.

In the first place, he has plenty of help. The United States of America and the State of California get more than half of it even with the very best tax people against them. Add three wives. Then three or four bad guesses. A business manager with glue on his fingers and bad judgment: poor Sid: no anger for he was after all dead.

And a very good time for most of the thirty years. Even so. If it had not been for Sid he would be worth seven hundred thousand now. Still Sid had worked out the San Diego thing for him. That was enough of that. All of that.

He started toward the cameras: crewmen were hauling these into position on wooden supports. The position was at the edge of the plain, halfway between the Greek and Trojan armies. The papier-mâché walls of Troy were behind the Trojan army. Beyond the plain was the blue sea.

Garrett stopped where the cameras would stop and watched the armies milling in boredom: each was a regiment in the real right-now Greek army. Korbin and three assistant directors were on the plain. Korbin spoke only to the first assistant director, Josh Duncan, who was handling the movement of the armies. At that job, Josh was the best there was. All the top directors wanted him. He was the most successful career assistant director in the Industry. All assistant directors were career assistant directors. Assistant directors simply did not become directors though almost anybody else did. Sometimes even cutters became directors, but assistant directors, never. Dick Powell had been a fine director, Paul Henreid was a good one. Garrett had never wanted to be a director, he knew his limitation.

He listened to the amplified electronic voices:

"Chariots up front. Chariots up front."

Strange words: a repeat in Greek.

The horses and chariots came up.

"Get the captain up here. Greek control, captain up front."

The repeat in Greek. These were actors. Garrett watched the AD's position them.

Dust began to rise. Josh Duncan had them wet the plain with hoses from a truck tank. He had them ready, he knew all about the dust from how many pictures.

Garrett watched with admiration, he was as always intensely interested in the control of screen armies, it was one of the few completely interesting things in the business he had been in thirty years.

After thirty years, though, he was no longer embarrassed by being an actor, nor did he fail to identify with the business. It was just that he had prior identifications.

His trouble, or his great good luck, was that he had never been able to take the business seriously. He had worked hard at it, he was one of the hardest workers there was, in the Industry he had the reputation of a rock. But it had always been just a job. He worked at it as he would work at any job, he liked it or at least he did not mind it, but he did not truly care about doing it. He had only deeply cared about doing two things in his life. One was to finish this picture. The first, and it was more than thirty years ago, was to be light-heavyweight champion of the world.

2

IN 1934, when his six-year hitch expired, he was a coxswain on the old *Greenville,* a six-inch cruiser in the treaty navy. He had lost a bad decision in the light-heavyweight semifinals in the All-Navy tournament two months before, and he was going to turn professional. That afternoon, two days before he was to leave the Navy, and the *Greenville,* he was talking about it to Jake Ruff.

"You still hell-set on fighting pro?" Jake said.

"Why not?" He felt good, he was walking back and forth on the well deck where the boxing gear was. He could feel the good heat of his body and its sweat soaking into the heavy soft cotton: he had done three rounds on the rope, three on the light bag, three shadowboxing, and finished with three on the big bag and loosening exercises. He had had the power on the big bag, the combinations had gone right, his last workout in the Navy was a good one, and he felt good, and he was going to fight pro and be champion of the world. He was hurt that his friend, and teacher, did not want him to fight pro.

"You'll get that pretty face busted up for one thing," said Jake.

"Don't you think I got it?" he said. He was feeling sad that Jake was not with him all the way. He looked at Jake, now a big belly and a flattened nose under a chief's cap, who had been all-service welterweight champion eighteen years before, and could have been, they said, champion of the world himself. "You know it was a bad decision," he said.

"Oh, I know you got it. I ain't got any doubts that you got it." Jake pushed his visor upward with the heel of his hand and looked,

sixty-five. After he had eaten a huge meal, and had drunk a quart of water in regulated but steady amounts, he knew he was up to a good one-seventy or seventy-one. Still the weight-making weakened him. He would have been stronger at an honest one-sixty-eight.

"We don't want to knock them out these first few fights," Gill told him. "It's going to be hard getting you fights at all because you're too big for a middleweight. Just win it on decision and don't scare them off. Later on it'll be different."

Garrett won by decision all the preliminaries, there were two four-rounders and two sixes. He won the first eight-round semifinal the same way, but had to take the second by a knockout in the seventh round because Gill thought it was too close.

Having almost nothing to do that interfered with fighting, he felt pleased with himself most of the time. Garrett going through half-darkness to the center of light that was the ring had shape and weight: he could see and feel him. His hands tight with gauge, his shoulders feeling the robe, his belly tight against the protector, all of it pulled Garrett together out of the spread shadows and made him firm. He had somebody to be: he was who he wanted to be.

The only thing he did not like was juggling with weight. It hurt him. He complained often to Gill. "It ain't for long," Gill said. After the sixth fight, the one he had to win by a knockout, Gill got him a main event. "You can start knocking them out now. You can handle most middleweights, all but the very best."

He won two knockouts over West Coast middleweights in his first two mains. Then they brought in an Eastern middleweight who had been a good name only two years before and who was only a little on the downgrade. Garrett lost by decision, clearly but gracefully.

After the fight he told Gill, "Making one sixty-five is killing me. When do we go up to seventy-five?"

"Maybe now," said Gill. "Maybe now. You got yourself a little bit of a reputation now."

And three days later: "There's a red-hot light heavy in San Francisco, maybe he wants a little action."

His name was Red Johnson, and he did. For the first time Garrett did not have to worry about making weight; he thought only about getting the best edge he could, and he went in at one-seventy-one in the best shape he had ever been.

He did not win a round and he took more punishment in ten rounds than he had taken in the rest of his life. Both eyes were black, his nose was broken, he had blue lumps on his face and purple lumps on his body.

"Man, you can take a shot like nobody I ever saw," Johnson said after the fight. "I thought I had you three different times."

You damn near did, Garrett could have said. What he did say was, "It's all shape, I guess. You were real sharp."

In the dressing room, Gill said, "I overmatched you, kid, I'm sorry. I didn't know he was that good. He's going to be champion."

"The hell he is," said Garrett on the table. *"I'm* going to be champion. The son of a bitch can bang though."

"He can box too, he can plain fight like hell. Jesus you can take it though. I didn't know you could take it like that." He turned Garrett's head, gently, so he could stare down into his face. "That pretty face ain't never going to be the same."

"Screw my face. I'll get him next time."

"Not no time soon you won't." He touched Garrett's nose, very gently, and Garrett made a quick soft sound. "That's busted, son. You better get used to it they ain't going to call you pretty boy no more."

"Screw pretty boy," said Garrett. "I'm no goddamn movie star. I'm a goddamn fighter that's going to be a goddamn champion."

"By God you may." Gill looked at him strangely. "You ain't going to be no pretty boy though."

That was the year Max Baer was going to fight Carnera for the heavyweight title, it had become fashionable for women to be interested in fighters or to pretend to be interested in fighters, and some dull sportswriter had called Garrett Pretty Boy Garrett. After he started in main events he noticed more women than usual around, some of them Hollywood women with fair names and one or two with big names, and always Lupe Velez, who loved the Mexican fighters but saw all the fights at Hollywood Legion whoever was fighting. Garrett was sure they did not care about him, it was just the thing to be interested in fighters that year.

Gill said, "I want to check you in at the hospital for a good rest and going over. I want you in tonight."

"I'm okay."

"It's just for a rest and checkup."

"Hell no."

"A favor for me."

"All right. Let me get my stuff."

He had his rub and shower and dressed and left the dressing room. He would get a cab and go to the Hotel Alexandria, where many fighters lived as he did, now.

He had the true, sad, sour feeling of defeat. He had had it in the ring at the last bell because he needed no decision to know he had lost badly; he had had it in the dressing room, where the permanent smell of ancient, dried sweat became the stink of defeat exactly as it had been, other nights, the scent of victory, and he had it in the shower which washed away sweat and dried blood but did not touch defeat. Now he had it, shrunk a little smaller but cold and permanent, inside him as he stood on the sidewalk in front of the Legion, feeling eyes on his wounded face that was the signature of defeat, and looked for an empty taxicab.

"Can I give you a ride?" he heard a woman's voice call to someone, he searched for a cab, and the voice called again, "Mr. Garrett. Over here. Can I give you a ride?"

He saw a black 1934 Cadillac, and a woman's white face, under a hat, behind the wheel. He could not tell who she was. He walked over to the Cadillac and bent to the window. His eyes tried to make out who she was.

"You don't know me, Mr. Garrett, but I see your fights. Get in and let me take you where you're going."

He was going to tell her no, thanks. Instead he walked around the car and got in the front seat beside her.

"Thank you," he said. "I appreciate it."

"*I* appreciate it," she said. "I appreciate the company." She started the car, he glanced at her face looking over the wheel.

"I'm Helene Lancaster." She said it with the kind of carelessness that meant it should mean something to him. It didn't.

"Glad to know you," he said. "I guess you know my name."

"I've seen your last three fights."

"You did?" He did not know what else to say. At a red light he got a clear look at her. She was about forty, maybe not quite, dark blonde, plump face, not bad looking. He couldn't see her figure except the upper works. They were all right.

"Yes I did." Shifting gears stiffly, not looking at him, she said, "Why did you take that beating tonight?"

He made a sound intended for a laugh. "I did all I could to stop it."

"Why didn't you just quit?"

"Quit?" It took him a moment to understand the idea. It outraged him. "A fighter don't quit."

"Well. I guess I'm put in my place. Forgive me."

He was embarrassed. "It's just that you always got the chance to get the shot in."

"It's all right. I know I said the wrong thing. You haven't told me where you were going."

"Alexandria Hotel, that's downtown. Then I'm going to the hospital."

"You were hurt then?"

"No. My manager just wants me to. You know, have a checkup, some rest."

"It's a very good idea." She stopped for another light, shifted, and started. "I know who you are. My feelings are hurt. You don't know who I am. Doesn't my name sound just a little bit familiar? He-lene Lan-caster."

His head hurt just above his neck. He did not care about her or her name. He cared about his head. Still he tried to please. "Oh, sure. Sure. Now it's coming to me. Helene Lancaster. I saw your last picture. I knew there was something about you. I guess I don't keep up with movies much."

He heard anger in her laugh. "My boy, you don't keep up with anything much. I, am, not, a, movie, person. Didn't you now, haven't you in some moment of your cloistered little life heard of *The Fury and the Flame?"*

"No ma'am. What is that?"

She was quiet. Then she said with a sweetness he understood to be dangerous. "It is a title. It is a title of a book. *The Fury and the Flame.*" She started to laugh. "It's the damnedest biggest book in the last twenty years. It's a household word, I thought. Well, I guess I bought it. What is a mere book to a prizefighter?"

In his defeat and weariness he was suddenly angry. "You knew I was a fighter when you picked me up. Why don't you just stop the car and let me out?"

"Oh shut up and sit still," she said, very pleasantly, and accelerated. "I apologize. I, am, sorry. No offense?"

"It's okay." He rested his head against the cushions, then lifted it. "What's the book about?"

"It is," she said very precisely, "about screwing in the thirteen colonies."

He felt a shock of surprise, and his cheeks flooding, and he caught her looking at him. "My God, I *have* upset you. You *are* an innocent."

"It's okay," he said uncomfortably, then aggressively, "I got nothing against screwing."

"Only you aren't used to the copulatory word in the mouths of ladies. This does seem to be my night for apologizing. So in self-defense I'll tell you something else. The book has been translated into nineteen languages. It has sold a million and a half copies in this country if you count book clubs. And I will tell you something else still. It, is, a, lousy, book."

"Looks like it's pretty good, everybody buying it like that."

"That's why they're buying it. It's lousy. I know more about putting a play together than anybody else alive, I am a great theater talent, and the way I have to make it is with a lousy goddamn book."

He wondered why she was telling him all of it, and he did not like it. He smelled something faint and sweet in the car: gin. She was not drunk but she was very loose from it.

Was she trying to make him, he wondered.

She had picked the wrong night.

His head was hurting, all over, the shots in the ribs that had not bothered him at the time were bothering him like hell now. A woman was the last thing he wanted or could handle. He thought of Rickie Lyman, a fair middleweight on the *Greenville,* who *had* to have a woman after every fight.

She was talking again. "I teach drama at this university in the deep, deep South. It has something called a drama workshop which is fairly famous. I have sent a dozen actors to what passes for success, one of my students is a veddy veddy fashionable goddamn playwright, and I can write rings around him, and I have twelve plays that have been produced in Drama Workshop and nowhere else, and I have to go and make it with a novel about screwing in the thirteen colonies. Biggest book since the Bible, my young pugilist, and I will never, ever, have a Broadway play."

"Why not?"

"Because they wouldn't like it *now,* even if it was *Hamlet* they wouldn't like it now. You have to make it through them first, or they won't let you make it at all."

"Would you like me to drive?"

"That won't really be necessary, I am not really drunk. I'm just talkative. Am I boring you being talkative?"

"It's okay."

"A woman can live without a Broadway smash. After all, I have quite a smash right now. They'll never write articles about it in *Theater Arts* though. You know, maybe they will somewhere else. *Pub-li-ca-tion of the Modern Language Association.* Or something like that. After I'm dead. Wouldn't that be a kick?"

Garrett had stopped trying to follow her a long time back. "You don't like the book, how come you wrote it then?"

"That is the question. That, is, the, question."

Garrett wanted very badly to lie down. He was now very glad he had promised to go to the hospital.

"Don't mind my talking," she said. "I've seen you fight three times and I'm very impressed with you and I want to impress you back."

"You don't have to impress me."

Something warm and hot was running down his upper lip and over his mouth and chin. He put his hand to it, he looked at his fingers, and it was blood.

Quickly he threw his head back. "Started a nosebleed. I never had a nosebleed before."

"I've got something for that." Steering with one hand, she reached in her purse with the other and handed him a white pad. He brought it quickly to his nose.

"I never had a nosebleed before."

"I'm taking you to the hospital right away," she said suddenly, competently.

He felt the Cadillac accelerate. "I guess I'm lucky you came along."

"I'm glad I did."

3

AT THE hospital they did things to check the bleeding, or at least the bleeding stopped, and then told him he had had a minor hemorrhage.

It did not hurt, then, but he was glad to stay in bed. He felt very tired. Gill left about two in the morning when there was no doubt Garrett was all right. He looked very worried. Does he care about me or his property? Garrett wondered. Both, he answered himself, don't look too close at anything unless you have to.

The next afternoon Helene Lancaster came to see him. The nurse stepped out and closed the door. In front of the white door Helene looked down at him. She was well stacked and sharp looking, he thought. He thought he felt the old reaction, then he discovered it was a reflex, with nothing behind it.

She said hello.

"I hope I'm not disturbing you. You started a hemorrhage in my car so I feel responsible. It was a hemorrhage, wasn't it?"

"That's what it was."

"I thought so."

"So you see you did me a hell of a favor."

"I'm glad." She smiled down at him. She had a pretty, strong, forty-year-old or maybe thirty-eight-year-old face. "I'm glad I had a chance to do you a favor."

"Maybe I can do you one sometime."

"I'll just bet you can."

Her lips curled, and he felt his cheeks get hot.

"You blush so easily," she said. "And you look so wicked."

"Nobody ever told me that before."

"Maybe you just look wicked to me. When do you get out of here?"

"Couple of days. I'm just resting."

"Will you fight again?"

"Why in hell shouldn't I fight again? You act like I was hurt or something."

"Do you like being a prizefighter? Or is that what you call yourselves?"

"Fighters call themselves fighters. It's other people call them prizefighters. Yeah. I like it."

They talked a few moments. Before she left she told him she would see him again soon. He hoped not, he didn't feel easy with her. He would have liked to have her all right, he liked them just a little bit old, but she made him uncomfortable.

Gill kept him in the hospital another day, and told him to do no glove work, no actual boxing, for a month. "Something could of got knocked loose. I don't want you to get hit for a while." He did everything else: roadwork, light bag, rope, shadowbox and big bag. He put all that he would have put into glove work into the big bag and into shadowboxing, and he worked on his next fight with Red Johnson. He went over every round of the fight he had lost. Johnson had moved faster on his feet and with his hands. He had gotten in first with the left hand every time, and then he had started to whang Garrett with the right in one-two's. Johnson had shown him no fancy combinations but simple one-two's and one-two-three's. He had got in first with the left hand so steadily Garrett had not been able to work his own combinations.

Now, Garrett worked on circling faster to his own left, staying lower, stepping in two inches more with the left and starting it faster than he had ever started it. He worked on a short, very high overhand right that he could loop upwards after taking a jab on the forehead and on a triple hook, one shot to the body and two to the head, getting them all off in less than a second, the first two easy and quick to set up the last that had everything in it.

He wanted Johnson again, when he was ready, and he worked hard to get ready. He had been working for two weeks when he saw Helene Lancaster again. He had finished work, and was walking out in a slow back and forth walk when he saw her smiling at him from just inside the door. She looked confused. He went to her to say hello.

"They didn't want to let me in," she said. "Ladies not permitted and so on."

"Guys wander around in their jo— without much on."

"I told them I had a message. How are you feeling now? Any more bleeding?"

"No, I feel great. Gill won't let me do any glove work, box that is, for a while."

"Well good for him."

He agreed to let her take him to the Alexandria. In the Cadillac, she said why not come to dinner, but he said no, he had strict training rules, strict diet, he couldn't mess around with either.

"Call me when you give yourself a day off," she said outside the hotel.

"Sure. Thanks for the lift."

But he did not call her, and he did not see her for a while.

In the gym, he tried something he had often thought about but never done. He did half of his shadowboxing and big bag work with ten-ounce boxing gloves on. He had never heard of anybody doing it, yet it was natural and logical. The punches felt different, slow with real gloves on. Why not get used to them?

The first day he boxed in the training ring, he worked as well as he had ever worked. He got the triple hook in every time. And he weighed seventy-three.

"You ain't never looked better," Gill said, untying the gloves, Garrett's chest rising and falling hard. "I'm going to find you some light heavies by God. You and Johnson drew pretty good. We might make this a light-heavyweight town like they made it a featherweight town, one good fighter drawing good can make a town for the division."

He found three light heavies. Garrett won a close one, lost a close one, and in a return, knocked out the man who had beat him.

"You do real good in these returns," Gill said.

"When you going to get me a return with Johnson?"

Gill smiled.

Not working it out carefully, Garrett thought that he had something more permanent than happiness. When he fought, even when he worked hard in the ring in the gym, he had instants as though he were outside the ring watching himself inside. He had not so much found as made a Garrett, and when he could see him and be him, he felt real.

And he wanted to fight Red Johnson again. Johnson was in eighth place in the *Ring* magazine's world ratings now. He worked for Johnson whenever he did not have to work on a particular strategy for an upcoming fight. He was weighing one-seventy-four, and Gill put him in twice with a good but light punching heavyweight. Garrett won a decision in the first and knocked him out in the second.

After that one he asked Gill, "How about some more heavyweights?"

Gill shook his head. "He couldn't hit like a real heavyweight, that's why. I got him for you. He was good for you but he ain't typical."

"I got stronger, I can fight heavyweights now."

"A good heavyweight can beat any light heavyweight, don't ever forget it. I ain't going to have you ruined by no heavyweight. You're drawing here now, that's the thing. Once a guy starts to draw good, it don't matter what weight he fights, he can get the action."

Gill got him another Johnson match, seven months after the first.

Garrett figured he won three rounds, held him even in two and lost five. The decision went the same way.

After it was announced, Johnson came over and put his arm around him. "You're the most improved fighter I ever did see."

"Give me another one?"

"I don't know man, you getting too good." He grinned and tapped the back of Garrett's neck. "Sure I'll give you another shot kid." He had a cheerful, friendly voice.

Garrett expected to find Helene Lancaster waiting for him in the Cadillac. He had seen her at ringside and she had disturbed his concentration for a few seconds. But she was not waiting. He did not see her in the next few weeks, either. He was annoyed with her. He had not been really nice to her, he knew that, and he had no feeling for her, but it was still annoying that she did not come around.

Red Johnson moved to Los Angeles from San Francisco. "It gets too wet up there," he told Garrett at the gym between rounds. "And I got to keep my eye on you, you keep getting better." The bell rang, the voice frogged, "Work!" Johnson stepped to the heavy bag. "I'm working out something just for you, kid." He threw a right hand deep into the bag. It jumped. He smiled delightedly, nodded his head, and elevated his eyebrows. "See? You see? Just for you."

He and Johnson worked out at the same time in the afternoons. They kidded a lot together, often they would eat together and afterwards go to a picture or walk around the town and talk. Johnson was the best friend he had in town, and he knew that they would be rematched and next time one would knock the other out. That one might go on and be champion. He knew Johnson knew it, too. They fought a double main, both won by knockouts, and the rematch was made.

Gill changed his workout time so they would not be in the gym together.

It was in the Hollywood Legion as always, in June. The night turned hot. Red was wearing no robe, just a heavy white towel over his shoulders. He waved at Garrett and grinned when he came in and after that they did not look at each other. During instructions they both looked at the floor. In his corner Garrett punched the air, revolved his head to loosen his neck, heard the bell, and came out to meet Red coming out, white body smooth and coiled behind the heavy red mat on his chest.

He circled fast, so did Red, the first left hands landed almost together. He moved faster that round than he had ever moved, and the next ones. Through the early rounds, they jabbed and crossed and one-twoed. In the fifth Johnson came in with a deep hard hook to the body that hurt. He had never seen it before. He would have to watch for it. Johnson hit him with it again a few seconds later. He had to hold on for a second. He made Johnson hold on with the good shot in the triple hook. Going into the seventh Garrett thought he had a very thin edge, which meant he was no better than even and maybe worse, for all fighters thought they had the edge in the close ones.

He tired a little in the round and he saw Johnson had more wind left than he did. In the eighth he started catching. He blocked or slipped the very big ones but he caught everything else.

In the ninth he felt he was going to get knocked out.

His chest was heaving, he had lost his wind. Red's chest was heaving too but he kept moving. Garrett saw his face, calm, resolute, unangry, framed by the red hair and the darker red gloves. He saw Red start the left, and saw him make every move in the one-two-three, but he could not move to miss them, and he felt them hit separately. They did not hurt, only orange exploded before his eyes, not stopping his vision and he saw everything. Red was still coming in, his face hard and calm, and Garrett felt a heavy shock in his arm and shoulder. He registered the shock before he registered what he saw: Red's head twist far to one side and come back while he was going backward in the air. Then Garrett heard: the loud *pom* as Red's bottom hit the canvas and the sudden noise of the crowd.

Red sat quite still with his legs stretched out. His eyes were open and not seeing. The referee had counted to six before Garrett understood he had knocked Red out. Red did not move at *ten* but sat staring idiotically. Garrett went over, put his gloves under his arms and pulled him to his corner. The corner men worked on him. It was a long time, maybe a minute, before he came back. He closed his eyes, shook his head, and opened his eyes. This time he could see. He saw Garrett, tried to get up and go for him, then fell back. Then be remembered and grinned. He got up very slowly and touched

Garrett on the shoulder. "That's the boy that murders 'em," he said.

"You all right?" Garrett was worried and yet he felt good.

"Except for my feelings. You can bang, you son of a bitch. I'll get you next time."

Garrett felt sad and sorry for him, and yet he felt as good as he had ever felt.

In the dressing room all the smells that had told him, once, he was a big loser, told him now he was a big winner. The shower was hot and fine. He dressed and went out.

He expected to find the black Cadillac outside, and he did, just in front of the taxis. She was watching for him through the window and smiled when their eyes met. He went behind the car to the other door and got in.

"The kayo king," she said.

He grunted.

"You were tremendous."

"I got in a good one. It could have gone the other way just as easy."

"How do you feel?"

"I feel good."

Later he saw they were heading west instead of east. "This isn't the way to the Alexandria. Where we going?"

"Wait and see."

He didn't fight it. He watched the street intersections and lights slide past the Cadillac going west on Beverly.

"I don't even remember starting the punch. I just felt it and there he was on the floor. I swung it like a tennis racket, and I felt it in my shoulder before I knew I threw it."

"It was very impressive."

They were in Beverly Hills and soon she turned into the driveway of a large dust-colored brick house. "This is where I live."

"Nice place."

"There are lots nicer in the neighborhood but I like it."

Inside, he looked around the room. It had thick carpets not quite white, strangely shaped chairs of different colors, strange pictures on the walls. He had never seen a room like it before.

"How about a drink to celebrate?"

"Not right after a fight. That's the worst time, right after a fight."

"A fighter might as well be a monk, I see."

"Oh I have a few drinks and blow off steam a couple of days after a fight. It's good for you, one night is, but not right after the fight."

"Well. Would you like something else to drink?"

"I could drink a quart of orange juice."

"A quart's what I've got."

She brought it with a glass and he drank off the first glass without stopping, she refilled it, and he stopped twice for breath on the second.

"Good."

"Is there anything *else* I can do for you?"

The way she said it, there was no doubt about it, but he was absolutely shot. "Gee no, I guess I better be getting back to the Alexandria. I guess I'm not much company tonight."

"Garrett. When are you going to do something about me? Do I look that old?"

"You don't look a damn bit old, you're a real good-looking woman."

She looked at him.

"It's just I had a real tough fight."

She raised her shoulders and spread her palms upward. "Okay, put me down for the first night you break training. You might as well stay here anyway even if you don't stay with me."

He said all right. She showed him to his room and brought him men's pajamas. "These may be small through the chest but they ought to be all right otherwise."

They were tight. He tightened his chest muscles, brought his arms down hard, and he heard a ripping. They were more comfortable then.

When he was in bed, she brought him a glass of hot milk. "I've got half an ounce of rum in there. Now damn it, it won't hurt you, it'll help you sleep."

"I'll sure try it, I play hell sleeping after a fight."

"I'll give you something else too, then."

She brought him two white capsules, he took them with the milk. In two years he could be champion, he thought before he slipped into sleep.

She was cheerful but a little distant when she fixed his breakfast and drove him downtown. In spite of what they had said about a date the first night he broke training, he thought he might not see her again. She looked fresh, and neatly sexy that morning, and he appreciated her but was still not up to her. He meant to ask her to meet him the next night, but somehow did not. Her face was composed and cool as he left the car.

Two days after the fight, he went back to the gym and did only light calisthenics and shadowboxing. He was strangely short-winded, but sometimes for no reason his wind was off, and he thought nothing about it. The next day, skipping rope, his wind was shorter still, and he had trouble finishing the first three-minute round. He forced himself to the end of it, gasping and wrenching and was confused and angry. He was angrier still when he had to stop, next round, after a few seconds. He fought for breath, and something hurt in his chest. He made it to a bench, sat, then lay back on it. His chest made short jumps, his breath went aahh-uhh, and the hurting kept pounding in his chest.

Gill came to him. "What's the matter?" Garrett saw his face was scared and over Gill's shoulder he saw other fighters coming toward him. They stopped work, he thought, why did they stop work? He heard Gill's voice, far away: "Get a doctor."

His breath eased though never completely, and instead of pain he felt something running very fast inside his chest.

The ambulance got him to the hospital quickly, they put him in bed, a doctor put a stethoscope to his chest, and they finally gave him pills. The next day they gave him an electrocardiogram. Two days after that, his doctor came in. He sat down by the side of the bed, and looking at him, Garrett was frightened.

"How you feeling?"

"Not bad. You guys ever figure out what was wrong with me?"

The doctor picked up a key chain clipped to his belt and began to swing it. "You ever have rheumatic fever when you were a kid?"

"Not that I know of. I had every damn thing else though. I was a real sickly kid till I was about twelve."

The doctor watched the keys on the end of the chain. "What happened then?"

"I just sort of came out of it. I started body building and working out at the Y and all at once I was real healthy."

"It looks like you had rheumatic fever." The doctor dropped the keys and looked at him. "It often happens that children have it and pull out of it without ever knowing it."

"What's that got to do with now?"

"It happens often that people who have rheumatic fever as children have trouble with their heart in later life."

Garrett laughed, not successfully. "Heart trouble, that's crazy, I'm twenty-five years old, I'm a rated fighter practically. I got no heart trouble."

The doctor looked at him and said nothing.

"What kind of heart trouble?"

"You have what is popularly called a heart murmur. The technical term is auricular flutter."

"How bad is that?"

"It's not too bad. You aren't going to die or anything. As I said, this happens very often with people that have had rheumatic fever. Your heart has been enlarged. You have a thrombus in your left atrium."

"What is that in English?"

The doctor smiled. "The atrium is a space, a chamber, in your heart. A thrombus is a blood clot. You have a blood clot on the walls of the left chamber. If that blood clot were to get a great deal bigger and fall off the wall, you'd have a stroke."

"Would that kill me?"

"It might. And it might not. That's something you never know till it happens."

"What can I do not to have a stroke?"

"Well." The doctor's voice was loudly cheerful. "The first thing you do is get yourself a new trade."

Garrett did not say anything for a minute. Then he said, "What would happen if I kept right on fighting? Would I be okay until it happened?"

The doctor understood him perfectly. "No, you'd get that acute shortness of breath and accelerated heartbeat. You couldn't fight well even if you killed yourself trying."

"I see." Garrett ran a finger over the top of his sheet. He heard traffic and horns in the street. "What else do I have to do?"

"Be careful. Don't get fat, don't eat too much or drink too much. One drink a day is good for you, but no more, not for a while. Plenty of light exercise but nothing like what you've been doing. Once you get rested up from this spell, women are all right. You can lead a perfectly normal sex life just so you get your sleep and plenty of rest, ah, between rounds. I'll write that all up for you."

"Thank you."

"We'll let you out of here tomorrow. You ought to come by my office every week though for a while."

"I'll do that."

Helene Lancaster did not find him for two weeks. He left the Alexandria after he left the hospital, and checked into a cheap motel in Oceanside a few blocks from the beach. Every morning he would go to the beach and take the sun and walk, but he did not go into the cold water. He forced himself to spend the mornings that way; if he did not force himself, he would never have left the hotel room. Though his days were despair, he did not drink, not even the one ordered. He thought of different kinds of suicide: the horizon of the Pacific suggested, but the water was too cold. A bullet was probably best. Still he might do it with whiskey, he could drink until that thing fell off the wall and he had the stroke, only that might take a long time and then it might not work. He finally decided that he was too afraid to commit suicide.

He was lying on the bed in thc hotel in the late afternoon when Helene Lancaster knocked and came in.

"You gave me some trouble," she said. She looked down at him.

"How are you now?" she said.

"I ain't going to die or anything."

"I read you had to quit fighting."

"That's right."

"What are you going to do now?"

"I don't know."

She sat on the edge of the bed and bent so her face was close to his. "Poor baby," she whispered. She kissed him on the lips and stretched her body alongside his. "Poor baby." Her hand touched him and she withdrew it instantly.

"You've had a heart attack, I don't want to kill you."

"I'd just as soon you killed me. The doctor says that's all right though."

"I don't want to kill you," she whispered again, and he felt her lips and breath at his ear. Gently she turned him toward her.

He felt her fingers work at his shirt, then he felt her smooth palm glide over his chest, then the warm weight of her body crept tenderly upon him. She took him: he submitted.

He came awake with the cool flat of her hand on his cheek. She was standing in the late sunlight lining through the window; she looked oddly formal in the green suit and high-heeled shoes, and her full face was smiling.

"Are you rested?"

He closed, then opened his eyes and shook his head, not to say no, but to clear it. "I guess."

"Get your clothes on then, I've already packed your bags. We're going to Ensenada."

"Ensenada?" He raised himself to an elbow, keeping the sheet over his bent body, and blinking again. "Why not?" he said abruptly, threw the sheet off, and walked naked into the bathroom.

It was dusk when the Cadillac passed the Mexican border into Tijuana, and dark on the road to Ensenada. It was a bumpy, narrow, winding road, and the headlights cast up large black mountains to the left and to the right, black rocks making jagged lines to the sea. They talked little, he saw she was looking calm, happy, and possibly triumphant. He would hate her for her contentment in his ruin, he thought, if he had it in him any longer to hate anybody.

They checked into a hotel overlooking the sea; it had once been a monastery.

He slept deeply and into the morning. When he awoke the air was warm and clear, and he felt very well for many seconds, before he remembered his life was over. The Garrett he had made had been wiped from existence. Now he had no Garrett to see or to feel, and he was not able to make up a Garrett he wished to become. He knew already that this last was much worse.

Every morning, they walked on the stretch of sand in front of the hotel, she taking his hand and he moving his feet as though they supported an egg.

"You aren't always that careful," she said.

"No."

"You'll get used to things."

"Will I?"

He did not believe it, but he did: in a week he decided he did not want to die after all.

"I've got to get out of here and find myself something to do," he said.

"I've got something for you to do."

"Can't do that forever."

"I could argue that with you, but I'm talking about something else. I'm going to put you to work when I take you back to town."

"*You're* going to put me to work?"

"I've got plans for you. But you've got to get over your disappointment first."

"Might as well start now. I ain't going to get over it."

"You're *not* going to get over it. Only you are, darling."

"I am like hell."

"You are. What we're going to do in these next years, you'll forget all about that bloodletting of yours."

"I thought you liked to see me fight."

"I liked to see *you*."

"What are we going to do?"

"You'll see."

"Tell me, goddamn it."

"I'll tell you when it's time to tell you. Oh. Stop it." She was laughing. "Stop it, you fool."

Later he said: "Now are you going to tell me?"

"Now I guess I have to, don't I?"

"You don't, I'll punish you again."

"Oh that's no *punishment* darling, that is no punishment *believe* me. But I'll tell you. I, will, tell, you. What I am going to make out of you is, a great, big, movie star."

"You gone all the way crazy?"

"Come here." She took his hand and led him to the full-length mirror. "Look at that goddamn face."

"It's a lousy busted up face."

"*Where* is it busted up?"

"Use your eyes." He pointed to his ear, then his nose. "I got scar tissue in both eyebrows, I got scar tissues inside my mouth, I don't look like nothing but a fighter."

"That ear can be fixed, it's a very simple operation. Your eyebrows hide those scars, even I can't see them, and nobody can see inside your mouth."

"How about this?" He touched his nose.

"There's nothing to a nose job. Only you aren't going to have one. That beat-up piece of flesh, my dear, is going to make a million women cream their little jeans. Why Garrett's a sissy, look at him blush. My God, you've got enough sex appeal for ten men and you don't make anything of it, you don't even know it."

"Oh shut up."

"No, without the nose you'd be too pretty, it's what saves you, and makes you. How did it get broken so interestingly, over to one side like that instead of just smashed flat?"

"God knows."

"That nose will make you. As soon as I get you to stop talking through it."

"What's the matter with the way I talk?"

"Everything. But I can fix it. Now. Walk across the room, walk just the way you did coming into the ring. Yes. My God yes. You'll never have to do the book drill. Just for laughs." She picked up her purse and balanced it on top of his head. "Walk again. See? It stays right there. Your walk was the first thing I noticed."

"I think you're the one that's punchy."

"Say *how now, brown cow.*"

He said something else.

She screamed a laugh. "By all means," she said. "Please do. Only not right away, you just did. Now you say what I tell you."

He said how now, brown cow.

"That's pretty bad. Don't say it up high. Say it down deep in your throat. Let it start down here in your gut. Better. Better. Don't forget, it comes from your guts. Now again. Much better."

"You really think you're going to make an *actor* out of me?"

"Not exactly. I'm going to make you a movie star. The two, believe me, are not the same. Let's work some more."

She stepped a few feet back from him. "Look fierce. Look sad. Look happy. Look sick. No, you don't have any idea how to do it but you will, that damned face shows everything. It's the most mobile face I ever saw. If you had talent, I could make a wonderful actor out of you."

"Look, I had talent. I could of been light-heavyweight champion of the world. Don't you ever forget it."

"I never will. I promise." She kissed him swiftly on the cheek. "And I think you're about ready to go back to town. You're going to marry me, aren't you?"

"Am I? Hell. Why not?"

They were married right there, after the honeymoon. All that he owned fitted nicely into two Navy footlockers, which fitted nicely in the trunk of the 1934 Cadillac.

In San Diego, she stopped at a drugstore, and Garrett bought a copy of the new *Ring* magazine. It was always one to two months behind the fights. Still at the newsstand, he turned to the World Ratings, and in the light-heavyweight listings he found it: Number 8, John Garrett, Los Angeles.

"Anything interesting?" Helene said behind him.

"Kind of," said Garrett.

4

THEY set up housekeeping in her brick house in Beverly, and an effortless housekeeping it was: she had a cook-chauffeur-butler, a maid, and a gardener who came twice a week. She was not working now; her role, essentially a symbolic one, in the preparation of the screenplay of *The Fury and the Flame* was done; and she poured her energy into the shaping of Garrett. Having authentic energy himself, he could perceive and be grateful for it in her. In a nervous, straining intensity that went unbroken for hours, she punched into him the elements of his new craft, which for a long while he found unbelievable and ludicrous.

She would sit forward on the edge of a chair, in a green or blue silk housecoat flecked down the front by ashes, smoke curling from the cigarette in her dangling hand. A thin line would show in the middle of her forehead, beneath her severely combed, dark-blonde hair, while the rest of her face would be tautly smooth in concentration. She would nod in approval, not altering expression, or shake her head in half-controlled impatience, the corners of her mouth twisting sourly. For punctuation, sometimes as she spoke she would raise the hand that held the cigarette, and lower it, and raise it again, in slow purposeful arcs.

"Your body work is very smooth," she said one morning. "It's your voice that's giving us trouble. And try to get that embarrassed look off your face. There's nothing to look embarrassed about."

"I feel like a fairy, all this crap."

"You shouldn't. And some of our best actors are fairies."

"I'll just bet."

"Don't be snotty. You can sit down now. Read these speeches I've marked to yourself, and then try them out loud." She handed him a book.

He read the lines.

She shook her head, flung her hands upward, and almost screamed: "No, goddammit, no, no, no. Get some feeling into it, get that goddamned voice out of your nose."

He tried again. She nodded. "That's much better."

His education was vexing enough, but no outlet for his physical vitality. Until his attack, he had been in training for five years without a break. And though the attack had left him a cripple, so far as the most arduous sport in the world was concerned, he still had left the residue of the vitality that had been so long building. He had one place to use it: bed. He had almost denied himself women during those years, and now he tried to make this one woman compensate for all the missed women, the lost years. And at the same time, he had to regiment himself in what he wished to be his excess. He had to watch himself constantly; he was both doctor and patient.

"Are you sure the doctor meant this is all right for you? You don't have some fool idea of loving yourself to death, now do you?"

"It's absolutely all right," he told her.

He rested a great deal, physically, lying in bed for hours. But he was usually reading something she gave him to read: a play, a movie script, or a book she thought would enlarge him. He had the grammar and the intellectual sophistication of a healthy, lower-middle-class American, she told him, and it had to change.

Garrett did what he did with energy, because he had energy and it was impossible for him not to do with energy. But he had no clear view of a shape he wished to fill. And so he had no clear view of himself. He could never feel solid: sometimes he could not even feel that he was there.

But he worked.

Sometimes she was able to rent prints of the pictures whose scripts she already had, and would run these over and over in her library, against a small screen hung before a wall of books. She had him study the male stars, particularly Frederic March, Gary Cooper, Clark Gable.

"You and Gable have a little bit the same style, that is you're both very masculine and you both look manfully wicked. Now he's very good in this one coming up. When you read it afterwards, try to imitate him a little. It'll come out quite different from him, you'll be surprised how different. Nobody would think you were imitating."

He watched Gable as Ace in *A Free Soul,* and then did his best to imitate him. He knew it was not a good best.

They did that many times in the next weeks. "Imitate Gable loosely," she said. "Follow him but don't follow him too closely. That way you'll have a track to stay on and still your own, *thing,* will come out."

For a month their procedure was to run a single Gable scene from *A Free Soul,* and then to have Garrett try it. One day at the end of the month, he said all his lines backward, out of pure exasperation.

"So we're bored, are we? All right. Let's try something else."

Then she had him rehearse two plays, *The Last Mile* and *The Petrified Forest.* In *The Petrified Forest,* he played the gangster who was willing to shoot a man as a favor to the man himself. When she was only mildly dissatisfied with him, she backed a semi-professional production of *Forest* in a little playhouse down the coast. It was her money, she directed the play, and he played the part he had been studying for weeks.

"In this depression, I can put on a two-weeks run in an amateur playhouse for a thousand dollars and the experience is worth ten times that to you. That's if I direct myself, of course, and I like to direct," she said.

"Have you really got all that money?"

"I told you, it's still pouring in from that damned book. When all of it's in, it'll be more than a million."

"Helene," he said. "Can I ask you something?"

"You can ask me anything."

"Why are you putting all this into me?"

"My God, I'm married to you, you're my boy."

"That's not a good enough reason."

"What in heaven's name is then?"

"I'm asking you. Maybe you're ducking working on your own things and I'm an excuse. Maybe you want to eat me alive."

"Do you really think that?"

"No."

"Thanks loads. I don't think so either. I am not too lazy to write, in fact I'm writing now. And I don't want to swallow you, at least if I do I don't know about it. You got any other ideas?"

"I think you're getting the same kick out of making me into something as you would making a book or a play."

"You are *not* a stupid boy, are you? You're probably right. But I wouldn't work anything like this hard if it weren't you. Believe me."

"I believe you." He understood that she needed to believe it herself.

After that first play, she continued to drill him in the morning but started, fairly ostentatiously, to write in the afternoons. She had a nap first, alone, with doors closed, and then she wrote.

"What kind of thing are you writing?" he asked.

"Oh, I'm working on several things."

He didn't press her.

Something changed between them; he was aware that it had changed before he even knew it was starting to change. For more than a year, he had fallen into her embraces like a man drowning and loving it. He had thought he would never have enough of her, not because she was herself but because she was, in herself, all the women he had passed by. But it finally happened, finally he did have enough. She became a responsibility to cope with rather than a delight to succumb to.

He began to feel the call of other bodies. He did nothing about it. But he knew the day would come when he would. He had long led the life of an ascetic. Now he knew he had nothing of the ascetic in him.

She took him through four plays at the playhouse in four months, the same way. He knew he was not good. He also knew he was not as bad in the fourth as he had been in the first. He was no longer embarrassed to be acting nor did it make him feel like a fool. Doing it before a live audience, he found, was not unlike fighting. Waiting for the curtain was like waiting to go into the ring, with the not entirely unhappy difference that he knew how it was going to come out, he knew he would not get knocked out. Or killed: he faced it the first time. Fighters could get killed. Now that he could never do it again, he could admit that for the first time: a fighter could get killed.

He might get used to being an actor in time, he thought.

She took him into an expensive plastic surgeon's clinic to get the cauliflower ear fixed, she was pleased with the result, and he had to admit he was, too.

She was still a figure of consequence in a town that despised writers but idolized success. *The Fury and the Flame* was still a world best seller, the "search" for hero and heroine of the film version was being intensely exploited by the studio, and with the shrewdness that Garrett respected more and more, she had hooked onto that campaign. She hired her own press representative, and–though the studio had no interest whatever in exploiting her–she got an almost free ride on one of the largest promotions in history. He drew some column mentions as her husband.

"We don't want to overexpose you right now," she told him. "I don't want too much pressure on you too soon. But I think we're about ready, to get you a test." She had enough influence to do it with no trouble. But she made another preparation first: she hired a journeyman cameraman to shoot him in two scenes from *Petrified Forest*. "This is very rough, not like a test at all," she said. "But we can look at it and correct from it."

It was printed, and he watched his own face on the little screen that flickered and jumped. His mouth said words without sound, his face moved from one contortion to another. Heat flushed his cheeks; he had never felt such a fool.

"Now do you believe I'm no actor?" he said.

She did not appear to have heard him. "That wasn't bad at all. I see some things. You've got a habit of licking your lips I never noticed, and the camera makes a couple of your expressions look too heavy. We'll have to fix those things."

They did, or she did, the cameraman did it again, and she said, "You'll do. You look more introverted than I ever saw you. And the camera shows, I don't know, a kind of sadness."

"How bad is that?"

"It's very good. I'm just surprised, I never saw it the way the camera did."

The test was not quite anticlimactic, but he knew he would make it, he felt just nervous enough to be adequately keyed up. Globe offered him the seven-year, six-months option contract, and Helene told him to sign it.

"It could be a mistake," she said. "But Torldson says they liked the test. The big thing now is to make sure they don't forget you."

But she didn't let them. They were grinding out pictures at every budgetary level–A down through C–and he worked steadily. The studio was a factory that fabricated pictures, stars, and myths, all to be sold at a profit. It did not make him a star, nor did it appear to be interested in making him anything. But with Helene's nagging, he got parts. He got them in one picture after another. Gangster pictures were not as big as they had been, but there were still a lot of them, and he had short lines in a dozen. Helene then wheedled Globe's casting director into a small featured role for Garrett in one. She gave a party for the director, and Garrett got a good close-up. It drew some mail.

"They consider that the test," she said. "You get mail and they get interested. Damn foolishness. People could write mail to themselves. Sometimes they do. In fact–" she grinned, almost lewdly–"in fact."

"*You* wrote the letters."

"Let's say I have quite a few friends here and there."

As a featured player, whose option had been picked up, he moved into a considerably higher status. He rather enjoyed it. He knew he was not a good actor and it did not bother him. He was beginning to like the life, the truth and he knew it was that he would have liked any life that kept him busy and moving in some kind of direction. He was liked on the sets because he was cheerful, worked as hard as he was asked, and never complained. And he always was prepared. He was not a quick study, but Helene rehearsed him and had him ready for every day.

She had her publicity man, whom she had been paying a continuing retainer, start a full campaign on him. "If things were as they ought to be, the studio would be doing this," she explained to him. "But they haven't decided to give you the development, not yet. This will help bring them around, I hope. We have some momentum going for us now and the big thing is to keep the momentum going. You're either moving ahead or back, you're never standing still. When you've got momentum, you've got to keep it going at all costs."

He was photographed in the standard masculine postures: on a horse, at the tiller of a sailboat, swinging a tennis racket (he did not know how to sail, even though he had been coxswain; he hated horses; and his heart kept him from tennis). The pictures appeared in newspapers, usually in sports sections where he had an entrée, and sometimes in fan magazines.

He was pleased by this, but nothing more; he knew that there were actors, he thought of them as "real" actors, who would have done literally anything for the public attention that Helene had conferred upon him. Having been shut out forever from what he wanted most, he was having things he did not really want always dropping in his lap. When he thought about it, he marveled.

Helene harassed Globe into giving him a succession of featured parts. They drew real mail, and those who decided things had to accept that he was a powerfully attractive figure to women. When his option was picked up the second time, she told him she had written a screenplay for him. "I thought about it six months and wrote it in two weeks. It's part *Manhattan Melodrama* and part *A Free Soul,* with some very special adjustments for you. I can sell it tomorrow for fifty thousand dollars, but we have to make sure you're guaranteed the lead. That will be the problem."

It appeared to be a problem she was not to solve. Conditions imposed on the sale of a script by the writer was something Globe-International was more than cold to. She finally made a deal with an independent producer, and persuaded Globe to let Garrett make the outside picture.

She had very shrewdly tailored the screenplay to Garrett's measure, and she won the ear of its young director. The picture showed Mace Garrett as a man who could dominate women and succumb to them, who could be heavily brutal or unbelievably tender, who moved mercurially from grimness to humor, and who had a deep vein of sadness that ran unbroken beneath his other moods. The picture established Garrett as a minor star, far from the first magnitude but one who might continue to develop interestingly.

The sneak preview, at the Hawaiian, excited everybody but Garrett, who was only conscientiously happy.

Two weeks after the sneak, Red Johnson won the light-heavyweight championship of the world with a knockout in the eighth round. Garrett sent him a wire of congratulations. Helene found Garrett in a beach house at Malibu, where he had been half-drunk for two days.

He watched her across the narrow table and the pale blue coffee cups from which thin white spirals rose. Her hair was combed, her face made up, she looked pleasantly attractive if not inflammatory. She made it a point to look well in the morning: clearly she knew how irretrievably old a freshly-risen woman could look to a man fifteen years younger. Her face was idle and semi-interested, then suddenly alert, then triumphant and increasingly amused. Her mouth curled upwards faintly, then markedly, then smiled broadly.

She looked up from the paper and handed it to him, her finger pointing to a place. "Read that," she said.

Under a picture of himself, wide and vacant-grinning, and Helene, looking up at him with an achieved expression of adoration, he read in black type:

"IT WAS MACE ALL THE TIME"

Smaller type said:

> Helene Lancaster—who wrote that book—admitted today she patterned the now-fabulous character of Andrew Allen on her own husband.
>
> The fair and fortyish author of *The Fury and the Flame* "confessed" to this reporter that its hero was indeed modeled on rugged Mace Garrett, whom the canny Helene masterminded to stardom.
>
> By an amazing coincidence, it just happens that Globe-International is "searching" for an actor to play the romantic Revolutionary War general.
>
> They're searching even harder for someone to play his wife, too —O'Neilla Allen. But there's a difference. Nobody, but nobody, has been able to see anybody but Clark Gable as Andrew Allen.
>
> In fact, it had been rather generally thought Helene had one eye firmly fixed on Gable in creating the character.

But she says no.

"It was Mace all the time," she confided. "All I did was imagine what he would be like if he were ten years older and a Revolutionary general.

"For years before we were married, I thought Mace was the most romantic man I'd ever known.

"Would I like to see him play Andrew Allen in the Picture?

"Why, who else is there!"

Mace looked at her across the table and said a short word.

"You're right, and it's what makes the grass grow. And in this case it was a damned expensive commodity, in trouble as well as money."

"What is it for?"

"For? It's for you to play Andrew Allen, that's what it's for. But there's a lot to do."

She put her publicity man on full time, he had been on a retainer only, and he had one objective: to get Garrett the Andrew Allen part. All at once Garrett found that he had been a Revolutionary War buff since he was fifteen and had a collection of curios that was the envy of many historians. The publicity man rented the collection, by sections, for one afternoon for an interview with pictures. He wrote a speech for, and Garrett delivered it to, the Pasadena Chapter of the Daughters of the American Revolution on the subject: "The Thirteen Colonies: What They Mean to Me Today." With changes, the same speech appeared under Garrett's name as an article in *This Week* and then the *Reader's Digest*.

This went on for three-odd months, and then Garrett and Helene were summoned, together, to the presence: Arn Torldson.

Arn Torldson was the executive vice president of Globe-International, formerly the son-in-law of Globe's chairman of the board, now a widower, half-Swedish and half-Jewish, and, possibly, the most able studio executive in town. He had been a producer of B pictures, a man without a destiny, when he married Nancy Teller. How did he do it, said the town, he has out-maneuvered everybody, he has tooled himself right into royalty. It occurred to nobody that he had married for any other reason; it shocked everybody when he disappeared after Nancy and their baby daughter were killed when she missed a curve on Laurel Canyon Boulevard one twilight. Old Man Teller found him in a Pennsylvania sanitorium (the story went), in a total emotional breakdown. Teller brought him back, gave him far more responsibilities than he had ever given him while his daughter was alive, and took great, strong satisfaction in Torldson's emergence as a more formidable man than Teller himself.

Torldson was rather less than average height, compact from twice-a-week weight lifting, smooth faced with a black moustache.

He stood and greeted Garrett and Helene formally and courteously. His face showed few gradations and Garrett suspected these were carefully ordered; yet the impression he produced was neither of bleakness nor of blankness, but of responsible, and likable, gravity.

He gave them no preparation.

"I want you to know, Helene, that all of this nonsense hasn't impressed me one bit. I wanted Gable for that hero of yours, and if I could have gotten him I would have, and believe me I tried like hell. However. Everybody concerned with the picture agrees Mace Garrett is an excellent second choice. We believe in you, Mace." He said that dryly, ceremoniously, and perhaps ironically. "As a mark of our belief and faith in you, we are pleased to inform you that we are casting you as Andrew Allen, in the Globe-International picture version of that great novel, *The Fury and the Flame*. I know it will make you very happy." In perceptible irony: "I hope it makes *you* happy, Helene."

"Oh it does. You see, I patterned–"

"I know, you patterned Andrew Allen after Mace. It's just a minor detail that he was a boy in the Navy while you were writing the book at that university."

"Why–"

"I know, it's just a minor detail."

He smiled at Garrett suddenly, almost warmly, as though he possibly meant it. "Good luck, Garrett." He stood and hurt Garrett's hand with his grip. "I really think you can do a damn good job."

Outside, she glanced at the sun, slipped her arm through Garrett's, and stared straight ahead, in her patented look of total satisfaction. "Son of a bitch. Not much he wasn't impressed by our nonsense. If we hadn't worked at it hard, we'd be nowhere."

It was eight months and two pictures before shooting actually started on *The Fury and the Flame*. Location was no farther south than San Diego County. A second unit was picking up exterior footage of orchards and stone walls in Maine; everything else was built by technicians, including a city for burning. Garrett's life was a cycle of dawn-rising, dust, fatigue, discomfort, and an existence as isolated as he had known upon ships at sea. But for the first time he was working with a great director: David Ransom.

Ransom was six-three, all bone, shock-haired, with a face that had the length of that of a horse and the diabolic mobility of a Regency rake's. Having had semiprofessional fights as a boy, he had great respect for Garrett, the once-rated fighter: he took pains with him that approached even the limitless limits of a director's duty. In urgent whispered conferences, he would press his instructions in fighter's idiom. "Shoot it hard now. Start it sharp but not too fast and then drive into it like you were throwing combinations with everything you got. Drive into it hard now, don't hold back, start it hard and *drive* into it." At the end of four months of shooting, Garrett was sick of his job, but felt for the first time he had put something of himself on a strip of celluloid. And for the first time, he cared.

He saw a rough-cut version of the picture when it was done, and he knew it was good as pictures were judged good, and he was good. He did not know how good until the sneak.

He and Helene watched a man who had his face and body but who appeared to have nothing else to do with him: they watched this man ride at the head of soldiers in ragged blue uniforms, they watched him face a hangman's noose and escape in a wild ride over broken country, they watched him renounce forever a wife who was a Tory spy.

While the man with his face, now set and stern, advanced toward them from the screen, Helene said, "It's happened. You're the biggest there is."

"Hell, no."

"Oh yes. You let it out this time. Ransom got it out of you." In her half-whisper he heard pleasure, some awe, and perceptible resentment. "You were on fire through the whole damned thing."

"Is that how it looked? Jesus. All I remember is how tired I was."

5

HE did not become the very biggest, but he was one of the three or four biggest. He was a great male star in a decade when stars were gods, and he found, a little to his surprise, and embarrassment, that he liked it.

His privacy was lost forever; eyes, personal and impersonal, were always upon him. He was photographed in everything but natural functions, and had he been willing, the fan magazines would have been delighted to oblige there. Yet he accepted, and was pleased to accept. He had been living in unreality for years, and considered he had simply moved to another plateau of unreality. He felt he was reaping some of the rewards of being champion without having earned them. With the real thing, of course, he would not have cared, greatly, about the rewards, only the thing itself. But since in his own view he had long since failed, he could accept these unearned rewards gratefully and without vanity. For this, he was well, if transiently, loved.

One thing disturbed him: Helene. She had spent three years pressing him into the mold of her own plan: he was the product not of his will but of hers. She had immolated herself upon her concept of him. Now that she had made him come true, now that he was exactly what she wished him to be, now that her triumph as fabricator was complete, she showed, often, that she hated her handiwork. But only sometimes. She acted toward him with fantastic ambivalence. Sometimes she would refuse to look at him, speak to him in cold syllables, and then totally ignore him. And she would jubilate over a review, a column mention, a mark of deference from the studio, as though he were, as completely as ever, an extension of herself bearing her own nerve-ends.

But the resentment slopped over, or spurted out, when he was least prepared for it.

One night he came home deeply tired from work on a picture on the home lot, and she greeted him.

"Ah. The great actor returns to his simple home and to his gray-feathered cherisher. Tell me, oh great man, what can your little gray-feathered cherisher do to make you happy?"

He controlled the flare of his anger before he spoke.

"Helene. Why are you bitter?"

"Bitter?"

"I'm nothing but an idea of yours that worked out. For you to be jealous of me is like being jealous of yourself. What in hell goes on?"

"I'm not jealous. As you say, why should I be jealous?"

"Aren't you?"

"Of course not. Yes. Maybe I am."

"Why for God's sake? Things have worked out the way you made them work out. It's your win, not mine."

"It really doesn't make a lot of sense, does it?"

"No."

"I suppose I resent the fact that you don't need me any more."

"You *know* how much I need you."

"Not really. You could hire a drama coach, you've already got an agent and a business manager. No, you don't need me now. But that's not all of it. I'm jealous of you in the most basic kind of way."

"It doesn't make sense."

"No, it doesn't."

That was the lancing of the boil. For weeks she was much improved. Then she slipped back; only now she covered it somewhat better.

One afternoon he came home two hours early, and found her coaching a pretty young man as she had once coached him. Only—Garrett acknowledged it cheerfully—only the boy was a more talented pupil. Garrett saw him many afternoons in the next two weeks, and then did not see him at all. She started with and abandoned others the same way.

"They don't have the drive. They don't have your drive." She looked at him assessingly, and spoke as though she were absolutely determined to be fair on a distasteful point.

"*My* drive. I didn't even care about it."

"You have a drive that hooks up to anything you do, whether you like it or not. Oh I recognize it, I have it myself. But what the hell can I do with it now?"

He was brutal because he thought she needed brutality. "You can get off your ass and write."

"Write? Write another piece of junk like *The Fury and the Flame?*"

"Write whatever it is you want to write. Write the play you're talking about."

"They won't let me. I've been smeared by that damned book. If I wrote *Hamlet* they wouldn't like it."

That sentence echoed from somewhere in memory. "You say that. I don't believe it. I don't know anything about it but I don't believe it."

"That's right. You don't know anything about it."

He moved slowly toward the final perception and finally grasped it. Then he knew why she was miserable. She could no longer create him because she had already created him.

When he knew this, he knew he could never truly reproach her.

Helene took on several new actors for development; two she signed to contracts, but she later released them. All of these were male. Then she took a girl.

Her name was Lauren Letrie and Garrett was very aware of her. She was about twenty-five and slim but round; she wore her black hair in a shoulder bob; she walked jauntily and with arrogance, flexing pleasingly under a tight skirt. Her face was changeable and pert. One swift look was a shaft of *knowing: I know exactly what you're thinking and you can't stop me from thinking it.* Garrett was aware of her because he wanted to go to bed with her.

But it was not he who did that.

Like every cuckold in every story, he came home early. He had no scenes that afternoon; the director told him to get off the set and relax. He entered the house through the kitchen, heard nobody, and walked down the carpeted hallway to the door of the little soundproofed room where Helene wrote when she wrote.

He rapped twice on the panel, called "Hi," and opened the door.

He had a sudden photoflash picture of two unclothed bodies and two upraised female white faces three feet apart, frozen in the blankness of sudden terror.

"Excuse me," he said, withdrew, and closed the door.

He drove out to the beach house at Malibu. It was dark when he came back. Helene was waiting for him in the living room, carefully dressed and made up, her face hardened in resentment.

"All right," she said. "Say whatever you have to say."

"What do you have to say?"

"Not one damn thing."

"What do you want from me? Divorce? Separation? Or do you just want to live apart?"

"You aren't–"

"Of course not. Did you really think I'd use that? I'm just not going to live with you any more. It's not because of this afternoon."

"You owe every damned thing you are to me, don't you forget it."

"I won't forget it. How does half the community property and half my picture earnings sound to you?"

Her face had been strained in defiance like a flag full of wind. Now the wind went out of the flag; her face sagged in folds, suddenly bereft.

"Get the hell out of here. Go on. Get out. I don't want your money." She started to cry and to come into his awkward embrace. "Johnny, I'm sorry. I don't know what's the matter with me."

He patted her, stiffly, on the shoulder. She worked her cheek against his chest.

"I guess it had to happen. Something had to." She drew back, sniffing and red-eyed. "Fifteen years is too big a difference, the wrong way."

"It's not your fault."

"It's not anybody's fault. Kiss me and get out of here. If you stay tonight, we'll put it off and just have to go through it again."

He kissed her.

"No. None of that. Go away. Go now."

He did.

The divorce was more than friendly. Once he had offered it, she refused his money. She had more than he did, she said, and it clearly proved something to her if she did not take it. But he knew how she spent money, he knew a time would come, and he set up a trust fund for her, of which she was not to know, into which he paid ten per cent of what he made. He felt criminally guilty it was not more–but he did not make it more.

The divorce left him feeling unmoored, drifting, and yet newly intact: as though some damage he had not known existed had been suddenly repaired. Shortly, he understood it: his self had been returned to him. It was not as it was, it would never again be as it was, but it was again his, and he was going to make possession permanent.

He meant to do so by the furious spending of energy–and of money. He dove into the life of a great star in the 1930's, and found he liked it. He discovered, all at once, that an involvement with his work had come to him: he was not a big talent but he had made himself into an honest workman. He wanted to be as good as he could.

He also discovered the pleasure of things. He bought a fourteen-room ranch house with a sixty-foot pool in the San Fernando Valley, a Bentley Continental, a thirty-six-foot yacht. He was getting a hundred and fifty thousand a picture, he would make at least three pictures a year for Globe-International, and maybe one more on loan. Taxes had become unbelievable, but he had a business manager who understood them.

Most of all, he was continually rediscovering how much he really liked women. He had always liked them but he had had to curb the impulse so consistently that he had not really known how strong it was. Now that he could indulge it, he found out. He still had to monitor himself, but this was perhaps as well; it occurred to him sometimes that if he had not had the heart problem, he could have killed himself of women in a few years. He went through them by the dozen: leading ladies or feature players in his pictures, extras, secretaries and female executives on the lot, and for a while, waitresses, cigarette girls, anything that he saw and liked. He had to cut that out though. It cost too much. His business manager, Sid, had to pay off two waitresses, and the studio had to exert itself to keep him out of court on a statutory rape charge. The girl had said she was twenty. Garrett had believed her, and she turned out, in fact, to be a sixteen-year-old senior at Van Nuys High.

Torldson called him in after that one. "This is on the line, Garrett. You've got to be more careful about this tomcatting. Stay away from tarts, stay away from schoolgirls, stay away from all of them outside the Industry. God knows there ought to be enough tail in the Industry to make anybody happy. Even you."

He became more circumspect.

Garrett's screen personality was somewhere between that of Clark Gable and Errol Flynn, a contemporary and now a big male star at Warner's. He was a little less earthy than Gable, a little less romantic than Flynn, a little more fierce than either. He played, always, the Mace Garrett character: a shell hurled forward by a mysterious explosive force, carrying a fuse that would blow it up on impact. The character could be a sailor, a soldier, a race driver, a flier, a gambler, a young tycoon, a diver, a wanderer. He was always the Mace Garrett character. That was the way Garrett thought of him: not as himself, Garrett, but as the Garrett character. They took him away from the character only once, for one comedy. It was not a flop, but it was not a success, and after that they stayed tightly to Mace Garrett. They always got his shirt off. Garrett's deltoids and pectorals became his trademark. He never played a fighter: Torldson could cite figures to prove boxing pictures always lost money. He was glad he never played what he thought he truly was, or had been. He considered that he was living in a world that had been entirely made up, put together out of air. If he ever brought reality into it, the whole thing might collapse. It seemed to him, sometimes, that on the day of his heart attack, he had fallen into a dream as he had once fallen from his whaleboat into the water of Guantánamo Bay. He had been grateful then that the water was warm; he was grateful now that the dream was not a bad one. He did not spell these thoughts out completely but he was very aware of them.

A fan magazine writer asked him, one time of a thousand times, what did he think of fame.

Garrett told him in one word. "But good." He completed the joke. "I got no complaints."

"You know what it is, sweetie, and I know what it is, but my readers don't want to know what it is," said the writer, who was a tired and bored man. "So come on and tell me how wonderful it is to be young and handsome and famous and rich. Tell me how it is to have all that fine new stuff coming at you in a nice steady stream."

"It's not bad," Garrett admitted.

"You bet it's not bad, sweetheart."

Garrett's triumph coincided with Hitler's: the year he made it big was the year of Munich: 1938. Garrett saw before Munich that war was coming, he had felt it coming from the time he got out of the Navy, and he was astonished that everybody didn't. It was on schedule, nobody could stop it, and he raced against it. He had to run faster to cover the ground he wanted to cover. His doctor warned him: the thrombus was still there. He had two mild attacks. Garrett conscientiously took his intervals of rest, he held his drinking down, and he had never smoked. But he tried to engulf all the rest of it: women, trips, parties, possessions. It was in that year, after Munich and *The Fury and the Flame* that, single-handed, he created a tradition in the Industry.

This was the Garrett Good Luck Piece.

He tried to sleep with every leading lady at least once while the picture was shooting. He convinced himself it insured success. On two pictures he didn't make it, and while one of them was one of his most successful, the other was a flop. Conveniently he forgot about the first, and on the flop, he insisted that his failure was the picture's failure.

Having drinks with the director, months after the comedy, which was his only failure, he was mildly high and confessed.

"It's because Marian wouldn't lay it on the line for me. If she had, we would have had luck."

"What the hell are you talking about?"

Garrett told him. The director thought it was very funny–and on the instant, became a believer himself.

"I wish to Christ you'd told me before the picture, we would of gotten somebody else. She's the most virtuous woman in town."

"Maybe the only virtuous woman in town."

"You know better than that, or if you don't, you'll damn well find out. There are any number of *practically* unassailable ladies in the Industry. Remind me to keep them out of any future pictures we work on together."

After that, the word got around.

His leading women always looked at him strangely when they were introduced, or came together for the first time at the start of the picture. Some looked at him boldly, like co-conspirators suggesting: let's get on with it. Others looked defiant, and challenging, and still others blushed a little and looked embarrassed–as was he.

He regretted the legend of The Good Luck Piece, he asserted it was the handiwork of someone else's imagination, and he insisted at the end of every picture that it had been neither consummated nor attempted. Frequently, he was telling the truth; more frequently, he was not. It had been ridiculous in the first place–and yet. Often when he failed, the picture had not failed. But every time he *had* made out, it had been without exception, a success.

In spite of himself, he cherished the idea, and made the attempt every time.

A successful attempt was a young actress named, professionally, Eileen Travers. She was his romantic interest, though not his costar, in a picture in which he played a gunman for the Irish Republican Army. She was blonde and delicate, she was not really exciting in the hay for she was too delicate, and she was certainly not his type. But she made him feel fatally responsible for her. He could not break away.

She smiled resolutely and forlornly, her voice was always tremulous, and one night she wept and told him they must not see each other again. She did not want him to grow to love her too much because she had leukemia and was going to die in a year. She felt she should not see him again, she said, because she did not want to cause him pain when she was taken away. She loved him too much already, she wanted to squeeze every minute of happiness out of her last months, but she did not matter. They must not see each other again.

He married her the next week.

In the months after, he was surprised that she did not seem to be failing at all. Indeed, she appeared to be waxing–possibly on those injections which he supplied so dutifully. He asked her about it. She was bewildered herself, she said. Four days later, she came home, she said, with wonderful news. She didn't have it. The doctor who told her she had it was incompetent, she said. Her fine new doctor had decided she had only a nasty anemia which was already in remission. Wasn't it wonderful.

When they divorced, she waived alimony and took half of what he had in a settlement. This was far more than her half of community property, but he let her have it because she did waive alimony. A month after the final decree, she married a young producer, the son of an old producer. Almost a year after that, the young producer told Garrett at a party:

"A wonderful thing has happened. Eileen thought she had leukemia when we were married and now it turns out she doesn't."

"I'm very happy for you," said Garrett.

And so he sailed through 1939, 1940 and 1941, one of the great virility symbols with Flynn, Gable, and a few others.

He wished his rivals well, he wished everybody well. He wished Helene well though he seldom saw her, and he loyally resented the new best sellers by women authors that were bought for superpictures: Mitchell's *Gone With the Wind,* Betty Smith's *A Tree Grows in Brooklyn,* Elizabeth Goudge's *Green Dolphin Street.* He wished the whole world well, so far as he had it in him, and then Pearl Harbor brought the U.S. into the war.

6

GARRETT had been awaiting the war fatalistically for years, and when it came, he, the one-time mercenary, was in the same fever as the amateurs. He had to get back in the Navy. But he had the heart problem. He made it, the Navy was glad to have him on its terms heart or no heart, but its terms made him a limited duty lieutenant in public relations.

He made personal appearances at a few forward bases, went on a bond-selling tour, and narrated a commercial film based on the life and times of an aircraft carrier, and was promoted to lieutenant commander. He did nothing in uniform that he could not have done better out. He finally got attached to a staff at a forward base in the upper South Pacific where he was at least geographically close to the war. But the war was moving on: he was as safe as if he had been in Santa Monica (more safe than he would have been in Santa Monica in December, 1943, he thought). He was sick of his job, and of himself: he wanted in the war.

One afternoon in the officers' club he saw a face that tapped at memory: it belonged to a commander in faded khakis. The club was the Pacific equivalent of a frontier saloon: bare wooden tables and benches were on hard ground outside a shack that held a bar, a head, and nothing else. The commander sat two tables away, Garrett saw him staring and smiled a greeting, the commander came over and held out his hand.

He was captain of a 2100-ton destroyer in the harbor. He had stood junior officer of the deck watches on the *Greenville* when Garrett, the coxswain, stood wheel watches, he was flattered at being instantly recognized by Mace Garrett, the movie star, and after two drinks Garrett, the limited duty lieutenant commander, asked to be taken to sea.

The commander was clearly receptive.

"Can you stand deck watches?"

"No."

"What can you do?"

"Stand wheel watches." That was for enlisted men.

The commander laughed. On the *Greenville,* fresh out of the Naval Academy, he had had a soft-fleshed, petulant, baby-stubborn face. Now the flesh had wasted, the petulance had gone into hardness, the dogged baffled seriousness had become an aggressive competence. Garrett had looked on him before with well-disposed amusement; now he regarded him with awe, more for the process of change than the product of it. In ten years, the officer had aged twenty.

"I don't know." The commander was clearly reluctant to let the idea go, but he shook his head.

"I've got to get some real duty," said Garrett.

"Just for a couple of months," said the commander.

"I've got to," said Garrett.

"I'll do what I can," said the commander.

The commander petitioned the admiral solemnly that he wanted Garrett for temporary duty of a quite limited character. The admiral, a wise man, who liked Garrett, pointed out equally solemnly that he was glad the duty was of a limited character because of Garrett's classification. So the commander told Garrett, safely at sea.

Three days later the destroyer rejoined the large task force that called itself, by turns, the Third and Seventh Fleet. Garrett was formally designated as an observing watch officer. "There's no such thing," said the commander, now Garrett's captain. "But why not?" Garrett stood one watch in three on the bridge, learning intensely what he could never use, and took his turn with the enlisted quartermasters on the wheel. He felt he was in the war at last, though no one had shot at him yet.

When that happened, it was a formality, almost. The ship went to general quarters. Garrett stood at his station on the bridge in helmet and life preserver.

"Bogeys at six miles," a telephone talker told him swiftly, hand over mouthpiece. "Whole bunch of 'em. Kamikazes I guess."

Garrett did not see the planes and he knew no one else did; they were enlarging yellow blips on more than a hundred red, round screens.

But he saw the firing start.

And he thought, guiltily, that it was the most beautiful thing he had ever seen.

Great arcs of white, red, and yellow scored the black surface of the sky, and that surface exploded in quick yellow-red splashes. Garrett tried to identify the tracers and the shell bursts: twenty-millimeter, forty-millimeter, five-inch thirty-eight. As only the outer ships fired, the lines were separate and identifiable. Then the whole force was firing, and he could see only one huge boil of red-white-yellow that filled the sky. He could see faces on the bridge from the light. He watched, head upturned, self-reprimanding, *you cannot enjoy this while men are dying,* and he heard something very loud and felt a shattering pain, and then nothing at all in the calf of his left leg.

He realized he was on the deck and hands were trying to pick him up. "I can make it." He took a hand, pulled himself to one foot, and put his arms around two sets of shoulders.

In the wardroom, the doctor did something to his leg, and took something out of it. Garrett was aware of the strong smell of alcohol and little else.

"Spent twenty-millimeter, one of ours," he said to Garrett professionally. "We get a lot of these. How are you feeling?"

"All right, I think. I got a thrombus on the left atrial wall, though. Could you see if it's in trouble?"

"A thrombus. Good God. What are you doing out here?" He stopped and went to work with a stethoscope. "All right so far. You're a tough son of a bitch. I'm going to keep you flat on your back awhile. And you better hope we don't get sunk."

"I promise to. Can I have a drink?"

"It's absolutely prescribed."

The destroyer was neither sunk nor hit, Garrett was the only casualty, and he was put ashore at Ulithi ten days later. The day after that, he was on his way to Pearl, ostensibly for medical, actually for the full press treatment. After the stateside papers made him a hero, the studio arranged for his separation. It was fine with him. He had suffered two years of tedium and paid his dues with them; he did not want any more. And now he had the strange, powerful satisfaction of having been wounded in combat, coupled with the triumph and relief of not having been wounded badly.

He went immediately into a picture, playing the captain of a submarine who, wounded on the bridge, gave the command, "Take her under." (It was based on an incident Garrett knew to be essentially distorted.) He made two other navy pictures that year, and was booked for another when Hiroshima was bombed, the war was over, and the picture canceled.

The wound from the spent shell looked to be a sure enough million-dollar-wound for him. "It's added at least two years to your career," Torldson told him with the pitiless directness that Garrett found warmer than dubious cordiality. "Maybe five. Normally you would have been good for about ten years in all, which would have meant you'd be starting to get through about now. But you could be good for another five years." He looked at Garrett in his cold-eyed, not unfriendly appraisal. "I hope you will be, Garrett, you're a man. Not all of them are."

Garrett, too, hoped he would last a while longer. He was not yet forty, he had been at the top for eight years, and he wanted to keep working at something he was reasonably good at. But he was confused at the prospect. The picture business as he had known it had gone crazy.

The business moved out of town. Many studios had money frozen in foreign countries by war and postwar loans that prohibited its removal. The only way it could go out was as product: a completed film in the can. And it was considered, not always correctly, that it was cheaper to make pictures overseas; there were tax advantages; there were glamorous locales uniquely desirable in the public craving for exoticism.

Many stars emerged suddenly as their own producers. Some started their own companies; others put a corporation together for a single picture and then collapsed it. There were always more of these, pictures maneuvered and bankrolled into existence like Broadway plays, and the financing of the project depended overwhelmingly on the star. And the star had to be an established star; as the great studios decentralized, and shrank, the apparatus that manufactured new stars slowed almost to a halt. This worked in favor of Garrett and his contemporaries, particularly the male ones: challengers were no longer ready and armed for the killing of the kings.

And yet Garrett was aware of a paradox. The commercial dominance of the stars was greater than ever and always increasing. And yet they were no longer gods. In the twenties and thirties they had had authentic if transient divinity. Now they were simply celebrities. He did not know how it had happened, or why, but he knew it was so.

He himself did not turn producer. He stayed with Globe, which was still producing more pictures than any other single source, and he was content.

He made three pictures a year from 1946 through 1948, most on American locations. In 1948, he went to Berlin for a picture about the occupation and fraternization.

A brigadier's wife, who had met the director, gave the cast a party. Across a drawing room full of medieval relics and moving drinkers, talking to a one-star American general and a man in a dark suit, Garrett saw the most exciting woman he had seen in Europe. She was dark blonde, certainly no longer naturally, and he guessed her at just under forty. In a black cocktail dress, she had a severe chic that restrained and counterpointed her full body. Garrett stared at her shamelessly, watching carefully modulated shades of feeling move across her face. It was a beautiful, disciplined, and possibly arrogant face, and he found it disturbing. After she walked in the opposite direction a dozen steps, he looked for his hostess and an introduction: he was a committed leg and derriere man.

When she turned toward him as the brigadier's wife brought him to her, Garrett knew she had been waiting for him. He had a thrill he had not known for years: that of finding an attraction returned by a beautiful woman he had thought out of reach. He had not known it for years because for years he had presumed most women were not out of reach. This one awed him.

She was the Baroness von Woldeck, Hilda von Woldeck. She was the widow of a German army officer, she told him. She let him know, delicately, that her late husband's title was a very old one. He had suffered for being an anti-Nazi, she said. So had she.

"For years the Nazis punished us for not being Nazis. Then the Allies punished us for not being Allies. It is a little confusing."

"I can see it would be," said Garrett gallantly.

"These are difficult years for all of us, you know. We are bad people. All Germans are bad people and we must all be punished."

Garrett said something.

"Of course, now that all of you are having your troubles with the Russians, it seems we are not such bad people as we used to be."

Garrett said something else.

"I do hope we can stop being bad people for a while. I am so tired of being punished even though I am sure I at least deserve it."

"You don't look punished."

"Oh, I have been, Mr. Garrett. Most severely punished."

Garrett thought how he would like to punish her. He said, "*I* haven't punished you."

She gave him a brilliant look. "You will, Mr. Garrett, I'm sure you will."

He knew he had had an invitation, he was not sure to what.

"Are you free after the party?"

She looked at him quite directly. "Yes, I am."

She showed him Berlin nightclubs. In the taxis she sat close beside him, so that he was very aware of her scent and the warmth of her leg through the silk, but he did not kiss her. He brought her to her apartment after two, and then she kissed him with great deliberation, moving her arms methodically about his neck, at last opening her mouth and pressing her lower body to his, then stepping back, still deliberately.

He saw she expected him to press her, and was poised to keep him off. Instead, he said, "Good night. Perhaps we can do it again."

"I should like to very much."

He could not read her face.

He took her out, almost but not quite nightly, for more than a week. She permitted him slightly increasing but carefully regulated intimacies. He understood she was teasing him. She probably wanted to get to America. He was annoyed that she thought she could work him up and make him marry her.

He brought her home from dinner and dancing one night.

"Why don't you ask me to stay over?" he said lightly, but looked at her quite seriously.

She looked back at him, consideringly; he saw she was reestimating the whole situation, weighing the possibility of a mistake, and making a decision.

"Why not?" she said. "We are not children. Are we?" She smiled at him suddenly. "I've wanted you to stay for some time, my dear. I did not want you to take me lightly."

She had an education in, an experience of, an intuition for, the art that transcended his own conception of its possibilities.

When he left her the next afternoon, he had made up his mind to take her to California with him on whatever the terms were. He had always despised men who could be bribed by bed into marriage. Now he was unashamedly willing to become one if that was what it took. He was only slightly annoyed that she had divined him so truly, and had gauged her strategy so well.

For her long-term availability, marriage was what it took. She had the kind of success in Southern California that was assured by her authentic previous title. They were much in demand not only among the most prestigious of the picture people, but among those glittering transients from the Mediterranean and the northeast coast of North America. One producer wanted to make a picture of her life story: certainly–Garrett thought–her version of it sounded very much like a picture. She gave every appearance of enjoying herself, though she reminded Garrett often what a cultural sacrifice she had made for him.

"They are all barbarians." She made a sound of scorn. "Though truthfully I prefer barbarians who know they are barbarians to bourgeoisie who think they are aristocrats." She made a sound of dismissal. "Aristocrats. In a country not yet two hundred years old."

"Am I enough of a barbarian for you?"

"You are a magnificent barbarian."

"Good enough to stud the princess?"

"Quite good enough."

And he took her again, and tried again to break through the thin impenetrable armor in which she was encased, and he failed again. From the beginning he had tried to break through and touch her personality, to know her in another way than carnally, and he had never succeeded. She was determined that he should not do so. It was a war. He waged it with resolution and exasperation, she with resolution and amusement, both with intense satisfaction. For him the struggle was emotional caviar: he relished the contest more than he desired victory.

The word love was never used between them. He had never known a physical passion more devoid of affection; he had never known one so deeply pleasurable.

When he caught her kissing a young actor on the balcony of a high-rise apartment in Beverly Hills, his first reaction was one of triumph: he had scored a point by catching her. His second was that it was actually she who had scored by embarrassing him. It was only his third that was jealousy, and it was not the jealousy of a lover but of one who sees a possession handled carelessly by another.

He saw them go through the open double doors, and shortly followed. They were embracing. From some strange decorum, he waited for them to end it. He saw Hilda open her eyes and look over the man's shoulder to see him. She did not stop the kiss. Instead–with a murmur, a twist of arms and body–she renewed it. When she did step back, she was smiling boldly at Garrett.

He tapped the actor on the shoulder and said pleasantly, "Get."

Turning, the man looked terrified as he first saw Garrett, then smug as he perceived Garrett was not going to hit him.

"Must I?" he said. Garrett slapped him lightly and he fled.

His wife was smiling, and he saw there was nothing faked about her amusement. She was enjoying herself. She did not stop smiling or enjoying herself when he slapped her.

"Don't do that again," he said easily.

She did not even rub her cheek. "My dear. I did not know you were so jealous."

"I don't like to be embarrassed."

Two days later, she told him she was leaving him. She looked impregnable in a fortress of fashion. He wanted to throw her on the floor and rip off the clothes that had cost him so much. Except the ermine coat, that was not from him but from some Nazi years ago, he would leave that on her.

"I am going back to Germany, Johnny." She spoke directly and unequivocally. As always, her precise yet differently accented English both irritated and aroused him.

"Are you?"

"Oh yes. I have a cousin, that is a good word, is it not, I have a cousin of whom I am very fond and who needs me. He has just been released from prison. It seems he was not so, democratic, as he might have been during the regime, and now he needs me. He needs me because he is a very soft man."

"So you like them soft, is that it?"

"That is it exactly. I am afraid it is the soft ones that appeal to me. There is nobody better than you, you are really very good, but you are too much man. I like men who are shall we say decadent, corrupt, who are shall we say a little, yielding. You are a splendid man, my dear, but for me you are not weak enough."

"I'm not?"

"No, my dear, you are not."

His left hand had knocked the coat from her shoulders to the floor before her face registered it.

"So I'm not soft enough," he said.

The hand went out again and ripped the black dress from the throat to the middle.

"No," she said.

The dress hung to one shoulder by a strip, and he yanked that in two with the same hand. The top of the dress fell forward and hung down from its middle and she was in her slip.

"No," she said again: the quick shock and anger had gone from her face and she smiled at him possibly cruelly.

He ripped the straps of the slip and the brassiere under it with both hands, and she aimed her breasts at him in the unchanging arrogance.

Then he tore everything off: the dress at the waist and her pants and her garter belt and then her hose. The noise of the ripping gave him great satisfaction. She did not move, nor stop smiling, nor permit her face to ease its cast of superiority while his hands slashed at her garments. She did not move while he savaged the garter belt hanging behind her, from her hose and threw it away. She stood before him in nothing but torn hose and high-heeled black suede shoes, and he fell upon her and bore her to the floor.

She still mocked him with her face, and he hated her until he made her cry in pain with his entrance. Then she fought, then she surrendered, then she met his drive with her own.

When it was done she said, "You see? You are not soft enough."

"I'll buy you a new dress."

"You will, my dear. You will indeed."

And he did: his inadequate store of weakness cost him half a million dollars.

That was all the cash he could immediately lay his hands on. He hated to part with it, and yet he had to admit that this time he had received some value for his money.

So he moved, shorn, into the century's fifties and his own forties. Quite early in that decade he was aware that he had slipped measurably and would slip still further. Yet the chief of the strange new characteristics the Industry had acquired kept him up. A picture had to have an established star to get financing, and he was an established star. More often than it used him in its own pictures, Globe lent him out to independents, and pocketed the difference between his salary it paid him and the fee it collected. His contract was renewed when it came up to 1953, but he was cut to $50,000 a picture. So he survived, holdover from another age, with a widening gulf between himself and the handful of new names. At a party after the Academy Awards one night, the size of the gulf was made clear to him.

A pint-sized dancer named Banty Forbes, one of the secondary figures in something called The Troop, saw Garrett enter alone.

"Hey guys, it's Valentino. Good old Clyde Valentino." He approached Garrett, his hand out, his face sweating, his eyes luminous with something stronger than alcohol. "Clyde *Burford* Valentino!" He grabbed Garrett's hand. "Tell us about Theda Bara, Clyde. How was Clara Bow, Baby? Give us the word, give us the word, Daddy. How was that fine old stuff?"

"It was too good for you bastards," said Garrett, and walked away.

Forbes himself howled with delight. The remark was repeated, and warmed up, expurgated, in a column. Garrett even got an invitation to dine with The Troop, but declined.

So he sat, alone, in the middle of a slowly shrinking pool of fame. He might have been better off if he had not renewed his contract with Globe six years before and gone the route that some of the others had gone: forming a company around himself. A few of his contemporaries had done it, but the truth was that he was too late for it. The ones who were doing it most successfully—John Wayne, Burt Lancaster, Kirk Douglas—had all come along five to ten years after him. And he did not think he had a brain for business. He might have lost it all.

When his agent of twenty-odd years retired from the Artists Corporation of America, richer from his half of ten per cent of Garrett than Garrett was from all of ninety, Garrett did not renew with the agency. He signed with the eccentric Nelson Glassgow. He suspected the agency was not severely displeased.

But he was not bitter. And he was not simply without bitterness: he was genuinely grateful that events had kept him professionally alive so far beyond his reasonable expectancy.

He understood, not one day or one week but possibly one year, he understood he had received a greater gift. Now that great success had left him, now that he was on the permanent reverse slope of his career, he had an unblurred view of a Garrett for the first time since he quit boxing. The Garrett he had made was Garrett the professional. He could do the job, he could do a good job with any job they gave him now. After twenty-odd years of acting, he had become an actor. He had a Garrett he could *be,* again. He had liked Garrett the fighter better, but this one would do.

7

IN 1961, he was cast with a young girl named Margaret Dayton in a picture to shoot in Arizona. She was not so much "big" as she was "hot"; that is, she was rising swiftly, she was on the threshold of very large success, but at the same time she was not certain of making the step across. If she took it successfully, she was likely to enter the most dazzling career of the decade. If she did not, she could fade swiftly. By one of its paradoxes, this either-or possibility carried more interest, more authentic glamour in the eyes of the Industry, than did absolutely attained and impregnable stardom. The first-magnitude star was a conceptualized institution, fixed, unambiguous, without mystery. The Margaret Daytons, almost but not yet to the summit, were breathless life and terrifying chance.

Garrett perceived and applauded the strategy: a rising personality had been paired with one established, respected, but descending. He was Dayton's insurance. It was an excellent move by the studio. The studio was interested in Margaret Dayton, not himself, but if it could prolong his career, quite incidentally, while pushing Dayton's, it would be good business to do so. And he was liked: Sidney Tate cared. Tate would be genuinely happy to help him; he simply would not risk a nickel to do so, and he was perfectly right. This way, he had been able to make an extremely shrewd business move with a favor to Garrett built in. It was Garrett's best break in five years.

The desert heat had solidity; to walk in it was not unlike walking under water. Garrett walked in it wearing an old-fashioned sun helmet, memento of his exploits as a white hunter in a fifteen-year-old picture.

He took it off, wiped his head with a handkerchief, and put it back. He stared at the dark wave of mountains lapping the edge of the flat empty sky. Behind him a woman said "Hello," he placed the voice and turned. Margaret Dayton was wearing a bandana over her head, her face had no makeup, and she wore a blue-checked cotton blouse and jeans. Garrett liked the way she looked, she looked very appealing, but she looked nothing whatever like America's fleshly dream.

"Hi," he said.

"Isn't it awful? I'll buy you a Coke."

"I'll buy you one."

"Whoever buys it, let's get it in a hell of a hurry." They started toward the commissary tent.

"You aren't like I thought you'd be," she said.

"I'm not?"

"I thought you'd be, you know, arrogant. Not really arrogant. You know. The Mace Garrett character. Kind of *bristling*."

"God save us from our public characters."

She laughed. "I'd sure be a little whore, wouldn't I?"

"Now you wouldn't be that."

"Oh sure. Sure I would, that's the way they like to see me. I don't care."

"That's right. What the hell."

They finished the Cokes.

"Could you hear me do the honky-tonk scene? The one we do tomorrow?"

"Sure."

She did it.

"Well," she said. "How can I improve it?"

"Honey, you could tell me, I'm no actor, everybody knows that. A couple of things that might help though. That next to last line, a little softer, like you're giving yourself away, and the next one, make it a little harder, like you caught yourself being soft and you want to toughen up."

"You're right."

She did it his way.

"Real good," he said.

She looked at him. "It sure is a shame you're no actor," she said.

When he left her at her trailer, for a rest and a nap in its air-conditioned comfort, he knew that the figure of Margaret Dayton's fantasies was a father figure and that he approximately filled its outlines. He knew what was coming and he did not look forward to it: in that sense, he was not in the least in search of a daughter. And yet he knew he would not put her off.

He stood, looking across sage and rock towards the dark mountains in the north. The sun, almost down, made them a heavy purple. He turned abruptly and started for his car. He had to blink against the low sun and keep his head down as he moved through the long shadows; his own fell behind him.

He spent the night in the motel ten miles from location, drove to the set in the Imperial, and by seven o'clock had changed into the jeans and boots he was to wear for the day's shooting. The picture was art cowboy, that was Garrett's own term, and it was about three competitors on the rodeo circuit. They traveled with each other and with a blonde waitress who had joined them. She was the sweetheart of all and the woman of none. Not in the picture. In the novel from which it came, Garrett had read it, in the novel she had slept with all of them with friendly impartiality, offering the service out of good simple comradeship. Her generosity was the emotional essence of the book, so it had of course been eliminated in the script. Yet Margaret was getting it into the picture anyway. Garrett wondered if she knew what she was doing. He did not think so. He thought she did the important things without knowing.

The day's first scene was a spin-off from a famous scene in *Snow White*. Margaret soothed the jealousies of the three cowboys and sent them to bed, with each other and without her (it had been *quite* different in the book, Garrett remembered, involving a hand of high card stud).

When it was done, he sat with Margaret Dayton while technicians made the last preparations for the next scene.

"You were great," he said honestly.

"Not all that great. How do you think the picture is going?"

"It's going to be good, it's going to be very good. I don't know how commercial it'll be."

"Don't you think it'll make money?"

"It'll make money because you're in it," he said.

"Because *you're* in it."

Garrett laughed. "God bless you for a liar. I'm just a, what do they call it, a Clyde. They think I go back to Valentino or something."

"*I* don't think you're a Clyde."

"Don't let those new guys hear you say that."

"*Them.*"

"Those guys." He shook his head and laughed again. "They wind up in a Tijuana whorehouse, they put out telecasts on it. They make a public thing out of their, well they make a big public thing out of everything. In my day we had a good time, sure, but we tried to at least look dignified to the public." He suspected it was not so even as he said it. "I'm talking like an old man, ain't I?"

"You could never talk like an old man."

In the next week, he spent much time with her. They fell together, almost automatically between scenes, at lunch, and sometimes for dinner. He did not touch her, however. This was not because he wished to be virtuous but because she did not excite him. He liked the way she looked, the way she looked appealed to him strongly, but not in the least the way Margaret Dayton was *supposed* to appeal to every man who still had them where they belonged. In her cotton dresses and blue jeans, with the bandana over her head, she looked like a Hollywood High girl, only more wholesome.

One afternoon, as they were walking off the set, he saw two assistant directors staring at them and grinning. He saw two electricians staring and whispering behind their hands. He was suddenly aware of the stares everywhere, and he wondered for just a moment before he knew. Of course it was The Good Luck Piece. He felt unreasonably guilty. He felt guilty because he knew that he could score easily and that he probably would. Because he was angry at himself, he spoke to her brutally.

"Look. Do you see them sniggering over there?"

She glanced in the direction he nodded, and smiled. "Mmm-hmm."

"Do you know why?"

She smiled straight at him. "Why?"

He spoke more brutally. "Do you know what the Garrett Good Luck Piece is?"

"Honey, everybody knows what the Garrett Good Luck Piece is."

"Well hell, doesn't it *bother* you?"

"Oh no."

"All those guys looking at you and smacking their lips and wondering if you are or you aren't, you mean that doesn't *bother* you?"

"Honey, I *expected* it. Everybody knows about that. Everybody knows about your lucky charm."

"And it really doesn't bother you?"

"Oh no. Do you really think that brings good luck? If you really think so, I mean if you want me to. For the picture and everything. I'll be glad to if you want me to."

"It's a lot of damned nonsense." He was surprised at how angry he was. "You can't believe that stupid nonsense."

"Oh I believe in luck, honey, nobody really knows anything about luck, whatever works works I always say. And if that works. Well. I mean it wouldn't be any trouble or anything."

"If we ever make it it won't be on account of any fool superstition for Christ's sake." He felt his face burning.

"Whatever you say."

"I thought you were too intelligent to swallow some fool superstition."

He saw a tear on her cheek and he understood what he had done. He took her elbow in his hand and steered her to a tiny space between trailers.

"I'm sorry," he said. "Look. I appreciate it, I appreciate it very much. I just didn't want . . . I mean I didn't want you to think you had to do anything. I mean on account of that nonsense."

"You don't like me that way."

"Look, I'm crazy about you that way. I told you how it was."

"You don't like me. I can tell."

"Yes I goddamn do like you and will you please shut up."

Then she did cry. He tried to comfort her, very awkwardly, and he drove her back to the motel. She left her car in the lot. In her motel room she wept much more freely, he tried much harder to comfort her, and it worked out, quite shortly, that they were in bed.

He thought he should leave her sometime in the night, he did not want to cause her any embarrassment or discomfort at all. But when he started to rise, she pulled him back and held him and he gave up the thought at once.

In the morning, sitting at the dressing table powdering her face, she looked at him over her shoulder and giggled. "I guess we're going to have a real lucky picture."

So it began. A *good* woman, his mind catalogued her: he had never known anyone so free from malice and meanness. She was generous, self-effacing–off camera–and deeply shy. In tranquillity her face said: *please don't hurt me, I can stand anything but being hurt on purpose.* It was a mobile face, that flicked from mood to mood as by a switch. It showed every emotion Garrett could think of except two: it never showed cruelty and it never showed vindictiveness. When she thought she had pleased him, it shone with delight. In the slacks and the kerchief she wore over her head when she was not before the cameras, she looked nothing like America's new orgiastic vision. Not to Garrett, she didn't.

From the first he cared for her, and he kept on caring more and more, but she never really stirred him.

Their intimacies were casual and affectionate, rather than great passages of passion. They moved into friendship ratified with an easy and incidental carnality. He could not remember it quite like that with any other woman. He understood that his recollection could not be infallible: he was more than fifty years old, and so he had had a good thirty of activity, and so he had had about a thousand women, at least a thousand counting all the one-shots, and how could he remember everything about all of them?

Through the furnace days he came to long for the surcease of her motel room, not for the phallic conjunction–he came quickly to consider that to be the chore he performed for benefits received–but for the sweet and enveloping attentions she paid him. After they closed the door, they always exchanged the ritual kiss, her tight young loins wriggling against him in hard but strangely antiseptic greeting (*everything is fine, here we are*), and always she sat him down in the pink plastic-covered chair. Then she acknowledged his sovereignty and her pleasure in it:

"Let me get you comfortable, honey. Let me get that sweaty old shirt off you. Put your head back now and let me put this nice cool towel on your head. There. Isn't that better?"

"That's fine, that is just real great."

"Now the shoes. Now this old belt. Now you just stretch out there, darling, and I'll bring you a nice cool drink. You want gin or vodka or rum tonight, daddy?"

"Vodka, honey, please."

"Vodka it is."

And she would mix their drinks, her face absorbed as a child's in the blending of liquids, the million-dollar hips innocent and guileless (and sometimes pantsless) in the May Co. slacks, the upper body working with a faint awkwardness that was its own grace. Then she would bring the drink like an offering.

"Ah. Ah that's good. You're too good to an old man like me, sweetheart."

"I love to take care of you daddy. Do I take good care of you?"

"The best, baby. The best."

And after his bath, and hers, and dinner sent in, they would fall into bed. Often he went to sleep immediately. Sometimes, when he did not, he thought of Hilda and tried to make believe that the woman in the bed was Hilda. But they were the light and the dark, Margaret was the light, and for the occupation of darkness it was the dark that he lusted for.

He understood that he loved Margaret Dayton in a warm passionless fashion. She brought him more contentment than any other woman had done. If she had not been an actress, or even if she had been just an actress and not the new, almost-arrived Marilyn Monroe, he would have married her.

But he did know what an actress was, most particularly did he know what an actress was who was or was about to be a star in motion pictures. Such an actress carried inside her a self-worship that was a bitch-wolf: in the end it ate everything else. Margaret was young, and she had been unbelievably lucky, and the wolf had never been turned loose for its run. Probably she did not know it was there. He himself had never seen it, but he knew it was there, it had to be. If it had been visible, he would have liked her much less and loved her not at all—and he knew, sadly, he would have found her infinitely more exciting.

But he knew it *had* to be there, and he knew if he married her it would devour him. Even if he were wrong, even if by some miracle she was born without the wolf, and for an actress that would be a miracle comparable to the Immaculate Conception, the pure external momentum of her career would smash him down. He had no idea of so sacrificing himself. He could not have accepted such a sacrifice, and he would not make it.

She wanted him to make it. That is, she wanted him to marry her, she did not know the price tag on it for him. He knew she did not want to know it.

"Why don't you marry me, poopsie?" she said one twilight, not for the first time.

"Because I know better, sweetheart. I would plain love to marry you but I just know better."

"What do you know better? Don't you love me?"

"Let me tell you something nobody has ever said before. An actress. Is married. To her. Car-reer. You can frame that and put it over your mantelpiece. I won't charge you."

"Merde." She had just picked up the French word, and said it as though she felt very daring. "That's old stuff, it's not like that anymore."

"He he."

"Well damn you anyway."

He reached up to her elbow, she had walked over and was standing in front of him, and pulled her down and kissed her, and she dropped the subject in favor of another.

And suddenly the picture was over. Garrett knew it was a good one, he knew he himself had been good, he thought Margaret Dayton had been very good.

The company completed the last day of shooting with ritualistic observance of what was known as "horsing around." Ransom, the director, placed on the chairs of the women certain Hindu art objects carved of wood. These were superbly detailed but extravagantly proportioned male organs: the women proclaimed their shock with loud screams that were, perhaps, not undelighted. In turn someone left a pie in Ransom's chair; he dutifully sat in it and rose with the proper expression of dismay and fury.

Cameras rolled on the last scene at eleven in the morning, and by eleven-thirty bottles were out all over the location area. Ransom took Garrett into his trailer, he placed a bottle of Early Times and a pitcher of water on the postage-stamp table, and they sat in the built-in seats on either side and started to get drunk.

Garrett was dehydrated, and on the doubles Ransom was pouring he got drunk fairly quickly.

"I think we got ourselves a good picture," he heard himself saying for the fifth or sixth time.

Ransom's long creased face shifted slightly upwards as he smiled. "Sure we have kid, sure we have a good picture, but the question is, is it a *lucky* picture? Is it, a lucky, pic-ture? Now I know you've done your part in that direction, kid, and I want you to know I appreciate it. I ap-prec-iate *it.* It must have been one hell of a sacrifice to go through that with Margaret Dayton, it was just as selfless as hell. To get in the hay with America's wet dream, now a man that will do that is all heart, Garrett. He, is, all, heart."

Garrett abused him and the creased face smiled back.

"Yessir, a man who'll do that is a real team player. Anything for the good old picture."

"Let me tell you something. You want to know something, you dumb bastard?"

"Sure I want to know something," said Ransom.

"Sure you do, and you know what? I ain't going to tell you."

"Aw come on and tell me. Picture's over. No secrets. One for all. All that. Tell me now."

"Well I will tell you cause you're too dumb to ever know it if I don't."

"All right tell me."

"I will when I get ready. You're like all the rest of these jerks, you think Margaret Dayton is the greatest thing in the sack since. Since who. I don't know since who. But. But I'll tell you something. Listen, she is the greatest kid on two feet, I mean she is the sweetest kid on two feet, and I would marry her this second if she weren't in the stinking Industry, but in the sack she is a nice kid period."

"I'll be damned. Big star on screen, no star in bed, huh. Won't be damned either: been lots of cases like that. But I wouldn't have figured *her* like that. No I wouldn't."

"Now look, don't you get me wrong, I love that girl. I mean I'm not just talking, I love her, but she ain't. She ain't like you think. She's sweet. That's the thing. She's too sweet to be sensational. You know what I mean. A woman can't be that sweet. A woman's got to be a devil to set you on fire."

"So Margaret Dayton is a lousy lay."

Garrett cut in. "Look, I didn't say that. She's all right. It's just that Nazi bitch spoiled me. She was the damnedest bitch there ever was but she was the best there was. She took me for half a million, and you know what, it was worth every nickel. That was one bundle I didn't mind dropping. Like I say, Margaret's a sweetheart, she's the sweetest there is, only, that way, she's not exactly my type."

He had said too much, he thought, he and the Early Times had said much too much, and it was time to shut up. He knew it was time to shut up even before he felt someone there, and turned to see Margaret Dayton standing a little behind him and already crying. The little muscles were working under her white cheeks, her teeth were clamped on her lower lip, and her whole face was one second before breaking up all the way. She came in the door at the end of the trailer, he thought fuzzily, she heard them and came in to join them, and then she really heard him.

"You're not so great yourself," she said. "You're old. And you're mean." Then the face did break up all the way and with it her voice. "You're not so great. You're not so goddamned great."

"Baby–" His palms pushed against the table top and he was on his feet if not solidly.

"You told about our things."

Her voice was all the way gone now, he stretched his hand to her shoulder, she twisted it off and ran out the door at the end of the trailer.

He heard her flat heels clack on the steps, he ran after her down the steps and into the night, but he was after all drunk, and he stumbled, and he had lost her. Maybe two hundred yards away he heard a car start, and go through the gears, and he watched a pair of headlights thread out to the highway and turn right, toward California.

In town, he got no further than her mother when he called. A few weeks later, he went to the sneak at the Hawaiian, hoping he would see her and afraid he might. If she came, he did not see her. He saw her only on the screen, and on the screen it was all there, the camera had caught it all. It had caught her charity and compassion and universal tenderness, and for him these filled the screen. She sang a song that was supposed to be a scorcher: he thought of a delightful child playing at being really grown-up.

Walking out, he heard a teen-ager say, "What would you give for a little of that, man, what would you give?"

"Whooo-*eee!* What wouldn't I give."

He heard the same thought a dozen ways. And he himself could only see the face full of delight, and a desire to please.

There must be something wrong with me, he thought.

8

GARRETT not only did not marry Margaret Dayton, he did not see her after the picture was done. Not quite a year later, he read she had married a novelist, and a few months after that, he married again himself. He married a girl he met at a supermarket in Northridge, who reminded him of Margaret. The girl, wearing the kerchief over her hair as Margaret had done, asked Garrett to hand her a bottle she could not reach. He did, she recognized him, and the slow coloring of her face reminded him of someone. He knew she reminded him of Margaret when he had watched her face for half a minute: it was full of the will to please, it was totally vulnerable, and, quite unwittingly, it begged for love. He carried her groceries to the car, dated her for seven weeks, and married her. Her name was Arlene Hill, she was thirty-three years old, and a divorcee with two children. In appearance, she did not look like Margaret at all. She was taller and more heavily built, she had brown hair, and actually she had quite different features. She had nothing whatever to do with the Industry.

He thought, he hoped, he was taking the best of Margaret and separating it from the rest. He knew that he himself would be consistently if infrequently unfaithful. He now accepted that his glands and his affections were not on the same frequency. It did not bother him, he did not consider it important.

He bought a ranch back in the hills of Ventura County, in a valley far enough from the freeway so the developers had not yet started on it. It was not really a self-supporting ranch but still was one that could be called, for vanity, a working ranch. It had fifty head of cattle on thirty acres of pasture, a five-horse stable, a pool, and a hundred-thousand-dollar ranch house. All of it cost him two hundred thousand, which could have been worse, but it cost him thirty-odd thousand a year to run it and for him that year, that was pretty bad. Still they made it. His manager sent him checks on his investments that almost covered the monthly nut, he got two pictures at fifty thousand each, and he thought he was set. He thought he had never been so set.

Then he had an attack, the fourth one. It was like the first one in the gym, almost thirty years before, though not so bad. He still had the same doctor. Their fortunes had risen together in the decades though not of course at a comparable rate: Garrett's had shot up and slipped down; the doctor's had risen more slowly of course but had never reversed.

He had ordered Garrett to the hospital and now was visiting him before his release. He had aged much more than Garrett: the black hair had gone to gray, the face had taken deep lines and jowls. He had had no reason not to age, Garrett thought.

He looked at Garrett with the same air of deliberate, ponderous consideration: he had had plenty of time to perfect it.

"This is the worst one you've had since that first one isn't it?"

"Easy," said Garrett sitting on his bed.

"Well, that thrombus is still there, and it's more dangerous than ever."

"What do you mean?"

"I mean at your age it's liable to drop off at any time, and when it drops it's liable to kill you."

"What do I do?"

"Not one damn thing you don't have to. I'm not fooling."

"Can't I work any more?"

"Do you want to die?" he was serious.

"No."

"Then don't do anything but take it easy. You must have plenty socked away. You don't need to work."

Garrett laughed. "If I told you you wouldn't believe me. I guess I can make it though."

The doctor studied him. "You remember the first time I told you about that thrombus? And I told you you couldn't fight any more?"

"Sure I remember. Why?"

"Nothing. Only if I were you I'd hate me."

"I don't hate you, I'll even buy you a drink. If you let me have one too."

"The one you have will have to be pretty damned weak."

He told Nelson Glassgow, who had been his agent for years now, and he declined an offer Glassgow had for him.

He and his wife let all the servants go except one man, sold all but two of the horses, and kept only his three-year-old Imperial, a Citroën for her and a very old pick-up truck. They were not exactly a hardship case, but they had cut out most of the fat, and for three months they stayed inside the budget.

Then Garrett's business manager died of cancer after an illness of only a few months. A week after, Garrett got a letter from him. Sid's name was handwritten in the left-hand corner of the envelope; the letter was not simply from his office. Garrett looked at the handwriting and felt very strange to have a letter from a dead man. He had the feeling of something very bad about to happen. He opened it. It said:

Dear Johnny,

My doctors tell me I could be in better shape and I think the time has come, old buddy, for me to tell you that I screwed you. I didn't really mean to but it looks like I have. All of that loot going through your fingers, man, it's just hard to say no. I guess like the song I'm just a guy who can't say no. Big joke huh? Well anyway, those rental checks you've been getting, they aren't from rentals at all. I've been paying them out of your capital. There aren't any rentals, kid. There isn't much capital. I blew it, just about all of it.

There's nothing you can say about me I haven't said about myself a damn sight worse, I know I'm a bastard. I want you to know though I didn't really steal it from you. I just borrowed it. There was this big syndicate deal in Kern County and I put it all in. I was going to give you all the dough back and part of the profits when it came in, but of course I was going to get myself set up pretty good by just hanging on quietly to a chunk of the stock. I had it set up pretty fancy so I could do that. Something happened, the guy running it used the money to cover some other operations, it's an old story and he'll be in jail if he comes back to California. The funny thing is I checked him out very carefully, he had made nothing but money for his investors in a dozen other deals. If I haven't done anything else, I've proved you *can* lose money in Southern California real estate. Guess I'd be in jail myself huh, if I was still around when you got this.

You went down the drain for six hundred long ones on that, more or less. That as you know was all that was left, it cost a lot to settle those last two divorces, and your brother's business cost you a hundred, and you know what your taxes have been. So I've been paying your rental checks out of the fifty you got out of your last picture. There's about twenty of that left and that is it except for one thing.

Now one thing I have done, I sold all my own stuff and got seventy-five together and bought into another syndicate in San Diego County for you. This one is real conservative and blue chip as you will see from the names on the enclosures and if you can hang on for five or six years, it ought to be worth four or five times what you put into it (papers enclosed as I say, take 'em to a good lawyer). Only thing is you've got to come up with another seventy-five in five months. Get it somehow kid, and you'll get back most of what I blew for you.

Like I say, I'm sorry. Believe it or not, I meant well. Fairly well anyway.

Yours,

Sid

P.S. Most important of all, you can get a real nice tax refund on the loss. I wish I was up to taking care of it for you. Joris Arlen would be a good guy to work it out for you.

Garrett pushed the open paper, the ends folding upward, back on the red checked cloth of the table. He looked for a moment over the table to the paneled pine walls of the kitchen. Then he took the handwritten pages, refolded them, put them in the slit pocket of his Western shirt, and went out the back door.

He stood for a moment in the late morning sunlight. In front of him the hills rolled back to the horizon, yellow-brown and smooth as stone, broken only by wide-apart clumps of green-black live oak. Fifty feet to his right was the red stable, the two-board white fence lining from it on either side and squaring off the pasture that a sprinkling system kept a deep green.

In the pasture one horse made a dark statue against the blue and brown far off behind it. Garrett walked to the stables.

Inside in a stall Arlene was currying the bay mare he had given her. In a blue checked shirt, her body leaned down and to one side, her left hand rested on the mare's neck, the right worked the comb. Sweat beads hung on her lip, dirt streaked her cheek. She looked deeply interested in what she was doing. She looked up and saw Garrett, smiled, and said, "Hi." Her voice had a happy climb.

"Fixing her all up?"

"Like a movie star. I'm just done."

She came out of the stall, put the curry comb on its hook, and came to Garrett. She had wisps of yellow hay on the blue shirt and a trace of manure on one of the reverse calf boots. She kissed him. "Hello again."

"Hello yourself. How was your ride?"

"Real great."

She put her arm around Garrett's waist and they went into the yard. "Did you ever see anything as beautiful?" she said looking at the country. "I've never loved any place like I love this place."

"It's not bad. What have you been doing today?"

"I cleaned the kitchen, I got the mail, I rode the mare, I curried the mare." She ticked those things off on her fingers. "There was a letter for you from Sid's office."

"It was from Sid."

"From Sid?" Her eyes opened wider as she looked at him.

His fingers slipped into the slit pocket and took the letter, and he handed it to her. As she read it, he saw her dirty pretty face move from surprise to anger to resolution. He saw no panic or fear.

"The son of a bitch," she said.

"I don't think he was really a son of a bitch. He did try to make it up."

"For my money he is a stinking son of a bitch." Her teeth clamped on her lower lip a moment, and she turned to face him. "How much can we get for the place?"

"I don't want to sell it out from under you."

"We have to sell it."

"I know how much you like it."

"I love it and I can leave it this afternoon. It's just a place. How much can we get?"

"For ourselves maybe fifty thousand. I figure we can get two hundred and at that figure our equity is fifty. It may take time to move it."

"I guess we'd better get at it as soon as we can then. Johnny."

"Uh-huh?"

"Don't worry. We'll make it." She kissed him.

He went to see Nelson Glassgow the next day.

"That was rough about Sid," Glassgow said. "I'm sorry."

"It was real rough. I got to have a job."

"I thought you couldn't work."

"I can work if I have to."

Glassgow looked at the forefinger of his left hand which tapped lightly on the top of his desk. "It's not worth it, Johnny, if you really shouldn't work."

"I can do one picture all right."

Glassgow breathed fully and looked at him. "Okay. I can sure get you a picture."

"Nelson." Garrett spoke carefully. "I need a hundred thousand for it."

"I could get you two pictures for a hundred."

"You want to know something? I don't think I can last through two pictures."

"Jesus."

"That's why I need the hundred for the one."

"Please don't do it. If it's like that I beg you not to do it."

"I got to do it. And I think I can get away with one picture. But I've got to have the hundred."

He explained why.

"It won't be easy," Glassgow said. "I'll try."

"Thank you."

"Try is *all* I can do, now. The chances are damn slim."

It was three weeks before Glassgow asked Garrett to come in again.

"We've got it," he said.

"For heaven's sake how? How did you get it?"

"It's Margaret Dayton's next picture."

"Oh." Garrett did not speak for a moment. "She got it for me, didn't she?"

"That's right."

"Did you tell her how it was?"

"Yes."

"I wish you hadn't. Well. Thank her for me."

"I think you'd better do that yourself."

"I will."

"Johnny. This could be a fairly rough one. It's shooting in Greece. I hope. Well. No point in worrying about it now, is there?"

"No point at all. I am very very obliged you got it for me."

He wrote Margaret his thanks and ended his letter, "I would like very much to have you meet my wife. You and she remind me a great deal of each other."

He was sure she would receive that clearly.

He knew she had when he saw her on the Globe-International lot a few days after.

She was standing outside the door to the long white building in which Sidney Tate had his offices, where Garrett had been summoned for a conference. She blushed deeply as she smiled at him, she came to him and embraced him hard, and kissed him lightly on the cheek.

"You look great," he said.

"You look pretty great yourself."

"I didn't know you could be early for anybody."

"I wanted to see you."

"You've done enough for me. I guess you know you pulled it out of the fire for me."

"I'm so glad."

"I'm the one that's glad, believe me." He looked at her. "You're the biggest there is now."

"This month."

"You know better than that. Let's go see Sidney."

She put her arm through his and they went into the building.

9

THAT was how he had got the picture, and he remembered it, now, as he sat in the camp chair and watched the preparatory movement of the armies in front of him. It seemed much longer ago than it was.

Josh Duncan, commander of armies, saw Garrett and stopped

beside him. Sweat beaded heavily on his forehead, and ran down his cheeks.

"Oooeee," he said. "It's going to be a poozer today."

"Yeah," said Garrett.

"You ready to get it shook off on the machine?"

"Ready as I'll ever get," said Garrett.

"You don't have to drive the bastards anyway. Suppose you had to drive them."

"There's that."

Duncan smiled, saw something, and ran into the Trojan army. Garrett watched the gray head bob and the arms wave in the red jacket.

Garrett knew this company liked him as his other companies had all liked him. It did not pay him super-star deference and he could not care less. He told himself.

But he did care that they were now trying to rush the picture, that for the next several weeks he would be working harder than he would like to work. It was a speedup, a real speedup, if the picture were not so far behind, if Margaret had not gone, if he had not been getting a hundred thousand instead of the fifty he was supposed to get now, he would raise hell. No he wouldn't. He had never raised hell about work in his life. He had never done anything about work except do it. Temperament he had never had: if a man does not have talent, he works at being a good guy.

A few more weeks: that was all now. He might make it. He might be there when Arlene had her baby. Why did he always call it her baby? It would be his, too. He was afraid of being a father. Yes he was. Well he would get used to it. No he wouldn't, he wouldn't have time to get used to anything. That was all right. Just let him finish the picture. He did not ask for anything else, only to finish the picture.

He sat down in the chair with his name on the back. He was five minutes early. When Korbin stood beside him, looking still at the armies, Garrett said, "Ready any time you are, C.B."

Korbin smiled, tokenly.

BOOK 6

HOWARD SILLS

1

ONE curved sheet of iron was both roof and sides to the hut. Its corrugations ran from a closed front door, past four desks occupied by three women and a man, to a partition at the end that extended across the hut but did not reach its top. A door on the left of the partition, closed, bore a sign: MR. TATE. Another, on the right, also closed, was lettered MR. SILLS.

Behind the door marked MR. SILLS sat a tall man with very white wavy hair (he used bluing almost unashamedly). Over a black knit sport shirt he wore a light blue alpaca cardigan. He was a handsome man, though not obviously so: a label he had borne for almost thirty years was *distinguished*. He did not object to it.

He was staring at the top of the portable desk, U. S. Army surplus, and the fingers of his left hand tapped against it. Pale sunlight fell through the window into a rhombus on the desk: outside it sat a field telephone in open leather case. Sills was not idle: he was awaiting the outcome of a call placed seventeen minutes before to Beverly Hills, California. Finally, the phone buzzed: he had it off the receiver at the first note.

"We have Dr. Bernberger," said the voice of his secretary, who had confronted traffic problems.

"Carl? Hello, Carl, Howard Sills. How are you? Good, I wish I could say the same. I daresay you've read about our problem."

Over seven thousand miles of cable, the Atlantic Ocean, and one hundred-odd miles of Aegean Sea, Bernberger's voice was thin but clear: "Oh, yes."

"Do you have any thoughts? I didn't hear you, Carl. Yes, Sylvia's gone, too. Now I hear you very well. Do you hear me? Good."

"I've always discouraged the relationship between Margaret and Sylvia. There are certain, hazards, in it. Are you hearing me, Howard?"

"I hear you fine, Carl."

"You understand I have no information or actually any reason to. I talked to Margaret last week and she seemed all things considered to be not really too bad. Certainly I got no hint of, I saw no signs of any crisis."

"Could you come over for two weeks, if it seems advisable? Assuming Margaret comes back."

"I lost that, Howard."

"Could you come over, if necessary?"

"It would put my patients out a great deal, Howard, and it would cost me a lot of money, I mean a lot of money. If we face a real emergency with Margaret I would drop everything else, of course. But I'd have to charge you a thousand dollars a day and expenses just to avoid a loss."

"That's no problem."

"I'd lose that much, Howard."

"I appreciate that, Carl, truly, and if we have to have you, why, no problem. Now, do you have any advice for me?"

"Nothing new. Remember, Margaret is in constant need of reassurance. Give her all the reassurance you can possibly give her. There's something else I think I have to tell you now. She was better before she took up with the Korbins."

"I know that."

"So the more you can minimize her contact."

"He's directing the picture, of course."

"I appreciate the difficulties. However. Margaret's not *very* sick, and you know how we use the word, everybody's a little sick. I don't *think* you have anything to worry about."

"Oh no. Nothing at all."

"It'll work out. And I will come if you need me, Howard."

"Thank you, Carl. We'll be in touch."

He heard the placing of the receiver and the strange seashell roar, and he hung up his own phone in the leather case.

He had expected no help from Bernberger and that was what he had got. He wondered . . . When he was himself Bernberger's patient, he had had touching faith. Now . . . But he rejected doubt. After all Bernberger had said Margaret was not *very* sick.

The situation was certainly absurd, and still it was certainly perilous. After his decades in the Industry, he was aware, with no particular amusement, that most situations in the Industry were absurd with both small and large *A,* and were intrinsically comical. And yet the consequences were not comical at all. No they were not.

Sills had an exact appreciation of the consequences to himself of a disaster on the picture.

In those years which he had survived, almost incredibly, he had had considerably more than simple ups and downs. He had known triumphs that were almost absolute and catastrophes of perfectly tragic proportions. In retrospect, the catastrophes were the most flattering: they suggested he had suffered because of an integrity so inflexible as to be quixotic. This was not so, he knew it was not so, and yet he wanted it to be so. And if it were not completely true, neither was it completely false: there was truth *in* it. He had not achieved that perfect, imagined self and he knew it; yet detoured as he had been by weakness, he had always moved toward the idea and he could affirm it.

For Howard Sills, once the arbiter of what passed for elegance in his métier, now again a totem of its clear (if unadventurous) good, he wanted no more catastrophes. He did not want him to lose a picture. He did not want him to sustain that disgrace. The fact that it might end his professional life, already overage, was less important to him than that it would deface the painfully restored self-portrait of Howard Sills.

He was relieved when Starnes confronted him with tangibles.

Starnes was number two man in Globe's publicity department, and for several weeks had been assigned solely to the picture. He wore horn-rims and so appeared studious: his only concession to location was that he wore no necktie under his jacket.

He sat at Sills's invitation and put a small load of papers on Sills's desk. Sills averted his face and trembled in burlesque.

"From Rome," said Starnes. "I talked to them this morning and to New York last night." The island was seven hours ahead of Eastern Standard Time.

"It's still the big story at home but it's getting a tongue-in-cheek treatment."

"It would," said Sills.

"And Vern McGaughey is still raising hell."

"He would," said Sills, and sighed.

"The European press is treating it much more melodramatically. They're rather taken with the idea that Margaret's been kidnapped by some wealthy lover."

"Of course they always mention in the next paragraph that Haratunian is somewhere in this part of the Mediterranean."

Sills frowned. The full irony of that was not known to those who perpetrated it.

"I think we can anticipate a small invasion of media people today."

Sills sighed again. "Yes."

"The only thing to do really is give them everything. It's better not to hold back. Get it over with, and if you level with them they'll give you a better break."

"I'll take your word."

"Do we have anything on Margaret?"

"Not a thing."

"Any suggestions on what to tell them?"

"Something. That there's unquestionably just been some kind of communication failure, and we're confident Margaret is all right, she's giving a marvelous performance, we have a marvelous picture, et cetera, et cetera, and et cetera."

"Not much else to do."

"No."

Sills looked at Starnes's back in the blue-yellow-green Madras jacket move through the doorway and the gray door closing after him, then at the clear limitless blue through the high window, then at the smooth desk top gashed with sunshine and telephones. And then he considered Margaret Dayton. Technically, it would have been remarkably easy and not truly expensive to replace her completely: they could shoot her replacement only in close and medium shots. Yet the picture had to have her, indeed could not do without her, for the first and final reason of the picture business: her name. They were in for so much money that only a super-name could pull them out, and there were now, with the passing of Marilyn, only three or four super-names among women. And Margaret truly interested him. Quite beyond her value, she interested him. There was something there. There had always been something there. It was a mistake to overvalue it, but it was a much greater mistake not to value it at all. It did not transcend her fixed dimensions as the great repository of sex so much as exist totally apart from it. Was it personality or was it talent? And was there a difference? Yes. There was a difference. He did not know what it was. Nor did he know, finally, what she had. Yet, in the most precise, and profound, sense of the word, he found her interesting.

He not only wanted her to return and finish the picture, and save it, and himself, and others. He hoped, for her own sake, that she was safe. He hoped it with measurably less intensity for her own sake than for his own; he knew it, and he wished it were otherwise. But he accepted it philosophically: everyone was the sun of his own universe.

So. What had she? What was her quality? Toward her, someone had once directed Fitzgerald's epiphany of Dick Diver (Sills was one of the few to recognize the source): she "had a trick of the heart."

But it was not a trick. So perhaps it was not talent after all. No. Simply because it was not a trick was it the clearest, purest kind of talent.

It would be sentimental and lumpish to say Margaret might have been his daughter. Yet he had slept with her mother. How, something, it would have been if he had retained a recollection of Margaret in, say, a Brownie uniform. But though Octavia had been his companion in bed and out, for almost a year, he had in truth never set eyes on Octavia's daughter until she was a young woman working for Globe-International Studios, Television Division, and for Howard Sills.

There was no profit in either nostalgia or speculation.

All at once he was aware that the office was oppressing him. When he was in it for long, it acquired the character not of a simple prison, but of his mind, a more complicated prison. From it, indeed, he must escape. He put on his long-billed baseball cap and left.

He stepped out of the hut and sudden sunlight blinded him. His eyes tightened: ahead he saw white clouds far apart in bottomless blue, long blade of horizon, dark wind-stirred sea, and hard plain with indolent armies drawn apart under the Trojan walls. On his right the impromptu parking lot with its dozens of cars, on his left two more Quonsets, the trailers of disparate function, the low side of a mountain.

Sills moved slowly in the sun, not really caring for an objective but heading finally for the cameras and director.

Any ordeal was less fearsome when he moved into it physically: the problem of Margaret shrank if it did not disappear. He remembered battle reports of combat officers who were completely controlled in action and broke up only on leave.

He smiled at Korbin and watched his preparations silently. He spoke lightly to crew members. One blonde camp follower of the Greeks, kept herself determinedly in his eye, tossing her head to show her hair, elevating her shoulders to present breasts he acknowledged were impressive. He smiled politely and looked elsewhere.

Starnes led to him almost a dozen men and three women in city clothes: the new media arrivals. He talked with them affably, at length, and with genial amusement at the importance they gave Margaret's absence. Just a quick vacation, of course, they expected her back at once, it was a trifling thing really. They left unsatisfied, but not hostile. At the border of vision he saw a stocky figure walking with slow heavy sureness to the production hut, and started towards it himself. He gave Tate two minutes and knocked on his door.

Looking upward across the desk, Tate's face was smooth and pink and solid. Sills found himself taking unwarranted assurance from it. Tate smiled.

"Sit down, Howard. And congratulations, or did you know?"

"Oh?"

"You've been elected to the Club. Vern McGaughey says *you're* incompetent too."

"I'm honored."

"Absolutely," said Tate. "We'll both get medals. He's demanding a special stockholders' meeting, by the way."

"Can he get it?"

"Certainly not. Unless. Un-less."

Sills said nothing.

"He's due in today, you know."

"Haratunian?"

"Who else is there?"

"Will he be very disappointed? About Margaret?"

"Yes. Yes, I think you could say that. I think you could say, he'll be, disappointed."

Sills started to say, *I'm sure he'll understand,* and did not.

He studied Tate's face now turned to the wall: the fold of skin beneath his chin hung easily but did not sag.

"Do you know something?" Sills understood Tate was not really talking to him. "I've never been truly dependent on anybody before. That I remember. I probably have I suppose, but I honestly can't remember it. This is, quite an experience."

Sills could have said, *you've been kind of lucky.* He did say, and he worked hard for absolute ringing sincerity, "Sidney, it's going to work out."

He liked Tate very much, and he would have spared him the novelties of total dependence if he could have. It was not, however, a novelty to Howard Sills.

It would not be accurate to say that he had more to lose than Tate, Sills thought. They both faced precisely the same loss: everything. And because he had known disaster before and Tate had not, because Tate therefore had a kind of virginity as to defeat, and he had not, it was even possible that Tate stood to be the greater loser. Nevertheless Sills refused to accept the proposition: nobody stood to lose *more* than he. "She'll be back today or tomorrow," he said. "And even if she doesn't we can shoot around her another week."

"A funny thing," said Tate. "They're associating Margaret and Haratunian. They can't know a thing and they're all wrong and yet isn't it funny how they're a little bit right? I mean, the press. You've heard the broadcasts and so on?"

"Some. Starnes brought in some European newspapers this morning, I thought exactly the same thing about the Haratunian business. They make him sound like an Armenian Daddy Warbucks, don't they?"

"You know what? He *is* an Armenian Daddy Warbucks. With Spanish Fly. Let's hear the latest."

Sills watched Tate's gray-haired secretary come in with the recorder, set it on the desk, connect and start it. She stood back, having the gift of seeming to be absent while being in attendance. Sills wondered if she were in love with Tate. Then he watched the spool turn and listened to the replay of the shortwave newscast.

The announcer invoked the presence of Haratunian in the Mediterranean. He produced, quite originally, a rumored love affair between Margaret and Mace Garrett, Margaret fleeing because of the tension it created. He concluded facetiously: was it possible that Margaret, notorious for her tardiness, had simply overslept?

"The son of a bitch," said Sills.

Tate's telephone rang. Sills watched the wall of his face as he said only "Yes?" and "Thank you."

Tate stood in a heavy, springless effort. "My lookout thinks Haratunian's ship is in sight. If it is him, I'd better be ready to render honors."

Sills followed him out and went into his own office, his concern for Tate and for himself gathered into the tightness at the solar plexus which he had long ago learned was fear. He was not at all sure he deserved survival, but he wanted it. He did not consider himself a great talent, but he felt, profoundly, that a large talent in his function would have been misplaced. His talent, finally, was to liberate the talents of others.

At the moment, on Mykonos, it was not the most useful talent conceivable. He sighed, and wished it were otherwise.

2

SILLS was often praised for the near infallibility of his taste, but this was not true and he knew it was not true. In the Industry, where power and a lack of taste so often were concomitants, he did appear to have taste. But he knew that, in this respect as in all others, he was mediocre. Affirmatively, constructively mediocre, he would qualify, but he was completely aware of his enduring and unchanging quality. He was not ashamed of, nor sad about it. Mediocrity was a misunderstood and maligned word, he often thought: worlds were built upon it. Certainly the Industry was.

And he considered that he had helped to raise the level of mediocrity in the Industry. It was his secret vanity that he as much as anybody had raised the Industry from mediocrity's ocean bottom to its middle depths. Let the *New Yorker* and *Time* critics say what they will, he thought, they can look at a sampling of 1935 pictures and a sampling of this year's, and they have to admit this year's are incomparably better. Movies really are Better Than Ever. He had had a great deal to do with that. He was not a genius nor did he approach genius; he was not an artist nor a theoretician of the art. He had simply proved that American pictures could be much better than they had been—and still be mediocre enough to make money.

Intuitively, he had set out to make himself the superior man of mediocrity, as though he had had a blueprint. By the time he was fifty, he knew that he *had* had a blueprint, though that aware portion of his sensibility had neither formulated nor identified it. The truer self, the one below awareness, had always known that mediocrity was his essence. That self had not despised but had used it, cherished it, built astutely and not in the least dishonorably upon it. He had longed for excellence, and found it, such as it was, in mediocrity.

In the end, he thought, he had had a more benign and enduring effect on the standards of Hollywood than if he had been a man of genius.

Finally this was because he understood, respected, and insofar as he was able, indulged talent. And because, so often, he kept talent from destroying itself. He was the gentle catalyst, the coordinator. Because he had won a true understanding of himself, he had done much good for others and for himself. He had succeeded. And he was able to forgive himself, finally, for his father's disapproval.

From the earliest he could remember, his father had employed two basic tones in addressing him. One was disdainful, disappointed impatience. The other was unconvincing, inattentive jollity. When he was fourteen, he was confronted almost exclusively with the impatience.

One afternoon he sat in his room reading, and raised his eyes to see his father in the doorway in white knickers and a blue sweat-streaked sport shirt. His father was bald, with a thick black fringe of hair and a heavy, jowled, bulldog face that was still fleshily handsome. A bag of golf clubs hung over his shoulder. His mouth shaped itself unpleasantly as he looked back at Howard.

"Don't you ever get out of that damned room?" he said. "Don't you ever *do* anything?"

"You mean like playing baseball? Or getting a paper route?" Howard said it with some nastiness. He was afraid of his father, but not entirely.

"Let me tell you something, you could do with a paper route. You've had it all handed to you, I've spoiled you rotten. By God, I just may put you on a paper route."

"Mother won't let you."

"Your mother's going to make a little queer out of you if you don't watch out. Maybe she has already!" His father's face lighted with malice and, possibly, triumph.

"I don't know what you mean." He did.

"If you don't you're worse off than I thought. I think I'd better take you down to Barbara Johnson's and get you taken care of."

"Don't you know that's the worst thing you can do?" he said with his own malice.

"What the hell are you talking about?"

"In this psychology book, it says that's the worst thing you can do. It says forced and premature sexual relations make homosexuals."

He looked smugly at his father and his father looked baffled.

"Let's see it."

He stood up, found the book and the page, and pointed out the paragraph with his finger.

His father read it, and looked baffled and furious.

"All right. All right. I'll think of something else."

Howard was sure he would.

He became aware that his mother's maid, Clarissa, was paying him more attention, and a different kind. Clarissa was a girl the color of tea with heavy cream, about twenty-five, slim but heavy breasted, and pretty to a point just short of beauty.

One day she came into his room—the door was open—while he was combing his hair.

"All right to come in, Mr. Howard?"

She was already in. "Sure."

She started to make the bed. In the mirror he saw her watching him.

"You a nice looking boy, Mr. Howard," she said. Her voice was different from any way he had heard it before. "I bet you got lots of girls."

"Girls. I don't care anything about any old girls."

"Oh, you got to like girls, Mr. Howard. A boy don't like girls, he got real trouble."

"Only sissies like girls."

"Oh no, Mr. Howard. It's sissies don't like girls."

"Where you get crazy ideas like that, you old Clarissa you."

"You find out. You get older, you find out."

"I ain't no sissy."

"How come you don't prove it?" She smiled at him, tucking the sheets under the mattress.

"What do you mean, prove it?"

She smiled at him, a long smile this time, and he felt his cheeks go hot. He fled from the room.

That was the day his father had taken his mother to the state capital, ninety miles away. That afternoon, he was in the library standing before the leather-bound collection of Sir Walter Scott, when he heard Clarissa's voice at his elbow. He started.

She murmured, "Excuse me, Mr. Howard, just one minute please."

She reached past him with a dust cloth and touched the shelf with it. She did not look at him. He looked at her, at the smooth tea-with-cream skin coming out of the blue cotton dress with the white apron. She was not six inches away from him. He smelled a strong perfume that was not at all like his mother's perfume, and then he felt the warm soft solidity of her breast against his shoulder. Her wide brown eyes looked at him and dropped and she smiled very faintly. He was aware as he had been that morning of the rush of blood to his face. He did not let himself move at all.

She still worked the dust cloth over the shelf. The pressure on his shoulder spread. Then he felt a long solid smooth warmth on the side of his thigh as her leg slid forward, and then he felt her firm hot body pressed against his. He turned, fire in his cheeks, and she looked at him boldly now and smiled. He saw her drop the dust cloth, and he kissed her.

"Not like that, honey man," she whispered. "Like this. Let me show you, lover man. Little bitty lover man."

Two days later, at lunch, he saw his father regarding him with a smug and self-congratulating look he knew well. Afterwards, he ordered Howard to present himself in the library.

He looked Howard up and down, with triumph and without hostility.

"Well," he said. "You may be all right after all. One way anyway."

"What do you mean?"

"You didn't really think Clarissa gave it to you on account of your big blue eyes, did you?"

"I don't–" Then he understood. "Goddamn you," he said, and ran out of the library and up the stairs, his father's laughter receding behind him. In his room, he pounded the door with his fists until his hands ached. Then he fell on the bed and wept.

By dinner, though, he was contained and–he hoped–distant. He responded politely to his mother's vagaries and looked at his father only once. His father looked bland, he winked at Howard over his soup spoon and Howard felt himself blush.

"Eat your salad now, son," his mother said. "You aren't eating your salad."

"This is my second bowl."

"You must eat it now, you must eat fresh green things, son."

"I said it was my second serving, Mother. I have eaten it."

"You–oh, I see."

His mother looked at him vaguely, and started to speak again, not exactly to his father, nor to him, nor, exactly, to anybody.

"I–so I told her, don't you know, I told her, you simply can't bid two spades with that hand, you simply cannot."

He looked at his plate carefully and ceased to hear his mother. He could throw a wall against her voice at will. He could not shut out his father's.

His mother was not forty, but he thought of her as old, he thought of most grown people as old. She had very fine blonde hair, carefully and expensively maintained by her beautician; she had deep lines at the corners of her mouth and little puffs of flesh on the line of her jaw. When anyone asked him, Howard said she was pretty. He never thought of it unless someone asked him. His great single impression of her was that she never knew what was going on.

Later in his life, he wondered why his father married her. And when he knew enough to wonder, he knew enough to understand that it was because she would create no problems. Then, he even knew enough to understand that his father had not figured this out, or planned it, or even recognized it. The submerged pilot had simply set the course and steered it.

Years after those first speculations, he wondered if his mother had possessed a totally unsuspected sexual facility, or intensity, that held the restless man. But even at fifty, after three decades of freedom and two of intermittent psychoanalysis, he was unable to consider, however abstractly, the bedroom scenes of his parents.

For his last two years in high school, his father sent him to a military academy. He protested, his mother wept, and it turned out that he was happier at the academy than he had ever been. His father was not there.

In all the passages of his life, he had felt himself enclosed by the hard superiority of his father. Finally alone, and free, he fought to break out: he wanted to become himself by becoming very good, at something. He did not care what so long as he was very good. He yearned for a nameless excellence as others might yearn for a Latin medal or a football captaincy or a decathlon prize.

He tried. He tried everything, at the military academy and then at one of the smallest, most expensive ivy colleges. He did not fail; he never achieved much more than adequacy.

In his freshman year, he was among fifteen who made the staff of the student paper, out of a hundred who tried out. He discovered his talent was possibly eighth out of the fifteen, and he resigned after one semester. He had made the swimming team at the military academy and he worked much harder at swimming in college: he started in the free-style dash events and won enough points for the letter. But he finished fourth in the conference tournament, he knew he could get no better, and he quit after the season. He went into dramatics, he was not a bad actor for college, but he did not get the really good parts, and he knew he did not deserve them. Later, he directed two plays rather well, but he was aware, again, that he did not have the resources for authentic excellence.

Then, against his inclination, he was persuaded to produce the varsity show his senior year. All the skits that were submitted, he had rewritten to match the known idiosyncrasies of the athletes; he supervised all details of production; and he maneuvered an unusual amount of publicity. In context, the show was an unprecedented success. It occurred to him then that there might be, after all, an avenue to excellence for the fatally well-rounded man.

His father was mollified by the letter in swimming, though he would have preferred football. And after he had to come up with some cash to silence a waitress who claimed she was pregnant, he appeared to become almost fond of his son for the first time. He had been hurt by the depression but not lethally, and when Howard was graduated in 1933, his father gave him twelve thousand dollars.

"Go raise all the hell you can with this. Then come to work," he said.

Howard knew his father expected him to spend the money in New York in a year or Paris in six months. He did neither. He got a job.

3

THE folklore of the motion pictures and popular magazines had it that it was so difficult to see a Broadway producer as to be impossible. Howard Sills found it as easy as anything he had ever done. He read in Winchell's column that Vaughn Pemble was looking for angels for a new show. He called Pemble's office and said he wanted to invest in the play. He got an appointment the same afternoon.

Sills looked at Vaughn Pemble, rising at his desk, and knew disappointment: *Is this it? Is this really it?* Pemble resembled, astonishingly, a friend of his father's, a president of the Rotary Club. His cheeks were pink and lightly fleshed, his hair was thin and gray, and gold-rimmed spectacles fitted his nose tightly. His only exoticism was the lapels of his double-breasted, blue chalk-striped suit: they were rolled long, to the lower button, as in certain photographs of the Prince of Wales.

Walking forward from his desk, Pemble smiled joyously and extended his hand. His grip was firm, his demeanor not simply warm but overflowing; it declared that he and Sills not only knew but were part of a most significant secret.

"Come in, come in, Mr. Sills. I am delighted to see you, sir, it's a pleasure."

"Meeting Vaughn Pemble is my pleasure and honor."

"You're very kind. And if you'll forgive my saying so, you're a much younger man than I expected from our conversation."

"I'm twenty-three."

"Twenty-three," Pemble said dreamily. "Twenty-three."

"As I told you on the telephone, Mr. Pemble, I read you're putting a show together."

"Yes." He nodded, perhaps encouragingly; the blue eyes stared serenely into space—no doubt at the produced, triumphant, already-become-history play. "Yes."

"Well, as I said, if you haven't completed capitalization, I'd like to participate, as I said, in the financing."

"Yes." The pink face turned to him now shining with compassion: *I do wish I could help you but*—"Yes, you mentioned that."

Sills wondered if he had breached some unknown decorum. "Have you, am I correct in assuming you haven't completely capitalized?"

Pemble looked at Sills with sad and infinite tenderness. "Nooo, no I'm afraid you aren't correct, Mr. Sills. I'm afraid you aren't correct at all. The truth—" he made a fatalistic gesture with hand and shoulder—"the painful truth is that the shares, have been, pre-tty, well, spoken, for."

"Oh, I see. Well. I'm sorry to have taken up your time." Sills started to go.

Pemble let him take two steps, and stopped him with a near-whisper. "Wait. Wait." He raised his hand, palm out. His face windowed the turning of massive wheels, all propelled by a loving, burning desire to help his dear true friend Howard Sills. "There ought to be. There just ought to be. Some way." The face firmed with decision and resolution: nothing was going to stand in the way of helping Howard Sills. "What figure, ah, did you wish me to accept, Mr. Sills?"

"Ten thousand dollars."

"Mmmmhmm." He looked thoughtful, and he did not look particularly unhappy. "Ten thousand dollars. I see."

"I understand you can put on a straight show, nonmusical, for about twenty, now."

Pemble looked at him, suddenly reproachful. "My dear young man, what you can put a show on for is something you can never be in the least sure of. I put on a show last year for fifteen, and the year before, in 1932, when money was tighter and costs should have been lower, it cost me forty."

"Of course, if you're already capitalized."

Pemble smiled suddenly winningly. "Mr. Sills. We know there never was a show that had enough money, don't we? I *think*—I think we can just find a place for that ten thousand of yours."

Congratulations, said the warm embracing voice, *oh, joy and congratulations.*

"How big a piece will that buy?"

The smile slipped and returned. "Why, about ten per cent."

"Well I appreciate your trying to work me in Mr. Pemble, I certainly appreciate it, but I want to buy half a show for the ten."

"Half a show." The shaking head pitied. "Well, if you find one let me know." Dry warm laughter.

He said good-bye and was at the door of the outer office when Pemble's voice checked him. He turned. Pemble was standing in the doorway of his inner office.

"Come in a moment."

He went back in.

Pemble's voice was business, "You can have a quarter of the show for ten."

"I don't think I want to back that expensive a show, Mr. Pemble."

"All right, a third then."

"I don't—"

"That's really the best I can do, Sills."

"All right. One condition."

"What condition?"

"I want to work on the show with you."

"You mean you want to be an actor, you want a part?"

"No. I want to be your assistant."

"We've got no budget for that."

"I'll work for nothing. That's why I want to invest, I want to work with you."

"Well. For nothing you've got a deal."

They shook hands.

Pemble's show opened five months later to mixed reviews, it ran four months, and Howard got eight of his ten thousand dollars back.

When the show closed, he continued to report to Pemble's office as before. Pemble said nothing about going on, quitting, or getting a salary. Howard handled the tedious trifles which were too much for a secretary and which Pemble had a tendency to slough, he read submitted plays and wrote short summaries and opinions, he saw people Pemble did not wish to see, and he made himself so useful that when he asked for a salary a year later, in 1934, he got it: twenty-five dollars a week.

For two years he worked with Pemble. He began to prepare pencil budgets and suggest casting. And he tried to be present at as many of Pemble's conversations as he could; when he talked to union representatives, when he heard actors and actresses read, when he charmed bankers into backing. He made himself very useful, and he had small pieces of the shows.

Pemble told him one day, "You know, you're really learning a lot more than I meant for you to."

Sills smiled deprecatingly. Pemble looked at him, perhaps closely.

One noon he brought the newspapers in to Pemble, who was breakfasting at his desk. Placing them beside the tray, his finger touched a picture at the bottom of a page: a man with a very long, very white beard surrounded by three pretty young women. The faces of the women were adoring, that of the man smirking. A caption said, "American students call on Gwylym Graeme, Welsh playwright."

"Behold our great writer," said Sills.

Pemble looked at the picture; his neat round tummy quivered in unfinished laughter. "That old goat. I wouldn't be surprised if he could still accommodate those young ladies. One of them anyway." He carefully cut his eggs Benedict with his fork and brought the small piece to his mouth. "You know." Chewing: "I'm told Globe-International wants to buy that philanthropist play of Graeme's. Which one is . . ."

"*The Benefactor.*"

"Oh, yes, that's the one. They want to buy it, they'd like to do it if they could persuade him to make some superficial revisions. They figure it's quite timely now. Dare say they're right."

"Who's interested?"

"Oh Torldson, Torldson himself."

"Why don't we tie it up? We could buy the film rights and sell them to Globe?"

"One reason we don't is I'm not enterprising enough. And I'm too busy. And I don't think he'd sell them cheap."

"You could go over and handle it in a week."

"No, no, it takes two weeks round trip."

"Send me then."

"There's a slight matter of money. Not to mention I need you here most badly as always. Besides, I don't think the old bastard would talk anyway, not without a lot of teasing. Let Globe worry it out of him, they've got the time. And the money."

That evening Sills stayed late to read and summarize two scripts. Walking to the water cooler, he saw the door to Pemble's office was not closed. He made sure the door from the outer office to the corridor was locked, and then he went into Pemble's office. He explored the drawers with the delighted and exultant guilt of the trifling sinner. He meant no mischief, he simply wanted to divine as many of Pemble's old womanish secrets as he could. Pemble was neurotically devious, and this was not the first opportunity Sills had seized.

He found carbons of letters from Pemble to three actresses, almost promising each the same part, he found three envelopes addressed to Pemble in the same hand and he did not go into them; and he found stapled sheets of typed paper. The cover sheet said: *Special Supplementary Budget, The Glass Door*.

He had worked on the budget for that show, he had seen no special supplementary budget, and when he scanned the entries on the sheets he knew why he had not seen one.

Item: Special assistant to the producer; Sills, H. . . . $300 (week).

He received his twenty-five dollars by personal check from Pemble every week. He did not need to wonder where the other $275 was going.

He restored the drawers to their order, closed them, and went out. In his apartment, he sat up until two, thinking. The next day, he began certain well-masked inquiries, and the next week, he told Pemble his mother was seriously ill. He would have to be at home for perhaps four weeks, he said. In two days, he was on the *Britannia* and in nine, he was in a room in an inn in a coastal village in Wales.

He had paid the landlord extra to keep a fire in the fireplace during all the waking hours; the coal crackled, the orange flames shimmied, and so he was able to thrill Byronically to a window view he would have found nothing but miserable without the counterpoint of the blaze: he looked out to gray sky, slate sea, and white breakers on black rocks. He tried to understand how a talented man could live there voluntarily in winter, and almost succeeded.

He was ready to execute his plan, and confident. From the beginning of his infatuation with the theater, he had encountered the mystique of Gwylym Graeme's unapproachability. Once he had believed it. Now he did not: he had himself crumpled the myth of the inaccessibility of the Broadway producer, and he was certain the same weapon would break Graeme's reluctance.

He sat in the chair before the coal fire, and committed to a page of his notebook a message he had already composed.

> Would like to pay you fifty thousand dollars as advance on new Broadway production of *The Benefactor*. If interested contact me locally at Sea Lion Inn.

He walked through the cold fog to the tiny railway station and telegraph office, sent it, and went back to the inn to wait.

Three days later, he left on the day's only outbound train with an option to produce *The Benefactor* and rights to represent the author in film negotiations for the run of the play. Like his first wedge into the world of the theater, it had cost him ten thousand dollars.

The proposal he had brought to Graeme was complicated and fairly unusual. He had paid the playwright ten thousand down, with forty more to be paid as soon as the play opened, if it opened. This was an advance against all revenue, not simply royalties from performances. The key clause, the clause which carried in it all of Sills's chances, was the one which gave him control of film rights during the run of the play. Because the play was an established work, he had waived the producer's usual share of film rights and had asked only the ten per cent that would normally go to an agent.

From Graeme's point of view, Sills's proposition must have seemed not only fair but almost foolish: as a playwright Graeme had enormous cartel but little current commercial appeal. The fifty thousand he would receive if the play did make it to an opening was far more than he could have reasonably expected. He had every reason to think he had driven a hard bargain.

Yet Sills knew something Graeme did not know: Globe-International was deeply interested in the play. Sills had gambled that it was interested to the extent of one hundred thousand dollars, and he had gambled on the basis of what he considered to be sound information.

He told Pemble all of it.

"You deceived me, boyo," said Pemble very gently.

"Only technically, Vaughn."

"Yes," Pemble breathed still gently. "Technically."

"You remember I urged you to contact him."

"You did that. Yes you did. Well. Let's just say you've graduated. After learning your lessons well. You did learn them well, yes you did."

"Would you say three hundred dollars a week well?"

Pemble looked at him keenly, and then smiled. "I told you you were learning too much. As I say. We'll just consider that you've graduated."

With tedious, occasionally frightening, but finally manageable difficulties, Sills made his deal with Globe. Globe paid fifty thousand for film rights and committed fifty thousand to financing the Broadway production. Under terms of Sills's contract with Graeme, this fulfilled his fifty-thousand-dollar obligation to the playwright; he got back his own ten, paid as an advance, plus five. And Globe-International was backing a major Broadway play with himself as producer.

Sills did not consider in the least that he had sold the author out. Rather, he had persuaded Graeme into a mutually profitable arrangement. He was relieved when it turned out exactly that way. His production was not simply a success: it had excellence.

He did not overvalue or undervalue what he had done. He had not had the pure creativity that made the play. But it was his choice and his decision that had put the production of it in motion. He might be only a man of energetic and tasteful mediocrity, but he had been responsible for excellence.

And he was a successful producer on Broadway, at twenty-seven. Globe brought him to the Coast as associate producer of the film. That, too, was part of his deal.

4

HE arrived on the Super Chief and was cared for like the transiently important arrival in all the stories: the driver and car at the station, the engaged suite (his not at the Beverly Hills Hotel of all the anecdotes but the Bel-Air, which he considered more tasteful); the leased convertible waiting.

He had an audience with Arn Torldson that lasted thirty minutes.

"I hope we don't dismay you, Mr. Sills," Torldson told him. Sills was relieved at the hard urbanity of his voice; he was not sure what he had expected. "This town and this business take a bit of getting used to, no doubt about it. Most people who come in from the theater find us sort of upside down. You're used to starting with the play, you consider it's your job to produce the play, and that's the way it ought to be. No doubt about it. But we've turned it all upside down. We've made the producer or the studio the starting place, we've made the writer a salaried employee who executes *our* ideas. You know all that, of course."

He looked quickly at Sills; Sills nodded. "I guess I do."

"It's obscene," said Torldson. "I know it's obscene. It's the crux of what is wrong with the business. I know it, you know it, Christ, everybody knows it. But it's the way it is."

He stopped. Sills looked at his smooth hard face: the eyes were staring straight ahead. Torldson spoke again, still fixed on the unseeable point in space.

"The picture business didn't start as an art form in this country, the way it did in most other places. It started as a business. A small business, in fact. There's a stock joke out here about candy stores. Most of them were not educated, and many of them couldn't speak good English, and some of our reigning monarchs can't speak good English today. The truth is they blundered into the business, and the truth may well be that the business grew not because of them but in spite of them, though if you ever say I said it I'll call you a liar. The business had no motive except the making of money, and it blundered and stumbled and sprawled into the pattern it has today.

Instead of doing justice to dramatic masterpieces, we make writers execute the ideas of garment manufacturers. Instead of talent, we sell faces and bodies and the names we have created for those faces and bodies."

"We hire the best creative brains on earth and ignore them. You know all this, too. What you may not know is that in spite of ourselves we are maturing. There are some of us who care about being good."

"I do know that," said Sills.

"Don't misunderstand me. This will never be the first consideration, that will always be black ink on the annual reports. That is absolution, and I mean absolution for everything. Let me point out that it is also absolution for being good. You can even get away with being good if you make money."

He grinned suddenly. It was as though an electric light had clicked on behind his face.

"Just remember that some of us care, and that we need all the help we can get. That's what I want to ask you, Mr. Sills. Help us. In the context of our imperfect apparatus, give us such help as you can."

"What I can do I will do," said Sills.

"I've made quite a speech, haven't I? I only make that speech to people I think I might like. Good luck, Sills."

If Torldson was nothing whatever as Sills had expected him to be, his producer, Bernie Huber, was a cliché intensified beyond credibility. But there he was: fat face and fat belly, harsh voice and squinting eyes, even bad grammar and black cigar. He took Sills to the Derby for lunch. Sills saw that Huber was awed by his Broadway background and was contemptuous of it; that he wished Sills to regard him as a comrade in taste and also to fear him, abjectly; that he wished Sills to understand that Huber was God and would tolerate no blasphemous interference; and that Sills's taste and knowledge would be warmly welcomed.

"Glad to have you, pal. Looking forward to working with you. Know you did a great job in New York."

"Well, we had a lot of fun with the play."

"On a picture, Sills, there is one goddamn producer and that's me, and don't you forget it."

Sills's eyes opened very wide.

"I consider it a privilege, a goddamn privilege, to have a fancy Broadway producer like you assigned to me. Goddamn it I mean it Sills, a real goddamn privilege. We'll do big things."

"Thank you."

"Don't you try to ruin my picture with any arty Broadway crap now. I know this business, been in this business twenty years, no arty crap."

It was quite a lunch.

Most of the pre-shooting preparation had been completed before Sills came to the Coast. This was as he had expected it. He had not expected to have a great deal to say about the fundamental decisions. He had dealt very astutely simply to get his name on the picture as associate producer, and accepted that he must be satisfied with that. He simply went to the office at nine, read all studio and interdepartmental memoranda, wrote two long ones himself on the necessity of holding closely to Graeme's play, and studied the situation as best he could.

The functions of the producer were not nearly so elusive as the jokes had it, Sills discovered. But his experience and researches taught him that the role of associate producer was like that of the vice president of the United States: it depended on what the number one man wanted to make it. Some associate producers were errand boys; some did so much of the work that they were the *de facto* producers; some appeared to do nothing at all; some said yes in as many different and pleasing ways as possible. Sills quickly and intuitively perceived the role for which he had been cast, and quickly and intuitively moved to the filling of it. He had produced a successful Broadway play by a "great" playwright. He was also young. Therefore it was assumed in the Industry that he was a Young Genius. It was also assumed that he could know nothing whatever about the "practical side" of picture making–and indeed he did not. When shooting started, he divined that he was expected to make profound but non-insistent statements about the "values" of scenes. He was supposed to speak learnedly–but never too precisely–about elements in the play. Most important of all, he was to imply that when it was so wished the film could be a far more artistic medium than the stage. He had an important symbolic value, and none other.

He was absolutely without power, he knew it, and he accepted his part and played it.

"What did you think of that one?" Huber asked him, typically, on the set.

Sills had a good ear for the nonsense of players and playwrights, and he had spent three years with them. "I liked it very much, Bernie. Irma caught the nuance and the dimension just as Graeme wrote it, I think. I think she had just the right amount of mystery. Wouldn't you say?"

"Yeah," said Huber omnisciently, past the thick black shaft of his cigar. "I think she got the mystery exactly right."

Whenever he patronized Huber (in his thoughts), Sills guiltily forced himself to recall how effectively the producer ordered the armada of details that furiously assaulted his office. He was not incompetent. The point was missed entirely if he was dismissed as simply incompetent.

It took Sills several weeks to learn that the most important thing about motion pictures was the motion picture camera. The discovery was not simply obvious, it was banal. But knowing it, knowing it all the way, was something very big. The camera was where it happened. The camera was the artist, it was the selecting intelligence without and the central intelligence within. In the box, he thought, was the true talent.

When he understood this, when he understood it so completely that the understanding was part of him, he was lost. He was irretrievably committed to the making of motion pictures. He had seen that in the sprawl of motion picture production, the capacity to fuse talent truly might be the biggest talent of all.

He went to the Pickwick and bought half a dozen books on film. One was Eisenstein's.

Three days later he was walking to his car in the lot when he heard someone call him. He turned. Miss Hogan, the script girl, was walking toward him swiftly, not quite running, with a book in her hand. Coming toward him she was very tall, with black hair and black-rimmed spectacles.

"You forgot your book."

He accepted it. "Thank you very much."

"Not at all." She was breathing a little hard from her hurry. She looked at him directly, stopped herself from saying something, and then said it. "I didn't know you took us so seriously. What do you think of Eisenstein?"

"He's made me want to see *Potemkin* again. I saw it in a history class at college and frankly it bored hell out of me then. I'd like to see it again now."

"That can be arranged. The studio has a beautiful film library. I'll run it for you if you like."

Her face suddenly was animated: Sills saw that he had touched the enthusiasm that she lived by. He also saw she was a physically attractive woman. On the set the only impression he had received from her was of competent neutrality.

He took her to dinner. (He already had learned about the caste system in the Industry, he knew he was violating it, but he did not care. Later he appreciated a subtlety of the system: all bylaws were waived in the sexual relationships.) When she came out of the ladies' room she had put lipstick on, which she was not wearing before, and had taken off her glasses. He would have liked her to put the glasses back on.

She had expected to have an academic career, she told him. But she had had the profound engagement with film. The English department at Columbia would not let her do the thesis on films, so she had shifted to Teachers College, and had written it there. She had come to the coast in her research, had come back after taking the degree, and had maneuvered the job as script girl.

"I don't have the drive for anything important. I just enjoy being around where it's happening."

She also told him she was married and divorced at Columbia and had a six-year-old son. She had a good collection of prints and a projector, she said, and after dinner they went to her apartment in West Hollywood.

The projector set up, she said, "Now how much do you know? What would you like to see?"

"Just assume I don't know a damn thing and show me what you think I ought to see."

He watched her face as she inserted the film: it was intense, dedicated, impersonal: the true believer with a new disciple. He also noticed the fullness of her hips in the severe tweed skirt. And he was pleased that she had the black-rimmed glasses on again.

"Now I'm going to start you with Edwin S. Porter's *The Great Train Robbery*. It's supposed to be the first time the camera was ever used to tell a whole story all by itself. Watch the way he moves the camera around to follow the actors instead of shooting from one fixed spot. Watch the way the sequences tell the story all by themselves, without any dissolves or words. Watch how he gets two parallel lines of action going at the same time. And watch the close-ups. This all looks pretty elementary now. It wasn't then."

Sills watched masked cowboys tie up a telegraph operator and board and hold up a train. He watched the telegraph operator try frantically to get loose. And he saw at the very end of the reel a cowboy turn and fix his grin into the camera. It took less than ten minutes.

"That was 1908. The really strange thing is he didn't in the least know what he had done, it was the shooting outdoors that had forced him into it. His imitators in Europe knew what he had done before he did."

She turned the lights on. "Here's a shorty called *The Pumpkin Race,* by Emil Cohl. French. Sennett got a lot of his stuff from it."

She cut the lights, ran the film for less than five minutes, and cut the lights back on. She looked down at him from behind the projector. "When was the last time you saw *Birth of a Nation?"*

"To tell the truth I never have."

"Good God. You can't have anything to do with the picture business and not have seen *Birth of a Nation*. Have you got three hours?"

"I'll take them."

Sills stared at her back as she opened a large wall cabinet and looked at small labeled boxes. Earlier, he had been pleasantly aware of her body: like any man with no reason not to, he had desired it with no special urgency. Now, having seen her immersed in her chosen and intense reality, his desire took on an edge.

She found the film and stepped back to the projector. "This is the film's encyclopedia of technique, it's like *Madame Bovary* for the novelist. The funny sad thing is it's really an evil work. It glorifies the Ku Klux Klan, it makes villains out of the Negroes, it tells you slavery was a fine noble institution. It's as though right now, in 1937, you got a sublime masterpiece which equates Hitler with Jesus."

She had the first reel in and faced him.

"Watch how he cuts back and forth from one scene to another. And notice how he controls the tempo, like a piece of music. He can make one object or one piece of business or one scene show the idea of the whole thing. Now when you see this, you may not see anything so startling. But remember you're familiar with the imitations. This is what they imitated."

He watched the domestic scenes with the Little Colonel enlarge into battle scenes and then subside into his return home.

"See? Low, swelling, crescendo, and back to low."

Later:

"Watch this very carefully."

The screen was full of a tight close view of women and children weeping on a hill. Then country swept across it and movement stopped on Sherman's army far below. Then quick scenes of pillage and slaughter. And finally a reverse of the beginning: the long view of the army, the sweep back, the view of women weeping on the hill.

"That was the greatest single sequence ever made at the time it was made."

Sills went deep into the picture as he watched, and then he was also watching her face and body in the light flickering upward from the machine. He tried dutifully, like a man in church, to think only sanctioned thoughts, but he had difficulty. She was standing almost against the arm of his chair, his hand extended along the arm, and the back of his hand very lightly touched her high on the hip: a compact firmness inside a hard girdle. He felt the shooting authentic thrill: for him, there was no aphrodisiac like flesh packed hard within that elastic armor. She permitted it for a long instant and eased away. There was assent in the seconds she allowed him: he felt his face go hot.

Her features were carefully set, he learned nothing from them. Yet he sensed now that she welcomed and responded to the clear strong excitement he felt for her, and at the same time resented it as an intrusion upon that rite of induction in which she was priestess and he acolyte. He was intensely interested in the art of film but more interested in getting her on her back. She was (he felt) intensely interested in that ultimate project, but more interested in film. The positions could accommodate each other superbly: in the end, each would have had his way. For himself, and for the moment, he decreed patience.

Finally the picture was over and he was suddenly aware that he had not thought of taking her to bed for more than half an hour.

She turned on the light. "I guess that's enough for tonight, don't you think?"

He rose to help her put things away. "When can we do it again?"

"You name it."

"I don't want to monopolize your time."

"I have lots of time."

"Tomorrow then?"

"All right."

At the door she stood still for a moment as though to accept a kiss. On impulse, he did not kiss her. If she were disappointed, she did not show it.

Driving home, he continued to think about her, and only partly in erotic fantasy. She had taken him on because she had seen in him or wanted to see in him the possibility of that religious passion she herself felt for motion pictures. He thought he could care a great deal about pictures, he also knew he would never care as she did, and he did not want to. It was not healthy. No permanent mystic exaltation was healthy. Yet he was intrigued by her as a phenomenon: a script girl who turned out also to be historian, critic, and prophet. He had a large respect now for what she knew and what she saw, he had learned a long time ago that competence and recognized standing are not the same, and he was seriously grateful for the opportunity to learn that had fallen to him. Yet he could not concentrate fully on the learning: her not-quite pretty plainness and the powerful, strong femaleness of her body inflamed him far more than did the cynical displays of the women at the studio considered to be the most desirable in the world. If the girdle were the right kind, he thought, it would not have to come off.

When she greeted him at the door the next night she was wearing not a suit but a dress, it was blue silk and fitted well but not too tightly, and she had a soft wave in her hair. Oddly, he did not find her as disturbing. The severity of her working clothes and the volupté of her body had set up the tension that exists between opposites. He was pleased when she put on her black-rimmed glasses and started the projector that was already loaded.

She showed him single reels of pictures by Thomas Ince ("note the marvelously realistic backgrounds"); Mack Sennett ("it's fashionable to see these now as great parables of human nature");

Chaplin ("he's a loser but won't admit it, that's his triumph"). From German films, *The Cabinet of Dr. Caligari* ("the business of the madman telling the story and not revealing his madness may have been old stuff to Henry James but it was new to pictures"); *The Last Laugh* ("the camera assumes the identity of an old hotel doorman who's been broken to an attendant in the men's room").

"Those are the early German prints I have," she said. "The twenties was their golden age, they've done nothing really since Hitler came in. G. W. Pabst was a big figure in the good ones, lots of social realism and all. I don't have any Scandinavian prints either, and they made some marvelous pictures, particularly the Danes. The Germans stole all their talent though."

He saw she was exulting in the role of teacher with disciple: she had taken on, even, a sexual bloom from it. He wondered if she knew that, and decided not. So far as she was aware she had no motive but generosity.

But he knew she was aware of his increasing urgency, and was holding it off with her own psychic pressure. Yet she was going to accede finally, and that they both knew.

It came suddenly and surprised him completely.

"You aren't following me," she said. "You aren't concentrating."

"Yes I am."

"You can't think about anything but making love to me, can you?"

"No," said Sills.

"All right. All right then. Let's get it over with. Let's get it behind us so you can learn something about films."

She led him to the bedroom and started to undress.

"Let me do that."

"Go ahead."

She stood quite calmly under his hands, then had to help him work the dress off. She stood before him in girdle and hose and his legs trembled.

"You'd better let me get this off," she said, still calmly. "It's a little bit of a production."

"Keep it on." He heard the thickness in his own voice.

He felt her shiver with laughter. He kissed her and took her to the bed.

There, he understood she was not simply acceding to his pressure, pacifying and even rewarding him. She was taking their relationship that one step forward without which it would go back; she was taking the prophet-disciple thing to another level. Even in bed she wanted to maintain it. Yet it crumbled, the dominance she took from it crumbled, and she became an importunate woman who not only begged passion but love. Yet, half an hour after she had sobbed, "Love me," she had put back on the robes of the prophet.

The projector whirred, the square of light flickered, her voice was again didactic and serene.

"You ought to see *The Lodger*. It's as good a picture as was made in England in the twenties."

After *The Lodger,* Sills started to go. At the door, she kissed him and then pushed him away.

"No, you can't stay. You absolutely cannot. I'll see you tomorrow night if you like."

Then he saw her open the door and stand framed in the doorway, a martini in hand and dispensing a provocative scent she had not worn before. She did not set up the projector until the more urgent business had been attended to. It was somewhat more than an hour after he had arrived that Sills was watching René Clair's *Entr'acte*.

"This is the way a seminar should be run," he said.

"Be quiet." She said it with the first note of playfulness she had shown him.

On the scene a camel drew a hearse. Mourners followed in a stately procession. The hearse broke loose and sped through the streets. Sills was able to make no sense or logic of the images shuttling on the yellow square.

"What in heaven's name is this?"

"This is Dadaism. They say. Clair is better known for his more conventional things. The sophisticated comedies and so on. He finally left Paris and came over here.

"They made wonderful films in France in the twenties, in spite of or probably because of the lack of big studio organization and money. Every picture was made on a shoestring. Independents might make just one picture and no more. Clair came out of this free-for-all, and so did Jean Renoir, Jacques Feyder, and Louis Delluc.

"The culmination of all that was done on the Continent, outside of Russia, in the twenties is *The Passion of Joan of Arc.* Carl Dreyer wanted to make this a talking picture but he didn't have the money. Instead of the first masterpiece in sound, it was the last Continental masterpiece of the silents."

Details: Joan's dirty fingernails, the cobblestones of the street, a bell tower far off, a cross against the sky. The picture had a sense not of perceived but of lived reality. This sense intensified in the inquisition as the screen was filled with huge mouths firing at Joan like cannon.

It was done, the room lighted. He turned his head to see her looking at him from beside the projector, staring at him in triumphant joyous interrogation: *Do you see now? Do you see how it can be?*

"It's life," he said.

"Yes."

Looking at her, he was aware that he did not at the moment desire her.

As he left, she kissed him without passion. "Tomorrow?"

"Yes."

"Tonight we'll start on the Russians." She was ready at the projector; full-hipped in the tweeds that constricted and so counterpointed her pleasure-promising body, the black horn-rims primly, erotically, fixed on her small nose.

"Let's skip the manifesto and go straight to Putovkin and Eisenstein. Putovkin studied Griffith like a textbook, he and other young film makers took the great pictures and tore them apart in a workshop and put them together in different ways to see what editing could do. Putovkin tells a story about this, they put a perfectly expressionless close-up of an old actor into a picture at three different places. Besides a bowl of soup, a child playing with a teddy bear, and an old woman in her coffin. It was the same shot, remember. Reviewers praised his look of hunger at the soup, his delight with the child, his grief at the old woman. It was exactly the same picture for all of them.

"I'm going to show you one reel of a Putovkin picture, *Storm Over Asia.* Watch the sequence of shots now. They tell a story and create a line of emotional development exactly the way a good novelist does."

On screen: a British soldier was instructed to shoot a prisoner. Clearly not wanting to, he put on his equipment with great slowness. Every move showed his distaste. The Mongol prisoner waited for him outside the stockade, smiling, not knowing. Marching away the prisoner plowed through a puddle of water; the soldier behind him stepped around it. At the place of execution the soldier, delaying, offered the prisoner a cigarette. The prisoner smiled and refused. The soldier motioned him forward, and was unslinging his rifle as the prisoner turned suddenly. The prisoner understood and screamed. On the way back the soldier plowed heavily through the puddle.

"Each shot not only built the drama but showed more and more about each character. Now. Eisenstein. I've got the *Potemkin* print here."

Sills watched her load it, eyes behind lenses fixed on the film spools of the machine, capable versatile fingers manipulating the strip as competently as they had performed other, recent tasks, the lines of her hips roundly, yet sharply thrust against the tweed. He had thought himself pacified; he found he was not. Conscientiously he looked away from her body to the screen.

"As I said, as you know, Eisenstein like Putovkin was committed to the effects he could get out of the joining of shots. Everything depended on what could be done with editing. It's like Japanese picture writing. They put two word pictures together to make a new one. The word picture for *crying* is made out of the picture for *eye* and *water*. Sorrow is made out of *knife* and *heart*. You see?"

"I see that," said Sills still conscientiously.

"You'll see in *Potemkin*. Let's get started."

On the screen rough waves getting rougher hurled themselves against a quay.

"See how the turbulence increases? That stands for the increasing turbulence in the Navy and society."

Shortly, a dejected sailor was washing officers' dishes. He looked at a platter with Slavic writing on it.

"That says, give us this day our daily bread," she whispered. "This scene is where the revolt, the mutiny, really starts. Watch."

The sailor raised the dish and broke it on the floor. But he did not do it at once: he was seen before, during, and after the act from several different angles in overlapping shots.

"You see what Eisenstein's done? He's expanded time. He'll draw out a critical moment for all it's worth. That breaking of the dish catches all by itself the whole spirit of revolt on the ship, in the Navy, in society. You'll see the principle several times."

Sills did. When the Imperial Marines were ordered to fire on their shipmates, the ordeal was protracted by shots of fists knotting, eyes turning, and rifles shaking. Until, finally, they did not fire. And as the victorious crew waited to see if the fleet would fire on them, the cutting from engines to faces to guns to prow drew seconds out and out.

She said, "Now we're coming to the Odessa massacre," and she stopped the projector. The picture of the advancing Cossacks was suddenly frozen.

"This sequence of the massacre has been called an editor's handbook. Let me tell you some of the things. He puts some shots together according to light, each one will get darker and darker or lighter and lighter. This is called tonal cutting. Sometimes each shot will follow the other in a straight unbroken path of direction. This is called directional cutting. He will cut on the shape of an object: the curve of an arm will be followed by the curve of a parasol and that by the curve of an arch. That is cutting on form.

"The massacre scene is broken down into many parts. You see the Cossacks advancing. You see one group praying. Another begging for mercy. A woman carrying the bleeding body of her child. A legless cripple. And the mother, baby carriage, student sequence. I told you about it."

Sills saw: time swelled beyond itself; instants on the screen lasted well beyond their span in literality.

She stopped the projector. "I'll run it again."

Knowing what was coming, he watched even more carefully, and felt he understood it, or much of it. He also understood that it now possessed him. Not the event: the possibility of what could be put on that rectangle. He wanted to throw images on the screen and he wanted them to be his images.

She started the projector again, and they watched silently until the last image: the battleship sliding smoothly over smooth water. "He makes one part stand for the whole and you can see it all. Call it symbol or metaphor or whatever you want, just so you know what it is." She cut the projector, turned on the light, and reversed the spools to rewind the film. "That's it," she said. "When you get right down to it, all you have to see is *Birth of a Nation* and *Potemkin*. They've got it all. The two great masterworks of the medium. One's as Fascist as Hitler, the other is a propaganda piece made for and by the Communists."

"You could probably come up with an epigram."

"*I* couldn't. You know what happened here in the twenties, don't you?" She was threading the film into the machine. "Very little artistically. A great deal in terms of business. These years are the years when the Industry saddled itself with the star system, once and for all. They sold the picture with faces and the names of faces. The thinking was that these are what the public would pay to see. Sadly enough it's true. I think. Remember these? I made this montage myself."

On the yellow rectangle, he saw Douglas Fairbanks as the thief of Baghdad, Valentino as the sheik, Harold Lloyd in a freshman cap, Pickford, Garbo, Nita Naldi, Buddy Rogers, Emil Jannings. Chaplin's tramp again.

"That essentially is the Hollywood contribution. The star."

Chaplin raised his hat, bowed, and gave way to Moses, who was followed by covered wagons against the sky, which were replaced by an Eskimo whipping ahead a dog team.

"The advances we made were almost all on the level of technology. We imitated the Europeans, particularly the Germans, and brought several of them over here. The Industry had absorbed what it wanted to absorb from other countries; it had fixed the star system; it dominated world markets. It was upset when sound came along but it seems to have recovered completely."

"I've heard a lot about that. What really *did* happen?"

"First they went crazy about sound itself, and it didn't matter what was going on, just so there was noise. Then they started shooting what was called canned theater, you know, stage plays exactly as they were on the stage. Then somebody saw how foolish that was, to throw away a whole art form, which the silents were, and they made some pictures you could call talking silents. Now they've passed all that, they know that talking pictures are neither the stage nor silents with noises. They're hitting a kind of balance. Where we go from here, God only knows. Maybe the rank and file pictures will get more intelligent."

"Do you think it can be done?"

"Not really. I think we'll always make a few very good pictures. I think that most of the others will be from poor to bad."

"Why?"

"First the money. Then the machinery. Too much money is involved, and too much machinery has been thrown together haphazardly. The Industry gets the best creative brains on earth out here and then gives them no authority."

"I know."

"If you stay out here and make pictures, that's something for you to shoot at, give the geniuses more room to work."

"How do you know I'm not a genius?"

"Are you?"

He only hesitated a moment. "No."

"It's always better to know." She put the reels of film away. "I guess the seminar is over, huh?"

"Maybe the seminar. Not you and me."

She smiled at him in a certain way, he felt uneasy, and he did not answer.

"Would you like to go to Mexico this weekend?"

"Is there anything we can do in Mexico we can't do here?"

"No."

He rented a beach house at Malibu with a telephone call, and she arranged to leave her son with a friend.

They could look through the picture window to the gray sea vanishing on the far side into thin mist, and on the near making a dull white surf on dull sand. The sound of the surf was muted and elegiac as they made love.

In two days and nights she receded from prophet to gentle and almost shy woman. At the end of the weekend they had run their course: he understood she had permitted the coda so he would know they had run their course.

They parted with deep affection and finality.

5

"I WANT to make pictures," he told Torldson.

Torldson nodded: the smooth hard cast of a face assumed no expression whatever: yet it conveyed to Sills that its wearer was pleased that his expectation had been met. "I thought you might," he said, and his voice, too, performed the same feat: it was studiously toneless and it implied approval, almost pleasure. "Yes, I thought you might."

"Could you give me a picture?" said Sills.

"No."

Sills looked at the gold-plated electric clock on the desk: the red second hand moved from one numeral to another on the black dial. "I guess that's plain enough." He started to rise: even as he did so, he wondered if he meant to go or was trying to prod Torldson.

"Sit down. Don't you want to know why I won't give you a picture?"

"I suppose you think I don't know enough."

"You know twice as much as you need to know."

"All right. Why not?"

"The caste system. You have produced one Broadway success and have been associate producer of one picture. According to the caste system you don't rate a picture of your own. Not on assignment from a major studio."

"I see."

"Now. Are you aware of the zigzag principle?"

"Vaguely."

"Don't be vague about it. You have to use it. What it involves for you is zigzagging between here and New York. Every time you come in from New York you're a little bit bigger. Maybe a lot bigger."

"I see."

"That is of course if you've had some luck. If you can possibly arrange it, always try to have a little luck." Torldson smiled just visibly.

"I'll try to arrange it."

"If you have one wish in this town, wish to be lucky."

"Do you really believe in luck?" Sills asked seriously.

Torldson said as seriously, "The older I get the more I believe in it."

It was seventeen months later, and a successful production of another Gwylym Graeme play later, that Sills came back to the Coast.

Through the doorway, he saw Torldson writing on a long yellow tablet. The granite face just above the black-suited weight lifter's shoulders rose and trained on him as he passed through the doorway and as he came closer to the desk, it smiled quite pleasantly.

Torldson stood to shake his hand, he hurt Sills's hand with his grip, and he looked to Sills as compact and bleakly elegant as ever. He had been one of the first in the Industry to take up the black suit. With it he wore a black silk tie with tiny gold figures of, perhaps, demons.

"Well here you are," said Torldson, politely, and then he smiled in that explosion of warmth. "It worked out pretty well, didn't it?"

"I tried to follow your advice. About the luck."

"You followed it very well. Let's see now. How long did the show run?"

"Seven months and sixteen days."

Torldson nodded. "That was all right. That was all right. Now. The budget for your picture is one million one. I've done a few things, the pencil estimate, casting possibilitics, and so on, but that's just preliminary. You have as much authority as any producer on the lot, you'll make the final decisions on just about everything except the budget. That you damn well have to stay inside. You'll pick your own director, at least you'll pick him from those that are available. Don't worry, they're all good. One version of the screenplay has been done. You can do anything to it you want; you can bring in your own writers. Okay?"

"Fine, I'm very obliged. I'd like to get going right away, of course."

"Of course. I need your help on something first, though."

"Anything at all."

Torldson looked at him quickly and humorously. "You better

learn to hedge a little if you stay out here. This one is a little sticky. As you know, we've got *The Blue Leopard* and Charles Boston is doing his own screenplay. Has done the screenplay in fact, and it's very good. He knows the camera. Did you know he wrote Westerns right on this lot for two years before he became the avant-garde hotshot?"

"No, I didn't."

"Well he did, he wrote them very well and he wrote them very fast. He accounted for eighteen final whites in the two years he was under contract, which must be a record. Between us, I think he wrote *Leopard* or anyway the first couple of drafts of it on our time, too, but God knows we got our pound of flesh and I'd never kick. Anyway, *Leopard* won the Critics Award before we ever bought it, and he has a very smart girl for an agent, and so he got script approval. He used to be a very reasonable man so I didn't worry. It turns out I should have worried. He won't budge on the ending. He wants that damned Broadway ending and for us it's murder."

"It's certainly no ending for a picture. I thought it was a weak ending for a play."

"What I wanted to ask. Would you read his screenplay, and an alternative ending our best regular writers have worked up, and see if you can talk him into it. Or into something. He just might listen to you."

"I'll certainly read both of them."

He still found Boston's ending despondent rather than tragic, but he liked the alternative, hack ending even less.

He could tell Boston honestly, "That ending they whipped up for you stinks."

They were walking in a corridor of the writers' building, Sills had wanted the encounter casual. He had to look down to Boston for Boston was a short man. His face was fat and today as always it was set in semi-agony: he looked perpetually as though he had just awakened from a monstrous nightmare. Yet in only two Broadway productions, he had made a reputation as an immovable defender of his work from the assaults of producers, directors and those most notorious vandals, actors. He would rewrite a line or a scene only if he could be convinced it should be rewritten.

"I'm glad we understand each other," Boston said in his soft frightened voice.

"So am I," said Sills. "Because I have to tell you yours is wrong for the picture."

"We don't understand each other."

The play was about a talented young painter imprisoned by his obligation to make a living for his mother and aunt. He finally chose freedom over duty, his life over theirs, and left them. In the final scenes, the mother and sister embraced in their hopelessness, and the son fled before the furies of his conscience, still not free.

"Look," said Sills. "What does the play say?"

Boston looked up at him with suspicion, the permanent fright, and immovable stubbornness.

"Doesn't it say life is a trap?"

Boston looked at him then with a splinter of respect. "That's exactly what it says."

"All right. I wouldn't ask you to change that. Now in your last play, in *Express to Memphis,* don't you say life is a trap but we have to keep fighting to get out of it? Don't you say we have to keep on hoping? Don't you say hope is man's final necessity and only salvation?"

Boston looked at him with a great deal of respect. "Yes. Yes, that's what I say."

"All right. I beg you. Please give us an ending to this picture that says what you say now. Nothing less. Nothing different. Your ending. Your theme. Will you please give that to us?"

Boston stared up at him with his fearful incorruptible eyes and walked away.

That was at ten-sixteen in the morning. At twelve-five Sills was straightening papers on his desk, getting ready to go to lunch, when the door opened and he looked up and saw Boston walk in unannounced. His face was red, and sweaty, and almost relaxed. He extended one sheet of paper. Sills took it, read it, and said, "It's great."

He caught Torldson before he left for lunch, and watched him read it, looking down on the smooth black hair and impassive features.

"It's pretty good," Torldson said.

Boston had written the one page of new dialogue. Without altering the substance of the play, he had changed its last note from unrelieved despair to courageous hope.

Torldson said, "How did you get him to do it?"

"I told him to be true to himself," Sills said with proper irony.

"If that idea ever gets around, this whole town will shut down in a week. Well. If it works it works. It's your picture now, by the way."

"What?"

"That's right. You've got two to handle. You damn well better handle them, too."

"Two at once?"

"I guess I can stagger them for you. This time."

But Sills's "own" picture, the one based on his second production of a Graeme play, was postponed a second time. He agonized through the planning and shooting of *The Blue Leopard,* losing twelve pounds by the time the shooting was half-done, and then he suddenly decided there were only three tricks to producing a picture. The first was to get the right script, and the right director, and the right actors assigned to the script. The second was to leave them alone, and take care of the organizational work so that everybody else would leave them alone. The third was to keep them inside the budget. When he made what he considered this personal discovery, he operated only as expediter and coordinator of the details that were always slipping out of ranks, and he stayed away from the set almost entirely. At the end of each day's work, he watched the rushes—the screening of the rawly edited film shot the day before. From time to time he had reservations about points, but he had no serious reservations about the whole picture, and he said nothing. He gained back four of the pounds he lost, the picture was finished only three days behind schedule and only sixty-three thousand dollars over the budget, and Torldson pronounced satisfactory the print as finally edited. While Sills was still sitting at conferences on exploitation and distribution, Torldson postponed the Graeme picture again and gave him the picture on Charles Boston's second play, *Express to Memphis.*

The play appeared on its way to becoming the most commercially successful play ever produced, including Shakespeare's. It had opened almost two years before on Broadway and was still running, it had not one but two national companies, it was a great success in London, and an Act of God in Paris. There people stood in line four and five hours to buy tickets. It involved scene upon scene of sexual and fistic conflict; yet it was a careful and deeply felt production rather than an opportunistic one. One drama professor pronounced it "architecturally the best play ever written."

For the sum of those reasons, in 1938, in Beverly Hills, USA, it was a hot potato, and it belonged to Howard Sills, producer.

The first major crisis came immediately after Sills was assigned to the picture.

He looked at Torldson across the desk and was aware, he was not sure how, of the other's powerful will aimed for the first time directly at him.

"That ending." Torldson looked very hard at him. "He's really got to change that one. No motion picture audience in the United States of America in the year 1938 will stand for a rape on screen even if just the first half of a rape."

Sills breathed deeply and softly. "Arn, this is a famous play. This is the most performed play of our time. Changing it would be like changing *Romeo and Juliet*."

"I've nothing at all against changing *Romeo and Juliet*. If I want to. Also this ending is not happy. It is not one damn bit happy."

"If we change it, there will be howls all over the world."

"Are you trying to tell me it's happy?"

"No, it's tragic. But it has the kind of affirmation the best kind of tragedy has. It—"

"Af-firmation. Now let's see. That means upbeat, don't it?" The bad grammar was heavily deliberate.

Sills flushed.

"Ve-ry upbeat. We have a girl being carted off to the hospital with an incurable illness. Would you mind telling me exactly how that is upbeat?"

"It's not conventionally upbeat. But you watch her go, you know her courage will never run out, she may be destroyed but she'll never quit."

"And you think a picture audience will accept it and the distributors will accept it and the stockholders will accept it?"

"In the end they'll have to."

"Suppose I told you I think any man that wants that ending is crazy as hell. Suppose I told you I seriously question the competence of anybody that wants to stay with that ending."

"You'll have to question mine then. I urge you as seriously as I possibly can, keep the ending as it is."

Torldson looked at him extremely coldly. Sills forced his eyes to meet the other's. Then Torldson smiled his sudden sun-breaking-through smile and pushed a memo sheet across the desk to Sills. It was addressed to himself.

"It is my feeling that there should be no significant changes in *Express to Memphis*. We do not want to make canned theater, of course, and we want a picture that is a *moving* picture, but we do not want to alter in any fundamental way what has proved itself an extremely dynamic property."

"Wrote that two days ago," Torldson said. "I wanted to see, let's say, how interested you were."

It was a famous trick of Torldson's.

"Suppose you hadn't agreed at all and I had gone on and raised hell. I wonder if you wouldn't have fired me."

"That's something to think about. Isn't it?" Torldson said agreeably.

In his first two years at Globe, Sills understood that Torldson had typecast him as though he were an actor: he was the Broadway producer turned maker of films, and his films were expected to display the virtues of the live theater.

He wished that he really did make them, that he could make them. It was the hand of the director that was the hand of the artist. The producer only provided the materials; what he could do was see that the materials were as good as possible. And that they were always at hand, unimpeded.

Sills thought of turning director, after *Express to Memphis* was completed. He went through one script, making notations for camera shots and for business by the actors. Two days later he went over the notations and his thoughts. He decided he could never be more than ordinary as a director. He never considered the possibility, as a possibility, again. He accepted that it was his destiny to provide the very best grade of materials, for others. He found that for this, he had a gift.

The pictures to which Torldson assigned him were topical or ostentatiously philosophical. Almost all were made from successful plays. Sills always got an excellent director, stars who were also good actors, and, when he drew the picture soon enough–writers who were good writers too in another medium. He looked for a sympathy of insight between his director and writer: he was convinced that the successful wedding of these creative intelligences was what produced successful films. He viewed his own function as one of liaison, and with absolute detachment he could see that in this function, he had a really extraordinary competence.

In those two years, his name acquired its resonance. When someone spoke of a "Sills kind of picture," it was understood what was meant. Sills was not a great film maker, and he made no great films. But within the strict borders of orthodoxy, his films had "quality." He respected his people, he disdained cheapness, and always he was finely attuned to what were considered "the realities."

By the end of 1940, it was whispered that Torldson had draped his own mantle upon Sills, that Sills was the heir apparent.

In 1941, his image as crown prince fleshed out ever more: fame touched him: he was pushed from behind the spotlight into its glare. He was caricatured by a Nobel Prize novelist.

Sills had tried, unsuccessfully, to protect the novelist from his own drunkenness, when they were together on assignment in Virginia in 1940. The novelist was preparing, or was in precise fact supposed to be preparing, a screenplay from a Reconstruction novel schoolteachers pronounced a classic. Globe had bought not only the screen rights but the handwritten manuscript, and Sills and the novelist were to present it to the university. The novelist came on for his speech falling-down drunk. Sills finally fired him. When the novelist struck back in his novelistic account, Sills appeared, just barely disguised, as the archetype of the anticreative philistinism of Hollywood. Since he had spent weeks exposing himself to protect the novelist Sills was fairly bitter. The final word was always the writer's, he decided, and it was not always a just word.

Yet he did not suffer. He profited. In the inverted cosmos in which he lived and worked, where lust for the name in print was the life-force, the attack had enlarged him. It gave him "star quality." *Life* asked him to write his account. He did (assisted by contract writers), with restraint and charity. When it was over, Torldson told him:

"You've come out of it smelling like a rose."

In those years he had no serious failures and only three partial ones. He felt Torldson's glacial displeasure on occasion but not frequently, and he knew Torldson esteemed him. Their personal relationship was confined to the studio, as were all Torldson's relationships. Sills preferred this, he had found that a sudden and close intimacy, in business, always had its backlash.

He wondered why Torldson so often gave him preferment. Globe had other producers who were more successful, others who were harder driving, others who had greater personal elegance. Sills decided it was because he had some of all the qualities Torldson valued, though he was champion in none. He was a kind of a decathlon entry. Always the man of mediocrity, he sometimes reflected. At least it was superior mediocrity. And directly out of it, he had achieved his soft excellence. He was even the standard by which it was measured in his métier: he was regarded as the leader of the new men, those producers just approaching or just past forty who were raising the level of taste and sophistication in the Industry. Among them were Clarence Brown, Edwin Knopf, Darryl Zanuck, Walter Wanger, Lawrence Weingarten, Sidney Franklin, Hal Wallis, Pandro Berman, and several others. Their careers had many points in common, and at one time or another each of them had been referred to as the "new Thalberg."

Sills got his full share of new Thalbergs, and for a long time it looked as though he could do nothing very wrong. It looked, indeed, as though he had the world by the handles.

And then one Sunday morning, as he applied tomato juice and vodka to a mild hangover, he turned on the radio.

". . . including the battleship *Arizona.* The Japanese force is believed to have been launched from an aircraft carrier hundreds of miles north of the Islands."

Weeks later, he went in to tell Torldson he had been offered and was accepting a captaincy in a special training unit.

It was a bright day outside. From his own chair he watched a bar of sunlight move across the severe planes of Torldson's face.

"Are you really that much of a patriot? Or are you just a goddamn fool?"

"I'm not a patriot."

"How come then?"

"For one thing the draft. I'm thirty-two and single."

"You know we can handle the draft for Christ's sake. You're not an actor, you're not notorious, for you it's no problem." His voice rose very slightly. His face aimed at Sills showed an incredulous disappointment. "It's no problem at all."

"It's not really the draft."

"What in the name of God is it then?"

"I just have to."

"Do you know what a goddamn fool you're being?"

"I guess I do."

"Do you also know you're my replacement?"

He hesitated. "Yes."

"Well you were. You go off playing soldier, it's over. Think about it."

He thought, and he went anyway.

He was not sorry. Like so many others, he did nothing he could not have done better out of uniform. He produced training films for the Army Air Corps, and he had to go into capital to live on an officer's pay. On the face of it he had been wantonly foolish to no purpose. Yet he had fulfilled an imperative. He had had to go: he had gone. He had that kind of contentment, which (he had learned) comes only from hearing the inner command absolutely clearly, and obeying it with absolute fidelity.

6

In the course of his duties, Sills managed to fly three combat missions on a B–24, he said he needed to observe the crew in action for his films, and he got a Distinguished Flying Cross and, finally, the Citation of Merit from the President. If he had destroyed his favored position at Globe, and he was sure he had, he still would have done what he had done in exactly the same way. He came out of the war a full colonel, with the minor decorations.

He was astonished at the attention Globe's publicity people gave him when he returned.

"You've done us a certain amount of good, I expect." Torldson looked at him assessingly. "I don't mind telling you I was pretty browned off when you left. Still and all you may have been right. I could have been wrong."

It was a major concession. Sills was appreciative. He appreciated, too, that Torldson had welcomed him back to the lot with a champagne-out-of-paper-cups interlude in his own office, attended only by those of moderately exalted rank. Now that was done and he and Torldson stood at the window and looked through it to the same world they would have looked at four years before. Almost. It was noon: over driveways and sidewalks and through empty spaces, on their way to the commissary, marched the troops of the Industry. There were secretaries in tight blouses and skirts, suddenly elevating chests and lengthening stride as they passed the palace, burning still with vision unquenched and unquenchable: *The one with the boobs! Perfect for the part!* And actors in sideburns and bare to the waist, actors in buckskin and in frock coats, actors with shaved heads and their hair below the shoulders, actors, actors, actors. Across the green lawn he saw Mace Garrett in khaki coveralls (an auto racing picture?), advancing in the fluid and menacing walk, the threatening face greeting a passing electrician with a smile of astonishing amiability and sweetness. Actresses in the long pantaloons and rudimentary breast covering of the harem, in bustle and long skirt and contemporary evening gowns and slacks and street dresses, hair piled high or worn to the shoulder or bunned in back, all with cheeks painted so deeply as to be almost purple.

"The more change," said Sills.

Torldson acknowledged with an elevation of eyebrow and a twist of mouth. He looked at Torldson in profile: there were only the slightest alterations. The hair was as black (he must have a good barber), the face no heavier, or barely perceptibly heavier, the thick body as well conditioned. But now there was a long line from the inner corner of the eye to the edge of the mouth, and it was already deeply grooved.

"You want a picture?"

Torldson turned his head toward him.

"You mean right now?"

"Right now."

"To tell the truth, no. I'd like to fool around and get the pulse of things. I've kept up as well as I could, reading the trades, seeing every picture I could see, talking to people when they came along and all that, but it's not the same. I'm not really in touch."

"Take as long as you like. Take all afternoon." Torldson grinned at him electrically and he felt he was really home.

He took somewhat longer than that. As he had been instructed by his reading, he found the Industry seething with "neorealism," a label that had attached itself to Italian films. He himself liked the pictures: *Paisan, Open City, Bicycle Thief,* and others. He thought the direction was admirable if a bit improvised, though certainly not the breakthrough in technique that its claque declared. Everything he saw in De Sica and Rossellini, he had seen in the pictures Miss Hogan had shown him in that seminar a decade before.

(The afternoon he saw *Bicycle Thief* in a studio projection room, he wondered what had happened to her. Personnel checked and told him she had resigned two years before, to marry a major in the Air Corps.) He gave the Italians their own clear feeling about the way things were, and their sharp skill at getting it on film.

It occurred to him suddenly that he was jealous: their pictures were uncontaminated; his represented tasteful and intelligent compromise. And his were not really his. It was not he who made them, it was the director who made them.

He acknowledged his jealousy, pulled it into visibility, and faced it calmly. It disappeared. Almost.

The Italian pictures were splendid pictures, he would have been proud to have them, and he was certain the American public could not endure more than half a dozen like them.

He tested the state of mind of 1946 as thoroughly as he could, and was convinced that the public would shortly realize it wanted the kind of almost high comedy it had loved in the thirties: *It Happened One Night, The Awful Truth,* naturally, streamlined, refinished, and arranged of course in the tempo of the new age.

Torldson let him make three. The last parodied the radio quiz shows, and he was convinced it was the most graceful comedy ever made in California. Among them, the three lost four million dollars.

He expected brimstone from Torldson: he got commiseration.

"You know how it works."

"I certainly do," he said with the desperate cheerfulness of the man resolved to be a *good* martyr.

"I thought they were good pictures. I thought the last one was one of the best comedies I ever saw. I'm sorry, Howard."

Again, his debt to Torldson was staggering. Torldson could not justify to the board of directors giving him another chance. By the bylaws of the game, he should have bought up Sills's contract, or found a way to break it, or hit him with such calculated indignities that he would ask for a release. Instead, he placed Sills in charge of projects which in another business would have been called programs of research and development.

He disclosed nothing to Sills. But Sills knew he had been protected again by the powerful hand; he had been pulled out of the area of fire until his wounds were whole and he was no longer a slow and easy target. He was to mend, and to wait for orders. He felt again the profound gratitude to Torldson he had had occasion to feel many times.

But he knew, too, he was sentenced to ordeal by failure, and he summoned his strength for it.

And so he presented himself to failure. Which, he found, was a most subtle torturer. Failure did not strike with insults direct, nor sneers, nor friends forgetting his name, nor in snubs by headwaiters. Its weapon was careful politeness: *be as nice to Howard as you can. Poor guy*. The character of the politeness dismissed him completely and almost forever: the fact that its disdain was not intentional made it far more profound, and vastly more painful. It was all contained in the different way people now spoke two words: "Hello, Howard." His failure was in the difference. He tried to identify the difference, it was not easy, and then finally it was remarkably easy. To a success, the words were spoken with a rising inflection. The last syllables had the quality of a miniature explosion. "Hell-LO How-ARD!" To a failure, they glided downward and trailed off: "HEL-lo HOW-ard." In the different accenting was a world. At thirty-two he had been a success; at thirty-nine, he was a failure. He remembered for the first time in twenty years a poem by Emily Dickinson, and looked it up:

Not one of all the purple host
Who took the flag today
Can tell the definition,
So clear, of victory

As he, defeated, dying,
On whose forbidden ear
The distant strains of triumph
Break agonized and clear.

But he learned he was tough. Failure he could endure. What was black was that he could no longer claim excellence. For in the metrics of his art, or business, or whatever it was, success was indispensable to excellence.

He looked for consolation, and he found it in starlets. He had never had a starlet phase before, and now he entered one. Before, he had always gravitated to women of sophistication, maturity and position, and he had preferred that they not be actresses. Actresses were not really people. His women had been, usually, the divorced wives of rich men who might or might not be figures in the Industry; he preferred not. Sometimes they were the restless and indifferently married wives of such men. Once in a great while one might be an actress of a certain caliber. He had not cared at all for those young girls, between eighteen and twenty-three, twenty-five was old, who were still maintained by the studio for cheesecake publicity and, quite rarely but sometimes, a picture.

Now it changed. Their awe of his position, corroded though it was, gave him a tepid reassurance. They did not excite him: they were healthy young animals, reflexively, ferally, and unreflectingly quick to couple or otherwise oblige as desired. Something was missing: he decided it was mystery. He remembered how he had baited Bernie Huber with the word a decade before. The word had truth, after all. The young ones had no mystery. Or perhaps it was a trick of tempo. Perhaps they just did not understand tempo.

There seemed to be many black-haired girls who were tall and long-legged and slim-breasted, and several blondes who were shortish and plump and lubricious. And there was one sharply differentiated redhead who was nineteen, thin-flanked, high-bosomed, and who moved with the loose laziness of a female basketball player and went into action in the same quick explosion of motion. The sequence of their voices made a soothing long play:

—Honey, you're the most *distinguished* looking man, I just love to be seen with you—Thirty-nine is no age for a man, sugar, no age at all—Howard honey, take me to Romanawff's so I can show you off—Let's just stay here lover and do what we been doing—Good God honey, you don't want no romance at eight in the morning—If I could jus say a couple of lousy lines—just one decent part—I bet you're so important at the studio you could even do something for *me*—For *me*—For *me*—For *me*.

He could not help them much of course, he did what he could and thought he should and did not worry. He had a big turnover, and before they could become too importunate or too indignant, they were gone. Always with suitable mementoes of his honest appreciation.

Bore him they might but comfort him they did. You cannot escape history, he thought: beautiful libidinous young women have always conferred something upon a prince by their very visibility in addition to what they contributed practically speaking. I wonder, he thought, have fading princes needed them more? Interesting item for research department. (I wonder if I ought to kill myself. Of course not.)

All the time he was trying desperately to understand what was going on in the Industry: he fought to *see* how he had so misgauged its current. But he was unable to define a main current: only eddies showed. 1946 was the year of the Great High in motion picture grosses: never before had so many dollars been pulled through box office windows. And quite probably never would they again: grosses were down in 1947, and further down in 1948.

More than ever did the American films show the signatures of the individual studios. The personalities of directors and writers increasingly were pressed into a mold by the processes of each studio: story selection, editing, musical score, special technical effects, as well as its most basic philosophy. A professional could tell instantly whether a picture was from Twentieth or Warners or Metro or Globe. He would have an increasingly hard time telling which of the directors and writers on the lot were responsible.

As confused as were the years, never had the studio so dominated the American film as it did between 1946 and 1950.

And the antitrust division pushed a whole series of suits, and more and more city-dwellers bought television sets to see prize fights on local stations, and every year motion picture grosses dipped.

In the confusion, however, certain signs were visible, and certain facts were established. Andy Hardy was through. *The Awful Truth* was as deeply entombed in history as *The Way of the World*. The ticket buyers were not having a great deal more of the Production Code: it appeared that the war had taught them sex was permanent. And violence. The simplicities of Sunday School were no longer quite enough: the Industry had to accept that humans have their complexities.

The pictures themselves were diverse and so were the urges they represented. For a couple of years, problem pictures were very large; *The Best Years of Our Lives* might have been the best of them. Yet two years after its release, its director said he would no longer be permitted to make it: the Industry had been thoroughly scared off social commentary.

At the same time, foreign pictures became increasingly popular —the public responded nobly to art if it had enough sex and violence in the composition. The Italians understood this admirably.

He thought, finally, that he saw what the core of change represented. The taste of people who paid money to see pictures had advanced. They demanded a higher level of mediocrity than they had ten years before.

The irony of his predicament engulfed him. He had committed his career long ago to the proposition that mediocrity could be greatly improved and still be mediocrity, and thus still successful. This had now come to pass. And instead of riding the wave he was drowning in it, because of a tiny error in navigation.

Meanwhile, his old contemporaries and rivals were continuing to grow. Wanger and Franklin flourished; Dore Schary, an esteemed screen writer, was producing at MGM; Clarence Brown and Lawrence Weingarten were developing acclaimed works of fashionable writers; Zanuck had emerged as the new titan. And he, once their prince, had gone under.

Yet nothing was ever totally irredeemable.

He planned as he waited. He read as many contemporary novels as he could, not simply the best sellers but those that were literarily esteemed and sold only thirty-five hundred copies. He saw pictures in some of these, and acquired options on half a dozen. Then, in 1950, he was developing plans for two artistic, violent sexy pictures, budgeted at only $650,000 each.

He was considering whether he should ask Torldson's nod when Torldson called him in.

Hollywood Reporter was on his desk. Sills read the black type:

FINAL DECREE: STUDIOS, THEATERS MUST SPLIT. He had read the story earlier in the *Times*.

"I guess you saw it," said Torldson.

Sills nodded. "Any new thoughts on where that leaves us?"

"No place we'd like to be. Well, we've had five years to get used to it." The first court decision against studio ownership of theater chains had come down in 1945. This was the last. "I guess we won't be in the factory business anymore. I'm damned if I know what business we will be in."

"The B and C pictures are through, I guess."

"That's what I mean. None of the bastards will take those if they don't have to, and now they don't have to." He grinned. "That's roughly what I wanted to talk to you about. Very roughly. How much do you know about television?"

"Only what everybody knows. It is or is not responsible for the drop in grosses in the last four years. It may or may not kill the picture business. It will or will not destroy us all. That do it?"

"Just about. Just about. Myself, I don't think it's touched us yet. There are only four million sets in the country, the big cables aren't in, I don't blame bad business on TV. So far. But we are going to have to deal with it, we certainly are, and that's what I want you to do. Go into this whole box business and see what you can see. What it's going to do to us. How we can live with it. All that. I want figures, projections, all that. I'll give you some good guys from statistics. Now I'm not interested in some day. I'm interested in the next five years and particularly in the next two years, and I want some recommendations."

Sills spent four months on his study. His recommendations were, he thought, simple and obvious and incontrovertible. He said in effect: Nobody can be sure how this thing will work. We should be in on it as soon as possible and control it as much as possible. We will then be in a sound position however it turns out; if television should someday destroy the picture theater, we will already be in it and will not be left outside. He did not think television would destroy the theaters, he said, but it was well to be prepared.

He presented the report to Torldson, and did not hear about it for almost two months. He did not have a real conversation of any kind with Torldson for almost two months, and then Torldson asked him to come in. Their conference was set for five, Torldson liked to discuss long-range projects in the late afternoon. But Torldson's secretary did not call him until five-thirty. She gave him a glance that might have been expressive, and he opened the door and went in.

Sills looked the length of the room to a large open window backed by a gray twilight sky, through which sunless light flowed. Lined against the light, at the corner of the window, he saw the shape of Torldson's head, faceless for a moment. Then his eyes adjusted and he saw the features.

He wondered why Torldson had not turned on the light.

Torldson was sitting at his desk. He did not answer Sills's greeting or look toward him. His dark eyes were fixed on something straight ahead. They looked oddly lifeless in the gray light.

Sills hovered uncertainly near the desk.

"Hello, Howard," the bust behind the desk said, and finally looked at him. "Have a seat."

Sills sat down.

"Would you like a drink, Howard?" The voice was extraordinarily calm, he thought, and then he thought that it was simply without a feeling of any kind.

He contained his surprise at Torldson's question very well. "I'd like one very much, Arn."

"Help yourself."

Then Sills saw the bottle. It was a day for surprises, he thought.

He took a paper cup from beside the water cooler and poured whiskey in it. He raised it in salutation, waterless, and drank.

"Occasion?" he asked.

"Well. Yes. And then. No."

The light behind him was already deepening. Looking directly at him, Sills saw him more sharply than before as a dark statue. He shifted to the side so he could see the face.

"That was a very good report, Howard." The curious voice rolled ahead without inflection. It suggested to Sills a disengagement so profound he could only guess at its depths: its tones were valedictory.

"I'm glad you approve, Arn."

"Perhaps I like it because its conclusions are the same as mine." The words were unnaturally spaced in the same slow march. Yet

Sills, squinting, leaning to the side, thought he saw a smile. "That's always a good reason. Isn't it?"

"The very best."

"Would you be interested, in heading, the television operation, Howard?"

"Yes. Yes I would."

"I'll make that recommendation."

Sills was confused.

"At one time I had something larger in mind. As you know. However, luck is luck. You'll handle the television very well."

"I hope I will. If I get the chance."

"This is a strange business. Isn't it Howard?"

"I guess it is, Arn."

"But life is strange too, Howard."

Sills did not speak.

"Something very strange has happened to me, Howard. Something. Very. Strange."

"What is that, Arn?"

"I have found I am. Let us say. Not, as I thought, I was." The head silhouetted by the light swung toward him, and then away. "I am not what I thought myself to be."

"I'm not sure I understand."

He could hear the regular deep breathing.

"All your life you have a very clear idea of what you are. Or what you think you are, finally it's the same. Almost. You know what you want to be and you head for that. You think of that as what you are. You are satisfied. Maybe you are even a little pleased. Then . . ."

The voice stopped. Sills saw the eyes were no longer looking at him.

"Then something happens. It happens and you are staring into yourself. All the way to the bottom. The first time. You see. What you see is, you are no good. You are no good at all." The head swung, the eyes were upon Sills. "What do you do? What do you do?"

Sills knew the shock of confronting the nonconfrontable. "You get a good night's sleep and then you take a vacation."

"A vacation." The voice was amused beyond scorn.

Then the form moved in the chair. "Twilight thoughts. Always depressing. Good night, Howard."

"Arn." He stood. He felt helpless. "Get a real good sleep, will you?"

At the door Torldson called him back. His voice was like itself for the first time since Sills had come into the room. "That was bad luck about those pictures, that's all it was. You're a good man, Howard."

"Thank you."

"Good night."

"See you in the morning."

"In the morning."

The telephone awakened Sills; his eyes fell on the bedstand clock as he reached for the receiver: five-thirteen. He was suddenly wide awake, and afraid, and he knew what it was before the cold receiver touched his ear. It was Torldson's secretary, crying. The security officer had found Torldson in his office. He had shot himself in the temple, with absolute success, about midnight.

Sills never knew what Torldson thought he had seen. He was sure it was a straw, a nothing–some negligible flaw in the self he thought he had created. A nerve of cruelty, a cell of weakness, a harmless sexual aberration. It had to be trivial. But it had been enough.

Torldson had willed himself to be a god, he had made himself as nearly a god as any man Sills ever expected to know, and he could not survive the absolute knowledge that he finally was not a god. Put much too simply, and yet quite exactly, he had expected too much of himself.

In the correspondence he had signed, a few hours or a few minutes before his finger touched the curve of steel, was a long memorandum to the board of directors recommending Sills's appointment as head of a television division. The appointment was not made.

It was late in 1950 that Torldson shot himself. The Industry guessed frantically and never reached a consensus as to why. Business troubles were unlikely: he had shown a corporate profit every year during the decline. Globe had weathered those postwar years better than any other major, his hand even had been strengthened at the last stockholders' meeting. If there was a single studio head who was safe, it was Torldson. Speculation had to fall elsewhere: he had suffered a miserable love affair, he was incurably ill, he had had another mental breakdown.

Nobody believed any one of these absolutely. Just as Torldson himself instantly entered the Pantheon on his death, so his reason for squeezing the trigger became at once one of the legendary mysteries of a town that lived by its legends. It was right there with the suicide of Jean Harlow's bridegroom, and more mysterious.

Sills never described his last meeting with Torldson.

In the strange deadness of a great personal loss, it occurred to Sills that Torldson might be the last real genius ever to head a studio. Geniuses would come and go as always; it seemed unlikely that events would ever again put one in the president's chair of a major studio. Diverse talents converged in Torldson: he was a canny showman like his father-in-law Teller. He was an authentic creator, he had mastered the technique of the big corporations when the financial power shifted to New York. Sills thought he was a great pragmatic professional because he was at bottom a great romantic. The romanticism was harnessed and hidden, but it was inexhaustible.

When Torldson died, there was no heir apparent. Globe had its share of intrigues but Torldson had minimized them: he resolved rather than played upon differences among men. Consequently, there was no immediate clash of commands. His office was not at once filled. Contenders moved quickly into the open space, however, and in a remarkably short time, there were two principals and factions.

One principal was Daniel Miller, who had been considered a representative New Man five years earlier because he had been a novelist and screenwriter before he was a producer. The other was Fred Kandel, an operator in an older tradition.

Miller won: his first year was totalled in red ink: Kandel got his job early in 1952.

Sills knew the time had come to save face. His contract had six months to run when he went in to see Kandel.

Kandel was bald with a black fringe, smooth-faced with a heavy second chin, and wore black horn-rims over eyes perpetually muscled in wariness.

They looked very bleakly at Howard Sills, who knew he had been an expensive luxury for some time.

"You ah wanted to see me, Howard?" He started writing busily on a long yellow pad and studiously looked at it instead of Sills.

"Yes, Fred. Yes, I did want to see you."

"Ah something I can do for you Howard." He wrote industriously.

"Fred, I've been with the studio fifteen years." He said it ceremonially. "That's a long time, Fred."

Kandel put down the pencil and looked at Sills. He was not stupid and he was clearly aware of the ceremonial note. His face altered tentatively, and his voice.

"Yes it is Howard. It's a long time."

"This association has meant a very great deal to me, Fred."

Kandel nodded massively and now agreeably.

"A man doesn't kiss off an association like that lightly, Fred." Sills saw from the suddenly pontifical set of face that Kandel now knew the name of the game. He went on. "I want you to know that. I mean I want you to know I'm not taking it lightly at all. I take my years with Globe with religious seriousness, Fred."

"I know you do, Howard. I know you do."

"You might even say Globe has been my religion, Fred."

"Yes, Howard, it's been my religion too."

"It's been the religion for all of us I guess, Fred. That's why this is such a painful moment for me. I mean I just don't know how to say this, Fred."

"If there's anything in this whole world I can do for you, Howard, all you got to do is just name it. I mean that sincerely, Howard."

"I know you do, Fred, that's what makes it so hard. What I have to ask. What I have to ask, Fred, is, that you release me, from my contract."

"Howard, I just don't know what to say. I just am kind of shocked. I mean that sincerely, Howard. I am kind of shocked."

Sills bowed his head in appropriate sorrow. "It's just that I want to form my own company, Fred. Believe me it's a very painful decision."

"Globe-International Studios without Howard Sills. It's so unbelievable I just can't believe it. However, we won't stand in a man's way. We won't do that." His stomach rumbled, he took a pill from a small bottle on his desk, poured water from a pitcher into a glass beside it, and swallowed the pill with the water. When he spoke, his voice was different again.

"If you don't hold us up for any dough I can get this cleared up in about fifteen minutes."

7

SILLS had a sense of holiday, though he was not sure whether he had achieved liberation or formalized failure. Looking back at his life, for the break with Globe had a quality of catastrophe that made him look back at his life, he saw two major movements. Up, and down. The course had started upward the day Clarissa initiated him; he recognized that starting point with surprise, and certainty. It had moved upward—with tiny detours, halts, descents—until he went to war. Then it turned down: he had lost the demi-divinity of crown prince, he had lost the glitter of his reputation, and now he had even lost his job. Yet he had an unexplainable sense of wholeness. It was as though he had recovered from an illness he never knew he had. Perhaps the descent was over, and it was time to climb again.

It came to him that he was free because now his life was totally his own responsibility. He had surrendered too much. Now he had it all back. The choices were his and the responsibility was his. He could make of it what he would.

Up to a point, he cautioned.

He knew his exaltation would leave him as all states of mind left him. Yet on the day he lost his last security, he felt as complete as he could remember feeling.

Sills had only two hundred thousand-odd dollars of his own, and he could afford no expensive mistakes. He looked closely and awaited his hour.

He decided his first picture should be a low budget but still an A picture. He bought for only ten thousand dollars a French novel that was an international *success d'estime* but which had sold only three thousand copies in America. Its title was *Julien.* It had such a dramatic structure Sills suspected it had been written first as a play.

It was carbon copy Sartre but good carbon copy: its existential hero was Rimbaud, slightly disguised, in his gun-running days in Africa. He moved from despair and total passivity into self-definition by seizing an ordeal. There was plenty of action to show the ideas, the characters were highly theatrical, and Sills saw a sharp picture that would spin off the novel's prestige to brilliant reviews. And it would make a pleasant profit if the budget were kept to $650,000. It would fail if it cost too much to make. He would put up a quarter of the $650,000 and borrow the rest.

A top American director would not only be high priced himself, but would insist on circumstances that would kick the picture from the $650,000 to the million three category. Sills decided to get a brilliant foreign director not yet discovered by *Time* magazine. He found him: a young Czech making films in Paris. Sills flew there, signed him to do the picture for ten thousand plus living expenses on a thousand-dollar binder, and signed him and the author of the novel to collaborate on the screenplay for another ten between them. The screenplay came to him in six weeks, and he thought it was the best he had ever seen. It was not the most commercial but it would be commercial enough given an American star.

Sills could afford either a rising star not yet at his peak or a big one not too far on the downgrade. For him the last was better business: he chose Rod Robin. Robin had been a solid though not a super-star at Globe, he had not been renewed in the panic of 1951, and he could act some. Though he was an enthusiastic and openly practicing homosexual, he projected a vivid, decadent virility that Sills thought perfect for the Rimbaud character. Inevitably, he was known in the Industry as Cock Robin. Sills sent him the script and then met him for lunch in Romanoff's.

By coffee, Sills was fighting boredom. The only bigger bores than most actors were most singers, he thought. And some writers. This actor was not one of the exceptions: self-admiration shown steadily in his long smooth face that was almost girlish under waved black hair. He was very lucky, Sills thought, that the camera somehow toughened the softness.

Robin said: "I read your script."

That was the way they said it: *I read your script*. And the significant pause. Sills had learned there was only one thing to say into it if you had to say anything. He said it: "Oh?"

"I liked it."

"Oh?"

"I really did. It's all right, it's got a nice story line."

"Think you might be interested?" said Sills very very carelessly.

"Well. I'll tell you. I *might* be. That would depend on a lot of things."

"Mmm-hmm?"

"There'd have to be a few changes of course."

"Mmm-hmm. What changes did you have in mind?"

"Now this guy. What's-his-name. He's a good character all right, he's got balls, lots of balls, but you've got him doing some things and saying some things. I mean, Howard, my public just wouldn't stand for me doing and saying those things. That scene where he abuses the native boy and talks about cutting his heart out. Howard, that's just not wholesome now. I couldn't afford to play a guy that unwholesome."

"Well, Cock, the character's whole motivation is shown in that scene. He's sick with despair, that's the whole thing."

"That's what I mean, Howard. I can't be sick with despair–you know? Maybe you can have him sad because of a love affair or something. Something noble, you know? Fix it up real noble. Keep the rooting interest, you know?"

Sills ordered himself to calmness. It was wasteful to fight at this point. "Why, I think we could make you happy with the script, Cock."

"There's a couple of other things, Howard."

When he was done with the script, there was no script, or would have been none. Sills thought wistfully that twelve years ago he could simply have *assigned* the idiot to the picture. But then there were other idiots to cope with.

He said reasonably, "As I said, Cock, I'm sure we can satisfy you with the script if we get together on everything else."

He had no idea of abandoning the best screenplay he had ever had. He was simply sure that he could bait the hook artfully enough when the time came: Cock needed a prestige picture; this would establish him as a *serious* actor. And so on.

"Glad you see it my way, Howard. Now there is that little deetail."

Sills smiled. "What figure did you have in mind?"

"I leave that sordid dee-tail to my agent of course, but just to give you a general idea. To give you a general idea, let's say three hundred thou against ten per cent of the gross."

"You've got to be kidding."

"Oh no Howard. No, I am not kidding. I, am not, kidding."

"Cock, last year you got one hundred thousand even at Globe. I know what you got."

"That was last year, daddy. This is this year. You know. Big star. Bank financing. Money in the old cigar box. You know the bit."

"Not any ten per cent of the gross, I don't."

Later, Sills and Robin's agent had almost agreed on one hundred and fifty thousand against five per cent of the gross. It depended on their ability to talk Cock into the script.

Sills was wondering what would happen to his producer's profit when the agent called very apologetically.

"Howard, I'm afraid we have to pull out. Cock has decided to set up his own company, he thinks he'll do a lot better that way."

"He's not that big now. I don't think he was ever that big."

"You know it and I know it but the banks may not know it. He was in some good pictures at Globe not too long ago and the grosses make a pretty persuasive case to a guy with money to lend."

"I know those pictures. He was just the leading man. It was the girl that brought them in. Not to mention Globe's advertising budgets."

"As I say. I know and you know it."

"Well. Tell him good luck."

Robin might make it, he thought, even on the downgrade. The habit audience had been shattered by television, the captive theater market had been lost, and every studio in town was in decline and most in red ink. Yet the *established* stars had never had it so much their own way. Many whose name was bank collateral were deciding to use it for themselves, and more would. The boxes of cereal were coming off the shelves to take over the store.

At least, Sills thought, no idiot actor had ruined his screenplay. So far. He decided, casually and implacably, that he would not make the picture at all if making it meant changing the screenplay for an actor.

Four months later, he had not cast it or capitalized it. There were enough stars free of studios, that now was not the problem, but the big stars wanted to organize their own companies or they wanted an impossible share of the gross. Those stars who had descended a level in marketability found the script too highbrow, or the character deficient. He was lacking, they said, in "heart": it was a death sentence.

He considered making the picture without a star, with rising stage actors. He could still make money if it only played art houses. Any picture could make money if the costs were low enough.

The loan officer of the first institution he approached did not encourage him.

"We have to have a star. For a motion picture we consider a contract with an established star as collateral, Mr. Sills."

"I thought my own experience might be collateral."

"It is, Mr. Sills. If you have a star to go with it."

He was still determined to make the picture on his own terms, and he was sure he would find a way.

That night, he went to the first black tie dinner party he had attended in six months. He had been invited by telephone only two days before, he had no doubt he was a fill-in, for his social desirability had declined with his career. Yet he accepted on impulse, and cheerfully. He sat next to a dark-haired woman who had a vividity that had not quite started to erode. She was Amanda Pathfinder from San Francisco, she said, and he identified her then. Her family was rich and old: she had been wild and often in the papers.

They talked about the San Francisco Opera Company's Los Angeles performances.

"Tell me," she said. "Where do you keep your artists around here, anyway? I haven't seen a musician or a painter or a writer or even a scientist since I've been in town. Every party I've been to has been all picture people or all Rotarians."

"We aren't San Francisco, I'm afraid."

"No."

Planning nothing, exactly, he achieved one of the better intuitions of his life. He said, "What this town needs is a hostess with a real interest in the arts and sciences."

"You could be right." She stared at the table in, possibly, speculation.

He managed references to painters and novelists and his own meeting with Gwylym Graeme. And he told her about his script.

"You're going to make a picture out of *Julien?* Well good for you."

He saw her looking at him assessingly.

He did not admit to himself that he had a tactic.

Her visit was long and indefinite, he went punctiliously through the minuet of seduction, and they had an affair for the next three weeks and pleased each other. In that time, two more stars said no to the script.

It was she who said it.

"Why don't we get married?"

"Why?" he said.

"It might be a rather good idea."

"Don't tell me you're in love with me."

"Well I am in a manner of speaking."

"Well in *that* manner of speaking so am I," he said. "You don't want to blow the whistle on a nice sexy romance, do you?"

"Not the whistle, guvner, not the blinkin *whistle.*" She giggled. "Think of how convenient it would be."

"There's that."

He looked at her: she was lying on a chaise on his terrace, the upper body almost erect, her legs sheathed in a long white skirt.

She smiled at him in a sudden, omniscient, amused complicity. "Howard honey. There's something else, you know."

"Mmm-hmm?"

"I could get you that loan for *Julien.*"

"Who would ever have thought of that?" he said.

"Who indeed?"

They were married in the house of her friends, she cosigned his note for half a million dollars, he started to plan the picture, and she started to give parties. She gave many, and her guest lists were mixed and brilliant. One representative dinner included a Latin American ambassador visiting his consulate, a Nobel Prize winner in science from UCLA, a very rich publisher, an American playwright, and an intelligent actress. In a remarkably short time, she created and filled a unique role for not only herself but for the two of them. This and the fact that Sills was "developing" a fashionable French novel restored a provisional gloss to his reputation. Without having made a picture in years, he was dimly seen, again, as an example of the very best grade of Hollywood producer. He had always savored ironies; this one he quite particularly enjoyed.

"When are you going to get *going* on that picture, darling?" his wife said to him one day with elaborate playfulness. "When are you going to become the great international aesthetic impresario?"

She did not say: *When do I get something for my money?*

He said equally playfully, "Aren't you satisfied with the benefits of this organization?"

"With certain of them I'm deliriously satisfied."

In point of fact, he had received no money from her: her endorsement of his note had simply made it available. However, that conversation exposed certain unpleasant possibilities; he resolved not to forget it, or them.

He cast the picture with excellent actors but without a star, though the leading actress had a qualified box office value as an intellectual sexpot. He shot it in leased space on the RKO lot. His initial budget shooting in town would be higher, but he could be reasonably sure of what to expect.

What he did not expect was confused direction. It was what he got. In the shifts from Czech thinking to French translation to English commands, the direction got very confused.

Sills had hoped for victory and was fortified for defeat. What he got was a draw. The picture was reviewed but the reviews did not establish it. Sills did not create a new reputation but lost none. The picture did not make much money but recovered costs.

"It didn't really hit, did it?" Amanda said six weeks after the release.

"No."

"Well, it doesn't *really* matter, I suppose."

The reception left Sills with a feeling of inconclusiveness: he lost the sense of complete responsibility for his life that he had held briefly. He was in a thwarted and diffusely angry state when Sidney Tate asked him to his office.

Tate had become president of Globe about ten months after Sills had left it. He was the third president in the three years since Torldson died, and he had been summoned by the board of directors in desperation. He was famous for revivifying shaky corporations, and he had no experience whatever in entertainment.

Many saw his assumption as a symbolic act: corporation finance had closed its cold hand on the flamboyant creativity of the motion picture studio. A television play dramatized it. Sills was amused. As a symbol, Tate was obsolete before he appeared. Corporation finance had taken over the studios more than a decade before; what was happening in 1953 was that the stars were beginning to close *their* hands on the corporations.

But perhaps that was the way it always was: the event that dramatized a movement perfectly came along after the movement was spent. Engrossed as Sills had been in his own problems, he had watched with fascination Tate's early moves.

Almost instantly, Tate had consolidated several departments, fired a great many people, and sold a slab of the Beverly Hills real estate that the studio occupied. He got so much money that there was serious speculation that he meant to move Globe entirely into the real estate business. What he meant to do about making motion pictures was not immediately made clear. He had been in office two months when he asked Sills to come to see him.

Approaching, Sills looked through the open doorway as he had done so many times to see Torldson's heavy head bent over the desk. Now, behind the same desk, he saw a gray-haired man in a blue-striped, single-breasted suit, of the kind that was almost a uniform for diplomats. The face turning towards him was authoritatively lined and faintly tending to plumpness, the eyes were astonishingly clear and blue, and the effect of the smile was that of grave and unfeigned courtesy. This was Sidney Tate, the savior of ailing corporations, whose chair Sills was once heir to.

Tate rose. His clasp was firm if well-fleshed. "Mr. Sills," he said. "Good of you to come."

"Not at all."

"Sit down." They both sat. "I read your report last week. With great interest, may I say."

Sills questioned with his eyebrows.

"Your 1950 report for Torldson. How Globe should live with television, you might call it. It seems rather timely this year."

"I dare say," Sills grinned.

"I was impressed with your conclusions, I suppose because they were so close to my own and they were three years earlier."

"I can't give myself much credit. They seemed inescapable."

"It never ceases to amaze me, Mr. Sills, how many people manage to escape the inescapable. I make my living out of that, in fact. The point is that if this report had been implemented in 1950, this studio would never have showed a single annual deficit. But then I wouldn't be here, would I?"

He smiled; Sills smiled agreeably.

"I've found all businesses to be a great deal alike, Mr. Sills. Their problems fall into one or another quite well-defined areas. The problem of the motion picture business right now is one of marketing. As you suggested. We lost a basic market when we lost the theaters and block booking. We have to find a new market."

"That's the whole story."

"Exactly. And the thing is, a new market already exists in television. Instead of making inexpensive pictures the theaters have to take, we make inexpensive films for television. You pointed that out."

Sills nodded.

"We don't even have to change the product. All we have to do is modify it."

"I wonder why the Industry has fought it so," said Sills.

"Everybody hates change, Sills. That's why a man with a new perspective has to be brought in from time to time in any business. He isn't committed to the status quo. Now. To get to the point. How would you like to head up our new television program?"

"I don't know," said Sills. "I have my own company now, I'm getting to like the idea."

"We can make an awfully good deal financially. A hundred thousand a year with bonuses and stock options."

"Stop me if you heard this, but I really like the freedom I have."

"I feel certain you'll have opportunities to do some things you like artistically. In fact I guarantee it. I found out one thing a long time ago, every good program that has a really good man running it has got to have a corner where he can indulge himself."

"I'm flattered, Mr. Tate, I'm very flattered and honored, but honestly I don't think so."

"Think it over for a week. Will you do that?"

"I'll certainly do that. May I ask you something now?"

"Of course."

"Why do you want me? All my experience has been in a very different direction." He did not say, *And Globe was very glad to get rid of me not so long ago.*

"Two reasons. First, you believe in the program, what we're going to do is just what you wanted us to do three years ago." He paused.

"What's the second?"

"The second thing is that I think you're an extraordinarily able man."

Driving, Sills acknowledged that the offer had shaken him. It had dropped like a depth charge through defenses as yielding as water, and had detonated on the real and unalterable floor of vanity. He was appalled at the vulnerability of resolves that he had thought irrevocable, at the loss of a serenity he had thought would last forever. He wanted to take the job.

It was not for the challenge, though he would welcome it. It was not even for the power, though he would love it. It was for one thing: he would be important. He would be very important again. He could shatter Howard Sills, the cultivated man who gave cultivated parties and produced not quite successful pictures. He could become Howard Sills, *important* Howard Sills again, who created and directed Globe Television.

Temptation took him like a swift hot illness. Nor did he wish to resist it.

The infection came from vanity, and only vanity fought against it: he did not want to think of himself as a man too weak to overcome his own germs of corruption.

The counter-vanity won, for the instant: he made up his mind to turn Tate down. He would *choose* to prefer freedom to importance, even if it was importance that he truly lusted for. If he were not in his own natural strength the man he wished to be, he would make himself a good copy of that man by what he did. He could not help what he wanted; he could control what he performed.

He would say no, that was all there was to that. And he knew that that was not all there was. He could lose his resolve a dozen times in the week, and, perhaps, get it back almost as many.

Twenty minutes after he left the Globe lot, still inside Beverly

Hills, he began the turn into his own driveway. From the street, he saw only the Normandy spires above and splashes of white through the tall green wall of hedge. Past the wall, he was looking suddenly at the huge white provincial that his wife had paid $265,000 for.

He parked the Bentley (it was nine years old and he had got it, rebuilt, for the price of a new Cadillac) in its space in the six-car garage (they only kept three), and took the door that led to the pool area.

He saw Amanda at the far end of the pool: red bathing suit framed by white deck just detached from turquoise oval pool. He walked toward her. It was after three, the sun was hot, the pool fence knocked off the wind, he felt himself perspiring.

She was sitting on a white chaise, her back against the cushion and her feet planted on it so her knees thrust into the air. Her tan skin shone with sun lotion, her black hair swung loose to her shoulders. She was holding a green telephone in one hand and waved at him with the other.

"I don't give a goddamn how difficult it is," she said. "Those are the decorations I ordered, those are the ones you contracted for, and I expect them in place by three o'clock tomorrow afternoon. Tha-ree o-clock. Yes, I'm sure you can too. Good-bye." She said the last word with a sudden seraphic sweetness, hung up the phone and smiled at Sills and offered him her hand. It was wet with sweat.

"Sonsofbitches," she said.

"No damn good," he said.

"Thank God you're home. Look, I've got to get my hair done. If you've got nothing to do this afternoon, would you mind calling the caterers and make sure the hors d'oeuvres are right. And the agency, make sure they're getting us the two extra bartenders like they're supposed to. Here. I'll write you a list." She looked at him and dropped his hand. "For God's sake. What's the matter with you?"

"Why nothing. Nothing at all. Any small services. Any little functions."

"You don't really have anything to do, do you? If you don't, I certainly need your help."

"As a matter of fact," he said.

She was suddenly angry. "You're a liar."

"I have a very great deal to do, and I think I had better, go do it."

"I think, you had better, go screw yourself."

"It might be an improvement."

That was a foul: he regretted it.

"Why you son of a bitch, I've helped you, I've helped you big even if you couldn't do anything with it and you get high and mighty. When I ask you for a little help."

"All right. All right. I'm sorry. I'll do what I can."

He understood that he was the offender in this one, even if he were the offended in the total pattern. That was the really lousy thing, and it happened to him often: to be specifically wrong though generally right.

"Don't *concern* yourself. I'll take care of *everything*."

"Goddamn it. I *said* I was sorry. I *want* to help you."

She got off the chaise, and not looking at him, walked away.

He would not have to take that any more if he went with Globe.

He waited four days before he called on Tate and, after some bargaining that he considered astute, took the job.

Whatever he had lost, it wasn't pure freedom, he thought: the only real freedom was to spend your energy in a way not totally distasteful. Wasn't that a rationalization? Wasn't everything?

He told his wife with malicious, triumphant and smug pleasure.

"Television?" Her face swung toward him blank, then surprised, then outraged. "You're going into television?"

"Why yes. Sidney Tate made me a very attractive offer." He purposely withheld the magnitude of it.

"Has something happened to you or was I just wrong in the first place?"

"I really couldn't tell you."

"You certainly aren't who I thought you were."

"At least you won't have to worry about, let's say any financial responsibility for me."

"So that's it."

"You indicated you were concerned, if you remember."

"You're a damned fool, Howard. The one thing I never thought you were is a damned fool."

Then he told her what the job was; she was gratified at its importance but was not ready to stop being mad. She resolved the conflict by saying, with a certain ominousness, "I hope you know what you've let yourself in for."

8

ONE thing Sills had let himself in for was a totally new series of problems. He began the television operation with one very serious handicap: he had never produced really low-priced pictures that had to be quickly made. So he brought in as his assistant a man who had.

He wanted to approach his job as always: to get good people, to clear obstacles for them, and to let them alone. Yet the urgency of production and the tiny budgets made that impossible. He had to be a policeman. He policed the scripts doggedly. He knew they could not be truly good: he was determined they would not be blatantly bad. Though his target for every effort in the first two years had to be the uncultivated audience, he fought to avoid notorious lapses of intelligence.

His wife made a performance of repenting her open censure, and standing by him no matter what. She forgave him (she indicated) for having become a six-figure-a-year television executive instead of the standard of excellence for the handcrafted film. It was perhaps her fault too (she intimated) for having made the mistake of believing him her equal in taste, discrimination, and creativity. She was nothing (she suggested) if not good-humored and tolerant.

"The best any of us can do"–she did not *say* after all–"is to find our own talent and pursue it."

"You're quite right, my dear," he said agreeably.

The second year, he had four series on the air, three Westerns, one comedy and five pilots accepted. The television operation was in black ink, if not spectacularly, and he persuaded Tate to let him do a serious anthology show. "You remember I told you a really good man has to be indulged. So long as he makes his profit overall, of course," Tate told him.

The anthology was the final piece in Sills's plan: he had paid Caesar in Caesar's coin with all the commercial series, and now he was going to do something he wanted to do. In the New Theater Hour, he disregarded his mass audience entirely. He indulged himself completely—or at least as completely as he would in the New York or London theater. English-speaking reviewers and audiences were still ten years behind Paris (Sills was sure that Sartre, Giraudoux, Anouilh, or Beckett would have been condemned in New York had they not come in as European successes). He was determined to keep the show pure theater. At the end of the Theater Hour's first season, Sills considered that of the thirty-nine shows, eleven had been absolutely first-rate, fourteen good, and fourteen weak.

"How long can you keep it up?" a newspaper critic asked him.

"As long as the show lasts."

"How long is that?"

"Not forever."

He hoped he could keep it alive for at least three years. He was not confident of more. The year Theater Hour ended its first season was 1956, and a pattern and a future were already established. The advertising business had not only taken over the medium, the agency men were intruding more and more deeply into the making of films. Even on Theater Hour, a comparatively sophisticated sponsor blurred out by sound device a reference to dead fish; one of its fifty canned products was tuna.

Theater Hour was only one Globe production, and Sills could not neglect the others. He worked harder than he had ever worked; he continually missed the luxury of quietly superintending the best films the Industry permitted itself to make; he had the frustrating awareness that he was spreading himself too thin. Still he had an enormous satisfaction in his work. He knew absolutely that he had made two incalculable contributions to American commercial television. He had proved that a film series could be commercially successful without being absolutely and embarrassingly bad. And he had forced the medium to sustain a vital movement in pure theater—for however long it lasted. He had touched excellence again, soggy though it might be.

His wife was intensely pleased by his creation of, and association with, the Hour. It bestowed *almost* the kind of aesthetic eminence she had wanted for him, so to be transferred to herself. In its good and celebrated days, she picked her guest lists with the Hour always firmly in her eye: the people at her parties were likely to be highly appreciative of the man who brought real theater to television. Her own conversation invoked the accomplishment:

"Did you know, Howard is working on Sartre himself for a TV play of *The Flies?*" (He wasn't.)

"There's nothing *in* those long pictures any more but swords and bosoms. I don't see how sensitive people stand it."

And so on.

The bloom had passed from their pleasant, pleasurable, but not truly remarkable physical passion. It had done so, almost formally, when *Julien* did not really make it. After he had gone back to Globe, they had moved into a relationship that was warmer than coexistence but still carefully measured. It was some months after the job started that he got around to being technically unfaithful, with an attractive thirty-five-year-old actress looking for work (Sills gave it to her). He did not start or want an affair. Flaubert was right: an extended adultery had all the banalities of marriage. He had quite enough complications in his life without an official, regular mistress: for me (he thought) the happy unending stream of one-shots. His situation with his wife could continue indefinitely without change. It did.

And in a sense, so did his work, which was full of half-satisfactions, and not-quite-fulfillments. Then, in 1957, audience ratings on Theater Hour were so low it found no sponsor and was cancelled.

The advertising agencies were more pervasive than ever, and he had to go with the wind. He developed two dramatic series with continuing principals but a totally different action each week. One was *Barbados Run,* whose center was a young captain with a trading schooner in the Caribbean. The other was *The Capital Crime,* using the same police characters and involving them with a different murder in Los Angeles each week. With the first, he had hoped for the level of Conrad, but settled gladly for that of Maugham. He had wanted Dostoevski on the second, but got no better than the *New York Daily News*. The shows were almost as good as the medium would accept in 1958. He could not get around the almost, though, and this bothered him.

In 1958, five years after he started Globe's television, he understood he had become more of a businessman than a creator. He did not fret because he considered it inevitable: when big money came in, something always died. Instead, he looked back at the five years and was surprised to perceive how much pure joy had gone into the total effort. Not simply from himself but most connected with it.

"The great days of television are over, I guess," his friend the newspaper critic said sentimentally one day. "How can real talent operate under the thumb of the advertising agencies?"

"I don't know. Some of it will though. For a while."

He did not say that talent was the most perishable commodity of all, which had the whole world as its enemy and which could only have a limited time of survival at its luckiest. All talent was engaged in a siege action, it fought to hold out as long as it could, it was doomed from the very beginning by the sheer mass of the enemy. Of course it was much luckier if it did not know it was doomed.

Once Sills had learned that talent was always doomed, he had committed himself to giving it as much protection as possible so it might last as long as possible. Though he did not always succeed, he always tried.

He did not see immediately that Margaret Dayton had, or was, talent. He would not have seen her at all if Nelson Glassgow had not told him she was Octavia Dayton's daughter. He was fond of Octavia: she had been the permanent woman in a period when he discarded temporary women like leaves of a calendar: the starlet period.

"Sure I'll let her read, Nelson," he said to Glassgow. "She'll have to satisfy Barney too, you know, he's directing."

In his office, waiting for Margaret, he saw from Barney's closed face that Barney had already rejected her. Sills knew Barney was sleeping with a girl who surely wanted the part: Barney almost surely had promised it to her. Sills was sorry. Perhaps he could do something else for Octavia's daughter.

Margaret came in, Glassgow's hand on her elbow. Her hair was redder than Octavia's, she was wearing a tight, knitted green dress to match the part, and her face looked open and faintly frightened. Sills found her sexy, amiable, and pleasant. The town was full of girls who looked sexy, amiable, and pleasant.

After introductions Barney said, "Have a seat and we'll start."

"Have her walk when she does the lines," said Glassgow.

"Why?" Barney's face closed tighter.

"Just have her walk."

"Let's do have her walk, Barney," said Sills easily.

Sills watched the impressive undulations of Margaret striding, he watched Barney, and he saw the walk had changed nothing. He could of course overrule the director but he would not. He often vetoed: he never forced his own choice for a character down a director's throat. His directors did not have to be perfectly happy, but he did not want them actively unhappy.

He thought Margaret did the lines rather well, she certainly had the walk, and two days later, he asked her to visit him, alone. He wanted to soften the turndown.

He noticed again the openness of her face.

"He didn't want me, did he?"

"No," said Sills. "I did but he had someone else in mind."

"I'm glad you wanted me, anyway. Would you mind if I broke it to Nelson? His feelings get hurt awful easy."

"Not at all," said Sills.

When she had gone, he switched Barney to another episode and cast Margaret as Sadie before he had assigned a director.

All of which had certain consequences.

When Margaret said, "You're nothing but a *peeg,* Mr. Crawford," and swung her hips through the door with the camera following a foot behind, he thought she was all right, sound, no more. He was astonished at the furor the scene created: he reviewed it several times and was not sure he had seen anything extraordinary. Finally, he thought: maybe.

He put her in other very brief spots, for she did not have the techniques for longer ones, and watched her carefully. There were certain roles in which she created much more interest than in others. He studied these. When he understood, he had to laugh.

She was essentially a variation of the most stock of stock types. She was the Whore with the Heart of Gold.

And she was breathless, young, and virginal with it. The tension between the opposites was unique, and so she was a unique personality. She was a *psychic* virgin who could love you purely, and still with everything a good whorehouse could teach. She sent this with no planning, no conscious art, so far as he could see. It was intuition. She had talent then, but it was an intuitive, spontaneous talent and so a narrow talent. The spontaneous talents were the small innocent birds: the hawks got these quickly. He wondered what names her hawks would have.

He signed her to a three-year contract, it would have been seven except for Nelson Glassgow, and he told Sidney Tate. Very few long contracts were being signed that year.

"It's your operation," Tate said. "You have more confidence in her than I do, though."

Tate did not hesitate to have opinions or to suggest the development of projects in that purely operational area where his comparative lack of experience might have made him timid. Sills did not resent it: he admired it. Tate had understood almost at once how fanciful most opinions were in the Industry.

"Look at what happened over that one line," he said pleasantly.

"That isn't really important, it didn't really have anything to do with her. It was just an accident. I don't consider it important."

"I think it might be, Sidney."

"I have no doubt she'll earn her salt in your operation. Beyond that, well. We'll see what happens."

Sills continued to see that she got what appeared to be a wide range of roles. Yet almost all of them, certainly all that he could manage, were variations of the Whore with the Heart of Gold. He saw to it that the publicity department gave her an effort. It was a small department for the area it had to cover. He was completely aware that the press attention she received was too large to be accounted for by that effort.

Never again did she approach the sensation of the first part. Yet, as a minor actress in television only, she was already conceptualized. The words "Margaret Dayton" had a definite and clearly understood value: a "Margaret Dayton character" was an ingenuous sexpot, a girl who did not know her sexuality was a highly explosive cargo.

Sills was always fascinated by that phenomenon of conceptualization. Some entertainers (or politicians, or writers) with superb abilities and dynamic personalities could fail, simply because they did not throw a single, simple picture on the screen of public consciousness. Others who were less skillful, and even less endowed with the indefinables, could succeed just because they made a clear, oversimple picture. Margaret Dayton was extraordinarily lucky: at the outset of her career, she had found a highly effective *persona.*

And she had talent. How much, he did not know. What kind, he thought he did know.

"How do you plan your work?" he asked her one morning on the set of *The Capital Crime*. She was playing a maid, seduced by the husband of the house, who saw him shoot his wife. Her face was full of unreflecting enjoyment; they had just watched a scene in which she did not figure.

"Plan it?" Her eyebrows pulled together. "I don't exactly plan it the way some of them do. What I do, I figure out what I would do if I were that girl and then I just go ahead and do it. That's all I do."

"That's enough," said Sills.

He was glad to lend her out on the stripper picture. After its success, Glassgow came to him.

"What can Margaret expect if she stays with Globe, Howard?"

"As much as anybody can expect in television. Good parts, exposure, if we come up with the right pilot maybe her own series."

"I don't mean in television. I mean in major, full-length, theater pictures."

"Television is all I can speak for, Nelson."

"Sidney Tate isn't really with her, is he?"

"He's not against her."

"But he's not *with* her, is he?"

Sills hesitated. "Not yet."

"Will you give us a release then? I can move her after that stripper picture. If she's clear."

"That's up to Sidney. I'll do what I can, though. I think she ought to get her chance."

He put it to Tate on grounds of intelligent self-interest: since Tate did not want to take a big risk on her, the studio should let Glassgow develop her while keeping some hold on her future services. It was both fair and apt to be profitable: he had found that any proposition that combined those things always had a good chance with Tate. And after a conference with Glassgow, Tate did give her the release.

He was interested in seeing what might happen to her, what she and Glassgow could make happen. Sills felt she was already more nearly a star than even Glassgow guessed: stars after all came in various magnitudes, and after three years in television, Margaret Dayton was established. He was certain she could carry a series at that moment, and she was barely twenty-one. If he had had the right series, he would never have let her go.

Ricci's art picture (how he hated the provincial epithet) had put a seal upon her: she could not only maintain a lead in a real picture but could even carry it. When he had seen it, Sills knew she was ready (and when he had seen it he had hated Ricci automatically for doing well what he himself had done in mediocrity).

He was not surprised when *Redheads* made her an authentic commercial star, and her next picture confirmed her. One hot picture was all it took: she was lucky it came early, but she was not atypical. She had caught the big luck on a rising tide of personal fortune. But if she had not caught it fairly quickly, say in three years, she would not have caught it at all. He knew several whose course had been remarkably like hers–except the Big Picture did not come at the sensitive moment.

There was Susan Prentiss whose career had strong parallels to Margaret's. She was a strong and skillful dramatic actress rather than a sex symbol, but she had done the same apprenticeship in television and attracted quick attention in young character parts in theater pictures. But if she did not get her Big Picture in about two years, her chance would have passed. A big star could not be made from material grown too familiar.

There was no absolutely standard pattern for the fashioning of a star. Margaret's was as nearly standard as there was at that historical instant: training in television, success in small pictures or parts, the lucky part in the big lucky picture.

His interest in Margaret was intermittent and professional, though keen. It was not part of his own life, which was complex and arduous.

He and his wife had their continuing situation, which was not as bad as the situations of most of his friends, but still was not a good situation. Guarded was still the word for it.

He could come home tired, but with urgent work to do at once. She might greet him dressed for the theater, or even the ballet.

"We're going to *The Blacks* tonight, there's a ticket for you."

"I wish I could. But I *have* to go over these schedules. I mean, I really *have* to, I have to tonight."

"Ah. The busy businessman."

He did not acknowledge the barb. "I'm awfully sorry. I really am."

"Well. We'll miss you." And she embraced him almost cordially, touching his cheek with hers, carefully, so not to smear rouge or lipstick.

He had been thinking about it for nearly a year before he told Tate, at a time he picked carefully.

"Sidney, I've been wondering if I might not be more useful to the studio if I went back to feature pictures."

Tate's kind grave face rose to him with a judicious shade of polite surprise.

"You're awfully useful where you are, Howard."

"A man can get stale on a job."

"Are you stale?"

"Not yet. It could happen."

"It can always happen to all of us."

"I think I may really need a change in perspective." He was playing to a Tate absolute: perspectives had to be changed.

Tate looked at him keenly; he knew Tate knew he was playing to an absolute. "Is that your only reason?"

"You know better." He smiled with suitable candor. "Right now, I can do what I want to do better in full-lengths. This is the real, true reason, Sidney, but I think it's just as true that I'll be more valuable to the studio back in pictures." He looked at Tate openly. "Globe TV might be better off with some fresh blood."

"You aren't asking me to fire you, are you Howard?"

"Not ex-actly."

"I'll think about the switch. For quite a long time, I warn you."

Sills knew Tate, and so he knew better than to press him. He worked, and waited.

9

He was used to being a man of mundane consequence again, and he did not want to lose that. It was not that it gave him positive pleasure; it simply would have given him pain to be deprived of it.

He had massive stature in television: a move from that comparatively safe eminence to the extraordinary risk that the big motion picture had become was more than a calculated gamble. It was a wild, foolish wager in which he could lose almost everything and win very little. Yet some interior gyro pointed him: he wanted to make "real" pictures again. He acknowledged the excitement of what television had been, and its serious contributions. But the very existence of television and the fact that it now supplied the lowest-level market had freed the Big Picture; the Big Picture could be consistently adult in a way it had never dared to be before 1950. It was possible to make in America the kind of picture he had wanted to make twenty-odd years before.

He knew he could leave and resume independent production, but he preferred to stay in the Globe framework. So he waited. And because he knew Sidney Tate well, he waited in silence.

Suddenly, unbelievably Tate had his problems, too. He had a deficit for the second straight year.

"We're crapshooters," he said to Sills, his face and voice still unable to accept it. "I've never gambled in business in my life, I've never had to. And now I'm face to face with the fact that this business is built on the big gamble. We're crapshooters, when we lose we have to keep doubling to get it back."

"You always build in the percentage, Sidney."

"I'm not so sure, anymore."

In the most difficult years of the studios, Sidney Tate had found the handle to survival and had held it firmly. Now, when others who had learned from him were flourishing, he had a balance sheet problem. It was serious, and it could become a great deal more serious. Unbelievably, Tate himself was in jeopardy.

Tate had made no mistakes, Sills thought. He had simply been unlucky. The bad luck had come all at once, and in a package.

"Do you still want to go back to full-lengths?" Tate's face was ordered, decorous as always, and yet Sills was at once aware of tension.

"Yes. Yes I do."

"I, have something. No, *no,* I am doing you no favor, believe me. This proposition is something I would order nobody into."

"It's that bad?"

"It's that bad and worse. It's *The Admiral's Lady*. Marlow is a maniac." Marlow was the star who had made direction of the picture part of his price.

"That's been suggested."

"He waited a week to get just the kind of waves he wanted." Tate raised his hand, fingers outspread; for him it was a theatrical gesture. "I'm taking Hinds off as producer. I'll have to let *him* finish directing but he must not affect production decisions any more." He stopped and looked at Sills, and Sills thought there was a cast of apology to his face. "It's your picture if you want it."

Sills looked over Tate's head through the window to the distant joining of hills and sky. Smog blurred the horizon brownly and thinned upward into clear and untouched blue. The day was mellow, and unfateful.

"It's a very bad situation," said Tate.

Sills felt in his stomach that it was a bad situation.

But if he saved the picture–

"I don't think I'd take it myself," said Tate.

But if he saved the picture?

"It's a very fine screenplay," Sills said. "It could be a truly fine picture."

"It could. I had hoped it would."

Sills recognized his feeling but not completely. He framed a conceit to understand it: it was as though he could see certain points fixed in space before him, and a line moving to join them in a long parabolic curve. He made it two such systems of points, one on either hand, and he could see the line of each system curving outward without end. They confronted him; implacable, ambiguous, riddling. There was more to the feeling than that.

Yet, if he saved the picture. There would of course be no truly creative role for him in it, not now. But to be *in* on a good, maybe great picture. And if he saved it. *If* he saved it. Save it and he would be again what he was *supposed* to be.

He identified the remnant of the feeling by a counterpart. Once, having lost, he had bought five thousand dollars' worth of one-hundred-dollar chips at a dice table at the Thunderbird in Vegas. Buying, he had known he would lose them, and he had, and he had lost more after that. He felt now as he had felt buying the chips.

Yet the here and now of the office was workaday and pleasant, there was nothing to mark off the undramatic instant from any other.

"It's a wonderful screenplay," he said.

"I'll consider it very carefully," he said.

But he already knew what he was going to do.

Five months later, he sat in the same chair, and looked at the same man wearing the same gold on blue necktie. It might have been the same meeting, thrown on the screen after a brief reversal and rewinding of a film spool. Except it was not.

"It was all in the letters," he said. "The reports. You know all about it."

Tate nodded.

"What final figure did accounting come up with?"

"Ten million three hundred and eight thousand, two hundred thirty-one dollars and seventy-one cents. That's what it cost."

Sills said nothing.

"I want you to know I don't blame you," Tate said. "I don't think anybody could have pulled it out."

"Maybe you could have."

"No, it was too far gone."

"A good gross can still get it back and more."

Tate hesitated. "The exhibitors aren't responding. We tried for the kind of advance commitments that saved Twentieth with *Cleopatra*. The exhibitors are not responding at all."

Sills made an exaggerated wince.

"I guess I should have arranged a romance between the principals."

"It might have helped."

"Matter of fact, there was a red hot romance. Only they were both men."

Tate smiled faintly.

"How bad is it?" Sills said soberly.

"Very bad. I'm in a proxy fight. Vern McGaughey is after me and he could get me, he's got an awful lot of votes."

"How are our chances?"

"Not good unless a certain thing works out. If it does they're better than good."

Haratunian, Sills thought.

"Am I a liability, Sidney?"

"No more than I am. Anybody connected with *The Admiral's Lady* is a liability of sorts. Forget it."

"Sidney, be candid now. Would it take some of the pressure off if I resigned?"

"I honestly don't know. I honestly don't."

That was answer enough. Sills swung Tate's yellow pad to him, took the gold-plated pen from the desk set, and wrote. He tore off the sheet and handed it to Tate.

Tate read it and his face grew troubled.

"I ought to tear this up," he said.

"Sidney, is there any purpose served by us both going down?"

Tate said after a moment and reluctantly, "No."

"That's the computerized solution then, isn't it?"

"Howard, I promise you I won't forget this."

It was better than a contract with anybody else in town.

"I resigned today," he said to his wife. He had been home less than a week.

"You what?" Her face turned toward him, her brown eyes opened wide, and the cords in her white throat tensed and stood out. For an instant she looked much older.

"I quit."

He saw her fight for and gain control of her anger, and she spoke as casually as he. "I guess it beats getting fired."

"That's what they say."

"What do you do now?"

"Await further developments," he said ironically.

"I see. Of course. You'll just lay back and enjoy the kudos from *Admiral's Lady*."

"Of course."

He had not had relations with her since his return from Tunisia, and they did not resume. She gave him no invitation. The long resentment which she had kept in shallow burial was now uncovered and open to the air. She was bitter and viciously ironic to him: her great grievance against him was finally insupportable, she implied. His own attitude altered from forced tolerance to weary disgust, and then, when he made a certain discovery, to cold outrage.

The discovery was in two parts. The first came when he picked up the telephone and heard her talking to a man on another connection: when his receiver went up their conversation was apparently innocent.

But Sills was not insensitive. The next afternoon when she was out, and with no compunction or conscience whatever, he checked the drawers in her bath where she kept her contraceptive device.

It was not there.

That was not quite evidence. He checked the drawer daily during the next ten days, and saw that twice the device was taken out and returned. Which was evidence.

Having recently read the Mary McCarthy novel, the one with the clear, definitive, and much-needed codification of contraceptive protocol, he considered this a betrayal of a particularly insulting kind. Miss McCarthy had decreed that a true lady should use one apparatus with exactly one partner—no matter how many partners she might acquire: no false economies. He also considered that it was precisely the kind of gratuitous over-injury Amanda would inflict.

Had he had his "normal" stability, he would not have brooded: he would simply have left.

But the disaster of the picture had dropped him into a quiet, disciplined, calmly reasonable hysteria. In that state, his discovery gave him a diversion. Now he had a game: to catch her. And he played it with hysterical exultation and zest. Six months before, he would have found his own condition at that moment slightly mad.

He watched her, cunningly, for signs—betrayals of betrayal. He depended on the game more day by day. It not only kept him sharp, it gave him pleasure. He suspected her of knowing the game, too, and playing it, on a level just beneath awareness, and also with pleasure. She might have been teasing him as some women tease their not-quite lovers, only her insinuated promise to him was not of surrender but of incrimination.

The game cleared the air: they were both better dispositioned: the game had in fact become the engine of Sills's life.

He bought a .22 caliber Hi-Standard target pistol. Buying it, he felt masterful, effective, and marvelously calm. For the first time in years, he had a highly satisfying picture of himself.

This is you, he thought, *this is really you.*

One Thursday Amanda said, "I have to go to a charity thing in

Newport this afternoon. Would you like to come down and spend the weekend?"

She looked at him boldly, with the hint of a dare: *Here's a chance, let's see what you can do with it.* He received it as though it were a clear electronic impulse: he felt his own zest leap to answer hers.

"Nooo, no, I don't think I can get down before Friday," he said blandly. They kept a weekend apartment in Newport.

"Guess I'll have to spend the night without you then." She gave him a quick, arrogant shaft of a glance, and left him.

Exaltation rose in him like a tide. Moments after she was gone, he took his .22, drove the Bentley to Rent-a-Car and took a Chevrolet, and arrived in Newport half an hour after he estimated she had.

He drove by the apartment house in the back bay area, saw her XK–E in its place in the garage, circled and parked a block away. Within an hour she came out. He followed her, saw the little red car stop by a parking lot and a man get in. The red car pulled out, and headed towards the Coast Highway.

The XK–E was in the right lane. He stayed in the left, almost a block back, to keep it in view, and then saw it turn right into a parking lot by the bay front, near the berth of their own 37-footer.

He turned left two blocks down, came around and reentered the highway and parked in front of an ice cream parlor on the inland side.

He looked across and down the pavement and to the far side of the lot and saw the red rear of the XK–E between two bigger cars. He looked at it appreciatively, he was very pleased. He studied himself impersonally, from somewhere outside, and found it interesting that he was so pleased. His pleasure was really very keen. And so was his gratitude: he was really tremendously grateful to her, he had a much warmer feeling for her than he had had for years. She had really been tremendously sporting, sporting was the only word, she was playing the game as it ought to be played, giving him a chance. They would be on the boat, of course: very sporting. He would have to wait a suitable interval of course: be sporting too. He felt his pleasure, and his gratitude, mount by the moment. He was surprised, and tickled to find his pleasure manifesting itself physically: he laughed out loud. Passing on the sidewalk, a man and a woman in sailing jeans turned to look curiously in his direction.

He gave her fifteen minutes. Then he left the car, walked half a block so he could cross the highway virtuously between the two white lines of the crosswalk, and then moved through the yacht broker's lot to the piers. He pretended to study the power cruisers on blocks, edging toward the water very slowly. He saw the black crosses of the masts lining jagged and uneven against the gray twilight sky. He felt the moment as one of those clear intense significances that time brackets: he felt himself resolute, cunning, magnificent.

He was closer to the water and saw the white, dark-trimmed, rounded hulls, side by side as in a nursery. Then he was on the boardwalk. He kept his face turned away from the left and his boat; he pretended to study carefully a broad-beamed 60-foot motor vessel in front of him that filled a slip by herself. He glanced furtively to the left, saw no one on the decks of his boat, and moved slowly toward her, still trying to avert his head, still stopping in front of and regarding each craft as he came to each slip.

He scorned the banality of the letters on the sterns: *Lady Gay, Easy Days, Joan III, Balboa Lass.* He approved one, *Nefertiti,* and filled with satisfaction at the chaste unbourgeois sweetness of his own as he approached her: *Børeas.* He had brought her from Norway.

Still no one on the decks. His face toward *Nefertiti,* he came to *Børeas*'s slip. She was portside to the pier, her stern toward the boardwalk. He would have to come aboard at the stern softly, without betraying himself: the boat was big enough so he could do it if he managed it properly. He turned from the boardwalk to the pier.

Trying to look supremely casual, and still to jar the boat not at all, he thrust his foot past the gunwale to the deck and put his weight gradually upon it. The boat gave, but slightly.

Then he was aboard, successfully. The design of the boat favored him: the doors at the entrance to the cabin were closed: the glass-covered ports to the cabin were all forward.

For the first time it came to him that they might not be aboard after all. He moved very slowly toward the doors and then sat on a bit in the dark.

He heard a noise beyond the doors, and then he heard it again, and then he identified it. It was a woman's laugh. Inside something struck the floor and then something else: shoes, he thought. He waited for the working of springs, then remembered the bunks were kapok mattresses on wood. But shortly came an unpatterned sequence of sounds—not words—that was unmistakable.

Now of course he should go in. But he did not wish to end or even to hurry the game. The hell with anybody outside seeing him: he crawled on hands and knees to the first port and slowly thrust his head to the glass. There was still gray light: across the little cabin on the blue padded bunk, he saw a man in the embrace of his wife. The man was completely naked. His wife wore only her hose. They were loose about her knees which were raised to make a rocking cradle. Sills saw the back of the man's head but he could see her face clearly.

It was most interesting, Sills thought, it was a better game all the time.

When the two inside left each other, he crawled back to the stern. Noises sounded on the other side of the door: some he identified as giggles. He sat on a wooden bit in the deck and waited: decorous, patient, interested not unsympathetically. It was not until his wife stepped out, followed by the man, that he remembered with dismay what the game now required of him. As he stood and as Amanda's eyes fell upon him, he noted that her face showed surprise but no real shock.

"Howard!" she said with just the proper mixture of anger and fear.

Embarrassed, apologetic, very regretfully unable to avoid the obligation, he shot the man with the .22 Hi-Standard as considerately as he could. He shot him accurately in the fleshy, outer part of the thigh (he had not aimed, as the sensational press later implied, to achieve a particularly punitive, poetic justice).

It was not until he heard the polite little explosion in his hand that he recognized the other as Nelson Glassgow. Glassgow's face showed only the absolute and injured conviction that a mistake had been made.

"Howard. What the hell. What the hell, Howard."

He sat on the bit, put his hand on the bleeding leg, and said the words again and again. "What the hell, Howard. What the hell, Howard."

By that time the policeman was there. The policeman looked frightened and bewildered. Sills extended the Hi-Standard butt first.

Glassgow called from the bit, *"No,* Howard, *no.* Officer, it's just . . ."

The officer looked scaredly at Sills who shoved the gun toward him sadly. It had been a wonderful game, except for the end, it was a shame it was over. The officer took the gun and dropped it on the deck.

Sills turned to Glassgow sitting on the bit with his hand still on his leg. "Gee, Nelson," he said. "I'm real sorry."

Glassgow was out of his hospital considerably before Sills was out of his. (At that, they told Sills at his sanatorium, he was recovering remarkably quickly from acute if temporary schizophrenia.) So it was Glassgow who called on Sills.

"How are you, Howard?"

"I'm fine. How are you?"

"Oh I'm fine. Just fine."

"Leg all right?"

"Oh the leg's fine. Just fine."

"That's fine. I mean, I'm glad the leg's all right."

"Oh the leg's all right. I'm glad you're all right."

"Oh, I'm fine."

Sills was sitting in a chair in pajamas and robe. Glassgow was wearing a loud expensive sport shirt.

"I thought you two had separated. I mean, hell I'm sorry, it wouldn't have happened if I hadn't thought you were separated."

"Actually we had kind of separated," said Sills helpfully.

"Well, that's what I thought. I mean, well, hell, I didn't mean to, I just thought it was all over and everything. You know."

"I know."

"Well I'm sorry."

"That's all right."

"Just so you understand how it was."

"I understand."

"What now? Are you getting a divorce now?"

"Oh yes. She's divorcing me."

"That's very gentlemanly of you."

"Oh, no."

"Howard. I would like to. I would like to do, something, to make this up."

"That's very generous but you don't need to do anything, Nelson."

"Well I would *like* to, Howard. What I would like to do is, now that you're at liberty, I would like to represent you, Howard."

"That's most generous of you, Nelson."

"The thing is, I think we could do big things."

"Why, I think we might."

"Absolutely. Big things."

"Yes indeed. Big things."

"Is it a deal, Howard?"

"It, is, a, deal, Nelson."

They shook hands, and Sills for the first time in his career had an agent, one he had shot up only a little bit. In six months Glassgow had him under contract again to his former employers, Globe-International Studios, as executive producer of its biggest production. Its shooting title was *Helen of Troy*.

10

To Sills, now, reflecting upon the ordeals of *Helen of Troy,* those steps by which he became involved in the picture (*enmeshed* was the word, he thought) seemed in another lifetime. Yet it was in the same life. And though Margaret was gone, neither life nor the picture stopped: the minor problems were unwilling to await the solution of the major. He checked his appointments: at ten, Brigadier Thazantis, the C.O. of the Greek troops, no clue as to his problem. At ten-thirty, the cost accountant: to discuss expenditures and authorizations, and that was enough to destroy anyone's day, if it had not been destroyed before it started.

He finally got his assistant director in Athens, who had nothing to report, and another call came from Beverly Hills.

He did not know who it was until he had said "Hello" and was answered by the voice of his wife. She was still his wife because they were between first and final decrees.

He was somewhat surprised to hear from her, but only somewhat. She was, after all, a worldly woman and he hoped he was a sophisticated man, although there was certain evidence to the contrary. Yes there was.

"Hello, Amanda," he said flatly.

"Darling, are you all right?"

"I'm fine."

"Why I thought from the papers the world was coming to an end or something. Has she really and truly disappeared?"

"She has really and truly disappeared."

"Come now. Are you and Sidney that hard up for publicity?"

"I'm never hard up." He said it deliberately with double meaning.

"Well good for you darling. I often am myself."

"Not for long, I'm sure."

"Ooooh. Take that stiletto out. I called to wish you well, you know."

"That's very kind and I appreciate it. Thank you."

"Howard–"

"Yes?"

"Nothing. Good luck."

He heard her hang up, and then for several seconds he heard the strange emptiness of the transocean connection. Then he hung up himself.

He looked at his watch: he could give himself five minutes. He walked outside and to the sea cliff, to the right of armies and action. He saw four vessels: a tanker, two caïques, and, inside the horizon, a gray one-stacker that looked not unlike a destroyer as she headed toward the island.

Poor Tate, he thought, and then he thought, nonsense. Tate was not only capable of taking care of himself but everybody else in sight.

He hoped so. He did not want to lose what he had fought so hard to get back. He did not want to. It was selfish to think of himself, and he did not want to be selfish, but he did not want to lose it.

BOOK 7

THE GODDESS AT MYKONOS

1

FROM behind, beneath rather than against a downward sun, the man was not tall nor short nor heavy nor light. The shoulders of the blue nylon windbreaker across the back shook in the sea wind, and the ends of his long blond hair moved too in the wind. Beyond the man were the piers, the caïques and other craft tied to the piers, and the green water in the harbor. Beyond the harbor was the sudden blue dark of the sea, and above the sea the sharp irregular dark of the islands of the Cyclades.

Seen close, and in profile, the man's face was regular in feature, though abstracted and tense in concentration. He was Grover Brand. He had just walked along the piers, hoping for information about the departure of his wife, if departure it was. He did not know what, or whom, he was looking for, and he had asked no questions, and he had learned nothing. He was aware, again, that his isolation did not help in this, as it did not help in so much.

In a spasm of conscience, he turned his head toward a man in a black watch cap. Brand had heard his footstep on the boardwalk, and said, "*Kalespera.*"

"*Kalespera,*" said the man pleasantly enough and went by.

He walked along the boardwalk, knowing he was not so much looking for information as simply looking. The caïques called to his blood. He had seen their sails white against the sky and full with wind, pulling their sharp bows across the scored floor of the sea, and he had longed to be of them. Some made livings for their owner captains in a small neat trade among the islands. They started at Piraeus, the seaport of Athens, ran from island to island in the

Cyclades picking up and selling cargo, and then returned to Piraeus with a full load. Brand would have given, perhaps, one finger to make the round trip.

At one of the piers, now, a large caïque was unloading. A block and tackle on a boat davit on the pier was swinging a sling of boxes off the deck. Brand watched the sling move black against the sun and come slowly to the dock. He watched the tall man in the open gray double-breasted coat standing beside the engine on the dock, his hands on its controls. Watching the empty sling arc fast and wide back to the caïque, Brand walked down the boardwalk and down the pier and stopped beside the man in the gray coat and black cap.

"Kalespera," he said.

"Kalespera," said the man.

His face was so stained and figured by his trade that it was beyond the words suntanned, windburned, weatherbeaten. Its brown was there forever. So too were the gullies about the eyes and nose set by permanent squint into sun and wind. There were none of the lines between mouth and nose that show failure, disappointment, and self-contempt. Brand wanted to paint the face, and the cap, and the open swinging double-breasted coat, on paper with words. He wanted to get too the smooth clean wood of the deck, and the open hatch to its hold, the thick long yardarm, now bare of sail, and beyond it the narrow jut of rock that rose sharply from the water and ran back to the high ridge of hill which was the spine of the island.

The captain smiled at him, and Brand saw it was a shy, delicate, and flattered smile.

Brand took his phrase book from his shirt pocket and tried to ask him what was in the boxes.

"The boxes," the captain said in English. "The boxes have toilet paper."

"Toilet paper. Ah," said Brand.

"It is in demand. Also the Kotex."

"I am sure. What else do you carry?"

"All things. Carry wheat, grapes, wine, lemon, olive oil, much olive oil. Carry this to Piraeus. You understand? From all islands–" a sweep of hand–"to Piraeus."

"What from Piraeus?"

"Excuse me?"

"What from Piraeus to the islands?"

"All things. Toilet paper, Kotex, can goods, clothing."

"Passengers?"

"Oh, yes, yes. Sometimes passenger. One island, another island, you know?"

Brand nodded. The captain's name was Constantin, he said. He spoke four languages. He went from Piraeus to Naxos, to Paros to Mykonos to Rhodos and back.

Brand had seen only the picture of the islands, and he thought of them coming out of the sea above the caïque's bow.

He talked, and then knew, suddenly, that he had talked for almost an hour, and had not thought of Margaret for almost an hour, and he was ashamed. But he knew he would do it again and exactly the same way.

He had asked about passengers for himself, wistfully, and now in penance he asked as part of the search. He was without expectation.

"Have you carried any women? American women?"

"Oh yes, yes. I carry them back to Piraeus. I stop here last, go to Piraeus, then stop here first on trip out."

"You carry them? How many?"

"Two women. Yes, I carry them to Piraeus."

"Beautiful women? One beautiful woman? Red hair?"

The captain smiled beautifully and sympathetically and shook his head. "Dark woman. One dark woman. The other with, you know," his hands cupped air above his cap, "cloth on head."

"When did you say it was?"

"Excuse me?"

"When?"

"Three, no four nights. Four nights."

Brand shook his head and ran, noticing for the first time that the sun was down.

In the hotel he did not stop for his key but ran straight through the office and the courtyard to Tate's door in C Bungalow. He knocked, turned the knob, and was inside before he heard Tate call, "Come in."

Tate was seated in an armchair, Glassgow on the edge of the dresser, and Sills was standing. They all were staring at him.

"I've got something," he said, and drew a breath. "Margaret and Sylvia went to Piraeus on a caïque four nights ago."

He saw the tensions leave their bodies.

"We just had a call from Sylvia, Grover," Tate said gently. "They'll be in on the *Leto* tomorrow afternoon."

2

AHEAD, target of the high white wave at the *Leto*'s bow, the island was beneath the sun and so a long black shape in the distant sea. Drawing closer, the blackness expanded, altered, and in an hour and minutes became a steep mountainside of brown sprouting tall white houses above the line where it met the sea.

On the port side of the sun deck, just behind a manila line that barred passengers from the wheelhouse, two young women sat side by side. Both wore cashmere topcoats and were of a size. One wore a big red kerchief over her head and tied under her chin. The other's dark hair blew in the wind. She smiled occasionally at the one with the handkerchief, and once patted her hand.

"You're feeling better already," said Sylvia Korbin and left her hand on Margaret Dayton's.

Margaret smiled slightly.

Sylvia studied her, and the island rushing toward them, and knew how afraid she herself was. She was returning to retribution, and knew she deserved retribution. The purgation she had won so briefly was gone, and she was only miserable and afraid. Watching the island rear up over her, she remembered how she had left it four nights before.

They had not been on the Cyclades' fastest mode of transport then, but on its oldest: a boat under sail: a caïque with olive oil for Piraeus: themselves supercargo at twenty dollars each. They had slipped away like thieves in the night, and Sylvia knew herself to be a thief. She was stealing an article worth an unfixable number of millions of dollars.

To a question, she would have had great trouble explaining why, and to herself, she could not have begun to explain why.

Sylvia was aware that her motives were contradictory and absurd.

She knew that she did not know, herself, the real shape of them. Yet she was luxuriating in as profound a satisfaction as she had ever known; she was "hitting back." She had shaped the words with unnatural formality, again and again, and warmed with each silent reiteration.

Had anyone put it to her that she did not know *how* she was "hitting back," that her strategy was as formless as her recent tactics had been sharp-edged, she would have been incensed.

It was exactly so.

She sat flank to flank with Margaret on the deck in the caïque, looked up at the dark square shadow of the sail above, heard the creak of the lines that was as regular as the rise and fall of the hull on the waves, and shivered. It was a cold wind.

Her complicity with McGaughey had begun shortly before the company left New York. Their acquaintance was much older.

He had reappeared as suddenly and as casually as Fate or a discarded friend. This was at a press cocktail party just before departure. She had felt a touch, and turned, and there he was, as ever: white-haired and Rooseveltian, ironic and humming with the adumbrations of power. She had five martinis: to him, she betrayed her anger at *them.* She remembered how urbanely he chatted, how easily he suggested they "keep in touch." She did not remember at all what she said. Of course he saw into her.

Two days later, he took her to lunch at the Colony. "Old times" were not mentioned. He simply said he would be grateful for a friend "in the camp of the unrighteous." He pretended to intend it as banter. But she saw he meant it completely: to him, theirs *was* the "camp of the unrighteous." He had a transparently clear conviction of his own clear virtue.

He repeated only his formless assurances of goodwill. He made no proposals. Nor did she. They simply understood each other.

Instantly and steeply, they glided into a conspiracy. Primly and absolutely, they refused to name it such. They maintained all the surfaces of a casual and correct business association.

She called him regularly from the island. And the content of their conversation might have seemed innocuous. The *fact* of it, of course, would have identified it unmistakably: nobody in Sidney Tate's Globe could have an innocent conversation with McGaughey.

She said: "I'm afraid it isn't going well. Margaret isn't doing well on her scenes, not well at all."

And he said: "That's a shame. But I do appreciate your keeping me informed."

And finally he said: "Perhaps it would be a good idea if you could get Margaret away for a good long rest. Say a month or so. Very quietly of course."

"Of course."

"By the way, you know about her first husband, well my people tell me her first husband is quite ill in Sicily. I understand she thinks quite highly of him, she might want to go to see him."

"Why, I think she would."

She wrote the name and address on a Kleenex with her eye pencil: Vito Stefano, Via Romagna, Palermo, Sicily.

By this time, she was sure Grover Brand knew something, she was not sure how much. Her husband suspected, but did not want really to know. She did not have much longer, she knew it, and she moved at once.

Margaret's "illness" was her chance: both Brand and Korbin were at location.

To Margaret, she urged a rest boldly. She saw Margaret's face awaken at the offered escape.

Margaret said: "What will they say?"

"Well they certainly won't let you if they know about it. But they don't have to know about it, do they darling?"

"Not even Grover?"

"Not even anybody."

"I can't just run off. *Can* I?"

She was asking permission.

"Just write Grover a note and I'll take it down to the desk and you and me'll go. Just like that. Right now. If we don't do it like that we won't do it at all."

Margaret protested once more, and surrendered with total gratitude.

In the hotel at Athens she moved to bring up Vito. Offering that intelligence to Margaret with any believable story was a problem. She finally settled on a course that was not totally improbable–she hoped.

After dinner, while Margaret was in one bed reading, and she sat before the mirror brushing her hair, she looked not at Margaret but at her image in the mirror and said, "Angela Rancalli wrote something interesting yesterday. I mean I got her letter yesterday." Angela Rancalli was a minor columnist who had swapped favors with Sylvia many times.

"Oh?" Margaret did not look up from her magazine.

"I probably shouldn't tell you."

In the mirror, she saw Margaret's eyes come from the page and meet hers in the mirror. "Why not?"

"I suppose there's no reason why not. Anyway." She looked at her own reflection closely and stroked hard with the brush. "Angela says she hears your ex is in Sicily and very sick."

"Vito?"

"Is that his name? Angela says a friend of *hers* says it looks like he's going. He's in Palermo or somewhere."

"Poor Vito. Poor old man. I was married to him less than a month. Mother had it annulled. I liked him a lot though."

Let her think of it. Sylvia kept brushing.

"I wouldn't know him if I saw him now," Margaret said. "He wouldn't know me."

"Oh, he'd know *you.*"

"I doubt it. I wish I could do something for him."

Let her think of it. "What *could* you do, honey?"

"I could go see him. I probably ought to go see him."

Careless now: "That would be an awful lot of trouble."

"You're right, we're in enough trouble as it is. Besides, I don't really *want* to see him. I'd feel funny."

"I guess you would."

"Do you know, I can't remember sleeping with him or anything. I mean, I remember *that* all right but I can't remember what he looked like or anything. I can't remember how he was built." She giggled, and Sylvia turned her head toward the bed and giggled. "All I remember about him really is how his eyes squinched over the adding machine."

"He's supposed to be very sick."

"Poor old man. I've really got to see him, Syl, I have to."

It *had* to come from her. "But we don't really know where he is, exactly."

"Could Angela get the address?"

"Oh I guess she could. It would take some time though."

"Would you call her, Syl?"

"Oh sure, I'll call her tonight if you want me to."

She talked to the operator and reported difficulties. "I'd better go down. Maybe if I write it out for them."

She came back in half an hour. Angela was working on it, she said, Angela was sure she could come up with it but it might take them a few days or even a week.

"I told her we'd pay for phone calls and so on. Okay?" That was corroboration: she admired it as she invented it.

"Oh, sure," said Margaret.

And they decided, somehow, that they might save time if they flew straight to Palermo and stayed in touch with Angela there. Sylvia booked them on an afternoon flight to Naples, and the day after that, to Palermo.

Sylvia and Max Korbin were both from the Bronx, and they met in Iowa City, Iowa, in 1950. Each wanted to be a director, and each had been drawn to the school of dramatic arts at the University of Iowa because Tennessee Williams had gone there (the folklore of the university was that *A Glass Menagerie* had been rejected as a master's thesis. It was, alas, unconfirmable). And to enroll, each had used savings–she had been a cocktail waitress a summer, he stock clerk a year.

In the second semester, Max Korbin maneuvered an assignment to direct *A Streetcar Named Desire*. She played Eunice and was also assistant director.

She discovered quickly that he was more talented: in revenge she married him.

His talent petrified hers. In turn, her ego tried to consume his, but with less success. She became extremely possessive; she created for herself the role of protector, guardian, and Svengali, and thrust toward that new identity as hard as she could.

Only he was not having any Svengali. He *was* willing, though, to let her support them when he got a graduate assistantship that did not cover much more than fees. And in Iowa City the best-paying job she could get, even with a college degree, was as waitress at the only fine restaurant, which was not in town but outside it.

Each of them held it against the other.

He was 1A, managed a deferment until he finished his graduate year and master's degree, and then was drafted. She went back to New York and became a salesgirl in an extremely fashionable shop that took only college graduates.

Something–in her eyes? her walk? her face?–something attracted one of her rich customers who was also a large stockholder. With exquisite and unexceptionable courtesy, he sought seignorial privileges. With a capacity for calculation unsuspected by herself, she teased him into the present of a moderately expensive diamond before she let him have them.

The arrangement was confirmed with the conventional ceremony, and then he brought to her certain subtleties.

At an appropriate phase of their next evening, she presented herself in negligee over lingerie. He ran his left hand over one side of his white hair. "My dear, do you have any, ah, black, ah, things?"

"Yes." She was annoyed but determined to be sporting. "You want me to put them on?"

"Would you please darling. And I have a present for you. It would make me very happy if you would wear these darling." From a parcel he had brought, he produced two black suede shoes with heels that came to a point no larger than a pencil.

She knew what they cost, and looked at them with a certain conflict. "If I can stand up on them."

She left him, and returned as he wished her to be. He kissed her, and knelt before her, and kissed her again. She felt his body trembling.

"Darling," he said.

"Mmm-mmm?" She caressed his hair lightly.

"Do you care enough for me to make me happy?"

"I propose to make you as happy as I can."

"I mean really happy."

"What does it take to make you really happy?"

"Promise you will."

"I can't promise till I know."

"It's such a little thing for you and it'll make me so happy."

"Tell me what it is."

He did. It involved the shoes. She was not shocked but amazed. That was not him, it was absolutely not him. Yet he was right: it was a small thing to ask: she did it for him.

And that was only the first time. She wondered often. The small service he wanted from her was simply not reconcilable to *him* as she knew him. He was so handsome, commanding, assured: everywhere else he had to dominate: he was well known for his resemblance to Roosevelt. His very career was founded on his capacity for aggression: his name was Vern McGaughey.

And yet. With her—

For the first time, certain platitudes won their reality: people *were* self-contradictory and complicated, they were made up of more things than one could imagine. For that knowledge she accorded to him a genuine gratitude.

That relationship lasted eight months. She conducted it (she considered) with enlightened self-interest and scrupulous justice: she felt an obligation to be fair to him that she did not in the least feel toward Korbin. When she understood this, she also understood she was unbreakably joined to Korbin. Not by love, but by something that perhaps included love.

She was dimly mystified, and vaguely frightened, by something else: she was exorcized by the exercises with McGaughey. And by the fact of her betrayal, some deep grudge of the blood against Korbin was stamped paid. She looked forward, almost tenderly, to his return.

When that happened, she had accumulated for him twelve thousand dollars and much goodwill. It was understood she had saved, and taken advantage of, a space stock tip by a customer.

She insisted that he study with Lee Strasberg at the Actor's Studio while she continued to work (she ended the McGaughey affair on friendly terms). He spent three months with Strasberg, and directed two plays in the Village. They were moderately well received but he could not get a Broadway play, and he spoke of starting a studio of his own. She had enough money for that and wanted to put it up. They agreed it would be futile to compete with Strasberg, and went to Los Angeles. There were a dozen such studios, in L.A. some good, and his did not make money, and they would not have survived if she had not gone to work again, as an assistant to an independent producer. She had to leave that when she would not go to bed for him, and then went with a talent agency.

Everything changed when Korbin finally published his book and his theory. He craftily merged the "intention" of the Actor's Studio with the self-plan of Sartre's existentialism: "The actor must understand his character's unconscious plan of himself, and thrust toward the fulfillment of that plan."

That was Thrust, which became obscurely famous. The studio turned the corner. Korbin was on the summer conference circuit, and the guest professor circuit. Then, one day, at a university in Los Angeles where he had a year's appointment as special lecturer, opportunity appeared in his class–not veiled like an Eastern bride but incognito and mousy in bun and horn-rimmed glasses. Of course it was Sylvia who first saw the largeness of the chance incarnated in Margaret Dayton. Or who first spoke of it. It sometimes occurred to her, uncomfortably, that Korbin was not only more gifted than she, but also more Machiavellian.

She watched the dependency of Margaret upon Korbin ripen, with wars of reaction. She was excited by the chance. She was rapacious to consume it. She gloated in manipulating Margaret. And she had other attitudes, that she did not at all understand.

From the beginning, Grover Brand was a corner in a four-sided situation. She was attracted to him, but not intensely, and was relieved when he married Margaret. She was also obscurely resentful.

From the days of those first lessons to the development of Brand's novel for filming, her feelings for Margaret became more and more contradictory. And more profound. The thing with McGaughey, the conspiracy, was as inevitable as the slide of a stone in an avalanche well started. One day on the island, it came to her that it was not McGaughey who had found her. She had found him.

In Palermo, they checked into the Mediterraneo Hotel. Sylvia left Margaret showering while she went downstairs to call from the desk. That would save time, she said: remember Athens.

When she got back Margaret was in the white terrycloth robe but it was not tied: she could see the inner curve of breasts, the smooth clearly defined musculature of belly, and the curly auburn hair of the triangle. She looked, and then made herself not look, looked again very quickly. Her thighs trembled, she swallowed with a dry throat, and she spoke as swiftly as she could. Angela could not reach her friend by phone, she had written him airmail and asked him to call her with the address and she would call Sylvia.

"Why didn't you just have her friend call us here," said Margaret.

"I didn't think of it."

Without embarrassment or haste, Margaret pulled her robe together and tied it.

Watching Margaret, she felt herself taken by the thigh weakness and a heaviness in the breasts and a certain languor. She excused herself, and began to draw a hot tub bath.

When she lowered herself into the water she was still weak and still excited. She had been excited since they left the island, but she had thought it was because of the risk.

Now she had to face that the excitement had another source. Her defenses made words as formally as if she had spoken them: *I'm not like that, I'm not, it's just Margaret and nobody else, I'm not really, not really, it's men I like, I do like men, this is just Margaret.* She sought the images of ancient illicit encounters with men–sight and touch and sound. These reassured her. So comforted, she found she could think of Margaret without self-condemnation, and she gave herself to her visions of Margaret completely.

Someone was pounding on the door, she awoke, and understood she had slipped into sleep after her gratification.

It was Margaret. "Sylvia, you in there?"

"Who do you think's in here, Queen Frederika?"

"Come on out, I've got news."

She came out in her own terry robe and felt guilty as she looked at Margaret.

"I've got it Syl, I got Vito's address."

"Vito's address?"

"Yes, and you know where? In the phone book. Can you imagine? The phone book's just like ours almost except for the front, and I looked it up and there it was. Vito Stefano, 1487 Via Romagna. Isn't that wonderful?"

"My yes. It certainly is, wonderful. Are you sure it's *your* Vito though? Often there are two or three with–"

"It's Vito all right, I *called* and I talked to his sister, she lived in California and she speaks English. We can see him tomorrow."

"We?"

"You'll go with me, won't you Syl?"

"If you want me to."

"Haven't we saved a lot of time?"

"We certainly have. My, yes."

"Vito?"

The old man in the nightshirt looked at Margaret as she spoke, and Sylvia Korbin saw that he did not know her and might not even see her. His face had just been shaved and had a morbid whiteness; his moustache was gray like his hair, and both made his white face look whiter.

"Chi è lei?" Now he at least saw her.

"It's Margaret, Vito. You remember Margaret?"

He stared at her.

"Don't you know me, Vito?"

Finally he did. "Sure I know you, cara. You came all the way from Los Angeles to see me?"

"Yes, Vito."

"That's real nice. Margaret." Sylvia listened to his breath: each intake was a labor. "I seen, all your pictures, Margaret. All the ones, that came here."

"Did you like them, Vito?"

"I liked them fine. You a real big star, ain't you, Margaret?"

"I guess I am, Vito."

"That's nice. That's real nice."

His sister gestured significantly. She was a large woman in what looked like an American dress made of brown seersucker. Her black hair was back in a bun.

They stood. "We have to go, Vito."

"Good, bye, Margaret. Come, again."

"Vito, I'll come."

Margaret bent and kissed him on the forehead.

At the door the sister shook her head and raised her eyes toward the sky. She was not displeased by the drama and her role in it. "Heart." She touched her own. "Any day the doctor says. And the poor old guy he might go on a month like that. You don't know what to hope for, you just don't know what's right to wish."

"Can we come back?"

"It's awful hard on him, Miss Dayton, I don't know."

"Maybe we better not."

"Miss Dayton." The sister produced from a pocket a square of paper and an American fountain pen. She had them all ready, Sylvia thought. "I was wondering, if you could sign this. Just say To Helena, who used to be my sister-in-law, and sign it." Margaret started writing. "Just say to Helena, who used to be my sister-in-law. Margaret Dayton."

On the hot street, Sylvia said, "Neither one of them had much of an accent, did they?"

"No," said Margaret. "I guess they lived in the States a pretty long time."

She started to cry.

The telephone between their beds rang. Sylvia came awake at once and picked it up. "Yes?" she whispered. She watched Margaret frown in outrage, still clinging to sleep. A rectangle of sunlight lay on the hump of her body under the pink blanket.

Long distance for Mrs. Kor-bana.

She knew she should dress and go downstairs to take it. But Margaret was breathing steadily and deeply again, and the phone cord was long. She picked up the phone very carefully, swung her legs and got up on the far side of the bed, tiptoed into the bathroom and closed the door with the cord running under it.

After the connection: "This isn't wise," she said softly. "Let me call again."

"I can't hear you, Sylvia."

"I said how are you."

"How is everything, Sylvia?"

"We saw Vito yesterday."

"That's not so good, is it?"

"No, Margaret found the address herself. Wasn't that convenient?"

"I understand. Can you keep her there any longer?"

"Oh yes, she wants to get right back. I think she needs a longer rest too but she wants to get back right away."

"That is unfortunate," said McGaughey's voice. "I'm sure she needs a much longer rest."

"Oh, I think so. I do."

"If you could. If you could keep her there just a couple of days more I might be able to find some help."

"Vern! You wouldn't hurt Margaret! I can't let you hurt Margaret."

It came out, too loud, too fast, and in the instant she knew she had ruptured something with absolute finality. *I'm still half asleep,* she apologized to herself, *I really know better*. And then: *Why did I really say that?*

"Sylvia, I have no idea of *hurting* anybody. I thought we might work out something to give Margaret a longer rest since she does appear to need it so badly. I thought it was understood what we were both interested in was Margaret's welfare."

"Of course, I'm so sorry." She was back in the tone and the deception that was for Margaret's benefit if Margaret could hear. But the door was thin, and she had cried out loudly, and all she could hope was Margaret was still asleep, because if Margaret was not asleep she had torn it with Margaret as she had torn it with McGaughey.

"Do your best for Margaret," McGaughey said very coldly. "And keep me informed. I'll do what I can."

"Wonderful, I'm sure she'll be just fine."

McGaughey hung up in her ear, she hung up and opened the door to see Margaret in the green sheer nightgown, breasts visible above it, maidenhair showing dark auburn through it, and judging at her.

"I tried not to wake you," she said brightly.

"Don't you know you wanted me to hear that, Sylvia?"

She looked as bewildered as she could manage. "That was Angela, I told her we'd already seen Vito."

"Why did you tell Vern McGaughey not to hurt me?"

"Vern *McGaughey?* That was Angela, I told you."

"Last night while you were in the shower the operator called and said she couldn't get Mr. McGaughey on your call. I didn't tell you because I thought you might tell me first."

"I haven't. Well. I'll confess. I'll just confess everything to you, darling. To tell the absolute truth I did call McGaughey. You see I used to date Vern, to tell the absolute truth I had, a, kind of affair, well I had an *affair* with him while Max was in the army. Years ago. I hope that *is* our secret. Well, he wanted me to do something for him, I had this letter the day before you and I left and he wanted me to get him some information. It sounded harmless, but I know how things are with him and Globe so I thought, no, I called him to tell him. He got a little upset."

Margaret looked at her.

"So you see how it is."

"Sylvia, why have you been trying to harm me?"

She tried to look astonished.

"You couldn't be jealous of Max and me. There's nothing to be jealous of and you know it."

"Margaret I don't have the faintest idea. Not the faintest idea. What you're talking about."

"I guess I know what it is."

"Margaret."

"You've always been sweet *and* mean to me and you meant it both ways."

"I don't."

"Sylvia. You're in love with me, aren't you?"

She heard herself saying quite casually, "Yes, I guess I am."

And she started to cry.

She felt Margaret's arms circle and press her, she began to cry harder, and harder, and then she was sobbing in a violent and total surrender to despair that finally brought its own peace.

"There," said Margaret. "There." And she did not try to stop her.

The shaking of her body and the ugly wrenching noises stopped, and she felt a hundred pounds lighter.

"I'll do anything I can to make you happy, Syl. I'm not wired into that but I'll try."

"Neither am I wired into it damn it. I don't know how it happened. Oh hell, I don't know anything."

"I'll try if you want me to, hon."

"No. No. No. I wouldn't let you. Just don't hold it against me."

"You know I don't hold it against you."

She left Margaret, went to her own bed, and cried herself to sleep. When she awoke, she felt more innocent than she had felt since she was ten years old.

That night, after telephone calls, they were on the plane for Naples. Several times Margaret reached across the armrest and squeezed her hand and she squeezed back. She had tried to—well, she didn't even want to think what she had tried to. And now she was returning, hand in hand with her intended victim, and she felt as innocent as air. She smiled at Margaret, who smiled at her.

For a span, their roles had reversed. She was dependent and grateful—Margaret was calm and protective. But the next day the swing back had started: on the flight from Naples to Athens, Margaret was tense and withdrawn, and she herself took back the burden of comfort.

When they were on the boat from the mainland to the island, Margaret was as frightened as she had been when they left, and threw herself on Sylvia, exactly as always until seventy-two hours before. Full circle. Only now of course she herself was a Better Person. How long would that corny purgation bit last? Maybe quite awhile, with Margaret anyway.

The day was brilliant and cold with wind. Under the high sun the Aegean was heavy blue splashed with dazzle, and the steady wind broke it with thin white ridges.

"I'm scared," said Margaret.

"Don't be scared, lov-honey. It's all right. It'll be, all, *right.*"

She watched the island grow larger still, the windows of the white houses sharp and square now, and the *Leto* was moving, suddenly very slowly, toward the entrance in the stone breakwater. On the end of the north pier she saw two men by themselves, their faces toward the ship, and she recognized Nelson Glassgow and Grover Brand.

3

THE JOURNAL OF GROVER BRAND

THE day has ended. Let me go back to the way it began. For it was not a good day.

Only Glassgow and I wait by the water for the boat. All agreed that this is best, that a larger deputation will upset Margaret more than she is going to be upset anyway.

Glassgow, waiting, twangs and twangs. I sit in the jeep and watch. He walks up and down the dock, in a kind of shackled dash, he throws cigarette after cigarette in the water as though they are rocks, he halts and stares at the wind-laced blue waves and the unproductive black wave of Tinos on the northern horizon. Then he climbs back into the jeep, and from the side I watch his face draw and twist.—That broad. That blank-blanking blank-blanker. That blanking Sylvia.—This with variations is almost all he says all morning.

Still it is I, walking on the dock myself, who see the *Leto* first: hull down and part of the stack and mast showing against the long black hump of the other island. I go back to the jeep to tell Glassgow, he jumps out, looks for and finds the stack, and comes back reviling Sylvia.

The mainland is about a hundred miles away and the boat is good for about twenty knots. Supposed to leave at nine and dock here at three, stopping first at Tinos. It is two-twenty when I see her first and almost three when she enters the breakwater. I wonder what Sylvia's story will be now. On the phone, first from Sicily and then from Athens, it was that they had left suddenly for Sicily because Margaret's first husband was dying there. That much would have to be true, she wouldn't dare invent it. But Korbin and Glassgow and I know that Sylvia has been in touch with Vern McGaughey, that probably she has been an *agent* something or other for him, and that she threw away a note from Margaret saying they were cutting out for an emergency visit.

(Question: why didn't Sylvia just tear the note in bits and flush it away? Why did she crumple it into a ball and throw it into the wastebasket? Fashionable analytic answer would be she wanted it found. But more and more do I mistrust cocktail party analysis.)

Inside the breakwater, the *Leto* turns her sharp bow toward the north pier and creeps toward it, the west wind striking her full length. It is a heavy wind though not the feared north wind, the Boreas, and I remember Ulysses' Cave of the Winds was in the Cyclades. I see the khaki-clothed, blue-bereted figure of the captain on the wing, I hear the heavy rattle of chain, the anchor splashes. A moment later, he swings the ship on her anchor and eases the stern toward the pier. A difficult maneuver. I watch the stern slip into place, the lines fly out, with the admiration I have for all artistic action (how can I at that minute? I can). Only after, do I see the girls in the twin cashmere coats. The gangway clatters to the planks of the pier, two Greek men in black sweaters come over at once, the girls follow quite slowly, redhair and blackhair close together over the tan coats. Sylvia shepherds Margaret over the gangway and looks at me as she steps off herself. I fancy her look admits guilt and avows repentance, quite meekly. I do not believe the repentance.

M. smiles, tiredly, and returns my embrace as though she is somewhere else. Sylvia touches my arm and looks at me with that unnatural meekness. I start to say something quite ugly but do not. She starts to speak and does not. I put my arm around M.'s waist and we go to the jeep (our jeep, there are two there). From the back seat I look to Glassgow and Sylvia still on the dock a hundred feet away. Glassgow's thin body menaces her, it is almost funny, it looks actually poised to strike her like a weapon. She stands quite still, as though accepting the stroke. She lifts her shoulders and lets them fall. It is not a shrug: it is a fatalistic, stoic, oddly elevated gesture. I am impressed for the first time; to me, Sylvia is a figure of dignity.

My concern of course is Margaret. She has that look that is her worst look: the look that precedes withdrawal, or informs that withdrawal has begun. She does not relax, or tilt her head back on the seat, but sits quite straight and appears quite small, her red hair blown hopelessly above the tan coat. I lay my hand on her forearm and feel the tautness of it through the coat.

—Are you all right, baby?—

—I'm all right.—

—I wish you had let me know, directly.—

—I did write, I guess I forgot to leave the note though.—

—We know all about Sylvia—

—Sylvia's all right. Don't you be mean to Sylvia, any of you. She's just been, confused.—

—Confused.—But I pursue it no further. I suggest she go back to the hotel and rest and not go back to location until the next day.

—No, I want to get it over with. Let's get right out there.—

—I'll be damned if I let you go right out there.—

We quarrel and compromise. She goes to the hotel for an hour's rest and a change of clothes, only she does not rest. On the bed, her body is stiff and her eyes open.

It is not much after three when we are back at Troy.

She cheers visibly from the warm welcome she gets from the Americans in the crew: hello Margaret, hello Margaret, hello Margaret. She answers each by name. The Industry prides itself on the cult of the first name, the all-of-us-workers-together thing. It seems an affectation to me but then I am not of it.

Sills and Tate greet her with strained warmth. They do not reprimand directly, however. I do not see Korbin. She has conference with the two of them, and then with Tate alone. I stay with her but I see she wants solitude and I let her have it. I see her standing on the edge of a seacliff, looking at water gone green with the changing slant of sun. This day is one of those Mediterranean days I hate—sunny and with the appearance of warmth and yet finally cold.

She comes away from the cliff and I fall in with her and without a word we walk to the jeep. Her driver, Hank, is waiting.

—You feel all right, Margaret?—he says.

—Hank, I've felt better, I tell you.—

—You'll feel great you get a good night's sleep, Margaret.—

—I hope so, Hank.—

In the hotel room she says—This has been the day. This has been really goddamn *it.* Like never before I see what am. I am a body, I mean a body like in a hospital, with all those tubes sticking out. Only they aren't keeping me alive by shooting stuff into me. They are taking it out.—

—It isn't really that bad, is it?—

—Oh you just bet it is. Mace Garrett, poor sweet old Mace Garrett, he thinks he's going to die. He doesn't say a word and every time I get near him I feel him begging, please finish the picture, please be good and finish the picture before I die. Please finish the picture so I can get my money and then die.—

I do not answer, for at the instant she does not want answers.

—Sidney Tate. The great wonderful gentleman Sidney Tate. Do you know what the great wonderful Mister Sidney Tate is up to? He is up to pimping for that Armenian. What's his name. Haratunian.—

—I don't believe it.—

—Don't you? Well I will tell you. Mister Sidney Tate asked me, he came as close to begging as Mr. Sidney Tate could come to begging, he asked me to save his job by going to a party on Haratunian's yacht. To *save his job*. Sidney Tate. I said, do I have to lay for an Armenian to save your job, Mr. Tate?—

—And he told you no. Didn't he—

—Oh he told me of course not. He turned six different colors and swallowed and said, of course, I don't want anything like that Margaret. All I ask is you go to his party. Go with your husband, by all means. I do not consider you a whore or myself a pimp, Margaret.–

–He meant it.–

–Did he? And Korbin there, Korbin wants me to give *him* a hit. For him, not for me. I know that. And Sills wants me to finish the thing so he can stay alive in the business. For him too, not for me.–

–Is that so terrible?–

–Terrible or not, they're two more tubes stuck into me and draining. And my dear mother. My dear dear mother is so terribly concerned. She says. I must compose myself and do my job, she says. And do you know why? Because if I don't my dear mother won't have a meal ticket and can't buy any more gigolos.–

–Your mother is not like that, your mother cares about you very deeply.–

–Sure she does. And Nelson Glassgow, I have to do my job for Nelson Glassgow too, so he can go on being a big man. He promises Margaret Dayton, he delivers Margaret Dayton. *Big* Nelson Glassgow.–

–Baby, you are just a little bit patho.–

–Oh shut up. All of you are tubes. Except you. You take nothing from me, you don't even need me. You don't need me or anything but that crazy thing in you. Grover baby, I love you, but you are a cold son of a bitch, do you know it? I do love you Grove, but you aren't really human.–

–No, I'm a writer.–

And then I say–What I depend on is what you must depend on.– But she does not understand.

In the night I awake and see the double doors to the balcony open. I rise and tiptoe to the doors and see Margaret standing at the handrail with nothing over her nightgown. The moon is on the other side of the hotel and though I do not see it from where I stand, it is so bright as to make, almost, a white night: sky is blue not black, rocks off from the hotel that I can see are black, water against them white. More black rocks and white water just under balcony but of course I do not see these.

I am afraid and I hesitate only one moment before I come to her. All I say is–You should have something on.–

She answers–I'm all right–but she does not resist as I guide her back in. Her body is cold and shaking.

4

FROM his window as he dressed, Tate could see only the far corner of the bay: a green flatness crested by a long black jut of rock that was a natural breakwater. He could not see the shore and the piers, and he thought it was as well. He knew what was there. Haratunian was there. The raked single stack and the gray blade-hull of *Cerberus* trembled against the lines that held her: Tate had seen as much of *Cerberus* and of Haratunian as he wanted to see.

He had been waiting on the dock, two days before, when *Cerberus* spat her lines to the dock and drew herself in upon them. He had paid his call, and his symbolic tribute, to Haratunian then. He had called again the next day. And now, before he was well out of bed, Haratunian's male secretary had telephoned a summons. He had accepted it with deliberate stiffness—but he had accepted it. He walked the three blocks to the harbor, and up the canopied gangway to the deck.

The military discipline of the craft had not slacked: a sailor in gunbelt led him to Haratunian's cabin. The memory of the two-winged room rushed into his present view of it as he entered. Haratunian, in white V-necked T-shirt stood erect before a full-length wall mirror. His right hand pushed an electric razor over the top of his head. The shaved smoothness of the skull accented the hawk profile; the cords of muscle moved visibly under the white cloth; turning toward Sidney after a long instant, the brown eyes were large and tender. Sidney acknowledged the success of Haratunian's creation: Haratunian.

Haratunian switched the razor to his left hand, he extended the right, and he smiled dazzlingly.

"Sidney. How thoughtful, how *considerate*. But you should not have. You really should not. Not this *early!*"

"You know I wouldn't have done anything else, Richard. I've been looking forward so keenly to a good chat."

"Sit down, Sidney, down." The right hand made great bestowing sweeps, then accepted the razor from the left, and brought it now to his face.

Sidney sat in an upholstered chair bracketed to the desk. Haratunian, shaving, looked at him and then back to the mirror.

"Sidney, dear man, I'd like to tell you how well you look: How very fit. Et cetera. Et cetera."

He opened his mouth and tightened his lower lip over his teeth, brushed it with the razor, and let it go. "But I can't. The truth is, Sidney, you look like the wrath of the devil. Dear Sidney, what *have* they done to you?"

Tate had had more time than he wanted to consider strategy: the choice was disarming, minimizing candor.

He said: "They've been doing quite enough, believe me."

"Oh?" said Haratunian interestedly.

"When I say they, of course I mean she." Tate laughed: he sought to be winningly deprecating. "Richard, I have had the most *harrowing* experience with Margaret Dayton." Watch it; he was slipping into Haratunian's extravagance. "I have handled hundreds of men with you might say a certain success, and do you know I am playing absolute hell coping with this one girl." He laughed, he hoped, carelessly and engagingly. "Sometimes I even wonder if it's worth twenty million dollars."

Haratunian's light climbing voice was authentically engaging. "Twenty million dollars, Sidney?"

"Why what the picture will bring us beyond negative and distribution costs. That's just a guess, of course, but I think you could say it's an informed guess."

"That's wonderful, Sidney, truly wonderful, that's almost as much as my best mine brought me last year."

One down, thought Tate.

"You've finished the picture then?"

"Nno. Not quite."

"Oh?"

"We've got to reshoot Margaret Dayton's scenes, most of them. She's been very upset, between us she hasn't been herself at all, not at any time during the picture has she been herself. This last episode, you know about that, this has just been one more episode."

"She is so difficult then?" Haratunian put the razor down and shut it off. He did not look at Tate, but walked to and opened a steel clothing locker that ran the length of the bulkhead. "Sidney, I must enlist your famous discrimination. Pick out a shirt for me. Pick out a shirt that matches the soul of your island."

"I don't know much about souls," said Tate.

But he went to the locker: one section of it was full of skirted, belted coat-shirts on hangers. They were identical in design and astonishingly varied in color and texture.

"As you see, those Cuban shirts are my true passion. I would never wear anything else unless I had to."

Tate picked one of bright blue raw silk trimmed in gold.

"Marvelous, Sidney, marvelous. I am overwhelmed that this is the soul of your island. Now. I will put it aside until I meet Margaret Dayton. When may I meet Margaret Dayton, Sidney?"

"*There* we have a problem."

"Oh? And what is the, problem?" Haratunian took a bottle from a wall cabinet, upended it, and let lotion flow to one palm. Then he brought his hands together, and patted the top of his head and then his face.

"She isn't. She isn't exactly well."

"Oh?" said Haratunian most agreeably. He flexed his fingers in the air to dry them. "But of course I can wait. She does mean to recover? I mean eventually."

"Richard. She'll be delighted and honored to meet you. Naturally. But she is, I think I should warn you, she seems happily married."

"Dear Sidney, did you think I was asking you to procure for me? Simply *present* me to this legendary creature. That is all I ask."

"She is very difficult."

"It does seem little enough to ask. To let me give a party for her. I should be desolate if my old friend could not persuade her to let me give a party for her."

Tate translated that with what he knew was absolute accuracy.

Haratunian put on a white coat-shirt and looked at himself in the mirror with admiration. He turned to Tate and smiled, tenderly. "Come, Sidney, you must forget your trouble and let me cheer you with a miracle of a breakfast. I demand it. In the name of friendship, I *command* it."

After breakfast, and Tate admitted it was indeed a *small* miracle, Tate went to his office in the Quonset. He was aware that the situation was absurd. He was also aware that it was totally serious. If the picture were on schedule, if it were inside the budget, if it were without problems, he would have no problems with Haratunian, even though he was ultimately dependent on Haratunian. Haratunian did not fire winners. He had departed from all normal accountability, but he was still a businessman: he did not fire winners. But at that moment Tate was not exactly a winner. And he was not exactly a loser. He was, quite simply, whatever Haratunian said he was.

He knew how this appealed to Haratunian: his breath would decide the matter of Sidney Tate, recently a titan, and he could blow it either way.

This transparently delighted him. His ego was as large and as active as his libido: only with overdeveloped self-esteem and glands, after all, did a modest millionaire by inheritance become a billionaire.

Perversely, Tate liked Haratunian, and was certain Haratunian liked him. He was also certain Haratunian would withdraw his support and leave him to McGaughey if he could not get Margaret Dayton to spend an afternoon on his ship. It was Haratunian's game: he was competitor, referee, scorekeeper.

All Tate could do was play.

And bear the displeasure of the master Tate: that shape and his own had drawn far apart. He wondered if he would ever pull them close together again.

He stepped out of his office, which he shared with Sills, whom he had refused to dispossess. It was the rear half of a Quonset marked *Production*. Beside it were three other Quonsets marked *Accounting, Publicity,* and *Costuming,* and in front of the Quonsets were the long trailers which had two dressing rooms each for the actors. He passed by Mace Garrett's, started to go in and wish Garrett luck, and decided not to. Garrett had a right to privacy. Particularly today: he had his biggest scene today: the fight between Hector and Achilles.

He wanted—he corrected himself, he and Sills and Korbin wanted—they wanted to get the whole fight on film today. If they got it all, they would have six minutes in the final cut of the picture today instead of the three that was considered. Good day's work. The background shots of the two armies had already been done. So had the chariot shots. Today it was the hand-to-hand fight on foot. They would do it without doubles, for it should not be dangerous, but it could certainly be strenuous.

"Sidney."

He turned and Howard Sills caught up with him. He knew what Sills was going to ask and was slightly, unreasonably angry. He had lost Haratunian for several minutes and now Sills had brought him back.

All Sills said was "Any news?"

"No news that's new. He still wants to give that party for Margaret and she still refuses to go."

Sills grimaced: a supposed parody of agony which (Tate understood) was unintentionally and absolutely truthful. "Maybe somebody can persuade her."

"I wouldn't count on it. Will we get the whole fight scene today?"

"I hope so."

"I hope we do more than hope."

Sills said reasonably, "I certainly expect to get all of it, Sidney."

Tate reprimanded himself: his thrust was not needed. He spoke reasonably. "I'm sure you'll manage it, Howard."

They had moved out of the area of the trailers into the plain between the Greek tents on the left and the Trojan walls on the right. These were about a mile apart. There was enough room for maneuver between, and the soldiers were a reasonable distance away.

These soldiers leased from the real Greek army lived in the tents. They made up both the Greek and Trojan armies of the film. The tents too had a double existence: as living quarters, real, and as the bivouac of the Achaean host, film. The two film armies now fraternized, idly, on the plain. There were some card and dice games. Even in the open, the sour odor of sweaty, unwashed bodies struck Tate powerfully.

"I guess our shower facilities are sketchy," Tate said.

"The real armies probably smelled a lot worse," said Sills.

"I dare say."

Sills excused himself, he had to check on something he said, and Tate wandered about alone.

He watched crewmen tug on pulleyed ropes to move the heavy cameras over planks on the ground. That was an awkward dolly, he thought. He saw Nelson Glassgow watching, too, and went up to him.

"What right have *you* got to look worried?" he said.

"Me worry?" said Glassgow.

5

WHY should *I* worry? Glassgow watched Tate's stately, plump back move in a slow straight line that cut through the sprawl of the armies. Why indeed?

He had one client, and friend, who was about to do a piece of work that could kill him. He had another client, also a friend (accept it: much more) who was one step from a screaming breakdown and possible consequences which he did not wish to define, or even to think about, except he had to. He had a third client who was a very strange friend, whom he had cuckolded and who had put lead in him, who was getting his last turn with the dice. He had a former mistress, brief but well-appreciated, whom he had to reconcile to her daughter, who was, not quite incidentally, also a former mistress. And he had a last friend, Tate himself, not a client but a man he admired infinitely, for whom he wished a triumphant valedictory and not an ignominious exit.

He just might *find* something to worry about. If he worked at it.

Garrett. Garrett at that moment had absolute priority. Try him one more time.

He walked to the trailer which was half Garrett's and knocked on the closed door. "Glassgow."

"Come in."

He opened the door and the light through the door fell on Garrett in full Trojan armor sitting in a chair in what had been half-darkness. His face turned toward Glassgow and his eyes blinked. Glassgow smelled bourbon and then saw the bottle on the floor by the chair: Grand-Dad.

"One," said Garrett. "Today I need one."

"Why not? How do you feel?"

"Great."

Glassgow looked at him. He was still a hell of a looking man if he wore something to hide the belly roll.

"One more time. Let me call it off."

"What?"

"Let me pull you out of this scene."

"You know you can't do that."

"Try me."

"I couldn't let you do it. I'm okay. I'm really okay."

"This is just what you aren't supposed to do."

"It's no worse than what I've been doing for weeks, not much worse. And Korbin wants me to do my own fight. I've always done my own fights."

"Don't do this one."

"I got to."

"We both know it could. We both know it's dangerous."

"It won't kill me."

"It could." He had not meant to say that.

"Okay, it could, but this is my last scene practically. Now I get my dough no matter what and that's the name of the game. That is, the name, of the game."

That was the wall. He said all he could say: "All right then. Take it as easy as you can."

"You can bet your ass on that." Garrett grinned and stood up. Glassgow left him putting on the helmet.

The next item: Margaret Dayton.

Approaching her trailer, he saw Grover Brand come out of the doorway, close the door, and come down the steps. Brand saw and started toward him in the swift compact walk, his figure enlarging and finally the eyes in his face showing clear hot blue. Under the blond shock that dropped over his forehead, his face was at once intense and remote.

Glassgow liked Brand, and still Brand always made him uneasy. By a not quite concealed, not very deep, strictly disciplined tolerance, Brand suggested to others that they were all playing games for children. And that only he was not: only he saw clearly: only he understood the real stakes and played for them.

The disturbing thing was that he could be right.

He said to Brand as they met, "How is Margaret?"

"How do you think?"

"I thought the rest might have helped."

"What rest?"

"That stinking Sylvia. Even with Sylvia working on her though, she shouldn't be in this bad a shape. She's never reacted like this to pressure before. She's worked under hell's own amount of pressure too. I'm not sure I understand."

"You ought to understand. You *were* an English professor, weren't you?"

"I was an instructor, what the hell has that got to do with it?"

Brand looked at him with some triumph and malice. "I knew you guys don't really *know*. You talk and you write criticism and all that but you don't *know*."

"Look, I'm not you guys, I'm an agent. Period. I've been an agent for fifteen years. What the hell are you talking about?"

Brand said patiently, "I've told you before. This time she is in the middle. She's caught between two forces."

"Oh Jesus not that again. Not that between money and art stuff again."

"Not between money and art for Christ's sake. Between big money and the academy. The textbooks. The rules. Between Globe-International Studios and Max Korbin. If you don't see that you don't see anything. Her work, call it her art if you want to, her true work is what can cure her and all that can cure her."

"You're really hooked on that, aren't you?"

"Has it ever happened like this before?"

"No. You're right and I'm stupid."

"You aren't stupid. It's just that I'm a prick." He smiled with a warmth so sudden it was almost a shock, he tapped Glassgow on the shoulder and said, "Why don't you go see her?"

Glassgow tapped on the door of Margaret's trailer and went inside when she called. She was sitting before the dressing table mirror, saw him in it, and said without turning, "Oh, it's you."

"We aren't using that line this year, hadn't you heard?"

"No I hadn't, and what do you want?"

"First, I want you to remove the corncob and be human."

"You are vulgar, Mr. Glassgow."

"Yes." He said, "You have to come out of this, you know."

He watched her study her face as she put on makeup.

"I don't know what you're talking about," she said.

"We aren't using that line, either."

"I do hope not. You never said what you wanted."

"I want you to relax and do your work."

"Oh go to hell. Go, to, hell. I am sick sick sick of everybody's being so damned concerned with their investment."

"I want my money out of it."

"Oohhh! Ohh you *shit!*"

She turned at the table and jumped at him, she swung, he ducked, she hit him in the chest, and he caught her wrists.

She said it again and spit in his face.

"Fine, that's fine, you look better than you've looked in months. Do it again now. Hit me. Cuss me. Do it again." He released her right hand and awaited the blow on the chest, but the hand moved swiftly like a claw and he felt a sharp burning on his cheek. He caught the hand again, she spat on him again, and she reviled him. He listened with admiration while his cheek burned and something wet oozed down it.

"Good, good. I wasn't sure you knew the words. It humanizes you remarkably."

"You son of a bitch I'll—"

She fell against him suddenly, no longer twisting. "You don't give a damn about me, do you?"

"You know perfectly well I love you."

"Nooo you doon't."

She bawled and went soft and he let her hands go and put his arms around her.

"Nelson, I'm so tired."

"I know you are, baby." He patted her. "The worst is over though. From here it's downhill." He wished he were sure.

She finished crying and stepped back from him. "God, I must be a mess. I've got to work, too."

"Korbin's not shooting you today. He's got the big fight."

"He's rehearsing me after. My scene with Hecuba. Right after Achilles kills Hector."

"I thought he shot that already."

"He did and I goofed it. It's got to go again."

"You'll be great this time," he said. "It's a good scene." It was: denounced by Hecuba after Achilles had killed her son Hector, confronting all her suddenly hostile in-laws, Helen defended herself in a speech that was both a definition of her life and the substance of the screenplay. Feeling awkward, he said again, "You'll be great."

6

WALKING from the trailer to the plain in Trojan armor, 1965 model, knowing he could die before the day did, Garrett told himself that he was beyond worry, that he had accepted the dice totally. It was a lie. He was afraid, and he knew he would not stop being afraid, and he had the sour, coppery, bad-winey taste of being afraid in his mouth.

He had waited in his own dressing room, one-half a trailer, as he had waited in the communal dried-sweat-smelling dressing rooms so long ago. He had decided not to wait alone inside four walls, but in sunshine tipped with human voices.

In front of the papier-mâché walls workmen pulled on long ropes to get the cameras in position. Korbin was using four today: he was going to shoot the whole fight all at once and edit in the angles.

The assistant director supervised the hauling. Soldiers from both armies clustered on the plain and beneath the walls. Achilles, looking very large, sat alone behind one camera in a canvas chair that had no name on it. Achilles had been Mr. North America six years before: his name was Hank Banks.

Garrett picked up a chair, walked over, and sat down beside him.

"Hello, Mace."

It had once been the thing to call him Johnny; it didn't matter now.

"Hi," he said. "How you feeling?"

"Quite well, thanks." Banks had the absolute, unhumorous seriousness of body-builders asked about their condition. "How are you?"

"Great."

"You look quite fit."

"You look in the pink," said Garrett.

Many of them had that half old maid, half YMCA way of talking, and of thinking. Garrett like most fighters despised body-builders. Still, Banks was in fantastic shape. Garrett had seen him working with his barbells, pressing 200 pounds, deep-knee bending with 250. Now he sat straight to show off his muscles: they had been oiled with the lotion that was called "sex" and they showed nicely: big arms and shoulders and pectorals, huge legs, all in proportion, all sharply separated.

Looking at him Garrett was aware that he was thinking in fight terms: in and out on this one, too heavy to stay inside, too much reach to stay outside, in and out and hook the chin, hit him right and he'll go down, they all go down you hit them right.

Of course what he would do was what Korbin told him to do. No real fight. No risk except the risk inside his chest.

He watched Banks automatically tense and separate his muscles. He did not exactly hold it against Banks, they had to be vain to lift, what was wrong with a little vanity. Still, lifters never made fighters. Slowed up. Henry Armstrong? Give them Henry Armstrong. He hoped he would not die today.

"Oh, I stay in shape," Banks said, and Garrett remembered he had said something to Banks. He had gone away. "I always stay in shape. I work on lighter weights though for muscle separation now, that's what you need for this job. Straight competitive lifting you get too heavy."

A muscular young man who had wavy blond hair, brought Banks a glass of milk. Fortified with wheat germ and honey, Banks said, would Garrett like some? Maybe after the scene, said Garrett. He always had it before any workout, said Banks.

The AD had finished the setup and brought Korbin to it. Korbin sat in a canvas chair with his name on it, head bare, eyes horn-rimmed. Noise stopped so sharply it called attention to itself. Korbin spoke conversationally: "All ready, Hank? Mace? Good. Now you understand your thrust here. Achilles is half-crazy, his whole life at this moment is killing Hector. He has to kill Hector to kill his own guilt feeling and to bring what he considers moral order back to his own universe. He has to kill Hector to achieve himself again. Got it, Hank?" Banks nodded.

"Now, Mace. Hector knows he doesn't have a chance. He knows this maniac is going to kill him. He's going to achieve importance by the manner in which he meets death, he's going to get the best possible price for his life. He defines his life by the way he loses it. Does that make sense to you, Mace?"

"I think so," said Garrett.

"Good. Now we start here where the chariot scene left off. Hector has been thrown from his chariot and Achilles jumps out of his and comes after Hector. First we get Hector pushing himself off the ground, then Achilles landing in a crouch and coming out of it."

He showed them, then shot Garrett's action, then Banks's. After these takes of each, he was satisfied.

"Now the fight. We'll shoot it straight through to the death scene. Now. Achilles comes at Hector swinging the sword hard. And fast. Hit each other's shields with your swords. Achilles beats Hector back, back, back. Now, Achilles, you're possessed, you're mad, nothing is going to stop you, see. You simply overwhelm Hector. Then he ducks one swing and throws himself at you. That's your one chance, Hector. You put everything in that one attack, and for one second you make Achilles break and go back. But just a second. Then Achilles comes back in an absolute fury and bowls Hector over and raises his sword and sticks it through him. That last is the next shot. We stop when Hector goes down. Let's walk through it."

They walked through it twice.

"For real now. Roll 'em."

Garrett saw Banks coming at him huge and theatrically scowling. They swung the swords on shields. Garrett's left shield arm hurt from the shock. Garrett moved back. Sweat hit his eyes. It went on and on. Time. Where was the bell?

"Cut. Not quite. You've got to make it more inevitable. Hector, your face has got to show you know it's hopeless and you're still going to try. Achilles, you're a natural force opposing a mortal man. Let's try it again."

Garrett felt his arms and lungs ache, but *it* was still all right.

A third time. He could barely get the left arm up, he knew *that* feeling. He got it up anyway. Laterally he saw Glassgow beside Korbin, he had not seen him before, and now he saw him touch Korbin's arm.

"Rest break," said Glassgow.

"Absolutely." Korbin looked at Glassgow resentfully and then at Garrett thoughtfully. "Take ten, fellows."

Garrett dropped into a chair, felt his chest rise and fall deeply, heard the hard draw of his breath, and thought everything felt right. The heart was all right.

Still he was tired when Korbin called them back. They went through the whole fight twice more, and the last part two more times after that.

His arms were as gone as after a full round of steady punching. He saw Glassgow speak in Korbin's ear: Korbin nodded.

Korbin called: "We'll print the last ones. And we won't need you for an hour, guys. Get some rest."

"I don't need any rest," said Banks indignantly.

Garrett started to say, *Neither do I.* He said, "You will when you're as old as me, junior. I'll take it."

In his bunk in the trailer he rested well. A good sign. He dozed lightly: the best sign there was. Almost an hour later, he arose, heated water in an electric pot, made half a cup of instant coffee, and returned to the cameras tentatively optimistic.

The death scene was nothing. He played it on his back. Korbin shot it eight times and said, "That's good. That's very good. Go home, you two. It was fine."

Glassgow followed him to the little dressing room.

"Are you *okay* you stupid bastard? Man that was great, it was just great, but are you okay?"

"I think so. Like the guy on the way down from the Empire State Building. All right so far."

He took two aspirin with water. "Don't you have Margaret in a scene this afternoon? What's left of it."

"Not shooting. Korbin wants to rehearse her. It's her biggest scene."

"She afraid of it?"

"Certainly not."

He raised an eyebrow. Glassgow grinned at him, twistily. "Sure she's afraid of it. She's hung up to hell on it, like everything else."

"Poor kid. You should never have let that Korbin near her."

"It's more complicated than that."

"It always is." He understood Glassgow did not want to talk about it. "You want to do something great? Fix us a couple with water. Mine real light."

The door opened without a knock, and a head through the doorway said, "Mr. Glassgow, they want you right away. It's Miss Dayton."

Garrett heard the fright in the voice. He heard Glassgow say, "Jesus." He saw him set down the bottle and move fast, not quite running, through the doorway and down the steps. And in the doorway himself, he saw the man in the jacket, the messenger, point with his finger and Glassgow did run.

If he could help, he would run himself, but he was sure he was not needed or wanted. He wondered what it was: he would find out later.

He did not have room to think about anything else except that he had made it. His scenes were done. You only made today, he corrected. No. I made it all. I get the money now, all of it.

He lay on the wall bunk. He did not sleep this time, but he rested well, and he thought again that it was a good sign. Poor Margaret.

7

AFTER the last take of Hector's death, Sills touched Korbin lightly on the shoulder. "That was marvelous, Max. Absolutely marvelous."

"Thank you." Korbin, in the chair turned his head to look up at him. He was pleased at the compliment and grudged his pleasure. Sills sympathized: Korbin did not want anyone looking over his shoulder. Still it was Sills's job to be omnipresent: others too had to adjust.

Korbin sat beneath and to the side of him, but still faintly turned in minimal courtesy. Sills nodded, confirmation of praise, and moved away in no special direction. The opposite armies had broken: soldiers in indolent motion carried helmets toward the tents.

Sills looked across the hard brown earth dropping at seacliff into rough blue water, the water turning smooth in the distance and sliding into the black swing of the low mountain of Delos. White clouds hung over Delos: it looked, for once, *like* an island sacred to Apollo.

Looking, Sills was aware, again, of an optimism so unreasoning as to be perilous. He had felt it first when Margaret Dayton came back, and he knew then there was absolutely no basis for optimism, her return had simply put them back where they were, which was nowhere good.

Yet–in some chamber below reason–he felt her return an omen. It was a turn, a massive turn, a tide which had been running out was coming in.

The picture was starting to work. The talents had come together; the meld was good; he had been, again, not artist nor alchemist but good grave catalyst. Of course he was overvaluing his role. He was giving himself too much importance. Yet he had had a function, and he had filled it. He had made himself Howard Sills again: he had fitted himself, once more, into the mold drawn by his imagination and shaped by his will. Into the space which the removal of Howard Sills had left more than once, he had once more returned Howard Sills. He resolved that there should be no letup, no ease: Howard Sills must not disappear again. To keep him present and alive would take a constant force of will. He promised that he would exert it.

He walked away from the cameras in winter sunshine with a strange and profound sense of elegy. He knew it was presumptuous. He did not know how presumptuous until Sidney Tate caught his arm and told him Margaret Dayton had tried to kill herself.

Not quite running, they made for Margaret Dayton's trailer.

"This is a finish, isn't it? Isn't it a finish though?" said Tate. He was breathing heavily: in spite of that, in spite of its plumpness, his face was set in planes of awesome judgment. "The final irresponsibility."

"How? What did she do?"

"The doctor just sent me word, I don't know how or when or who found her or how bad. Foolish foolish woman."

"I suppose she's had a bad time."

"So have we all had a bad time." His breath was shorter: looking laterally at him, Sills found his gravity intact.

"Some feel it more," said Sills.

"It seems they do. Here we are."

Tate went first up the three steps to the trailer door. Sills noticed incongruously the dirt caked on his shoe heels. Tate opened the door without knocking, and Sills followed him through the doorway to see a sweep of red hair on the white pillow of the bunk against the wall.

The bald young doctor, not in white but a brown houndstooth

jacket, stood beside the bunk. Nelson Glassgow in a gray sweater stood beside him. Moving, Sills saw the tubes connecting a jar to Margaret Dayton's forearm. On the pillow, Margaret's face was white and her eyes closed.

Tate touched the doctor's arm and gestured with his head. The doctor tiptoed with Tate and Sills to the opposite corner. Glassgow glanced at them and back to the bed. He did not move.

Tate said, "What happened?"

The doctor moved one shoulder. "All I know is, she cut her wrist with a razor blade. It looks like she changed her mind when she saw the blood spurt, that's enough to make you change your mind. Anyway she stuck her hand over it and stuck her head out and yelled for help and somebody heard her. I was here in a couple of minutes."

"How much blood did she lose?"

"That's hard to say. Maybe no more than a quart but that's a lot more for a woman than a man. Women are always short on blood. I'm giving her extra."

"Is she in danger?"

"There are always elements of danger. If she takes the plasma okay, if shock isn't profound, she could come back awfully fast. Sometimes recovery from blood loss is very dramatic. Sometimes it takes a while."

Tate nodded.

"I wonder why she did it," said the doctor. "What would *she* have to worry about?"

Sills saw the door open and Octavia Dayton rush in. He was angry with himself for thinking automatically of nights in another year. She touched Margaret's forehead with her hand and of course started to cry. From the opposite corner, Sills saw Margaret open her eyes and smile weakly, and he heard her say to her mother, "Hello, darling."

"She's coming back now," whispered the doctor. "Actually she's never been out, she's just weak."

Sills watched the plasma in the jar. He saw Margaret Dayton open her eyes again. She did not look happy. He walked softly to the bunk, feeling awkward.

"How do you feel, my dear?"

"I feel like I lost my nerve."

"You mustn't talk like that. You've been very lucky."

"Oh yes. I'm *so* lucky."

The door opened again and Grover Brand came in with Korbin behind him. Brand's compact muscular body moved like a shaft of energy to the bed.

He looked down at his wife. She looked back at him.

"Are you going to be all right now?"

"I guess so."

For a few seconds the room was absolutely quiet.

"Why?" said Brand softly.

"Because."

"What other reason, huh?"

He smiled, she smiled.

"I was just so horrible at rehearsal. That on top of everything else."

He took her left hand and held it between his. He said very gently, "I guess you think we're all against you."

"No. I'm not crazy. I'm just miserable."

"Well. Let me tell you something. We *are* all against you."

"What do you mean?"

"Don't cry. You aren't allowed to cry yet. I said we are all against you. No, you may *not* cry."

"You said you were all against me."

"Yes, I said it, we are all against you. You have to understand that. The time has come when you have to understand it."

"Grover," said Tate.

Brand said, "All of us in this room love you or need you and yet we are your worst enemies."

"Brand," said Tate.

"Please be quiet. You see, Howard and Sidney, they love you but they want to see you succeed. Big. It's their job. They want to see you make the big money picture and make big money for yourself and the studio. There's nothing dishonorable in that. In fact, they're very good men. They have no wish to be your enemies and no idea that they are.

"Max loves you and wants the best for you and he's put you in a straitjacket. Nelson wants you to be a success, it's his job to help you be a success and that pressure kills you. And I'm the worst enemy you have, I mean that your work has, just because I'm married to you. You have to survive all of us."

Sills looked at Brand: his face was concerned but relentless.

"You have to see that clearly. You have to survive all of us. Do you see it?"

"I don't believe you."

"You have to see it. Talent is Ishmael. It is never anything else. Every man's hand is turned against it. Nobody means for it to be that way, there is no malice and no ill will, but it is that way. Talent has to survive what everybody tries to do to it. It has to survive the best it can as long as it can. There are no guarantees and there is only mortality. The talent will die before you do. But there is an obligation. There is a responsibility. You have a real talent and you have to fight as long as you can and as hard as you can to use it. You can't throw it back."

"I don't want to fight any more."

"That doesn't matter."

"I can't."

"Yes you can. You'll know it when you're through. I mean really through. You aren't through yet. You know that, don't you?"

She didn't speak.

"Don't you know that?"

"I guess I know it."

"Do you accept it?"

"Yes."

"Yes what?"

"Yes I accept it."

"All right then." He turned to Tate and Sills. His face was totally bleak and its life was all in the eyes, and Sills thought he knew who Brand was for the first time. "She'll make her call tomorrow."

"Make that the day after," said the doctor.

Tate started for the door and Sills followed, looking at the tight framing of the four figures by the bed, the red hair on the pillow, the tube dipping. Her weak clear voice stopped them.

"Mr. Tate. I'll go to that party for you, too. If that's all he wants."

Tate said, "He doesn't have to get everything he wants."

He opened the door, paused, raised his hand, and let it drop. Sills followed him down the steps.

8

TATE tied the black bow carefully at his throat: it was wrong: he tied it again and it was still a mess. He glared at its unsatisfactory lines in the mirror, and loosed and pulled off the tie in one snap of his arm. From his bag he took the emergency item: a custom-knotted twenty-dollar clip-on. He put it on and looked at his improved reflection with a satisfaction distinctly malevolent.

He was annoyed that Haratunian had made his guests dress: black tie and dinner jacket on Mykonos was ridiculous. However. That made it appropriate. That made it just right. He had never been in a more ridiculous situation in his life than he had been since he received Haratunian's edict to produce Margaret aboard the *Cerberus.* A black tie party on location, on a boat, in Mykonos, was the perfect and culminating absurdity to what had been totally absurd from the beginning. So be it.

He should be indulgent, he thought, he should be amused and indulgent now that it had gone his way. There was just one thing, one small thing.

He was not sure it had gone his way, and would not be until he led Margaret up the gangway of the *Cerberus,* and he was getting more nervous with the minutes. She meant well, she meant very well, and if she set fire to the hotel it would not surprise him. He put on the white jacket, buttoned it, and held his right hand before him. It was perfectly steady. The moment of decision: not the clash of antagonists nor yet the counting of shares voted, but the appearance of a nice, wholesome, neurotic on the boat of a megalomaniac.

He went out of the room, along the passageway, and down the stairs to the next bungalow.

Please let her not be more than an hour late. An hour is all right. I'll be grateful for only an hour.

He came to the Brands' door and knocked. He relaxed for a short wait: Margaret opened the door at once.

She was in a green evening gown and her red hair hung to her shoulders.

"Hello, Mr. Tate." She said it with her artful breathlessness of the screen, and for an instant her mouth hung half-open and glistening. "I'm all ready."

"Why yes," he said. "You are indeed."

He felt a great deal better.

The night was windless, the sea flat, and, clearly for privacy, Haratunian had moved *Cerberus* outside the breakwater and anchored. Her whaleboat met them at the north landing; from the gangway of the yacht, an officer conducted them to the salon.

Haratunian came to greet them in his white captain's uniform, gold buttons to his chin, four gold stripes on his shoulder boards. It showed him to great advantage. That was why they had to dress, Sidney thought, in fury and hilarity.

But he spoke solemnly, "Miss Dayton, may I present Mr. Haratunian. Mr. Brand, Mr. Haratunian."

He stepped back. What, he wondered, what at this pinnacle of destiny would the two fabled creatures have to say to each other?

"I've looked forward so much to meeting both of you," said Haratunian.

"We've looked forward so much to meeting *you,*" said Margaret.

Tate wondered what would happen if he screamed.

The little salon was crowded–Haratunian had invited the principal members of the cast and administrative staff–and Tate stood discreetly in a corner and watched the party. What he really watched was Margaret Dayton and Haratunian.

Margaret Dayton was exhibiting the commodity Margaret Dayton to Haratunian, cordially but unattainably. Her face was as careful a composition as a camera portrait of *Margaret Dayton;* her soft red hair swung above the lime-green sheath through every thread of which thrust *Margaret Dayton;* she listened to Haratunian with eyes wide and direct; and a great part of the time her hand rested lightly in the crook of the elbow on her husband. Haratunian clearly understood; he could view but not touch the merchandise that launched a million ecstasies.

The fabled bosom hung within the orbit of his eager but properly disciplined fingers; he could only consider in frustration that a movement of arm would bring them to flesh. Tate watched his polite, never-betraying, smooth tanned face with interest and admiration.

He was taking it like a good true gamester. He had set a condition. Tate had met it. If he had achieved nothing tonight—Tate fancied he could see the thoughts arranging themselves—then there would be other nights. And other states of mind. In Haratunian's idiom, there were no defeats, only postponements.

Howard Sills came to his side. He murmured, "Who said happy endings are out of style?"

"Who indeed?" said Tate.

And Glassgow joined him. Looking across the room, at Margaret and Haratunian, he said only, "Ah."

"Ah," Tate responded.

It was a punctilious, uneventful, finally rather dull party and never for one moment did he forget it was a party that had preserved Sidney Tate.

Tate thought he had succeeded completely in suppressing every trace of satisfaction and triumph, during the party and at this moment, afterwards, when he and Haratunian stood on the forecastle of *Cerberus*. On the right hovered the black mass of hill beaded with yellow light. On the left, against star-shoaled blue depths of sky, another island made a ragged black edge. The point of the ship's bow and its dim white anchor light divided the immediate universe.

"It was a marvelous party," Tate said.

"Please, Sidney. You know I am embarrassed at my present lack of facilities."

"I'd be intimidated if you had any more facilities." Tate wished to minimize any loss of face the other might feel.

Haratunian laughed in appreciation.

He said unwoundedly, "Miss Dayton is charming. A bit more reserved than I would have anticipated."

"She's rather fond of her husband." Tate did not say, "As I told you."

"As you told me." Haratunian turned to him and in the half-light his smile was dazzling white. "Dear Sidney, I expected nothing, absolutely nothing, from Miss Dayton except the pleasure of her presence. There are periods in a woman's life when she chooses to be, devoted. There are other periods when she chooses otherwise. If she should ever become a free soul, so to speak, why—"

Tate inclined his head sympathetically.

"And I must express my appreciation for your difficulties and devotion, Sidney. I have some idea of the difficulties our charming friend has inflicted upon you these months. Now you and I will split a bottle of wine that is not exactly plentiful."

He said nothing about continuing to support Tate. He did not need to.

"How much longer do we have?" Lawrence said to him across the table and its depleted breakfast dishes.

"You have as long as you like." Tate studied him: handsome, wise, innocent face under heavy black hair, over khaki shirt and red pullover. "I'll buy the jeep from Globe for you and you can sell it when you finish. We're about through. I expect to close everything out in a week or so."

"This hasn't been an easy one for you, has it?"

Tate was pleased at his concern and his penetration. "None of them are easy. It's worked out."

"You worked it out."

"No," said Tate, he hoped not completely untruthfully. "I just did what I could."

"Why don't you retire?" It was the first time he had said it so directly. He said it off-handedly, but Tate knew there was nothing off-handed about his meaning.

"As soon as I put things in order, I am."

"You mean it?"

"I absolutely mean it."

"What do you know." He worked to hide his relief and pleasure: Tate was moved. "Time you enjoyed life a little."

"I've always enjoyed life. If it's worth anything to you, the way to enjoy life is to do a lot of what you do well. And to stay away from what you do not do well. In the end, you are what you do."

"A not unfashionable concept these days."

"I don't know about that," said Tate. "All I know is it's true. Now. Get out of here. I've got work to do."

He watched the red-sweatered, khaki-trousered, engineer-booted figure go through the doorway and the door close.

He took pen and notebook from his coat pocket and made figures. He studied them. Getting advance payment from exhibitors, he could count on eight million, and that was almost half cost. He was already savoring the hard sweetness of figures as he would speak them in his outgoing address. Sidney Tate, he thought, would end within the approximate outline of his conception of Sidney Tate. Almost. Reasonably within the outline. He worked to forget certain uncomfortable, recent ruptures of the outline, and for practical purposes, succeeded.

9

SHE was sitting on her bunk in the trailer with her back and red-topped head against the wall, reading a big paperback book. Coming in, Glassglow reflexively tried to see the title.

"Leftover Life to Kill," she said. "Caitlin Thomas. Mrs. Dylan. Ever read it?" She looked full of life and blood: it had been six days since the razor blade.

He said, "I only read my special three or four writers now, I'm a stick."

"No, you're sensible. It's just what I'd do if I knew who my three or four writers were."

He made a movement of shoulder that slid all writers into a sea, somewhere. "Anything in particular?" She had sent for him.

"Not in particular," she said. "The time of day and so on."

He looked at his watch. "Two o'clock. That's a fairly good time of day, isn't it?"

"It's not a bad time. It's been a funny picture, hasn't it?"

"All of them are funny. I don't mean comical."

"Neither did I. I suppose I'm chiefly responsible. No suppose about it."

"Oh everybody has done their bit."

Their eyes touched and they looked away.

"Do you think we did justice to Grover's script?" she said.

"Other writers should have such justice. The script wouldn't have had more respect if he produced it himself. I hope he knows it."

"I think he does."

They were looking at each other again and this time did not break it.

"Do you think I'm good for Grover?" she said.

"What I care about is, is he good for you?"

"No, he's the important one, he's a writer. I mean a real writer."

Glassgow said something about writers.

"You shut up."

"*You* shut up."

"Here we go again, huh?"

"Here we go again."

"You still love me, Nelson? I mean *love* me."

"Who knows?"

She looked at him quite steadily.

He said, "Did you think I ever stopped?"

"I wasn't sure you ever started."

"Neither was I. Till after."

"Till after what? Till after you slept with my mother?"

She looked at him tragically and then giggled, and he felt hot blood in his cheeks and ears.

"There'll be none of that," he said.

"No, sir."

"What is this all apropos of, anyway?"

"I wish I knew."

He looked at her and understood that she now touched nerves she had not touched before. Perhaps I am just queer for grown-up women, he thought. Did you have any doubt of it? he thought.

He wondered if he should go to the bed and kiss her and decided not.

"You can't think of anything else?"

"Not a thing." She smiled a little and stopped. And for the first time he saw the nose to mouth lines and he was strangely moved.

"I guess I'd better cut," he said.

"Thanks for coming by."

"*Nada*. Call if you need me."

"I will."

He did not move for a moment, then he turned, went out the door, and down the three steel steps.

Without a reason he walked in front of the Quonset huts, then among the white tents on the other side of the plain (the tents were quite dirty now), then because there was no place else to go he went back across the plain, to Troy and the cameras. This afternoon, Korbin was shooting two scenes without the principals. Or without the principal, for Margaret Dayton was to be billed alone over the title, though Garrett had star billing technically. That morning, Korbin had done the last of Margaret's scenes that had to be done over, and the picture was suddenly, practically finished. The shooting bored him, and he went out to look at the Aegean, which never bored him.

Brand found him there. They exchanged ritualisms until Brand came to what he had to say:

"I think you ought to marry Margaret."

"You know what, I thought she was already married. Can you imagine that?"

"You know she's in love with you."

"You are full of it. But then you're a writer."

"There's a certain amount of discussion about *that*. But I'm not fooling. I think you two ought to get married."

"You've decided that, have you?"

"Yes, I have."

"Suppose I said screw you," said Glassgow pleasantly.

"Suppose you said it," said Brand agreeably.

"Well I *mean*."

"I don't think I should be married to her nor she to me. I think you ought to be married to her."

Glassgow could not resist. "You're sure I shouldn't be married to you?"

"I'm *fairly* sure."

Glassgow shook his head.

"Think about it," said Brand.

"It would require a certain amount of thought."

Alone again, Glassgow decided he was frightened. He started to walk, found himself on the hard gravel road that ran around the island, and on the road took a conscious decision to walk to the end of the island three miles away. Troy was on the long western side.

There, he came to a kind of stone observation post. He did not know what it was called or how old it was: it could have been built in the Cretan age or two years ago for tourists. From it he could see three near islands clearly, though their colors had gone to black, and two more behind them black at a far distance. At the horizon was nothing except blue sea.

He wondered, as he did more frequently than he wished, if the total of himself was significant, if there was a total of himself. Communicant of Camus, explorer of Sartre, he could see in himself no Camusesque resolve against an enemy universe, no Sartristic self-plan that would make something out of nothing. He wondered if he truly cast a shadow.

He saw little to himself except motion for the end of motion, energy consumed in devotion to energy. He did not admire himself. Yet truly he did not feel unhappy, or sterile, or even purposeless. His simple exertions kept him balanced in trajectory, and they kept him warm.

When he moved fast, when he moved like Nelson Glassgow, he felt good. For Hemingway, Camus, Sartre, and Conrad that would take no effort at all to explain. They could fit it right in.

But he had not been able to.

Did he want to marry Margaret Dayton?

He might. That surprised him, but a brutal sense of fact was his curse and his gift, and he acknowledged it. Maybe he did want her, for good.

10

GARRETT had little to pack, and one day more to stay. His hands flat on the closed suitcase, he looked through his window; it was at the end of the hotel and he could see both sea and mountains.

On the right were the joined white houses of the village, and he could look across their rooftops to the breakwater and the three-sided harbor inside it, with the crossed mast of one moored caïque and the lumping gray bulk of *Leto* at the north landing. It was a good day and most caïques were at sea. Outside the breakwater, two big cruise ships stood at anchor, and beyond them the flat sun-polished silver of the Aegean lost itself in haze before it could make a western horizon.

Moving left, he saw the sea slip along the black edge of Delos ten miles away and then fall back to the headland that ran back into the low mountain that was Mykonos. Out of the dry brown side of the mountain cubed white houses rose singly, and stone walls cut the mountainside jaggedly, dark with their own shadow. Between straight walls a dirt road climbed.

On the road, upward, five black goats filed. Behind them walked a woman in a black and white checked dress with a black shawl over her dress and a stick in her right hand. Garrett felt great swift affection for the woman and the goats. He felt *with* them. Since he had not died, he felt a part of everything that was alive, people, animals, and things, and the things were as alive as the others.

He turned from the woman and the goats, put on a tan cashmere jacket, its lapels too wide for fashion, and left the room.

In the street he walked slowly over the stones. Between buildings he could see the caïques at the piers. He met and greeted an American tourist couple, dark-spectacled and camera swinging. And he smiled at the little brown boy with insincere concupiscent eyes.

The boy moved toward Garrett. No, thought Garrett. He cannot say it. Nobody can still say it. It has to be history: *hey Joe you fawki my sister?*

The boy said, "You want to screw my girl, Jack? Nice clean girl. Fourteen years old. From Athens. You want to screw?"

Garrett said no.

"You want to screw *me,* Jack? Ten dolla you screw me."

Garrett said no and handed him ten dollars. The boy snatched the money and looked at him, not quite sure it had happened, and fled. The little son of a bitch, thought Garrett fondly.

The wind was warm and dry and strong. It had picked up from the waterfront the smell of dead jettisoned fish, old bait, picked ripening lemons, wheat just ground into flour, goat hides fresh tanned with manure, human sweat, and from the wine shop down the street the smell of heavy, sweet resinated wines. Garrett liked the smell of all of them together, and he tried to pick each smell from the rest, and he liked each smell. They were the smells of being alive.

Never had Garrett known that it was so good simply not to be dead.

He knew his luck was in the end only temporary luck, and he knew he carried the end of his luck and of his days inside his chest. But so did they all. The difference was that he *really* knew it. Life and the death that was a part of life was as real as a loaf of bread, and half the size, and inside his chest they thumped seventy-odd times a minute as long as they were so minded. There was a definite limit to how long they might be so minded, and he had to make of that strictly measurable span of time what he could.

And he could say honestly that he had made much of it lately. He had decided exactly what he had to do, and with good luck he had done it. He was not simply satisfied but honestly, humbly pleased with himself for the first time in a long time, perhaps the first time since he could not finish skipping rope, that day.

He did not know how much time he had, but neither did anybody. All he knew, now, was that he was not going to waste any of it.

He turned down toward the waterfront to look at the small strong ships resting for the sea. Afterwards, he could call his wife on the studio wireless phone to the mainland.

11

Two raps: Octavia looked at the door, the open bags on the bed, the dresses piled, the lingerie strewn. The hell with it, she thought: "Come in."

Margaret came in: dark green capris, light green blouse, green handkerchief over red hair, no makeup.

"Oh, hi."

"Hi," said Margaret. "I thought maybe I could help."

Octavia felt joy, suddenly and surely. "Fine," she said lightly. "You think we can put this jumble together?"

"Oh sure. Just tell me what goes in what."

They sorted and assigned things. She'd brought no trunks but six bags.

"You didn't think I still needed those, did you?"

"Why not? You're only forty-five. You look thirty-five."

"Come now. Maybe thirty-eight."

They laughed.

"How would you like to stay over in Europe three or four months? With Grover and me?"

"Thanks but no thanks. That's too long to suffer a mother and much too long to suffer a mother-in-law."

"Oh come on."

"No. Thanks for the invitation though." Say it right out now. "Could that mean you aren't mad at me anymore?"

"I've never–" Octavia looked at her keenly, humorously, and she stopped. "Well, to tell the truth I was jealous. Of you and Glassgow."

"I know. You shouldn't have been though. That was just one time with Glassgow and it was only because he was sick over you."

"I assure you Mr. Glassgow's motives are of *no* interest to me. What *ever."*

"Of course not."

She looked at Margaret, who had colored deeply.

"You're sure you won't stay over with us?"

"All right then. I'll stay two weeks. No more. How's that?"

"That's fine."

They worked steadily for almost an hour.

"That ought to do it," said Octavia. "Save two bags to the last. When are we going? I *was* going to fly out of Athens day after tomorrow."

"We have to be here a couple of days longer. Where'd you like to go first?"

"Goodness, I don't know. Wherever you want."

"How about Rome?"

"Rome's fine."

Alone, she sat at her dressing table and considered. She must not think that all of her differences with her daughter were resolved, that all henceforth would be pure harmony. Yet there was a beginning, from beginning and no faith, and it was really more than a beginning. Now that Margaret admitted why she had *really* been hostile, because of Glassgow, she could dismiss it.

Octavia looked at her reflection: the hair was brown with a rich auburn luster, triumph of time, skill and money, and her face was smooth and lined only at the eyes. She studied herself without minimizing the truth or making it worse.

A woman forty-five who looked a *little* younger, still had interesting possibilities. She would have to find out–no, to *decide*–what they were, and who she was, and what she should do. There was time, but not to waste. The world, again, was an inviting circle of doors. But she would have to choose one, and open it.

12

THE JOURNAL OF GROVER BRAND

I FIND him loading his caïque with barrels of olive oil, two men lowering the barrels in a small cargo net from a boat davit on the pier, he guiding the net full of the barrels through a hatchway into his little hold. His face is creased brown hide under an old-fashioned wool cap. Over an unfastened white shirt he wears, hanging open, a double-breasted pencil-stripe gray coat, 1943 model U.S. He is alone on his deck, behind him are masts of other vessels, behind those the long headland, beside the headland the open blue sea. I would like to render him and all of it in one quick stroke. Perhaps I am in the wrong art. But I paint less well than a third-grader. Perhaps the fact that I have to use words for paint is what gives my work some value.

He sees me, takes one hand off the line and waves. I come aboard to help him secure for sea, and then we walk from the caïque to the open café on the street.

Thick sweet black coffee in small thick white cups. It is settled, he says. I give him one bill (bill like in a hundred dollars). Condescendingly, conferring a gift, he puts it in a large unbelievably worn wallet.

This is to take me on his run through the Cyclades to Piraeus.

"I show you the way we go," he says, and takes from his coat pocket and unfolds what turns out to be a U.S. Hydrographic Office chart of the Aegean Islands. It is worn and patched from behind with paper and paste but completely serviceable.

The thick brown finger traces the course. One island is almost the closest to the mainland and almost at the point of the Aegean group. From it we go out southwest to Delos, and Naxos, swing west to Paros, then northwest to Syros and then to the mainland and Piraeus.

The stubby finger moving across worn paper draws deep skies, high mysterious landfalls, and, yes, by God, *wine-dark* seas. It may not be the path of Ulysses but it is enough.

I ask him how long.

He makes a magnificent gesture consisting of a one-inch twist of his head and roll of his eyes. It says: Who knows? Who cares?

"Not long. Maybe two weeks. Maybe four weeks."

(He speaks serviceable English and better French, and some Turkish, and a little German, I learned before.)

I stare at the chart. A navigation chart is mystery, and glamour, and romance, all expressed in faultless mathematics.

I will finish this trip with him and make the next, the whole circle from Piraeus to Piraeus. I know nothing about sailing and will be dead weight but must not postpone. Have postponed too much. If I have learned one thing I have learned an artist cannot sit on his behind and still be an artist.

I will be two or three months. I may get a short book from it. But if I get only ten good pages from it, it will be worth it. If I get a fourteen-line poem from it, it will be worth it.

I excuse myself. He sails in the late afternoon, to pick up a light land breeze that starts then. So I must prepare.

Margaret will not be in the hotel. I am going to leave the letter and not see her. Coward? Maybe. But I think it is the kindest way for both of us.

I am leaving her in all love. Of a certain clear sort. We have given much to each other and the years have not been wasted for either of us. I have my book to be made of her, and I think I have given honest value for it, and I hope I have given much, much more. But it is time—

If I did not know she was irretrievably bound to Nelson Glassgow, I would not leave. But she is. Now it is inevitable that they come together, for good, unless their luck is far worse than either deserves, and it may be. But I shall hope that their luck is not bad, and I shall do what I can to influence their courses.

It will be hard for them. They are both positives and may tear each other apart. They will have to reach for each other *across* each other, and it will not be easy, but it is necessary. They must know it, and face it, and try it, and maybe they can do it.

As for me, I make preparations with a lightness of heart mixed with sadness. This morning, Margaret identified and smiled at me, blurred in sleep, not waking, as I kissed her very lightly: I will always love her but I do not belong with her. I do not belong with anybody.

By helping Margaret draw closer to her interior vision, I have come much closer to mine. Nobody makes it all the way, of course.

As I walk back to the hotel certain lines I once knew perfectly come back to me for the first time in years and years:

> "The spell of arms and voices, the white arms of
> roads, their something, something, and the black arms of tall
> ships that stand against the moon.
> They are held out to say:
> We are alone–come.
> And the voices say with them:
> We are your kinsmen.
> And the air is thick with their company as they call to me,
> their kinsman, making ready to go, shaking the wings of their
> exultant and terrible youth. Long something old father, old
> artificer, stand me now and ever in good stead."

I would like somebody to write lines as good.

13

TATE and Sills stood outside the production hut watching Troy go down. In the space outside the walls, a truck with a hoist equipment was backed to an open trailer. A big box marked *Camera, Delicate* hung on the pulley from the end of its crane: three Americans guided it toward the trailer. It went down too soon, they jumped back, "Son of a bitch WATCH it!" Into other trailers, up rigged wooden runways, men pushed smaller boxes by hand. Tate tried to pick out the categories: the baled costumes, the boxed weapons, the delicately packed lighting equipment, the camera stuff. The office furniture and records would not go until everything else had.

Josh Duncan was leading a file of Greek workmen toward the walls. All carried sledge hammers, almost all were dressed the same:

heavy shoes, bell-bottomed dungarees, naked waists, the short-billed black sailor caps. Duncan gestured: they began to swing the sledges. The heads of the sledges made smooth short arcs, they struck the papier-mâché and the wood beneath, the walls fell apart in pieces. Tate listened to the ragged, muffled blows.

"It's a little frightening how quick they come down," said Sills.

"I know what you mean," said Tate.

"The mayor wants the horse for a souvenir for the town."

"If they want it. I hope it doesn't bring them bad luck though. We can't say it's a lucky horse."

"We can't really say it's unlucky, either."

"No, I don't suppose we can. What do you think of *Helen,* finally?"

"We've only seen the rough cut."

"But what do you think of it? I mean really think."

"What do I really think?" Sills paused. The two of them watched a bare-torsoed man swing his sledge at a section of the wall. It toppled and struck dust from the ground. "I think it is an imperfect picture made by imperfect beings. It will be a disappointment to many and many will like it for the wrong reasons. And yet it amounts to something. For whatever motives, we have all collaborated in something that amounts to something."

"Yes," said Tate. "I think we have."

Some of the men with hammers started to knock the papier-mâché from the remnants and break the framing apart.

"We're selling that to the local lumber dealer," said Sills. "He's going to sell it to the peasants for fireworks."

Behind the rope barrier watched tourists and villagers, sport clothes and black shawls. Among them, Tate saw a gray-moustached man astride a donkey. He wore the black cap and dungaree shirt, and behind him on the donkey was lashed a full burlap bag.

"What will they do for comedy after we're gone?" said Sills.

"They'll survive," said Tate.

The man on the donkey started it on the road up the hill.

"We bored him," said Tate.

Tate looked from the man on the donkey to the swinging hammers, then to the spectators, then back to the donkey halfway up the slope. He saw the bag on its back, slip, slide, and fall to the ground and burst. From it potatoes bounced downhill. It was an easy slope and they did not roll far.

The old man jumped off, raised his fist, and Tate saw rather than heard him shout at the donkey. Stooped and lumbering, he picked up the potatoes, dumped them in the pack, and tied its ripped ends together. Then he carried it back to and lashed it on the donkey, climbed on the donkey, and started him up the hill.

His eyes moved from the old man and the donkey to the brown scalloped country and then out to the white-beaded blue Aegean and the low smooth curves of the dark islands against the horizon. It was a clear day and he could see all the way to Aghios.

"I'll buy you a drink," Sills said.

"I can use one," said Tate.